PRAISE FOR **POINT OF ENTRY**

"Intriguing . . . frighteningly believable. . . . As good as this kind of writing gets."
—*Chicago Tribune*

"The author presents a world of spies, greed, duplicity, and danger, but holds out the evergreen possibility that love can conquer all. It its execution, the novel is thoroughly entertaining."

—*Washington Post Book World*

"Schechter's depictions of smuggling uranium through the Caucasus mountains and shaky relations between the United States and countries around the world ring true—as do the relationships between powerful figures and their minions. . . . Motives for two of the novel's three nuclear-attack scenarios are believable . . . as is the clever way Schechter's bad guys try to move the uranium to its final destination."

—*USA Today*

"I couldn't put *Point of Entry* down. A must read for anyone who loves great fiction and superb writing. In this day and age of international terrorists who cause mayhem and horror without a care to borders or targets, and those who chase them, Peter Schechter enlightens, educates and most of all entertains. I have respected Peter Schechter as a superb political strategist with the best knowledge of the international players and countries of anyone in the game. *Point of Entry* puts him in the ranks of superb storytellers like Daniel Silva and Nelson

DeMille. The behind-the-scenes intrigue involving Syria, Pakistan, Colombia, Cuba, the former Soviet Union are all there. As I read, I kept thinking: Could this happen? Will this happen? When will this happen? Can we stop it?"

—Ed Rollins,
New York Times best-selling author of *Bare Knuckles and Back Rooms*, was manager for Ronald Reagan's re-election campaign in 1984 when he then served as assistant to the president and White House political director

"*Point of Entry* seduces the reader with a deliciously clever plot. It unfolds in exotic locales and international corridors of power that Peter Schechter describes with authority because he's been there. His insider's understanding of international politics and the personalities behind them make it all plausible. The surprise ending reminds that, in an age when those who pose the gravest international threats may make common cause, international cooperation might be civilization's only salvation. A timely thriller that ought to be on the Department of Homeland Security reading list."

—Richard Whittle,
Pentagon Correspondent,
The Dallas Morning News

"If I weren't married to Mary, I'd lose it for Marta Pradilla right now! This woman, the beautiful President of Colombia, has to make tough political decisions that end up saving the United States from terrorists. It's been a long time since I've heard a more compelling female voice in a thriller."

—James Carville,
political consultant,
author, and CNN commentator

"If you are addicted to political novels like I am, *Point of Entry* is pure narcotic. Peter Schechter gets it all just right from the White House to international summits in a smart, intriguing, and cosmopolitan book. He demonstrates he is a master note-taker at the highest levels of political thrill."

—Mike McCurry,
press secretary to former President Clinton

"The strength of *Point of Entry* is that it reads like nonfiction, great nonfiction. It's a nightmare scenario in which terrorists and drug traffickers exploit the security weaknesses of the United States. And, the presence of a female Latin American president is a refreshing and unexpected element of this fast-paced, intriguing book. The book's vivid details of the corridors of power clearly reflect Schechter's experience as advisor to influential leaders. This is a must read for anyone concerned about our porous borders and terrorists' threats."

—Jorge Ramos,
best-selling author of *Dying to Cross* and *No Borders*

"*Point of Entry* was sheer pleasure. Schechter's insights into the intrigues of political power were developed over fifteen years of political consulting; and the result is an international thriller that had me going—it's a mirror into the presidential palace! The novel's resolution is brilliant and it highlights the role of heroes that we in Colombia play every day in the war on drugs."

—César Gaviria,
former president of Colombia and
former secretary general to the OAS

"It's for good reason that Peter Schechter makes you feel like you're in the room where world leaders make critical decisions; he's been there himself, and now he brings it vividly to life in *Point of Entry*. The book roars ahead with the suspense of John Grisham, the wit of Nelson DeMille, and the eye for fascinating detail of Patricia Cornwell. All this, with a female protagonist that lives in the mind long after the book comes to its amazing conclusion."

—Brian McGrory,
critically acclaimed author of *Dead Line*,
The Nominee, and *The Incumbent*

"*Point of Entry* is to the War on Terror what *The Hunt for Red October* was to the Cold War—a timely and evocative piece of fiction set in the context of current history. The tense October days that unfold in John Stockman's White House also remind us of the harrowing days of the Cuban Missile Crisis in October 1962. Peter Schechter weaves together a thrilling tale through Washington, Bogotá, Rome, and Tblisi that deals with a number of relevant issues today, including the specter of terrorism by Islamic extremists, the successes and failures of the drug war, and the real possibility of nuclear arms proliferation. Most significantly, *Point of Entry* requires us to ponder the promise and limitations of intelligence, military action, and diplomacy in facing down the threats of the 21st century."

—Jack Devine,
former acting and associate director for
the CIA's directorate of operations

"First-time novelist Peter Schechter draws on his background as an international political and communications consultant for this . . . promising international thriller . . . Schechter deftly executes this spellbinding plot . . . the strength of Schechter's storytelling makes for an entertaining debut."

—*Publishers Weekly*

"Readers . . . will be treated to a host of delights: a well-constructed, tightly interlocked plot; international settings created through the close observation of authentic detail; an engrossing relationship between two heads of state, and an immensely satisfying conclusion."

—*Library Journal*

"What happens when you cross 'The West Wing,' 'Commander in Chief' and '24'? You end up with a rip-roaring novel about terrorists, nuclear plots and presidential dating."

—*Newsweek International*

A NOVEL

Peter Schechter

rayo

An Imprint of HarperCollins*Publishers*

HarperCollins books may be purchased for educational, business, or sales promotional use. For information, please write: Special Markets Department, HarperCollins Publishers, 10 East 53rd Street, New York, NY 10022.

FIRST RAYO PAPERBACK EDITION 2007

Grateful acknowledgment is made for permission to reprint "Ms. President" by Sandra Janer from *Semana* Magazine, copyright © 2006

Designed by Daniel Lagin

The Library of Congress has cataloged the hardcover edition as follows:

Library of Congress Cataloging-in-Publication Data

Schechter, Peter, 1959–
    Point of entry: a novel/Peter Schechter.—1st ed.
        p.   cm.
    ISBN-13: 978-0-06-084330-4
    ISBN-10: 0-06-084330-6
    1. Drug couriers—Fiction.   2. Terrorists—Fiction.   3. Smuggling—Fiction.
4. Uranium—Fiction.   I. Title.

PS3619.C338P65   2006
813'.6—dc22   2005051896

ISBN: 978-0-06-120564-4 (pbk.)
ISBN-10: 0-06-120564-8 (pbk.)

07 08 09 10 11 DIX/RRD 10 9 8 7 6 5 4 3 2 1

To my five girls—Rosa, Alia, Marina, and Gerda.
Yes, you too, Salsa.
And to my father; now gone, but never departed.

ACKNOWLEDGMENTS

In October 2003, a cold sweat ran down my spine. That was the month I sat down to try writing a first novel.

It wasn't the creative challenge that had me worried. I could forgive myself if my soul would prove unable to squeeze out a good story, fine characters, and a plot that quickened the pulse. Yes, I could live with that.

What concerned me was that, to get this book written, I would—alone—have to wrestle a blank computer screen into existence. This was the first enterprise in my life that had no deadlines. No timetables. No to-do lists. For that matter, there were no bosses. No clients. No colleagues.

Very scary for a type-A personality like mine.

It turned out all right. More than all right, actually. I had a blast. I loved the unexpected parts most. Feelings between two characters took on a life of their own and became deeper than planned. One protagonist I never thought of killing ended up shot dead unexpectedly. Friends that I intended as a symbol of deep closeness were suddenly screaming at each other, their relationship tottering on a huge abyss.

Writing this novel was one of the great, fun moments of my life. But the book you are going to read could not have happened without the sustenance of some people that need mentioning.

A kiss of enormous gratitude goes to my beautiful wife, Rosa. She was the first to say that writing this book was a great idea. She never wavered in that support, even when I forced her to read the manuscript again and again. And again! Each time, in her very Spanish way, she told me the straight truth. Even when I thought I'd fixed things, Rosa still pointed to parts of the story that weren't deep enough, believable enough. And she was right. Always.

To my parents, Edmund and Gerda, I can only say that without you I would never have had this thirst for culture, languages, and travel. I would not have appreciated a good story without listening to my father's passionate and funny narratives about life, friendship, and soccer. I can only hope that, forty years from today, my kids will feel for me what I feel for you.

Thank you to some of my good friends who were kind enough to read the early drafts—Ornella, Carlo, Marianne, to name a few—and still encourage me forward. Miguel is included in that list; but an extra measure of thanks goes to him for also reviewing the Spanish version.

To my partners, Bob and Charlie—I am grateful that you understood my desire to write this book. Thanks for being flexible, for taking the long view, and for the many years of friendship.

Thank you to Rosario for introducing me to my editor, Andrea Montejo. They say that editors have become paper pushers and account managers. It isn't true. Andrea brought depth and insight to the book. She gave it time and thought. She worked and mulled it over. What came out was thoughtful, shrewd advice. Thank you for believing in the manuscript, Andrea.

My sincere appreciation to the others at HarperCollins/Rayo. In particular to René Alegría, who thought it might be fun to have a thriller in Rayo's excellent collection. Rayo became a reality and a success through his energy, and you can understand why the instant you meet him.

To Cullen Stanley at Janklow Nesbitt, my agent, many thanks for taking on a new author and for imparting your sage knowledge of the business on my behalf.

Last, I want to thank many of the people I have met over the years in Colombia. Perched atop the South American continent, Colombia is better known for its problems. That is a pity because instead it is a magnificent, multifaceted country with dynamic, open people. I have had the privilege of working with four Colombian heads of state and met countless senior advisors and ministers. Many were talented women. Unlike other countries where this foreigner's political advice was often met with suspicion, Colombians listened and then agreed or disagreed on the merits. It is a place that is more grown-up up than most. I have made countless friendships in your country. Thank you to all those Colombians who treated me as a fellow citizen. I'm honored.

PETER SCHECHTER
August 2005

Rarely do great beauty and great virtue dwell together.

Petrarch
(1304–1374)
De Remedies

POINT OF ENTRY

In the Not-So-Distant Future . . .

PROLOGUE

"Bogotá Approach, Cuba Two is with you; flight level 2-1-0, beginning descent."

Pablo Vasquez, the manager of Bogotá's El Dorado Airport, was a proud man: proud of his personal professionalism honed over twenty-five years in airline services, and patriotically proud of his country on this very important day in Colombia's history. Pablo's senior flight controllers had already safely talked down French president Jacques Rozert's Airbus 340, Brazilian president Roberto Flamengo's sleek Bandeirantes, and U.S. president John Stockman's Boeing 747, Air Force One.

There were sixteen other airplanes—in the air and heading his way—each containing a head of state. More than fifty other assorted aircraft with the region's foreign and finance ministers, the secretaries general of the United Nations and of the Organization of American States, the presidents of the World Bank and Inter-American Development Bank, movie stars and scores of other dignitaries were due throughout the day. Just now on the airport's radars, Cuba One, with President Fidel Castro on board, was crossing the verdant Andes on final approach to El Dorado's high altitude runways.

"Cuba Two?" shouted Pablo, flipping through his log sheet of scheduled arrivals.

No flipping necessary. He had planned this day for months. He knew every arrival—the minute each plane would cross into Colombian airspace, the exact time it would be handed over to him for the descent into Bogotá. There was no Cuba Two on his list. "Who the hell is Cuba Two?" he asked anybody in the room.

"Bogotá Approach, this is Cuba One. We wish to advise that Cuba Two is part of our official presidential delegation," radioed Captain Osvaldo Torres, the long-time personal pilot of Cuban president Fidel Castro. "It contains the gift El Comandante would like to present to your new president. And by the way, am I cleared to land?" asked the Cuban pilot with an irritable voice that gave away the fact that he was not accustomed to providing explanations.

Vasquez kept calm and told his controllers to clear both planes. He flipped out his cellular phone and called Lucia Ramirez, the pretty, elegant chief of protocol. She was the Colombian official in charge of meeting the dignitaries arriving for the presidential inauguration. She had just gotten the twelve-car motorcade of U.S. president Stockman out of the airport gates and on its way toward the American embassy in downtown Bogotá. She was now busy lining up the far more reasonably sized motorcade for Castro when Vasquez told her of the second Cuban plane.

"Lulu, there is something strange happening. Castro is landing in three minutes, but he has a second plane landing right behind him that nobody knew about. I'm on my way down," was all Vasquez said as he sprinted down the stairs. He had one hour and forty-three minutes until the next plane—with Canadian prime minister Claude Sambert—was due in Bogotá's airspace.

"What the hell do we do?" asked Lulu. It was more a shriek than a question. "It's completely against protocol! He can't just land a second airplane without telling us. This isn't Cuba."

Pablo Vasquez shot out of one of the rusty doors that led to the airport's ramp areas just as Castro's first plane hit the tarmac. He dodged under the parked French Airbus, cellular phone glued to his ear. He was now close enough that Lulu could hear his voice both cracking through the air as well as in her mobile phone's earpiece.

"Not to mention that I have no damn parking space for another airplane," huffed the airport manager. By this time he was almost five feet away from Lulu, still screaming in his cell phone. She had already put hers away.

"Here's a thought," tried Lulu Ramirez. "How about if we land the second plane and tell them that we'll refuel it as a gesture of goodwill? But only if it leaves immediately."

No wonder she's the diplomat, thought Pablo. He nodded his agreement to her logical reasoning.

The two Colombians positioned themselves next to the black limousine at the bottom of the moving stairwell which nuzzled up to the doors of Castro's aging Russian-built Antonov now parked on the tarmac. Eyes were peeled to spot Esteban Montealegre, Cuba's foreign minister. The Colombians were ready to demand an explanation and lodge their official protest.

The doors opened and the aging Commander of the Armed Forces, President of the Republic, and Keeper of the Revolution stepped off the airplane. He was dressed in military fatigues. His unkempt beard was, as usual, unkempt. Castro beamed a huge smile as he walked down the steps. Before Lucia Ramirez could say "Welcome to Colombia," Castro took both Colombians in his arms.

"Yes, yes, you must not be angry with me," said Castro, his eyes sparkling. "Fifteen years ago, when your president-elect spent a year studying international relations at the University of Havana, I gave a banquet for some of the foreign students and faculty. At that time, your president-to-be was a member of the University's Foreign Students Association," he said, reliving the event a decade and a half ago.

"I remember it well. As soon as we finished dinner, I got up to sit next to this charming Colombian," Castro continued. "When we were drinking the after-dinner rum, I asked: 'What has impressed you most about the year you have spent in Cuba.' Do you know what your new president answered? 'The mango ice cream we just ate, Comandante. It is unbelievable. The waiter told me that there is no more, but perhaps you could use your influence to get me another helping?' "

As Castro threw his head back in laughter, they all had to cover their ears as the now-infamous second Cubana airplane slammed onto the runway. The three watched the aircraft turn off the runway and taxi to Castro's presidential airplane.

As the newly landed airplane's motors wound down, Castro opened the door to the waiting limousine, winked at Vasquez, and patted Lucia on the arm. "So, my dear, before you even ask what this second plane is doing here, let me tell you that it would be good if you parked it in a shady spot. It is refrigerated, but the last thing we would want is to melt my present of 250 kilograms of Cuba's best mango ice cream before your president tried some." Howling with laughter, Castro closed his car door and sped off.

Vasquez and Lucia Ramirez stared at each other. Both had the same exact thought at exactly the same time: "So this is what the next four years are going to be like with Marta Pradilla as president of Colombia."

PART I
COLOMBIA

REUTERS WIRE SERVICE

FOREIGN DIGNITARIES CROWD INAUGURATION OF COLOMBIA'S NEW PRESIDENT

Bogotá, August 6. Marta Pradilla was sworn in today as Colombia's first female president. She was elected in a landslide victory.

Pradilla, single, 43 years old, took the helm of this war-torn South American country and immediately promised to set a new course. Nineteen heads of state—including U.S. president John Stockman—and millions of Colombians seemed to have one purpose in mind today: to get close to the new president. Pradilla is a former Miss Universe, a Rhodes Scholar, and served in the Colombian Senate for six years.

Pradilla is not the first woman to run for president in Colombia. Noemi Sanín, a well-known former foreign minister, tried and came close. Colombia is unusual in Latin America, as it has fielded a number of active and popular women in politics and government.

Pradilla takes over at a delicate time. Colombia, a country of 45 million, defies common stereotypes. It boasts hugely successful business conglomerates with a strong export sector in fresh cut flowers, textiles, seafood, and natural resources. It is home to world-renowned writers and important Spanish-language publishing houses. It has one of the region's strongest democratic traditions. Yet it continues to suffer from an endless cycle of violence from guerrillas and drugs. Negotiations with guerrillas broke down late last year, and voters sided with Pradilla's hard line.

Fluent in four languages, the new president was raised from the age of sixteen in France by her uncle, Francisco Gomez y Gomez, after terrorists belonging to one of the principal guerrilla organizations stormed her family's ranch in the early eighties. Her father, then the country's foreign minister, and mother were killed in the attack.

Known in Colombia as a straight talker, Pradilla is hard to catalogue politically. Within minutes, her inauguration speech caused controversy by proclaiming a hard line against violence from all sides.

"Let us all be clear with each other and with the world about what we think here in Colombia," said the new president. "We Colombians believe the time has come for those fighting illegal wars and creating violence from both the left and right to put down their guns. If you do so, we will help you reintegrate into society and become normal citizens. If you do not do so, the Colombian state has a right to find you, to fight you, capture you and, if necessary, extradite you for trial to foreign countries. Impunity will no longer be a fact of life in Colombia," said the new president.

Pradilla's announcement of her intention to reinstate the extradition of violent criminals to third countries clearly took observers by surprise. The extradition of powerful drug lords or guerrilla leaders to the United States and other nations has long been controversial in Colombia. Past leaders avoided the extradition issue because of its implicit admission of the inadequacy of Colombia's judicial system.

The president caused a number of controversies when her speech turned its attention to Europe and the United States.

Referring to the inability of developing countries to convince the industrialized world to decrease its protection of agriculture and textiles, Pradilla said, "Now is also the time for the world to consider a new pact with our country—one which goes beyond the military hardware. My government will seek a comprehensive open-door trade agreement with the world's more developed economies. Imagine the hope that could be kindled in the streets of Nairobi, Rio, and Delhi if we in Colombia would become a symbol of what is possible—pioneers in a trade pact unlike those negotiated in the past. This accord would have more paragraphs of agreement than clauses of exceptions."

"Last, we cannot help wonder if the time has come to explore other avenues, including legalization of some narcotics. In this manner, countries that consume drugs can oversee and regulate what obviously is impossible to control. And Colombia can cease to be the source of an illegal business that corrupts with its billions. If U.S., French, or Dutch junkies need heroin, perhaps we should let Merck or Pfizer or Aventis make the drugs. That should make everyone happy," stated Pradilla.

White House press secretary Allyson Bonnet had no official comment on President Pradilla's speech. But a highly placed U.S. government source said, "Any talk of legalization will not make friends in the United States."

The inauguration ceremonies will be capped tonight by a gala event at the Presidential Palace in Bogotá.

- End Story -

The U.S. Embassy

President John Stockman hated overseas trips. It wasn't the travel that bugged him. Mostly, it was the people he met. Foreigners were way too complicated for his Midwestern practicality. They talked too much, wasted too much time. Their conversation was too flowery.

"Decisions need to be made; let's make them and move on," was how John Stockman viewed his job.

On the way back to the U.S. embassy from the inauguration ceremony, inside the black limousine, Stockman peered out the window. Here he was in a far-off South American capital and, for the second time in less than three hours, stuck in a twelve-car convoy. He hardly heard the sirens of his motorcade—the president of the United States was used to driving with the unbearable acoustics of squealing police cars.

John Stockman was grumpy. He was irritated with himself for agreeing to come to Colombia for this woman's inauguration. His staff—incited by Nelson Cummins, his national security advisor—had been nearly unanimous in recommending he make the trip when it was proposed two months ago.

"With so many dignitaries coming to Colombia for the event, your absence will be noticeable," Cummins had argued sixty days earlier, at one of the daily national security briefings. "She seems impressive, Sir. I think it's worth doing. And, after all, the United States has been Colombia's closest ally in fighting drugs and terrorism. So, lots of us feel that we really can't miss this."

Shit, why had he allowed himself to be persuaded to come?

The swearing-in itself had been a quick forty-five-minute affair. One oath, one speech. Nonetheless, three quarters of an hour was enough for Señorita Pradilla to get on his nerves. Where did she get the balls to hint at drug legalization and souped-up trade pacts?

He wasn't the only one unhappy with her speech, though; Stockman noticed that some Colombian VIPs at the inauguration didn't applaud her intention to revive the extradition of criminals. The president leaned back in the car and looked at his watch.

Nonetheless, he had to admit to a small, grudging admiration for the new Colombian president's speech. She clearly did not run away from controversy, thought Stockman.

He ached to get back home—to real work—and toyed for a split second with the idea of telling the agents to keep driving straight to the airport. Damn the gala affair tonight. But he knew he couldn't do it—the world's newspapers would ooze with the insult committed by the American president.

So, instead, he grumbled his annoyance under his breath. "Seven hours in a country, and most of them in a damn car," he muttered.

Resigning himself, Stockman used the free time wisely and pushed his weight against the leather-bound seats until his head rocked comfortably on the headrest. He closed his eyes.

The president's mind drifted—as it often did—to his dead wife. Stockman had been celebrating his thirteenth anniversary in the U.S. Senate when his wife, Miranda, was diagnosed with non-Hodgkin's lymphoma. She made it through a year of hell—chemotherapy and radiation, hair loss, muscle aches, and the endless exhaustion.

During Miranda's twelve-month emotional roller coaster, Stockman went from touting a near-perfect voting record to missing almost half the votes in the Senate. He stayed at his wife's side through the doctors' appointments, the trips to Johns Hopkins and the Mayo Clinic, the hours-long intravenous drips in the chemotherapy centers, and finally through the slow realization that the drugs were not functioning. Nothing worked. The cancer kept coming and, on a rainy May night, Miranda passed away.

Throughout the ordeal, Stockman often asked himself what he would have done without Julia standing at his side. The couple's nineteen-year-old daughter, away at college in San Francisco, flew home to be with her mother within months of the diagnosis. Both parents tried to convince her not to come—college was too important for her to make an open-ended commitment to a sick parent. She should not get behind in her courses, they begged.

"If you are skipping votes, I can skip art history," Julia told her father. Stockman thought about it for a second and concluded that one should not argue with that type of logic.

Julia came back to Washington to be with her mother, but the person her presence helped most was her father. For two months, father and daughter cried together. They returned from the hospital at the end of each day and sat at the un-set dinner table to spoon canned soups. They met in the morning at sad, wordless breakfasts knowing they again faced the same tragic routine.

A month after Miranda's death, Julia started talking about leaving Stanford and transferring to Georgetown or George Washington University to be closer to her father. At that point, Senator Stockman put his foot down. Weeks later, Julia Stockman was back on an airplane to San Francisco, hoping to make up the lost semester at the Stanford Summer Program.

After her departure, Senator Stockman threw himself back into his work. Anything was better than facing the large, empty house in the Cleveland Park section of Washington. In October, to everybody's total surprise, John Stockman made the decision that would change his life. Partly to alleviate his solitude and partly out of patriotism, John Stockman announced his candidacy for the presidency.

For nearly a year, Stockman's campaign ran hard against the administration. It was not so much that there were deep policy differences—there weren't. But, the ever-widening scandals linking corporate malfeasance to cabinet officials and even to the vice president made an easy target for his campaign.

While the senator stayed above the fray, his campaign attacked. Television ads accused the president and his associates of repeated conflicts of interest. Overpriced Pentagon contracts. Deals without competitive procurement. Illegally distributing government bidding documents to corporate contributors. Blocking foreign companies from important contracts. The media loved each new accusation, echoing and repeating every twist and permutation of the scandals. Within months, the administration and the president's polling numbers had sunk to the low twenties. Weeks after that, Stockman won the election.

John Stockman forced himself out of his reverie as he felt the motorcade turning left off the mountainside parkway, which served as an express road for traffic going downtown from the city's northernmost reaches. The views of the city from this high road were stunning—Bogotá's tall skyscrapers mixed in with older residential neighborhoods to create a demented, see-saw architectural jumble. A cool, light drizzle coated the sidewalks. The few pedestrians stopping to watch the police caravan all wore sweaters and raincoats. He was amazed at how green Bogotá was—the majestic mountains surrounding the busy city below shone with bright emerald pastures and dark green pines. He was surprised, and just a little bit irritated; wasn't South America supposed to be hot? It would have never occurred to him that the closest thing to Bogotá's weather was Ireland's cool dampness.

Stockman had traveled little in his youth. He did not choose a career in politics because he cared about the world—he came to public service because of a deep sense of duty to the United States. John Stockman, a Nebraska farm kid, had been home schooled by his devoutly Lutheran parents. He missed out on Latin, never learned geography beyond Rand McNally's road map of America, and did not read Milton. Notwithstanding his tall, lanky good looks, he also never learned much about dating girls. Miranda had been his girlfriend since the age of fifteen.

His parents inculcated the boy with tough lessons about discipline, hard work, and service. As a result, John Stockman matured with clear certainties illuminating his life. During his youth, it was his devotion to the Boy Scouts. Later in life, it was his dedication to his country with five years as a Navy Seal. His marriage. His belief in God.

Doubting was for university professors with time to spare, not for him.

He knew some people thought that his clarity made him shallow. He begged to differ—it made him decisive.

Stockman heard the dying siren of the lead police car as the motorcade halted in front of the U.S. embassy's residential compound. Ambassador Morris Salzer was there to welcome him. He held a large umbrella out as the president stepped out of the car.

"Mr. President, we're glad to have you at the residence, if only for a few short hours. The fact is we don't often get the pleasure of a presidential sleepover here in Colombia," said the ambassador. Stockman had read up on Salzer—the posting in Colombia would be his last prior to retirement from a successful diplomatic career. He appreciated the ambassador's humor.

"Mr. Ambassador, I'm pleased you're hosting me, though I don't know what the hell I'm doing here—seems like a long way to come for a pajama party."

"Well, Sir, to tell you the truth, I'm surprised you came. I'm frankly not ready to say that the young Miss Pradilla will be a good friend to the United States. She has gall, that's for sure; but the proof will be in the pudding."

The two men stepped into the foyer. The ambassador led Stockman to a partition closed by two large double doors.

"Mr. President, the national security advisor asked if you and he could borrow the living room for a meeting," Salzer added. "He is waiting for you in here." Salzer opened one of the doors, led the president inside, and shook his hand.

"I look forward to taking you to the party, Sir. We'll leave shortly before 7:00 p.m."

President John Stockman walked into the embassy's ornate living room to meet his national security advisor, Nelson Cummins. The two men were alone in the embassy's majestic—ridiculously majestic—sitting area. There were at least ten sofas in the room. Who needed ten sofas? Particularly when the couches lived in a building hidden behind ten-foot bombproof concrete walls peppered on top with sharp shards of broken glass designed to dissuade climbers. The United States embassy in Colombia had sixty-five diplomats, but it needed more than a hundred guards, security personnel, and armed Marines to protect them.

"Mr. President, I need to talk to you about the press release on Syria. Since you are leaving for the inaugural party with the ambassador, I thought we might have a word now as I probably won't see you alone until the flight back."

Cummins was one of the few persons at the White House who knew the president well enough to dispense with the usual niceties. They had met eleven years ago when Cummins was the staff director of the Senate Committee on Intelligence. The two worked together since then. Mostly, Cummins liked the freedom that came from being employed by a man who did not think himself a foreign policy expert. Mostly. Every once in while, though, he was bothered by the president's stubbornness and his inability to see that the world was not singularly colored in black and white but mostly made of grays.

"Fine," Stockman said as he settled into one of the deeper sofas, "but I would write the release straight—without beating around the bush or letting people see words between the lines. It's not as if my idea about Syria is nuanced; let's make damn sure they get the message."

Cummins cringed, but tried hard not to show it. There was one other thing about Stockman that drove Cummins crazy. Namely, he hated the president's intellectual stinginess. Other people's good ideas magically morphed into Stockman's, and credit was rarely shared. True to form, the president now conveniently forgot that the recommendation to put the question of Syria before the Security Council of the United Nations was Cummins's idea.

For years, Syria and its young president, Bashar al-Assad, had done everything possible to trouble and complicate the U.S. military mission in Iraq. Syria continued to harbor terrorist bases. It still functioned as a money funnel for Hezbollah, Islamic Jihad, and other radical groups.

Recent intelligence from senior al-Qaeda prisoners pointed to the involvement of Syrian intelligence officials and/or Syrian-based groups in the recent attack on a Continental Airlines airplane outside of Madrid. Two Saudi citizens had used a shoulder-launched missile to attack the airplane. It had missed, thank God. The terrorists had been so exorcised about the miss that they tried to launch again and locked the firing system. Spanish police captured both attackers and the weaponry. U.S. intelligence traced the hardware back to Damascus.

Four months ago, Cummins had recommended that the United States propose a resolution at the United Nations to send Syria a clear ultimatum: Desist now or suffer the consequences. Notwithstanding President Bush's UN fiasco prior to the U.S. invasion of Iraq, Cummins was certain that this time a well-orchestrated diplomatic effort would get the needed votes on the Security Council.

The decision to return to the United Nations for world approval of a U.S. policy initiative had been incredibly controversial among John Stockman's seven-person national security team at the White House. The secretary of defense warned that the United States would again become bogged down and limited by the UN's indecision. The secretary of state believed that America could ill afford another confrontation with its allies and recommended against any type of ultimatum. They all had objections.

"Tell the Pentagon that I don't want to read non-attributable statements in the *Washington Post* about how parts of the Stockman administration still believe that the idea of returning to the UN is an incredible blunder," said the president, cognizant that many of his senior advisors still harbored doubts. "I expect loyalty on this, Nelson. Pass that message on."

"Yes, sir. I'll pass it on, though I would not take a bet that the Pentagon will roll over and play dead. Those military guys sound so sincere when they talk about loyalty and patriotism, but they're the most experienced bureaucratic players in Washington."

"You tell the secretary of defense that we had this debate a few weeks ago, and it's over. He said his piece and lost. Tell him that I remain totally sure we'll be able to get a tough resolution out of the Security Council, Nelson. I can give you ten sophisticated sounding reasons for why the UN Security Council will give us what we want this time, but, deep down, we'll succeed for the simplest reason of all."

Stockman stopped for a dramatic pause to savor just how knowledgeable he was sounding.

"Namely, the UN and, in particular, the Europeans are tired of fighting and arguing with the United States. There is feud fatigue—no stomach for another transatlantic spat," the president concluded.

Cummins grimaced again. This time he was sure the president saw his irritation. But he couldn't help it: That nice turn of phrase, "feud-fatigue," was his, not Stockman's. Now the president was proudly parading it in his own rhetorical arsenal.

Cummins forced his pettiness to the mental back burner. This guy pays my salary, so my ideas are his to repackage as his own. That's how it works in Washington, thought Nelson to himself.

President Stockman was right about the UN. It would, most likely, give the

United States the resolution it wanted. And, once approved, the tough line against Syria would have a ton of side benefits. First and most important, a win at the Security Council would signal an end to the transatlantic skirmishes between Western allies. But it would also show up the important character differences between the previous administration and President Stockman. A few years ago, an exasperated U.S. government had decided to go it alone in Iraq. Stockman, on the other hand, would prove that he was capable of leading the world and, in turn, the world would allow itself to be led by America's president. Politically, such a success would be priceless.

"So, can't we use this little get together in Bogotá to rally the troops?" Stockman asked, getting excited about his UN plan. The president was now fired up on foreign policy, a state of mind that occurred very, very rarely.

"Except for Castro, why not have a meeting here to negotiate the UN resolution?" continued Stockman, further warming to the issue. "Jacques Rozert is here. The British foreign secretary is here. Colombia, Brazil, and Costa Rica are on the Security Council this year, and they're all here. Why don't we try to get them together and come out of here with a plan of action?" insisted Stockman.

Nelson Cummins did what staff around the world—no matter how senior— occasionally had to do. He lied to assuage his boss.

"Mr. President, your UN idea about Syria is brilliant. But this is not the time. Since Iraq, the United States government has repeatedly been taken to task for using every relationship to force friends into taking sides on the Middle East. The perception is that we're not really interested in the rest of the world or its own particular set of issues—only in support for our policies in the Middle East," Cummins reminded the president.

Stockman kept quiet, so Cummins kept going.

"Let's do things differently. Let's prove that we want to talk about what matters to Latin Americans. Let's start a dialogue about immigration. Trade. Debt. Economic reform. Poverty alleviation. Every Latin American head of state here except Castro is democratically elected. Let's create a hemispheric partnership on the stuff they want."

Cummins continued with his logic. "Think about it. The haphazard rotation of the Security Council places four Latin American countries on the Security Council: Colombia, Costa Rica, Cuba, and Brazil. We need their support, and it's far from a slam dunk. Remember that at the time of the Iraq debate, Mexico and Chile were on the council. Both voted against us.

"I know. What's your point, Cummins?" the president interrupted.

"Don't bully them," Cummins warned. "You will make a very good impression if you at least seem interested in their issues. Then, I guarantee that we can come back to them in a couple of weeks on Syria."

"What do I do with Castro?" asked Stockman, changing the subject.

Cummins knew he had won this round. John Stockman never conceded an intellectual point. This president was not a man who thoughtfully scratched his chin and said, *Nelson, I considered this and have concluded that you make a lot of sense. I want to do it your way.* No. The best victory you could get from Stockman was a change of subject.

Cummins answered, pressing his advantage. "Mr. President, why not acknowledge his presence? Doesn't mean you have to embrace him or love him in public. But, if he wants to shake your hand, take it. Everybody knows he is an anachronism—an aging dictator. But people down here love the guy, mainly because we hate him. Forty years of shunning him have gotten us nowhere. Let's show people that John Stockman does things differently," Cummins said.

President John Stockman stared at his advisor, thinking that sometimes Cummins transformed himself from a foreign policy genius into a complete idiot. Did he not understand anything of American politics? How could he be so knowledgeable about Turkey or Trinidad but know nothing of Tallahassee? Did he not know that there is a place called Florida and that it is full of people from Cuba and therefore very important politically? What a moron.

"Fuck off," said the president to his senior foreign policy advisor as he got up to put on his black tie for the inaugural dinner.

The Inauguration Gala
Bogotá, August 6
6:30 p.m.

This was President Marta Pradilla's first time alone that day. With only a half hour to go before the inaugural gala, she welcomed the temporary solitude of the private residence on the third floor of Casa de Nariño, Colombia's presidential palace. Casa de Nariño was an odd, turn-of-the-century building with heavy colonial overtones. Some rooms and halls were beautiful and ornate; others, drab and gray. There was little rhyme or reason to the decoration.

Outside, she heard the Palace Guards, a division of the Colombian Army, lowering the flag at dusk. She remembered the first time she had seen the ceremony. Dressed in blue, like German praetorian guards with cone-shaped metal helmets, the guards carried medieval lances and goose-stepped down the street, turning left into the palace courtyard, on their way to the flagpole. The army band played unintelligible martial music that supposedly syncopated to the rhythm of the guards' steps. The ritual was god-awful, and it was done twice a day.

She had first witnessed this surreal scene fifteen years ago with President Virgilio Barco, the aging Colombian patriarch with a doctorate in engineering from Yale. He had disgustedly slammed the window shut as the martial music began to play. "Pradilla," he had said—Barco never called anybody by their first name—"this is life in the tropics. You take the sublime with the ridiculous."

Marta laughed away the memory wondering whether the now-deceased ex-president would catalogue her present situation as sublime or ridiculous. She was president of Colombia now, for four hours. But she was not signing decrees or naming ministers. She was nearly naked in front of a mirror and wondering, like millions of women the world over, what she would wear that night.

She was beautiful. There was no doubting that. Brown, medium-length hair caressed broad shoulders strengthened by years of swimming competitively. Though her forty-plus-year-old body was no longer the vehicle that garnered the title of Miss Universe, she was still well formed and taut. Her breasts were slightly smaller than she might have liked. But that had never stopped any man from looking.

Her beauty was a political double-edged sword, and she knew that. Too many people had ascribed her victory to a vote for good looks. "Sure," they said, "she looks like a movie star. A problematic country like Colombia needs to drown its sorrows in the false pool of beauty. That is why she got elected." She had heard the same cheap psycho-babble during the campaign. But Marta Pradilla was way too practical to let this type of resentful rumbling worry her.

Marta dressed impeccably. Ten years with her uncle in Paris had taught her the French art of converting an already beautiful woman into an irresistible spectacle. Marta reached for a blue dress by Spanish designer Lorenzo Caprile. A few years ago, Caprile had designed the wedding dress for Princess Leticia's marriage to Prince Felipe, the Spanish heir. True to the couturier's unique style, this dress comfortably combined sexy and sedate in a single garment.

It was deliciously low in the front and cut off at the shoulders. It had two slits—no, *one* would not be enough today—not front and back, but rather on both sides of her strong, silken thighs. She would concede to protocol today and put on stockings although she hated covering her legs. Legs had to be free: They were, Marta Pradilla had always thought, what make a woman so special.

She finished with a pinkish-purple Burberry's cashmere Pashmina from London. She slung it over her shoulders, but was careful not to cover them entirely. "Great thing, being an ex–Miss Universe," she muttered with mock self-satisfaction. "The designers keep sending me clothes for free." As the mirror responded admiringly at how well the dress hung on her lithe body first from one side, then from another, she wondered if her closet would suffer during her presidency.

Ready for tonight's celebration, she opened the door to her bedroom and found Manuel Saldivar, her chief of staff, press secretary, and most trusted advisor, sitting—no, slouching—on one of the sofas just outside the presidential bedroom. Manuel was exhausted. He had held four official press conferences in the last six hours: one for the Bogotá elite press, one for television and radio, one for press from Colombia's smaller cities and towns, and one for the foreign press corps. He also had given twenty one-on-one interviews to the world's major newspapers and magazines, including the *New York Times,* the *Financial Times, El Pais, Le Monde,* the *Frankfurter Allgemeine Zeitung,* and *The Economist.*

Manuel Saldivar was one of a series of President Pradilla's young, cabinet-level appointments. Nearly thirty, he was officially part of what one of Bogotá's best-read old-school columnists derisively called "the kindergarten"—namely, the slew of young cabinet nominations made by the novice female president. Manuel wondered if the crochety old journalist would consider the thirty-five-year-old minister of justice too old for the kindergarten.

Saldivar was a boy genius. At the age of twenty-four he had written *Hooked*, a hugely successful novel about a fish's conversation with a scuba diver (from the fish's point of view), even though—in real life—he was afraid of the water. Critics and intellectuals swooned, concluding the story was a metaphoric mirror for the fact that Colombia's white-skinned elite lived amongst an oceanful of mestizo and mulatto countrymen. Saldivar always denied this. Fish had a lot to say on their own and did not need to be a metaphor for any human group, he had retorted with a smile.

At twenty-six he had been given the job of heading the investigative unit of *El Tiempo*, Colombia's largest and most prestigious newspaper. Saldivar had personally overseen a groundbreaking journalistic investigation that detailed the wide connections between drug trafficking and the purchase of illegal arms by Colombia's guerrilla groups. His investigative pieces on the guerrillas' addiction to the drug trade were admiringly translated into eight languages and published in magazines ranging from *L'Espresso* in Rome to the *New Republic* in Washington.

He met then senator Marta Pradilla while working for the newspaper. He went to see her to propose using her father's assassination as a backdrop for one of his exposés on the guerrillas' illegal arms imports. Saldivar felt instantly comfortable in Pradilla's modern, minimalist apartment. Instead of launching into the interview, they spoke for hours about rock music. She bragged that her collection of rock CDs and LPs was the best in Colombia and invited Manuel to rummage through her shelves. He countered strongly, claiming that his collection, numbering more than a thousand albums, was the best in the country.

He had Iron Butterfly's rare first album. She had a limited edition copy of a 1975 Rolling Stones concert given in a small two-hundred-person theater in Tokyo. Thus began an argument between them that rages to this very day.

But it also started a relationship of mutual trust and friendship that was to become the envy of Bogotá. Pradilla consulted Manuel on her speeches and political messaging. When she decided to run for president, the first call she made was to Manuel Saldivar. He had agreed to become the campaign's manager and communications director. Now, with his thirtieth birthday just a week away, he was the president's chief of staff and press secretary. He could hardly believe it—the campaign, the victory, the inauguration—it had all happened so fast.

"Nutty country," Manuel Saldivar kept saying to himself.

Manuel was shaken out of his exhaustion by the sight of his friend, the president of Colombia, coming out of the presidential private quarters.

"Marta," gushed Manuel, "you look perfect—a little too sexy for the new president of a conservative country, but that's the way it is with you." Manuel meant the compliment. Strong politics and relentless smarts coexisted easily with sleek sexiness inside Marta Pradilla. It was useless to tell his friend to opt for traditionalism on her first presidential outing.

As they walked toward the elevators that would take them to the palace's ballrooms, the two laughed as Manuel told President Pradilla that the palace's staff was in a twist about how to address the new president. As a typical journalist, Manuel had eavesdropped on Juan Pablo Ortiz, the chief butler for over twenty years, debating with the staff on whether to call the new president "Señora Presidenta," "Señorita Presidente," or just "Señora." Who knew? Colombia was unusual in Latin America because it had so many important women in politics and business. But actually having a woman as head of state was new territory for them all.

As they descended from the private quarters in the elevator, Don Ignacio, the delightful seventy-year-old elevator operator, cut through the problem with a simple "Buenas noches, Presidente." Don Ignacio just used with Marta exactly the same appellation he had used for years to address every male president before her. He finessed the gender issue by using the male form in Spanish. He was right. Why not just keep addressing the present holder of the office with the same title held by all previous officeholders? Marta winked at Manuel as the elevator doors opened before them.

Before walking into the ballroom, they reviewed the evening's plans. Of course, the idea was to impress all the foreign and local dignitaries. But the president of the United States was the evening's principal target. Marta would hit him twice—first with her knowledge of economics and trade when she would argue for a six-month, lightning timetable for a free-trade agreement between Colombia and the United States. And the second, ah . . . the second, would involve a little mischief that would make a lot of headlines.

She entered the ballroom one minute late at precisely 7:01 p.m. to the applause of the 150 invitees. Even as she made the rounds to greet her guests, the applause lingered for more than ten minutes. Most of the dignitaries pecked kisses on her cheeks. A few went their own way. Brazil's working-class, man-of-the-people president, Roberto Flamengo, delivered the obligatory kisses and then slammed her into a breath-removing embrace that was surely designed more to feel her breasts than to measure her politics. France's Jacques Rozert inclined his tall, lanky body and kissed her right hand with formal fanfare. Japanese foreign minister Yunchiro Hazawa bowed deeply. And U.S. president John Stockman, still irritated about her earlier comments on drug legalization and desirous that everybody in the room realize his dissatisfaction, just shook her hand.

Not everybody in the room was a fan. Juan Francisco Abdoul, the president of the Colombian Senate, did not clap and did not smile. He represented the sizable Arab community of mostly Syrian descent that lived in the city of Barranquilla, on Colombia's northern coast.

After two brutal decades in which many Colombian prosecutors, police detectives, and journalists were killed, Colombia was finally winning the war against the corruption of the country's political dynasties. It was getting a new generation of political leaders. Marta Pradilla was the prime example. But not the only one. On the other side of the ballroom two good-looking men, the former and present mayors of Bogotá, were laughing and drinking together. Between the two, they had started to cleanse the city of crime, endless garbage, and horrendous traffic. With smart economics and sophisticated international connections, they gave Bogotá back to the people by building bike lanes, parks, and, most importantly, real social security nets for the urban poor.

Juan Francisco Abdoul, however, was a big-time holdover from the past. Together with his brother, Ricardo Abdoul, the mayor of Barranquilla, the family represented the worst of Colombia's politicians—a mixture of nepotism, mafia tactics, and ruthlessness financed by their drug and contraband operations. Mayor Ricardo Abdoul had lost the Liberal Party's presidential nomination to Marta Pradilla. The fight had been brutal, but Marta had won by being straight and calling the Abdoul brothers exactly what they were: the worst of Colombia.

Juan Francisco Abdoul was only invited to the evening's gala because the president of Senate had to be invited. He came only because he had to come. But the Abdoul family had vowed never to forgive her.

Marta Pradilla went through the receiving line and was now at the end of her rounds in the ballroom. Abdoul was one of the last to be greeted, and she reached out to take his hand. Dressed in a black suit, white shirt, and cream-colored tie, Abdoul took the president's hand in his. He had golden rings on three of his five fingers.

"Marta, what does one say to a former Miss Universe who has reached such surprisingly high levels?" sneered Abdoul with a voice so loud that all nearby were able to hear his deep disdain.

Marta Pradilla kept his hand in hers. She looked at him—no, she knifed him with her dark green eyes—for what seemed forever. She did not smile but she did not scowl. She just stared. She would not let go. She would not stop looking straight into him. Time ticked by. Abdoul became increasingly uncomfortable at the realization that, first fifteen and then thirty endless seconds passed and she was still not letting go and was still saying nothing. Around them, silence slowly descended as the ballroom realized what was happening. Conversations between presidents, foreign ministers, priests, deacons, politicians, and artists slowly ground to a halt and all eyes turned toward the two Colombians.

After what seemed like a lifetime, Marta looked at Abdoul and spoke very slowly: "One says: Buenas noches, Presidente."

With that she dropped his hand and turned just as President Alberto Granada of Mexico headed her way.

After Dinner

Bogotá, August 6

9:45 p.m.

"Mr. President, if this hemisphere is to prosper we all need to change tracks," said President Marta Pradilla to President John Stockman. "In the last twenty years, we declared the war on drugs, the battle against poverty, and the fight against corruption. Yet, today the Americas together make and consume more drugs, have greater poverty, and suffer the same corruption. We can't keep trying to do the same things and pretend that this time they will work when we know they won't. Let's take the opportunity and try something new."

They were in a small alcove just on the right side of the immense ballroom. Dinner had gone well. Rather than the usual pseudo-French cuisine served at diplomatic gatherings, Marta Pradilla had asked Harry Ricart, Colombia's superstar chef, to prepare the dinner. It was modern, avant-garde cooking. Soup that began hot and ended cold; foie gras nearly reduced to foam and then lifted victoriously over sweetbreads and served in a cappuccino cup; balsamic vinegar reductions sprinkled over Caribbean spiny lobster; and, finally, playful sweets of 100 percent Colombian cocoa boiled and poured over tropical fruits and then served frozen.

Marta had sought out Harry Ricart's cooking to make a point about Colombia. Her country might be known as suffering a number of dreadful diseases—poverty, violence, drugs, and terrorism—but it was also young, hopeful, creative, and talented. Marta intended the dinner as a political statement. She wanted guests to know that there was a new Colombia. It was subtle gastronomic politics, but the message came through loud and clear.

As guests were milling about with after dinner drinks, she had taken President Stockman by the arm and led him slowly to the small alcove, decorated with huge renditions of Fernando Botero's world renowned murals of oversized women. She would have only a few minutes—it would not be polite or politic to leave the others alone too long.

"We in Colombia understand that the United States has been preoccupied elsewhere. We know that you are fighting in the Middle East for much of what we all hold precious in the West," continued President Pradilla. "But, sometimes it seems that America has forgotten that it was founded and built on hope. Every second word now coming from the U.S. government is 'terrorism.' You cannot build leadership if you talk only about your fears *of* the world. You must also talk about your hopes *for* it."

Stockman was irritated already. The last thing he wanted was to hear advice from a novice colleague whose total time in leadership was less than eight hours. He decided that the best move was no move, no comment. He knew she would have to get back to the party and that this lecture could not last long.

"At least she's good to look at," he thought to himself.

Marta continued, knowing full well that she was getting on his nerves. She had studied this man in depth—his speeches, his television interviews, his opinions, and his obsession with loyalty. "The guy does not respond well to dreamy proclamations," she had told Manuel. "He is all about the business of politics. And, deep down, he does not think women are pragmatic enough to be good at it."

So, to hook him, she would first launch an ethereal appeal about hope. It was not that she didn't believe in what she said—she honestly thought that America's fears were putting at risk the can-do, positive magnetism that was the core of its being. But she knew that he would be repulsed by anything sounding flowery. So, her plan was to make him complacent, confirming that she was the typical woman he expected her to be; then she'd surprise him with highly specific requests. She learned long ago that politics was a game of expectation. If you do better than expected, you win.

"Here in Latin America, we still want to hope, Mr. President," said Marta. "We have been your partner in the fight against drugs and have supported the United States in the war on terrorism. Be our partner back."

Stockman turned his eyes away to hide his exasperation. What the hell did this rookie woman want? He was about to answer that $7 billion in military and police assistance from the United States in the past three years was damn good partnering. But as he started forming the words, she kept going.

"I want to leave a thought with you: Join me in creating a free-trade agreement with our country—totally free, with none of the usual exceptions for agriculture, textiles, and manufactured goods," Marta argued, as she lightly put her hand on his arm.

"Mr. President—John if you will permit me—the issue is no longer about protecting the U.S. from foreign imports. The fact is that if you don't make a deal with us, you'll be flooded with Chinese goods. It's a choice you have to make: Either your neighbors and friends in Latin America can supply bras for your women, farm the soy you eat, and assemble the televisions you watch; or China can do it. But if you choose us, we need a better, newer high-octane trade deal."

Stockman was annoyed to find that he was actually paying attention. "Suddenly, she sounds so much more commanding," he thought to himself, wondering what it was about her delivery that had him listening from one minute to the next. The thoughts started piling up in his head, when he realized that she was moving on. He forced his mind to reorient its concentration.

"The United States has become a service economy. Old textile states like South Carolina now have high productivity levels in non-textile activities." Marta was accelerating strongly now. She saw that something changed in his eyes—the blue in his iris was sharp and focused. The irritable, distant glaze was gone. For the first time, she thought she might understand what voters saw in this man: When he was interested, he actually looked like he cared.

"The United States can afford—and benefit from—a serious trade agreement with a country like mine," she continued. "Don't answer me now, but I want you to consider a fully free trade zone with agriculture, textiles, and manufactured goods moving across borders without taxes or duties. This is more than a free-trade deal. It will be a hemispheric development pact. And we should negotiate, agree, and sign it in less than six months.

"This is what will give hope to Colombians and get them to once again believe in the United States." As she finished, her cashmere pashmina fell slightly, revealing over the right shoulder the deep sartorial cut in her dress.

Stockman could not keep his eyes off that shoulder. She was gorgeous and damned smart. She had turned an irritating lecture on hope into a cogent argument about prosperity and poverty alleviation. She even ended with a clear policy recommendation. Against his better judgment, Stockman admitted to himself that he was impressed.

It was then that he noticed that she had still not taken her hand from around his arm. He felt a passing warm tingle. After all, the world was not exactly full of gorgeous presidents.

"President Pradilla," Stockman began, "America needs to do what it is doing in the Middle East because we believe the Western world and secular democracy are in danger. I sure hope you realize that. I'll take your suggestion home with me because I know that trade is the only real door to economic growth and social peace in our hemisphere—but don't get your hopes up. Textiles and agriculture are still important political players in my country, and you don't just decide to hit them with a lightning agreement that may cause a lot of damage.

able to avoid others knowing it occurred. But nobody needs to know what was discussed. I won't tell if you promise not to."

She opened the door and watched the guests look agape as they witnessed the president of the United States and the president of Cuba, two of the world's oldest enemies, reentering the palace's ballroom in the company of the newly inaugurated president of Colombia.

Ernesto Cortissoz International Airport

Barranquilla, August 6

10:00 p.m.

One thousand miles to the north of the fanfare in the presidential palace, in the Colombian port city of Barranquilla, Alicia Ortega was at gate 6, ready to board Avianca flight 073 to Miami. Pretty with dark piercing eyes, Alicia just turned twenty-three. She had already taken this flight three times so she knew where to go and what to do.

Her new baby girl was three months old and she felt guilty leaving the gurgling infant behind. Alicia would be gone less than a week, but it bothered her to leave the baby with her sister, Gabriela. Gabriela had her own problems; she worked nearly fifty hours a week to make ends meet. Gabriela had pleaded with her sister not to go, but Alicia argued that the money would be too good to miss. With her earnings, Alicia promised to hire a maid to take care of the baby and cook for the two sisters. The money would even be enough to cover their rent for a few months. That would permit Gabriela to quit her waitressing job in a hotel and find better, less strenuous work.

Alicia looked around the gate area. She knew that there could be as many as five to ten other women just like her on tonight's flight. Some were with husbands. Some traveled with mothers or fathers. Some were older and others younger. Once, on a similar airplane, one of the women was wearing a nun's habit.

All of them carried a pound or so of highly refined heroin in their gut.

The previous trips had gone well. There were many stories about how hard it was to swallow the stuff, but Alicia never had any real problems. She swallowed over a hundred pills, each containing one or two grams, in a latex bag that resembled a condom.

She had become pretty adept at the preparation. At first, under the guise of "teaching" Alicia how to handle the narcotics, the traffickers had kept watch on her. Now she had earned their trust and was on her own.

Four hours before flight time, Alicia had carefully cut off the individual fingers of the latex surgical gloves given to her. She tapped down a couple of the pills into the bottom of the plastic finger and tied it tightly in place with a square knot of dental floss. Then she repeated the operation, first tapping down the pills, then using dental floss to secure the pills into place. In the end, she got about five little chambers—each separated by strongly knotted floss—into each plastic finger.

When she was done with a finger, she carefully folded it into two and tied the two ends together. That got her a plastic ball the size of four or five grapes bunched together. The balls were hard to swallow, but she ingested each bag with big swigs of Diet Coke as they were ready, rather than taking them in all at once.

By the time she was done, she had swallowed twenty-one bags equaling about 450 grams—about a pound. She recognized the feeling now slowly creeping into her gut. But, there was a difference from past jobs: This was the first time she carried heroin. On her previous trips, she had transported cocaine. A pound of cocaine got about $6,000 in the United States. With her handlers' heightened confidence, they had graduated her to the more lucrative stuff. The heroin now inside her had a street value of about $30,000–$40,000.

She was a "mule"—a carrier—one cog in the massive drug-trafficking machinery of the Abdoul family. Her controller had come by the house earlier in the day with her drugs, a counterfeit passport, some letters to stuff in her suitcase from a nonexistent brother in Charlotte, North Carolina—it was false proof that she was on her way to visit family in America. The letters were handwritten and even postmarked from Charlotte. These guys had planned everything, thought Alicia.

They had given her $1,000 for the trip. She would be paid $5,000 on delivery and would even get a bonus of $2,500 upon her return to Barranquilla. This was nearly 50 percent more than she got carrying cocaine.

Alicia knew there were many dangers throughout the trip, the greatest of which would come at the end. At check-in, the airlines had asked security questions designed to identify and weed out the nervous nellies. No worries. She had good answers to such questions as *How did you pay for your ticket? Whom are you going to see? Where do you work?*

As she went through outbound passport control, the agents of the DAS—Colombia's FBI equivalent—scrutinized her documents and again asked questions about her, where she lived and where she was going. They were looking for false passports and suspicious stories.

In the air, the flight attendants would offer her drinks and food. While she would accept the in-flight meal so as not to attract attention, she was strictly prohibited from eating or drinking anything but water. She had bought some souvenir bags of 100 percent Colombian coffee with the picture of Juan Valdez and his donkey at the duty-free shop and had flushed the black grounds down the ladies room toilet next to her gate. On board, Alicia would shove the uneaten food into the empty coffee bags to avoid raising the crew's suspicions.

Alicia could handle all those hurdles. But the big danger lay in the endless minutes after landing in Miami International Airport. She knew the airport's setup from previous trips. Unlike their practice with flights arriving from other countries, U.S. Immigration, Customs, and DEA agents met passengers from Colombia at the plane's door. Agents experienced in the creativity of the drug trade scrutinized passports and faces. There were cameras every hundred feet as passengers walked to passport control. There, Immigration officers would ask a lot of questions.

Once in the baggage hall, flights from Colombia were segregated physically from other arriving flights. U.S. Customs officials and DEA agents walked dogs around each traveler and their luggage. Passengers were routinely asked to join agents for interviews in small rooms adjoining the customs hall. Strip searches were common.

Alicia could not blame the gringos for their show of vigilance, but it was a ridiculous exercise in futility. They were good at what they did, but they just could not stop the volume. Narcotics by the hundreds of pounds crossed the U.S. border every day from South America, the Caribbean, and across the Rio Grande from Mexico. The drugs came by airplane, car, boat, drone, airmail, and FedEx. The drugs came and came because America was addicted. It could not be stopped.

Using mules—*mulas* in Spanish—was one of the Abdoul family's favorite tactics. The Abdouls were a diversified mafia whose businesses included control of ports, duty-free shops, and a bank, owned through dummy corporations used to launder drug monies. Since drugs were not all the family did, its narcotics operations did not have the flair of the legendary Medellín and Cali cartels. The Abdouls did not have their own fleet of airplanes, landing strips, and corrupted drug prevention officials. Instead, they smuggled in cargo ships and by airfreight, and sent the products to Mexico for reexportation across the Rio Grande.

But, their favorite smuggling mechanism was mules—lots of them. There was an endless supply of willing takers. And, in the mule world, there was a little of everything.

Some mules carried drugs because they owed something to the Abdoul family. Others were people—mostly women—who needed money. Some even did it for fun. Once, Alicia met a girl of twenty-one with a pompous-sounding, triple-barreled last name who had flown to Miami as an exception. "I prefer Madrid because that is where I like to buy clothes," the girl had told Alicia.

Mules were easy to manage. They obeyed orders. Upon arrival and once through U.S. Customs, all the mules on a flight went to predetermined hotels. There, they sat in their rooms until nature took its course. Once his or her bowels were evacuated, each mule removed the shit from the toilet bowl and carefully fished out the latex balls. The bags needed to be cleansed with great patience and opened. Each swallowed pill had to be counted and accounted. Counting was important. The same number that went in had to come out.

Sometimes the mules took Lomotil to avoid shitting during the trip. This was a curse, because once the mules arrived, the local handlers wanted everybody's merchandise within twelve hours. Those who took the powerful antidiarrhea medicine naturally had to wait longer than others to go to the bathroom. This just made operatives of the Colombian mafia's U.S.-based distribution machine very jumpy. Wreaking havoc on a mule's digestive system for weeks to come, the drug handlers often forced "tardy" mules to take huge amounts of cod liver oil to get the narcotics.

Sometimes things went wrong and a mule got busted—but most got through. Occasionally, one of the latex bags burst. This led to a fast but painful death as the body began to take in a massive amount of purified narcotic. It did not occur often, but it happened.

Such a loss was of little consequence to the Abdoul family or any of the other criminal organizations that trafficked Colombia's drugs. America's insatiable demand for the drugs meant there was an endless supply of carriers interested in taking a delivery to Europe or America for $5,000–$10,000 per trip.

Alicia handed the agent her boarding pass and walked onto the Avianca Boeing 757. She found her window seat and nestled in for the two-and-a-half-hour ride. She hardly felt the takeoff. She slept until the food came around and smilingly accepted her tray of lasagna. When her neighbors were not looking, she stuffed the pasta into the coffee bags she had bought at the airport. With about a half hour to go before landing in Miami, Alicia climbed over the two American guys who worked for British Petroleum and went to the forward lavatory to take a pee.

There, she heard the pilot announce the initial descent to Miami's international airport. She felt a tingle of nervousness but brushed it away. She was opening the narrow door to head back to her seat when she immediately heard the commotion.

"Come back here this instant," screamed a fat Spanish-speaking lady chasing after her six-year-old twin boys who careened straight up the narrow aisle toward First Class. Both twins collided solidly with Alicia's midsection and sent her flying into the galley. She slammed against the food carts that flight attendants were putting away for landing. Blood dripped from a small cut above Alicia's left eye.

John Ribeiros, the senior flight attendant, helped her up. Alicia felt okay, except that her head hurt. She was grateful for the purser's help in getting off the floor. He handed her a Kleenex for her cut and accompanied her back to her seat.

As she fastened her seat belt, Alicia smiled weakly to the two men and said something about all kids being beyond anybody's control. Just as she thought to herself that the last thing she needed was to be bumped around, a sharp piercing pain in her abdomen doubled her over. Alicia screamed.

"It can't be," Alicia shouted. She tried to calm herself down. She must have hit the cart harder than she thought. Everything was fine. Just as the initial pain subsided, a second massive burst struck her gut.

As the flaps of the 757 extended and the airplane banked left to line up with Miami's runway 27, Alicia began to sweat uncontrollably. Everything was not fine—she now knew what happened, and realized there was nothing she could do. Sweat rushed from her forehead, and her body and arms trembled uncontrollably. Her heart was accelerating out of control. One of her neighbors pushed the flight attendant button. But the plane was now lowering its landing gear as it began its final approach. No one came.

Alicia lost control of her physical functions. Her mouth began to froth, with saliva and mucous bubbling out of her. Her body was now in full shutdown as the narcotics took over. Alicia was shaking uncontrollably and did not feel the plane's wheels hit the runway. The petroleum workers would later tell the police that it looked like she was having an epileptic fit.

As the pilot pulled the throttle backwards to engage the reverse thrust, Alicia could not get one final thought out of her head.

"Goddamnit, the bags broke," Alicia repeated over and over, as she took in her last breath.

PART II
COLOMBIA

The House for Illustrious Guests
Cartagena, August 15
11:10 a.m.

Manuel Saldivar was sure no structure could live up to such a pompous-sounding name. But within two minutes of his arrival at the Cartagena House for Illustrious Guests he knew he was very wrong.

Cartagena, the magical colonial city on Colombia's northern coast, conjures up images of pirates and buccaneers. With good reason. Cartagena was the main port of the Spanish Empire in South America, the loading point for the Incan gold it plundered. For over a hundred years, unbelievable riches went through its two naval entrances.

One of the bays, called Boca Grande—"Large Mouth"—was indefensible. The entrance was too big to stop an organized attack from pirates or foreign enemies. So, late in the seventeenth century, the Spanish viceroy ordered Large Mouth sealed. In a line nearly a mile wide, hundreds of boats were sunk in the bay's shallow waters, forever impeding access from the Caribbean. Those obstacles still litter Boca Grande today.

Boca Chica—"Small Mouth"—could, on the other hand, be secured. A narrow waterway between two points only hundreds of yards apart opened to Cartagena's splendid curving bay. At each side of the bay's entrance, the Spanish built magnificent fortresses with the most modern arsenals. Boats that dared to enter without permission would be pelted from each side with cannon fire and incendiary bombs.

Next to one of those three-hundred-year-old castles, the one that sat on Boca Chica's easternmost flank, rose the House for Illustrious Guests. Built in the early 1970s and commissioned by former president Julio Cesar Turbay, the house was to serve the government of Colombia as a place to host international meetings and offer inspiration to important visitors. Like a Caribbean Camp David, the building also became the weekend residence for Colombia's presidents.

Manuel entered the house and drew in a deep breath. Earlier in the week, Marta announced that she wanted to spend her very first weekend in office at the famous Cartagena house. She invited Manuel to come along. He arrived a day after the president.

The House for Illustrious Guests was not at all what Manuel expected. He had imagined a glittering, over-the-top structure designed to impress those already rich, opulent, and famous. The building's reality could not have been more different.

Designed by prize-winning architect Rogelio Salmona, the house impressed guests by letting nature do the talking. Built of plain, exposed red brick, the main living area had windows and patios with nearly 270-degree vistas taking in the bay of Cartagena and the colonial city. As visitors moved from room to room, they were forced into porticos that took them outside, inside and then back out, each passageway laced with small rivers and canals of running water. Water was everywhere.

Manuel was shown to his room by a young naval officer. He was instantly impressed with the room's ascetic monasticism. Red brick, tile floors, and unbelievable views—that's all. He noticed that the ceilings were easily twenty feet high. The architectural restraint spilled over into his bathroom, which was small and tight, with its towering ceilings soaring over the simple shower, sink, and toilet.

Manuel began to unpack slowly, and wondered what Marta was doing, when he noticed a small note on his desk. He read it and panicked. The fact that the note was short didn't matter—what was clear to him was that notwithstanding all her charisma, Marta Pradilla was at times politically tone deaf.

The note read: "Manuel, welcome. Remind me to talk to you about my options on extradition. On Monday, I need you to see the legal affairs specialists in the office. Specifically, I want to know the procedures for removing the immunity of elected officials prior to extradition. Once you've unpacked, we'll meet for lunch."

Extraditing politicians. Marta was nuts. In a complicated country like Colombia there were fifteen emergencies a day that needed presidential attention. Guerrillas. Paramilitary violence. Displaced persons. Human rights issues. The tense border with Venezuela. Drug trafficking. And even with all of this, no president could ignore the normal, everyday stuff like poverty, children, healthcare, pensions, and education.

"You name the problem; this country has it," thought Manuel. Now this new president wants to take on corrupt and powerful political interests by threatening them with extradition. It meant opening a whole new, unnecessary and risky political battlefront.

"Does she think she won't be busy enough?" he asked himself irritably.

Manuel decided there and then to ignore her instructions to unpack and meet for lunch. Without taking his jacket and tie off, he grabbed the handwritten note and stormed out of his room, his elegant garb looking completely ridiculous in Cartagena's sunny heat. He found Marta in the small study off the principal living room.

She was looking out toward the bay, dressed in a bloomy white skirt curiously shorter in front than in back. She had on a blouse that looked like it was made of denim, but closer inspection would reveal a light linen fabric. She was smoking a cigarette, something she did very rarely and only when she was content.

He didn't knock.

Marta Pradilla smiled and stood to welcome him. She looked stunning.

"Marta, let's talk about your note," Manuel said, ignoring her cheery demeanor.

"Welcome to Cartagena, Manuel. I'm glad to see you too!" answered the president, still smiling.

He knew how she worked. Manuel was not about to let himself get charmed into a soothing chit-chat.

"Marta, you can't do this. You didn't even campaign on extradition. Your speech last week announced a tough policy reversal toward the guerrillas. We have three new decrees ready to go today—school lunches, human rights, and trade reform. Don't open this huge new political flank."

President Marta Pradilla sighed loudly. She was clearly not going to be able to avoid this argument.

"Look, Manuel, I have about one hundred days of honeymoon. After that, I become just another president—I'll get blamed for floods, highway potholes, and God knows what else. To really change this country, we have to go after the crooked politicians—and the only way to do that is with extradition."

They both knew that extradition was the mother of all judicial weapons. It meant arresting Colombians based on an indictment issued in a foreign country and putting them on a plane for trial overseas. The issue was incredibly controversial.

"Marta, I know we have extradition agreements with the United States and the European Union. But your predecessors chose to apply them sporadically. Why? Because every poll ever done in this country proves that Colombians are incredibly ambivalent about forcing their citizens to submit to foreign courts."

"I know," answered Marta, now totally engaged. "Lots of countries feel the same way and point-blank prohibit the extradition of their own citizens. We can't afford the luxury. The fact is that our courts are unable to withstand the threats and the corruption of powerful criminal bosses. What is a judge going to say when he gets a phone call at night saying that his daughter is going to be murdered?"

Marta's eyes shot hot rays of anger. She pointed a finger at him.

"No, Manuel, we have to do this."

He was not about to give up.

"Do you understand that this will bury all other issues? When it leaks out that you want to start extraditing some of the big, corrupt political families to Miami or Madrid, the entire country will be consumed by the debate. As much as you may want to make this about the administration of justice, the media is going to accuse you of giving up national sovereignty. Everything else you care about will move to the back burner!"

"No, I don't think it will. Most Colombians understand that breaking with the past will require some unpleasant choices. This will be easier than you think."

Manuel thought about arguing further, but decided that would be useless. Instead, he resolved to slow her down.

"Alright, Marta, I will check with the Ministry of Justice and the prosecutor's office to get a list of extradition requests from the United States and Europe. We can go over the list on Monday."

Marta Pradilla stared at Manuel for what seemed an eternity.

"That was not what I asked in my note," she shot back, eyes furious. "I don't want to study the list of present extradition requests. None of those names are big enough. What I want is to understand the procedures for removing the immunity of corrupt elected officials. You damn well know that anyone holding national elected office cannot be extradited without first being stripped of his powers. We will never change this place unless we expose and go after politicians like Abdoul. He and his brother are emblematic of the corrupt connection between mafia and politics in this country."

Manuel was speechless. It was worse than he thought. What she was about to do was not just politically insensitive. It was suicide. Hara-kiri.

"Marta, it's one thing to reinitiate a policy of extraditing Colombians that have arrest warrants pending in foreign countries. In my view, that's bad enough. What you are proposing is to go after some of your most implacable enemies by removing their political immunity to clear the way for extradition requests to be issued against them."

The gall of her proposal did not seem to bother her one bit. She just stared at him with a look of great calm.

Manuel continued.

"Marta, do you understand that you'll be accused of seeking revenge against your political opponents. Think of what Abdoul will say. 'She is attacking my family because we opposed her in the party's primaries.' Even if it isn't true, he'll manage to chink your armor, to inject a doubt. People will wonder whether Marta Pradilla really is the idealistic crusader for change they voted for."

Marta Pradilla got up and walked around the chair and put her left arm around Manuel Saldivar's sulking shoulders. With her right hand, she tussled his hair playfully.

"You need to start trusting your fellow citizens, Mr. Saldivar—these are the same people who voted for a single woman to become their president. They expect action, not caution. Don't lose the faith. We'll get the support we need.

"Now, go finish unpacking and come join me for lunch!"

The president had to practically shove Manuel out into the hallway. Closing the door behind him, she allowed herself a deep breath. She could feel her stomach in knots. It was the first time she put on a show for her closest advisor. It hadn't been easy.

Although Marta did a good job of projecting a certainty that she did not feel, she understood his desperation. What she was proposing was politically dangerous ground. But even a peek at her own doubts would have given Manuel enough ammunition to convince her not to do it. She did not want to risk that.

Marta Pradilla always considered that Colombia's future lay with creating a new political class. The country was changing. Over the past decade, many young Colombians with no corrupt family connections had reached key positions of leadership. Her own victory was but one large step in the same direction.

But her two-minute encounter at the inaugural party with Juan Francisco Abdoul convinced Marta that the slow process of political transformation needed a shove. Looking into Abdoul's eyes, Marta suddenly understood that she could not simply wait for the Abdouls of her country to die out and fade away. No, that would not work. These people claw back to power.

After the party, on her first night alone at the palace, she made a fateful decision. Accelerating the downfall of Juan Francisco Abdoul's family mafia was her responsibility to Colombia's future generations.

Her mouth was dry. Damn, my stomach is still tied up, she thought to herself. Marta picked up a bottle of water and poured herself a glass. The knots in her gut reminded her of the first time she met Senator Juan Francisco Abdoul.

It was twenty-one years ago and nearly ten months into her reign as Miss Universe.

Marta vividly remembered looking around the Bogotá Gun Club's main event room. She recalled asking herself why nearly a hundred members of the Colombian Chambers of Commerce—most of them conservative, older gentlemen clad in pin stripes and crisp white shirts—would show up for a lunch to hear a twenty-two-year-old beauty queen speak. They weren't coming for her looks. They could get those on pretty much all the magazine covers. It was some of her outspoken comments that were creating quite a stir.

She rose and smiled when the chairman called her name. Over that past year, she had done this countless times, yet there was still the ever so slight buzz of nervousness at the beginning of every speech. After winning the title, the new Miss Universe, like all those before her, was sent to a two-day media training course with a man whose curriculum claimed that he prepared politicians, corporate leaders, and even Hollywood actors to face the vicissitudes of public and media appearances.

"Marta," her trainer had then told her, "it's completely normal to have butterflies in your stomach before any public appearance. It's even good to feel those jitters. This course is not designed to get rid of the butterflies, but rather to teach you how to command them to fly in military formation."

Marta Pradilla had pecked the chairman of the Chambers of Commerce on the cheek and he hugged her enthusiastically. Pradilla drank a sip of water and ordered the butterflies to maintain military discipline. She adjusted the microphone to her far taller height.

She remembered starting slow and easy. She had learned that any audience must be warmed up, particularly if it's an audience of older men listening to a young woman talk. She told them how proud she was to represent Colombia at different events. She told them where she traveled and what she learned on the road. It was nice, innocent, and proper.

Then suddenly, without notice, her tone changed and her demeanor hardened.

"But I confess that I travel the world with my country's tragedy weighing on my shoulders. When taxi drivers, restaurant waiters, and businessmen in New York, Paris, London, and countless other places ask me where I'm from, I get a discreet silence and a sober nod of the head when they hear where I was born. 'Oh yes, Colombia,' they mumble.

"We Colombians always feel alone. Wherever and with whomever. We can always spot the look of others when we confess that we're from Colombia. There is an expression that is somewhere between pity and fear visible on the faces of the world's customs officials as they look at our passports to make sure that we have the appropriate visa.

"I know what they are thinking. They know all the bad things about my country: the violence, the narcos, the guerrillas, the right-wing paramilitary groups. I used to feel compelled to publicly recognize and atone for the warts of Colombia.

"No more. I want to talk about the mountains and the seas. About the fact that our country is as big as Spain, France, and Portugal put together. About our new export businesses in flowers, publishing, and textiles.

"We have towering problems to solve. But we can't find solutions if we are embarrassed about our nationality. We can't change it. We are stuck. You—we—are all Colombians. It's time to lift off the cloud of shame we carry wherever we go!"

Nobody said a word. The room had gone silent.

"When an American boy buys an American girl a rose, chances are better than seventy percent that the flower was grown here in Colombia—probably just a few miles away from Bogotá. We developed this efficient system of cutting, boxing, transporting, and delivering in less than sixteen hours. So why is it that our flower growers want their packaging to look like and be confused with Dutch flowers? Why are we not screaming: 'This is from Colombia and it's better than anything you can get elsewhere'?

"And what about our coffee? It's not only the best in the world, it's the most just. One day in the near future, the world will look for something more than good taste. It will ask that products stand for a greater value such as respect for the environment or social commitments. We will not have to invent it then, because we have it now. This is the only country in the world that protects and assists its coffee community—from pickers to owners—with loans and schools and medical services. Why aren't we talking about that?

"There is no doubt in my mind that we must all do more to solve the problems we have at home. They are grave and difficult. One almost does not know where to start. But we are not the first country to have problems or the last. Meanwhile, if we bemoan the fact that we Colombians do not get enough respect from the outside world, it is only because we don't demand it. The time has come to do that."

It's hard to pinpoint what moves a roomful of middle-aged wealthy businessmen to jump off their seats and cheer for a pretty young beauty queen. It was a strange scene. But there they were—over one hundred of Bogotá's richest and wealthiest—clapping and shouting their support. They had just been lectured to by a young woman who spoke in their language, had their accent, but seemed a breed apart. The old guys loved it.

The small reception following the speech was a simple affair. The board of directors of the Chambers of Commerce scheduled a private half hour with Marta Pradilla following her presentation. Ostensibly, it was to thank her for participating. In reality, it was because the seven gentlemen wanted a little time with Miss Universe to themselves.

The Bogotá Gun Club is a strange place, an elegant gentlemen's watering hole in the oldest of English traditions. Its three floors are a panoply of nooks and crannies carved into private dining and sitting rooms, each fitted with dark leather sofas, soft oriental rugs, and, obviously, all imaginable hunting regalia. There are rifles from Arabia, eighteenth-century pistols from czarist Russia, sidearms owned previously by Prussian Junker generals, and ornate weaponry that belonged to the grand names of Colombia's history.

They sat—seven men and one young woman—in a small sitting room surrounded by Scottish hunting pictures and hundred-year-old rifles locked behind glass cases. The men asked her about her travels and how other countries compared to Colombia. They chatted amicably about the pressures of her job. Someone asked the inevitable question as to whether it was a burden to always look beautiful. Men always liked that question, and each man who asked was sure that it had never been asked before.

The chairman had organized the little get-together because he felt it important to honor Marta with more than a podium from which to speak. It reflected the twisted logic of Latin America's elites—that offering someone the opportunity to speak before a hundred guests was really not sign enough of granted entry to the world of influence. No. Serious, ultimate proof of importance was to concede a few vapid, chatty minutes on a leather sofa with the deacons of elite power.

As the chairman signaled the end of the meeting by rising and formally thanking her for her time and visit, she noticed that one of the men, Juan Francisco Abdoul, was positioning himself to be the last to exchange a thankful kiss on the cheek on her way out. She didn't know him—he was a senator from Barranquilla and she'd heard he was filthy rich.

Although twenty years her senior, he was one of the younger members of the chamber's board, so she naturally gravitated toward him. During the small gathering, he had been particularly humorous and flattering about her speech.

"Ms. Pradilla, it has been a pleasure," Abdoul said, holding on to her hand just a tad longer than he should have. "You are not only beautiful, but I suspect we Colombians will have to contend with your brains long after you give up your title."

Marta remembered smiling placidly. Nice compliment. Well delivered.

"I'm leaving too. May I drop you somewhere?" Abdoul asked.

Her driver was waiting downstairs, but the offer seemed nice enough. He could continue fawning over her in the car. She said yes.

The ride home in the Atlantic-blue Mercedes sedan started out pleasantly, a chattier version of the mindless natter at the club. She had heard stories of the Abdoul brothers in Barranquilla and the accusations that their money was tainted with illegal drug trafficking and smuggling. But the man with her in the car hardly seemed a criminal. He was a charming, amusing storyteller. He told her about his horse farm, his speedboats in Barranquilla, and had her laughing with stories of his first political campaign.

"Its amazing what people ask of you during political campaigns," chuckled Abdoul. "Can you get my brother a job? Can you help my daughter to get a visa to the United States? Can you get my father out of jail? One day, walking through a poor section of town, a woman invited me into her house for a snack. What a mistake that was! She asked me to get five hundred green balloons for her son's birthday."

He sat close to her in the backseat of the blue Mercedes. Halfway into the thirty-minute ride home, the conversation suddenly and dramatically turned. Abdoul leaned over and came very close to her face.

"Tell me, my beauty, what are you going to do when this adventure of yours comes to an end in three months?" Abdoul had whispered. "You know, beauty queens have a very short life of glamour. You need to think about how to make the good times last."

She was somewhat taken aback by his new, somewhat invasive tone, but she did not yet fully realize that the car ride had turned a dangerous corner.

"Who knows?" she answered flightily. "I'm getting my law degree, and then I'll convince somebody to hire a retired Miss Universe."

He came closer. It wasn't a typical, subtle come-on move—he didn't try to hide the slight shift in body positioning behind an imperceptible cough or a re-crossing of the legs. No, she could recognize those desires. This was different. He wanted her to notice that he was coming closer. He wanted her to feel the distance closing. His precise objective was to make her uncomfortable.

"Marta, none of that is necessary, you know. Why should a woman like you have to study or work? You have become accustomed to living a certain way, and you should not have to change. I know your uncle is well off, but he can't provide you with what you really want."

Abdoul paused, now very close to her face.

"But I can," he said. "And, I will."

Seriously disquieted, she tried to laugh him off.

"What are you talking about?" She smiled, straining at the effort to keep the conversation on keel. "You can't imagine all the things I want."

"Yes, I can. And I will give you all and more. Everything your heart desires would only be a phone call away, Marta. Let me tell you how."

Abdoul now had his arms around her shoulder. She had only then fully understood how badly this situation had actually gotten.

"When you are done with Miss Universe in three months, I will give you a house—decorate it however you desire. A car—pick what you want. First-class airline tickets anywhere—wherever you want to go. And you will have a salary so that you can save or spend to your heart's content.

She tried to pull away and felt his arm tightening.

"And what do I have to do for all this?" Marta recalled asking.

"Only one thing. You have to be mine."

Right then and there, Marta Pradilla learned something. It was the first time she actually felt fear. Like an arrow penetrating her nervous system—every fiber in her body was reeling her backward.

She also learned another thing: that she belonged to those relatively few humans who, facing danger, somehow reach into themselves, grasping at a reservoir of control, to prevent the onset of panic. She showed nothing. Her face went blank. Her body hardly moved. Her mind went into autopilot.

She noticed that the car's doors were still unlocked. She took a deep breath and saw the red traffic light ahead out of the corner of her eye. Her stare penetrated into his.

"All those things sound appealing. But if the price to pay is to be your prize, I would rather eat shit for the rest of my life."

She felt the car slowing to a stop at the traffic light. With a quick, strong move she forced herself away from him, opened her door, and spun out of the car.

Abdoul never saw it coming. Jumping out of a prominent politician's car in the middle of city traffic was just not a consideration. Not in Bogotá.

Abdoul's face contorted in rage. His arms flailed as he tried to stop her. He managed to grab onto the right-side shoulder seam of her white blouse, but the material was too thin to hold. It tore nearly immediately. As the shocking sound of ripping clothes bounced through the automobile, he momentarily let go. That was all Marta needed; she was out of the car.

As she slammed the door, she looked back inside and shouted.

"There are still certain things in this country that are simply not for sale."

She turned around and stormed into the Bogotá traffic. Abdoul ordered his driver to the curb and hurtled out of the car. But it was too late. He could not get to her.

The instant she stepped onto the street, a passing pedestrian recognized her. Seconds later, she was surrounded by well-wishers and crowded by people wanting to shake her hand. Two or three of the lucky bystanders even had cameras. Bulbs flashed.

A mother and a little boy walked by and noticed the gaggle of people.

"There is Marta, the Colombian Miss Universe," the boy shouted.

The embarrassing news story plastered on the front page of the next day's newspapers featured her "not for sale" quote and pictures of Miss Universe surrounded by fans on a downtown Bogotá street. The shoulder seam of her white blouse was visibly ripped and, in the photo's background, Senator Juan Francisco Abdoul stood, glaring sullenly, next to his blue Mercedes stuck in the traffic.

Abdoul was disgraced. Somebody in the crowd had taken a picture and reported the incident to the press. With one single snapshot, two vast and seemingly contradictory Latin American taboos were being broken. On the one hand, even in macho countries, open violence against women was a code-breaking infringement. And there was no mistaking the ripped blouse. On the other hand, custom demanded respect toward a person of prominence. Yet, here was a young girl telling off a well-known political leader. Now the entire country knew about it.

Senator Juan Francisco Abdoul would forever become the butt of snickering jokes. Every speech delivered, each article penned, every interview engaged would be followed with nearly imperceptible whispering.

"Isn't that the politician who got told off by the smart beauty queen after ripping her shirt in the middle of the street?" somebody would always ask.

Marta knew well that Abdoul never forgave that moment of utter ridicule. It was then that he had vowed to destroy Marta Pradilla.

PART III
ITALY

Ristorante La Carbonara
Rome, August 26
1:05 p.m.

Syrian ambassador Omar bin Talman loved La Carbonara restaurant on Rome's Piazza Campo de' Fiori. He did not have to tell his driver where he was going. When Ambassador bin Talman got into the backseat of his Mercedes 450 SL, all he had to say was "lunch."

Hamid Tarwa, the Syrian embassy's longtime chauffeur, expertly maneuvered the diplomatic car through narrow streets to Piazza Venezia, the enormous square that functioned as Rome's vehicular epicenter. There, Tarwa would ignore the signs that said Taxis and Buses Only and turn right on Corso Vittorio.

Syria's chancery, close to Rome's Jewish Ghetto, was only a ten-minute drive to the medieval beauty of the Campo de' Fiori. As the ambassador read the day's e-mails from Damascus, Tarwa's mind drifted to the same thought that he had every day—namely, that La Carbonara was completely out of character for Ambassador Omar bin Talman.

Bin Talman was an impossible snob in every possible way, so why this restaurant?, Tarwa asked himself as he slowed to allow a blue and white Fiat of the Italian police to pass at sixty miles an hour. There was probably no police emergency anywhere; Italians just seemed to have a genetic need to drive at those speeds.

The ambassador drinks Johnnie Walker Blue Label scotch at two hundred dollars per bottle, Tarwa continued his silent dissection of his boss's personality. He spends thousands of euros on hugely expensive dinners, paired perfectly with twenty-year-old French wines. He gives me $10,000 a month to pay the expensive blond woman for his few hours of weekly pleasure. Why does a man like this go to La Carbonara for lunch? Tarwa was asking himself these questions just as he turned his Mercedes onto the Campo de' Fiori.

Ambassador Omar bin Talman stepped out of the car and drank in the view. Campo de' Fiori was an exquisite oval-shaped piazza in Rome's old historic center. Squished in between two of Rome's most splendid and far better known addresses, Campo de' Fiori had neither the architectural magnificence of Piazza Navona across the street nor the sedate French splendor of Piazza Farnese down the block. But, thought Ambassador bin Talman, Campo de' Fiori was the real Rome. True to its name, the piazza had functioned, for the last four hundred years, as Rome's flower market. Every day, it came alive with beautiful women, artists, and the hustle and bustle of the flower vendors haggling the prices of their bouquets. This place made him feel alive.

Ambassador bin Talman walked slowly to La Carbonara, perched on the far side of the piazza. Its red tablecloths were easily picked out—and, as always, it was packed. La Carbonara claims to have invented the spaghetti plate of the same name in 1877. Whether it did or did not is a matter of considerable argument in Rome, because a number of other restaurants have competitive claims to the great pasta dish. But no matter what side you take in this great debate, all Romans agree that La Carbonara never lost the special soul that had engendered its success for over 120 years.

Osman Samir al-Husseini was already waiting for bin Talman at the ambassador's preferred table. He had landed earlier that morning on the Alitalia flight from Newark. At the airport, al-Husseini had jumped in a taxi and driven to the Hotel de Russie, his favorite stay-over spot in Rome. The Hotel de Russie was an old palace owned previously by a Russian noble family forced to sell the building to keep up their storybook lifestyle. Now, its recent conversion showed off a spanking minimalism that was in complete contradiction to the building's turn-of-the-century architectural opulence. Husseini quickly showered under the massive onion-like showerhead of the Hotel de Russie's swank bathroom. The hotel's brochure said each room's showerhead contained 600 individual water sprinkles.

Al-Husseini's diplomatic passport identified him as the chargé d'affaires of the Syrian mission to the United Nations in New York. That was his cover. His real job was to be Syria's principal eyes and ears in the United States—the chief spy for Syrian president Bashar al-Assad. Al-Husseini was proud that, unlike other intelligence agents, his findings were not filtered through an opaque bureaucracy.

Al-Husseini never went through channels. He had only two reporting requirements. One channel was the president himself. The other was the al-Assad family's longtime ideological mentor, his luncheon companion, Ambassador Omar bin Talman.

The spy and the ideologue had known each other for years. Al-Husseini and bin Talman were both Alawites, a small, long-oppressed Shiite offshoot geographically concentrated in the remote Syrian province of Latakia. This tribal connection was important because, since Hafiz al-Assad's coup d'état in 1971, the Syrian government was dominated by Alawites. In the ensuing thirty years of family dictatorship, Alawites were the only ones allowed in the ruling inner circle.

But tribal and religious connections were not the only reason for the trust Syria's leaders placed in al-Husseini. The experienced intelligence officer had many successes in his long career. It was al-Husseini who cautioned the elder al-Assad of the impending collapse of Syria's Soviet patron two years before Gorbachev announced perestroika. And, more recently, at a time when most in the Arab world scoffed at the notion of a direct American intervention in the Middle East, he warned young Bashar, who assumed the Syrian presidency after his father's death in 2000, that nothing could or would stop George Bush and Donald Rumsfeld from invading Iraq.

To request this meeting in Rome, al-Husseini had called ambassador bin Talman the previous day from his office on the thirty-seventh floor of the United Nations. Bin Talman had agreed immediately; Osman Samir al-Husseini was not one to ask for a meeting to waste time.

The two weathered compatriots kissed on the cheeks and chitchated about the flight. They knew each other well and were comfortable together. They had an established routine of pleasantries to go through before the real conversation started.

"Osman, this time I am very angry with you," said Ambassador bin Talman to his New York guest. "Why is it that you again refuse my hospitality and my invitation to stay with me at the embassy?" inquired the ambassador in a mocking tone.

"Mr. Ambassador, forgive me for not accepting your generosity," answered al-Husseini. "If I stayed with you, I would be forced to use my electronic gadgets to sweep my bedroom for listening devices that you may have put there. When I do this, you would certainly be offended. However, when I would inevitably find those devices, it is I who would then become offended. Why risk a good friendship with such complications?" concluded al-Husseini.

Both men laughed at this old, familiar exchange.

Al-Husseini appreciated the fact that the ambassador did the ordering with the headwaiter, Maurizio. After all, this was the ambassador's city; he spoke Italian and knew the food. Bin Talman began with fried zucchini blossoms filled with mozzarella as antipasto. He asked Maurizio to follow with the inevitable spaghetti alla Carbonara for the pasta dish. For the main course, the two men would share a grouper cooked over an open grill then filleted and sprinkled with olive oil and lemon. This seemed ample.

After Maurizio brought the wine and the mineral water, the two men looked at each other seriously. "How can I help you, my friend?" inquired Ambassador bin Talman.

Al-Husseini took his cue and moved quickly through his script. "I am here to give you five facts that together cause me great worry.

"First, while they are denying this, the Americans have quietly increased their troop presence in next-door Iraq from about 110,000 men to 150,000." Bin Talman was impressed. He had not known of this military escalation.

"Second," al-Husseini continued, "the CIA last week delivered a report to National Security Advisor Nelson Cummins that, in essence, classifies our country as a military paper tiger. You remember Israel's recent bombing of a Hamas training camp just seventeen kilometers outside Damascus? It was indeed a Hamas camp, but this is the first time in twenty years the Israelis bring the fight directly to Syrian soil. The fact that we did nothing to retaliate prompted the CIA to take a closer look at our force preparedness and arms stockpiles. Their report is scathing and embarrassing, my friend.

"Third," said al-Husseini, "my sources tell me that U.S. president John Stockman's political advisors believe that their boss's reelection chances lie in his ability to walk a tightrope—he must both contrast and emulate the previous American government. They want to follow the tough line of the past, but Stockman's handlers also want Americans to see that the rest of the world will follow Stockman. So, they are looking for ways to demonstrate international leadership. Denouncing Syria as a roadblock to peace and democracy looks like a good choice of issues." Ambassador bin Talman wondered how he knew these things. Could it be possible that his colleague had such impeccable sources?

"Fourth"—al-Husseini was now speaking with great assurance—"the focus on Syria will be more than just rhetoric. Within the next months, the United States will present a resolution to the United Nations Security Council that will immediately and effectively isolate Syria politically, economically, and militarily. It will commence an economic blockade and will sanction the use of military force unless we hand over certain terrorist elements now residing in Syria. This is the first step toward an inevitable invasion of our country.

"And, my dear ambassador, fifth on my list is the fact that Stockman was in Colombia twenty days ago lobbying for the four Latin American countries on the Security Council. Together with Britain, Russia, Sweden, and Thailand, this could provide them with the majority."

Omar bin Talman, ambassador of Syria, advisor of presidents, scholar, diplomat, and ruthless tactician, knew then and there that without brave action, the end of the Assad dynasty's rule over Syria was near. As that day neared, he knew that their enemies—most of them belonging to Syria's Sunni Arab majority—would jump at the chance to hunt down Alawites.

It is sad, thought bin Talman. Here in the Roman sunshine, his friend had just informed him of the chronology of his nation's foretold future. The ambassador had known this moment would come—he had not gamed out how or when the end would come, but he knew that it would be inevitable. The Arab world was in collapse; not because it lacked power, but because it was reticent to use the little power it had.

For three decades now, Omar bin Talman had taught his patrons that power rested on one's willingness to use it. He had warned the elder al-Assad to ignore the irritating Western cries about human rights and freedoms. And for years his advice had been heeded. Hafiz al-Assad had remained in power because of his willingness to ruthlessly expunge Syria of the influence of the Sunni majority. Al-Assad would stop at nothing; in 1982, 20,000 men, women, and children had died in the vicious quelling of the Sunni Muslim Brotherhood's rebellion in Hama, Syria's fourth-largest city. After the uprising, Hama was destroyed, flattened, and paved over. This singular act of power created the fear that fueled the al-Assad family hegemony until today.

"This is what a ruler does to preserve power," bin Talman repeated over and over again to the al-Assad family.

But young President Bashar did not have his father's single-minded purposefulness. He vacillated. He was unsure. He cared too much about economics and poverty alleviation. These were effeminate Western precepts; what Arab leaders needed to care about was stopping the expanding political, economic, and cultural power of the West.

Ambassador Omar bin Talman had dedicated his whole life to ending the West's hegemony. Thirty years ago, at the elder al-Assad's side, he had created the Syrian Baath Party, a strong, secular, and stridently nationalistic movement that would protect Syria and the Arab world from the encroaching European colonialism. Now, the Baath experiment was sinking in the same quagmire of corruption and economic stagnation that ate away at the Syrian state.

With Baathism dying, the only ideological vehicle left was Islam. Arabs no longer responded to secular political movements, because Arab citizens no longer trusted their secular political leaders. Osama bin Laden, Hamas, Islamic Jihad had done much to delegitimize Arab governments. These were the groups that captured the imagination of young Arabs today. Now the time had come for an Arab government to take the flag of Islam and use it for action. Personally, Omar bin Talman had no use for religion. But if religion was the only way to show the West that Arabs were willing to fight, so be it.

Syria was perfectly positioned, bin Talman believed, to wrap itself in Islam's flag and "accept" its leadership role. Egypt, the largest Arab country and the Arab world's traditional intellectual epicenter, was in the pay of the Americans. Saudi

Arabia, keeper of the holy sites, was a land corrupted by a stagnant royalty. Iraq was no more. Syria, known as the Middle East's most strident and recalcitrant country, and now targeted by the Americans, was the only nation left to take the mantle of leadership in Arab Islam's struggle against the West.

Ambassador Omar bin Talman's mind returned to the reality of the luncheon table with Osman Samir al-Husseini. The time had come to bring his friend into the loop. He ordered more wine and told al-Husseini to brace himself.

"This will be a long afternoon," said the ambassador. "I want to tell you about an idea I have."

Fiumicino Airport

Rome, September 13

2:00 p.m.

As the Avianca Airlines Boeing 767 touched down at Rome's Fiumicino Airport, Senator Juan Francisco Abdoul, president of the Senate of the Republic of Colombia, thought to himself that it would be a pity if Colombia's flag carrier ended up disappearing. Avianca was in bankruptcy proceedings and most Colombians felt that the airline's financial problems were both self-inflicted and well deserved. Senator Abdoul, however, begged to differ.

He always liked the impeccable service, the old fashioned glassware, and the porcelain plates from Limoges that Avianca served up in first class. As Abdoul adjusted his watch to 2:05 p.m. Italian time, he thought again of how much he had enjoyed his eleven-hour flight from Bogotá to Rome.

As he filed off the airplane into the terminal area, Abdoul immediately saw a sign in Spanish and Italian that read "Europe–Latin America Inter-Parliamentary Summit." As he walked toward the sign, he recognized Massimo Feliciani, chairman of the Italian parliament's Committee on International Relations.

"Juan Francisco, welcome to Italy," shouted Feliciani as he reached out to embrace his Colombian colleague. Originally from Milan, Feliciani had lived in Rome for the last seven years. He had been the dean of the School of International Relations at Milan's renowned Bocconi University for more than twenty-five years. There, he had taught his students that Italy needed to play a more aggressive role in international affairs. But Feliciani was a relative newcomer to politics. While many in Italy's press corps saw Feliciani as a bright, serious player in parliament, the majority of the old foxes in the Italian legislature viewed him as an insufferable nerd.

"We are delighted you could come, Juan Francisco, truly delighted. Now that you are here, this meeting will be a real success," babbled Feliciani as he handed Abdoul's passport to an assistant who scampered ahead to clear the Colombian VIP through immigration controls.

Once through the passport and customs procedures, they walked out of the terminal to where Feliciani's chauffeur waited for the group in a black Alfa

Romeo with parliamentary license plates. Feliciani and Abdoul climbed into the backseat and the car moved quickly outside of the airport area and onto the highway toward central Rome. Abdoul noted that the car reached 150 kilometers per hour—about 85 miles per hour—within one minute of leaving the airport area.

"Juan Francisco, this is the first ever summit meeting between the heads of Europe's and Latin America's parliaments," explained Chairman Feliciani. "As Italy now has the rotating presidency of the European Union, this meeting is a perfect way to demonstrate that we Europeans hold Latin America dear to our hearts and to our future. This meeting will be the first step to the construction of a free-trade agreement between Latin America and Europe. Unlike our friends in America, we will talk less and negotiate more," said the chairman of the Italian parliament's international committee.

"While your continent is physically closer to the United States, we must not forget that you are the sons and daughters of Europe," added Feliciani, with demonstrable seriousness, as he handed Abdoul the list of participants and the schedule of the next day's events.

To the untrained ear, all this happy talk about Latin America's sparkling future with Europe would sound exciting. But Juan Francisco Abdoul was bored already. He had attended scores of such conferences. Interparliamentary groups of all sorts met all the time. Few achieved anything; most were exercises in futility. Yet, they still happened. The organizers of these ridiculous sessions of parliamentary "fried air," as Juan Francisco called them, astutely called the meetings to order in the world's most splendid spots. This was done to dangle an irresistible carrot in front of the parliamentarian's spouse as much as to engage the individual member of Congress.

"Massimo, I'm honored to be here, and I look forward to this unique opportunity to deepen the relations between Latin America and Europe," lied Abdoul. "You have put together an impressive list of attendees. One does not often get the heads of the Colombian, Brazilian, Argentine, Mexican, and Peruvian congresses in one room." This time, Abdoul was not lying: it was an impressive list, and together those men (and the one woman from Mexico) represented over three quarters of Latin America's population.

The two men talked for another ten minutes about scheduling, participants, and agendas for the next day's meeting. Feliciani even wanted Abdoul to have the prestigious honor of cochairing a meeting with EU president Romano Arberi. But Abdoul hardly listened. His mind was busy going over the details of the hours that lay ahead of him. Everything had to work perfectly. Tomorrow's meeting was of little concern; he would be on autopilot for the soporific event.

They arrived at the door of the Hotel Hassler. Unfortunately, Feliciani was still talking and offered to walk him into the hotel lobby. The Columbian visitor insisted that he not come inside—"the chairman has a great many other things to do than to watch me check in," Abdoul demurred elegantly. Once the Colombian politician escaped Feliciani's chatty clutches, he immediately felt free to concentrate on his real mission in Rome.

Juan Francisco Abdoul walked into the ornate lobby and checked in. One of Rome's best-known hotels, the Hassler was next to the Spanish Steps and, from the terrace of his fifth-floor suite, Abdoul had a wonderful view of the roofs, cupolas, and palaces of the Eternal City. The doorbell rang within minutes to deliver the bottle of crisp Verdicchio he had ordered from the concierge. Abdoul unpacked, carefully hung his clothes—blues in the left side of the closet and grays to the right—and put on his pajamas.

He walked out to the room's brick-layered exterior terrace, took the white wine from the ice bucket, and poured himself a glass. The day was cloudless. He sat on a swinging easy chair under a pergola of vines and felt the gravitational pull of his slowly relaxing body. He allowed this view of the world's most beautiful city to lull him into a precisely timed one-hour siesta.

At 6:00 p.m., Senator Juan Francisco Abdoul awoke in a deep sweat. He had dreamt that he and his brother, Ricardo, were on the beach together. They were walking and chatting placidly about the family; then, suddenly, Ricardo had taken a small pistol out of his pocket and had shot Juan Francisco in the head.

Abdoul reached for the white cloth wrapped tightly around the white wine bottle and dipped the linen into the cold ice-bucket. He wiped his brow slowly, sadly acknowledging the inescapable fact that the dream was revealing.

In the past months, tensions had grown between the two brothers.

The crushing loss of the Liberal Party's nomination to Marta Pradilla nearly a year ago had vastly different effects on each of the men. To Ricardo, who often spoke of signs and superstitions, it was a signal that Colombia was changing and that they could no longer act as if the country was a family fiefdom. The younger brother's view was simple: We have already made millions—forget it, billions—of dollars in illicit gambling, smuggling, and drug trafficking. Let's wash the money and invest it in legitimate businesses. With the family's connections, the wealth would inevitably multiply and grow.

Juan Francisco, on the other hand, became more embittered with every passing day. The ballot-box loss in the party primaries was a deep defeat, but he interpreted Marta's overwhelming victory in the national elections as a personal rejection of his family's name. He became obsessed with taking down Pradilla. He argued with his brother that this was the time to expand profits, not slow them down. Every time he saw Ricardo, he became agitated—screaming about the need to retake the family's "rightful place."

The disputes became increasingly heated and ugly. Juan Francisco accused his sibling of weakness and acts of treason against the family. For more than twenty years, the two men had talked at least once a day, in person or on the phone. But since the May election, days and even weeks would go by without any communication.

No wonder he was having nightmares about Ricardo.

Juan Francisco Abdoul mentally swatted away the dream and marched to the shower. Within a half hour, he descended the hotel's elevator dressed in a Zegna sports jacket, a "Polo by Ralph Lauren" cream-colored shirt, and perfectly fitting blue pants. He actually would have looked good were it not for the fact that he was thirty pounds overweight.

Abdoul walked out of the hotel and turned left. Should anybody be watching, they would see the leader of Colombia's Senate doing what nearly every man, woman, and child does upon arriving in Rome. He was taking a stroll in the city's historic center.

Juan Francisco walked the fifteen minutes to Piazza Navona and sat down at the Caffé Tre Scalini. He seriously considered and then resisted the urge to order their infamous chocolate tartuffo ice cream—a concoction of chocolate ice cream inside a chocolate crust with a frozen dark chocolate center. Instead, he asked the waiter for a Campari and soda and paid immediately. Abdoul knew that within the next half hour he would have to get up and leave at a moment's notice.

Taking in the vast oval-shaped square, Abdoul's mind wandered back to his first trip to Rome many years ago. He recalled how amused he had been by the stories of the disputes between the principal architects of the churches and fountains of the historic seventeenth-century piazza. He smiled as he looked again at the fountain in the piazza's center. Built by the great Giovanni Lorenzo Bernini, the fountain had a perfect marble statue of a bearded man at its center. It was hilarious how Bernini had sculpted the man's uplifted hand to cover his eyes. This was to block the statue's view of what Bernini believed to be the hideous horror of the church of Sant' Agnese just fifty steps away. Bernini's main Renaissance rival, Francesco Borromini, had designed the church.

Abdoul shook himself back to reality. Effete, insulting gestures may be how Italians like to deal with their enemies. It was not his way. This was too refined and indirect. Enemies were to be co-opted or discarded—those were the rules Juan Francisco Abdoul had lived with all his life. Some enemies did not even merit consideration; Marta Pradilla was one of those. She had to be removed. And that is what he was here to do.

At precisely 7:30 p.m., a Mercedes 450 SL with diplomatic plates maneuvered onto the historic square. While cars were not allowed on Piazza Navona, nobody paid any attention to this car because diplomatic vehicles regularly disobeyed Rome's traffic restrictions. The car stopped in front of the Tre Scalini.

Hamid Tarwa got out of the driver's seat and walked around to open the back passenger door. Senator Juan Francisco Abdoul got into the Syrian embassy car. As the ambassador's chauffeur put the vehicle in first gear, Tarwa told his passenger, "My instructions are to take you to our embassy."

The Syrian Embassy
Rome, September 13
8:05 p.m.

This was the third time in two years that he found himself in the basement of the Syrian embassy in Rome. Chibli Farkish was seriously beginning to wonder if it was going to last all night.

So far, he had been stripped totally naked, doused every five minutes with ice-cold water, and beaten with a horsewhip around his genitals and buttocks. The room was cold and dank. The walls were white concrete and the floors were lime-green linoleum. Both materials made for easy washing. A masked man had asked questions about his connections with other Syrian exiles in Rome, hit him, and turned on the ice-cold shower. This was pretty much how it had been the other times, too.

Five minutes ago, Ambassador Omar bin Talman had entered the room. As long as the ambassador stayed, Chibli knew it would not get much worse than this.

Except for these three uninvited visits to the Syrian embassy, Chibli Farkish was a happy man. At thirty-two years of age he was doing exactly what he wanted to do and was in love with the most beautiful woman in the world. His parents, Syrian diplomats, had been stationed in Rome during his teenage years, but Chibli never returned to Damascus.

Good looking and athletic, Chibli studied education at the University of Rome and graduated with a master's degree. At twenty-seven he began teaching the sixth-grade international baccalaureate students at St. George's international school in Rome. One year later, he fell in love with his boss, the principal of the school, Susana Saldivar. A towering, tough beauty four years his senior, Susana had come to Rome after paying her dues in the international school system with teaching positions in Ankara, Turkey, and Quito, Ecuador.

The daughter of Colombian diplomats and the sister of Colombia's newly elected president's chief of staff, Susana had built St. George's up from a small program for diplomats to one of Rome's preeminent international schools.

Today, under Susana's direction, St. George's graduates were eagerly scooped up by Oxford, Cambridge, the Sorbonne, Harvard, Heidelberg—the world's finest universities.

Susana and Chibli had much in common. As often happened with diplomatic children who spent their youth moving from one place to the next, there were two sides to their core personalities. Both saw themselves as true citizens of the world, comfortable everywhere. Yet both also knew they belonged nowhere.

Having found each other, their lives quickly entangled. You could see it in the detailed attention to their beautiful apartment, their love of cooking dinners for frequent guests, their long conversations before going to sleep. Neither had a country they wanted to live in, but they had each other.

Chibli was a wonderful teacher. His students adored him. Susana joked that the girls in his class loved him for his looks, not his teaching. And the boys, Susana teased, respected him only because he had the girls' unending affection. To his students, Chibli was an optimist, teaching that the young would fix the world's wrongs. But, behind his classroom smiles, he was angry about his country, about the Arab nation and about the endless cycle of violence that consumed his part of the world.

Two years earlier, Susana began to urge Chibli to put this frustration into words. He had always spoken privately about his country with vision and passion. She told him that others should have the chance to hear what he had to say. So he began to write articles in Italian and British publications about the situation in Syria.

This, of course, was the reason for these occasional meetings in the Syrian embassy's basement. The scathing articles had come to the attention of Ambassador Omar bin Talman, who decided to take matters into his own hands.

"Your parents weep—not because they miss you, but from the embarrassment you cause. How is it possible that the son of proud diplomats of our nation could become such a disaster?" Ambassador bin Talman asked the freezing, naked body standing in front of him.

"Your staff asked me to come because my passport required renewal. I knew this was false, but I came because I need my passport. You have had me beaten for two hours. Now, let me leave," begged Chibli. He tried not to engage the ambassador.

"Do not ignore me. You are a Syrian," shouted bin Talman, his face contorted with rage. "Our country is surrounded by enemies on all sides. The Americans are to our east in Iraq. The Turks to our west. The Zionists to our south. Fifty years have passed since our national liberation, but we are still fighting the same war against the Jews and the colonialists. They want to take our land and kill our culture. And you, the son of respectable people, write essays that accuse our government of wrongdoing. How dare you!"

Chibli was at once angry and very worried. He had always known that his articles could result in the occasional questioning and even physical punishment. But he also knew he was a small-time schoolteacher of little importance to his government. Why, then, was bin Talman so outraged? The ambassador's anger filled him with dread.

"Ambassador bin Talman, all I have said in my articles is that we Arabs must stop looking outward for scapegoats and that it is our government's responsibility to fix the things that are so wrong with our society. I have made the point that 65 million Arabs and almost two thirds of all Arab women are illiterate. Do you know that the United Nations has said that in the thousand years since the reign of the Caliph Mamoun, the Arabs have translated as many books as Spain translates in one year? I am a teacher and this is a sin against our children."

"Damn you and your obsession with education. The only path to freedom is to finish our project of national liberation. Personal freedoms or individual liberties are meaningless," said bin Talman. "Who cares if the daughter of the fishmonger can read?" spat the ambassador.

Chibli, still naked, shivering and dripping, was unable to contain his surprise at the gruesome ignorance. Here was a respected Syrian leader, a counselor of presidents. How could he not see the truth?

"We are becoming an anachronism in our world, Ambassador bin Talman," said Chibli. "The Arabs, who once led the world in science, mathematics, and astronomy, have become poor, ignorant peasants. Which side of the barrel of a gun one stands upon should not define right or wrong. I believe in what Imam Ali abi Taleb said 1,500 years ago: If God was to humiliate a human being, he would deny them knowledge."

Suddenly, the phone rang. Bin Talman quickly picked up the small, metallic phone and listened. "Escort the senator to the basement conference room. I will meet him there," bin Talman barked into the phone and hung up.

Turning to the masked man who remained in the dark room's back corner, bin Talman ordered, "Lock this pig up for the night. But keep him naked. This idiot needs to learn humility. He can have his clothes tomorrow." Turning to Chibli, bin Talman walked to within inches of his face, stared into his eyes, and cleared his throat deeply. He then spat squarely on the handsome young man's face. Saliva dribbled down Chibli's right cheek. "Tell Imam Ali that humility starts this way," said bin Talman, and walked out.

The man with the dark mask walked silently toward Chibli and without a word raised the leather horsewhip and banged it into Chibli's thighs three times. He raised Chibli's arms and handcuffed both hands above his head to a single iron ring on the wall. He turned on the faucet to let out a drip of cold water that would run unendingly through the night onto Chibli's right shoulder, down his stomach and legs.

The man walked out of the room without a further word. Chibli was both relieved and scared. He had never been forced to spend the night at the embassy. Bin Talman had been unusually aggressive and he desperately hoped that the ambassador's agitation did not reflect a newfound determination to silence him. Chibli knew well that when the Syrian government decided to quiet people, the victim could swiftly cross the invisible line from a chilly interrogation room to an ice-cold morgue.

Chibli forced his mind toward Susana. He remembered that last night they slept curled together on their sides, his face buried in her thick black hair, his body snuggling perfectly into Susana's curves. A wave of sadness came over him; he knew Susana would agonize over his beatings, blaming herself for pushing Chibli to become politically active and visible.

Footsteps shook him away from his mind's roiling emotional waves. On his three previous embassy encounters, Chibli had never noticed that one could hear outside of this room. He never paid attention because, on all past visits, he had never been left alone. They always released him within a few hours. This was his only time alone in the room and the first time he heard something outside the door.

Now the footsteps came closer. At first they seemed to be coming toward his cell, but the movement stopped and a door was opened. Chibli surmised that it was the door to the conference room next door. He had seen the room's open entrance, and it had caught his attention because it was full of plush carpeting on both the floors and walls. He now understood that the carpeting in the adjacent conference suite was to muffle any sounds of violence from this cell.

Voices lifted as the neighboring door opened. "Senator, welcome, the flight from Bogotá is long. Are you not tired?" Chibli clearly heard bin Talman's voice speaking perfect English. Then, an unknown, Spanish-accented voice answered in poor English, "Ambassador, I am not tired because I am on my life's most important mission. Let's talk quickly. I want to be back at the piazza within one hour."

The door closed and Chibli heard no more. He wondered who this was and what in heaven's name a Colombian politician was doing in the basement of the Syrian embassy in Rome. If the visit was diplomatic, why was he not received upstairs in the living room? What could Syria offer a Colombian politician as the most important mission in his life? Chibli's interest was multiplied exponentially by the fact that this mystery involved a man from Susana's country. Perhaps she would know.

The darkness of the room was total and it enveloped him. He felt the cold water numbing his muscles and burning his skin. He was shivering and hurting. He tried to concentrate on the outside to learn more from next door, but the silence was overwhelming. The trickle of cold water felt like a pounding as his muscles twitched into spasms from the icy drip. Chibli fell into and out of a dormant state of unrest.

In the Embassy Basement

Rome, September 13

11:15 p.m.

===

Chibli didn't know how much time had passed when he heard the door open to his interrogation room. A single flashlight pierced the dark and pointed straight at him. He could see nothing but the light moving toward him. He heard keys and felt his arms—now numb with reduced blood flow—fall down toward his body as his cuffs were released. A towel was thrown at his feet.

"Dry yourself and walk with me. You will get dressed." Chibli thought he recognized the voice as the masked man with the horsewhip of a few hours before. Chibli was worried. He was either being released or being shot. It was not yet clear.

He followed the flashlight out of the room and at the door found his clothes. He donned his white shirt and pulled on his socks. He started putting on his blue jeans and immediately felt the searing burns of pain from the blows he had taken in his buttocks and thighs. Wearing the tight blue jeans would be painful enough, but the effort of getting them on seemed a nearly impossible task. He managed to slowly pull them up and put on his moccasins.

Chibli was escorted past the slightly ajar door of the conference room where he had heard the snippets of bin Talman's meeting with the mysterious Colombian. He saw nobody there now. The corridor remained dark, but he could make out the mask of his interrogator. He followed the man up the stairs to an empty hallway. Instead of leading Chibli left, to the embassy's main entrance, the man turned right, toward the kitchen's open door. Chibli panicked. He was not going to be released.

The masked man pulled Chibli's arm through the kitchen and opened a service door obviously used for deliveries and trash removal. Chibli's heart was pounding. As the door to the kitchen exit opened, Chibli closed his eyes and grimaced. His mind instantaneously conjured up visions of two unshaven men dressed in dirty gray suits who would drag him onto the back of a black truck with diplomatic license plates. On the truck, he expected to be drugged and taken to a waiting Syrian military plane that would fly him to Damascus. There he would be tortured and shot.

When he reopened his eyes an instant later, he could not believe what he saw. Instead of drab men belonging to Syria's intelligence services, he saw Susana. Her black hair was uncombed and her dark eyes flashed anger and concern simultaneously. She wore a purple Indian tunic and khaki denims. Her favorite mother-of-pearl necklace was in place around her neck.

Chibli was pushed outside and the door shut behind him. Susana bounded up the five steps to the door and steadied him. "Come, my love, walk with me carefully, but walk fast. We need to get out of here," Susana whispered into his ear.

She led him through the embassy gates, past the Syrian guard on the inside of the property and the Italian police protecting the outside. Susana directed him to her parked blue Fiat Uno. She knew from the last times he had "visited" the embassy that the lack of any visible signs of beatings was no guarantee that Chibli was not hurt. Once she helped him into the car, Susana opened the button to his jeans and immediately saw the welts below his waist.

He waved her off and said, "Get in and drive us home. While you are driving, explain to me how you got me out. They were going to keep me all night this time."

Susana started the car and got away fast from the embassy. Traffic at this hour was light. "I came home from the school and heard the message on the answering machine that the embassy had called about your passport. I waited until 8:00 p.m. and I knew the monster they call an ambassador would be beating you again," said Susana. A small tear fell down her eye. "I'm so sorry, my love, I'm so sorry I pushed you to write those articles. I'm so sorry, Chibli!" Susana implored his forgiveness.

Chibli smiled and put his hand over hers on the gearshift. "This is not your fault. I chose to write. And, because of my parents, I doubt they will ever do more than this." This was, actually, more than enough, thought Chibli to himself, wincing at the pain. "Now, how the hell did you get me out?"

"I came to the embassy and asked to speak to bin Talman," Susana responded. "Of course, the efficient and horrible woman at the entrance told me he was unavailable. So, I wrote a five-sentence note. I asked that she either give it to him or read it to him over the phone."

"A note?" Chibli asked. "What on earth did you say in the note?"

Susana smiled, "The note said: Ambassador, Chibli Farkish teaches twenty-two kids that love him at the prestigious St. George International School. In his class are the sons and daughters of five foreign ambassadors, two Italian government ministers, the daughter of English soccer star David Mulham and the nephew of Joseph Cardinal Ratheuser, the Vatican secretary of state. As the director of St. George's, I will call these children immediately and ask them to come to the aid of their teacher and—trust my knowledge of sixth-graders—they will come. When they arrest us for trespassing Syrian diplomatic property, we will gladly give press interviews about why we were there. Please let Chibli Farkish go. I will be back at 11:00 p.m."

"That is six sentences," Chibli chuckled and moaned at the same time. His butt ached as Susana drove over a Roman cobblestone street. Typical Susana, he thought. Audacious, tough, passionate, and too creative for her own good.

They arrived at their apartment in the neighborhood of Monteverde. To get there, you had to drive up one of the city's seven hills and through the beautiful Piazza Garibaldi. Under the gaze of the statue of the mounted hero of the Italian revolution, lovers sat on the huge terrace and kissed as they looked out from the city's best view into the expanse of the Roman panorama. It was a middle-class residential area of Rome. Susana had spurned the offers of a home in the nicer, more diplomatic neighborhoods when she arrived a few years ago.

Today Susana ignored the view. It was nearly midnight and there was no parking spot. This was no time to make Chibli walk, so she pulled the Fiat onto the sidewalk and simply parked between two trees. To pass, pedestrians would have to walk onto the roadway and around her car, but this was Rome. In this city, all parking problems had a solution. In the morning, she would find the cop who walked her neighborhood waiting for her and wagging his finger. She would have to hold her head low and listen to his lecture. She would smile and apologize. He would wave his hand and feign fury. He would storm away complaining that women were out of control. But there would be no ticket, fines, or citations. It was the neatly choreographed dance of Rome.

She helped Chibli through the main gate of the building and up the elevator. Once inside the modern, minimalist apartment, Susana put Chibli on the sofa and promised him tea.

"Forget the tea," said Chibli. "Give me a large glass of cognac. And sit with me, because I have things to tell you, too."

She served them both unusually large portions of the tawny-colored liqueur from the open bottle of Hennessy VSOP. She also brought him two aspirin from the kitchen drawer. He swigged down the medicine with his first gulp. She listened carefully as he told her of the beatings, the horsewhip, the cold-water showers, and the humiliation of being naked. He told her of bin Talman's unusually agitated state.

Again the cloud of guilt passed through her body. This would not have happened were it not for her insistence. She gazed into his eyes, thinking that she would have never been able to forgive herself if anything serious happened to him. Never. She truly loved this man.

"Then something occurred that was very unusual," exclaimed Chibli, shaking away her thoughts of remorse. "Bin Talman ended our conversation when somebody was announced. They obviously did not want any noise in the basement, because they immediately halted the questions and the beatings. Bin Talman met with the person in a conference room next to where I was being held. I heard the person arrive and I heard the greetings," concluded Chibli.

"So, what is so strange about this?" Susana asked. She looked puzzled. "The monster had a guest and did not want the visitor to hear that somebody was being interrogated and beaten next door."

"Well, don't you think it's strange that the ambassador would choose to meet with somebody in the evening in a secret conference room in the basement of the embassy?" Chibli asked, building up slowly to reveal the big secret.

"Yes, it's a little strange but . . ." Susana could not finish the sentence before Chibli interrupted her.

"You see, I also heard who it was. Well, not exactly the name. But I did hear bin Talman call this man 'Senator,'" Chibli said, now speaking slowly and pausing so as to savor the coming surprise. "And the ambassador asked him if he did not feel tired after his long flight from . . . Bogotá." Chibli suddenly felt great. One look at Susana's face made this little tale almost worthwhile.

Susana Saldivar's dark eyes were wide open. Her mouth was agape. What was a Colombian senator doing in the basement of the Syrian embassy in Rome at night? Who was this? Why were they there? What did they say? The questions tumbled out like a waterfall.

"That's all I know," said Chibli, raising his hand to stop her questions. "The door closed; and after that I may have fainted, because I did not hear them leave. But these questions need answering because the Colombian senator called this the most important mission of his life."

Chibli and Susana's Apartment

Rome, September 13

11:55 p.m.

"Good evening, this is Casa de Nariño," answered the calm voice.

The telephone operators at Colombia's presidential palace were a legend among Colombia's political class. No matter what crisis erupted, what bomb detonated, or what natural disaster exploded, Casa de Nariño's operators could hunt down the most elusive human on the planet and connect you efficiently, quickly, and quietly. Nobody understood how they got the cell phone numbers of the mistresses of Bogotá's best-known politicians or how they had tracked the errant mayor of Cali to the Miami apartment number of his secret gay lover.

Over the years, many exhausted politicians tried to escape for a few hours or days. But if the invisible operator deemed it important, the inevitable call came through and the voice on the line would say, "Forgive me for interrupting, but this is Casa de Nariño and we have a call for you."

"Good evening, this is Susana Saldivar. I am calling from Rome, Italy, and I need to speak to my brother, Manuel Saldivar," explained Susana to the voice on the other line. She had previously tried her brother's cellular phone, but it was turned off. He had told her to call the switchboard in any emergency, but this was the first time Susana had used the palace operators. She was about to explain that her brother was President Pradilla's chief of staff, when the operator interrupted her.

"A pleasure, Ms. Saldivar. Please provide me a number where we can reach you," answered the efficient voice in Bogotá. Susana gave the man the number. The operator asked if this was her home number. Once given, this number would never again be requested. "We will do our best. Now please hang up and keep the line free."

Within two minutes, the same voice called back and connected Manuel Saldivar to his sister across the ocean.

"Hi, little brother, how does it feel to be in power?" joked the older sister.

"A month has gone by and I'm ready to come live with you two in Rome!" answered Manuel. "You can't imagine the hours. We're at work until midnight and back at dawn. Forget everything I've ever told you about the hardships of journalism."

Susana admired her brother's dedication to his country. It was amazing that two siblings could be so different. Like her, he had spent his life being dragged by their diplomatic father from one country to the next, yet he was clearly so happy back at home. She mused to herself that this must be Manuel's way of securing his own roots.

"Listen, little guy, I need to talk to you about something serious." Susana then told him about Chibli's ordeal at the embassy and what he had overheard.

Silence greeted Susana from the other side of the phone. She heard Manuel sucking in a deep breath of air. "Susana, did I just hear you say that a senator from Colombia was in the basement of the Syrian embassy in Rome at night? Is that what you just told me?" asked Manuel.

Though they lived thousands of miles apart, Susana always remained close to her brother. They were in touch by phone and e-mail. She could now imagine the squinty eyes, hands rummaging his jacket for the pack of Marlboro Lights. She waited a moment. Then, she smiled. Yes, there was the metallic click of the Zippo lighter he always used.

"Yes, Manuel, but Chibli did not get a name. He just heard the word 'senator,' " said Susana.

Manuel did not need a name. He had seen Senator Juan Francisco Abdoul's press release about his trip to Rome. In the release, he had pompously announced his intention to 'dialogue' with European parliamentarians about trade matters. Manuel would have to give the situation some serious thought.

"Susana, I will have to do a little research, but the senator could have been Juan Francisco Abdoul. Please stay out of trouble—both of you. I will let you know what I find," said Manuel. Manuel was, like Chibli, four years younger than Susana. Notwithstanding the fact that she was older, Manuel felt protective.

They chatted a while longer and then Susana hung up the phone. She went to Chibli's side. She could not get rid of the feeling that she was responsible. She loved this man deeply, more than she had loved any other in memory. She smiled and lovingly kissed his neck. Susana put her hands inside his shirt and slowly rubbed his skin as he closed his eyes. She shuddered to think what horrors he had just been exposed to.

Suddenly the phone rang. "Please don't answer it," said Chibli and she smiled her agreement. Nothing was further from her mind.

The machine in the kitchen picked up the call. "This is Casa de Nariño from Bogotá, Colombia. I have Mr. Saldívar on the line," said the same calm, efficient voice Susana had heard earlier in the evening.

Then she heard Manuel's voice.

"Susana, I know it's late there. I'm calling because I want to again tell you to be careful. Juan Francisco Abdoul is a dangerous man. Tell Chibli to be careful too. I will try to find out more. But, both of you, stay out of this, because it can only mean bad news."

The phone cut off.

PART IV
THE CAUCASUS

Tbilisi, Georgia
The Night of September 29
2:30 a.m.

===

Five weeks after his meeting with Ambassador Omar bin Talman in Rome, Osman Samir al-Husseini heard the British Airways Airbus reverse thrust upon touching down at Tbilisi's Lochini International Airport. Al-Husseini disembarked from the forward door with the other business-class passengers and stepped into the dingy terminal.

It was a ridiculous hour to arrive. He had challenged his secretary at the United Nations to find him a better flight. There was none. If you wanted to land in Tbilisi, Georgia, on a Tuesday night, this was your only choice.

A half-shaved, half-awake man—presumably he was some sort of official, but it wasn't clear because his crumpled suit made it impossible to discern any official identification—pointed the foreign passengers in the direction of a dark window with bars on it. The single, obscure opening looked scary and uninviting. It was in the opposite direction of the four plastic cubicles that stood under the handmade sign that said "Immigrashon."

When one of the passengers ahead of al-Husseini made an effort to ask a question of the crumpled man, he just grunted "Viza"—the z really zinged—and pointed to the dark window. Al-Husseini tried unsuccessfully to explain to the man that he was a UN official and did not require a visa to enter. The man looked at al-Husseini, pointed again to the window and grunted: "Viza."

Al-Husseini got his visa. Most countries requiring a visa asked a couple of details about an entering passenger's life, demanded a passport photo, or at least wrote the traveler's name in a register before providing an official stamp. In Georgia, you landed, queued at the dark window at 2:30 a.m., and paid eighty dollars to a faceless figure who asked nothing, wanted nothing, and gave nothing in return except for the sticker firmly placed in your passport.

As al-Husseini left the airport terminal, he spotted a tall man with a United Nations sign. The UN chauffeur did not much resemble a UN employee; rather he conjured up the stereotypical image of what al-Husseini imagined a Russian mafia hit man would look like. Sporting a leather jacket and sunglasses in the middle of the night, the man shook al-Husseini's hand and announced, "Temuri is my name. No English." That was the end of all conversation.

The silence suited al-Husseini just fine. Once registered at the Sheraton, al-Husseini would have to force himself to sleep for a few hours. He was officially in Tbilisi as the Syrian delegate to the yearly UN conference on Abkhazian refugees. Abkhazia was a forlorn province on Georgia's western Black Sea shoreline. In the Soviet era it had been a pretty vacation spot frequented by Russians and Georgians. Over the past decade, spurred on by a Russian-instigated bombing campaign, Abkhazian separatists had been scaring away the ethnic Georgians who had lived in the region for thousands of years. Now these homeless, pitiful families were scattered across the country. They lived in tent cities or as squatters in shabby hotels.

The UN had taken on the cause and much of the care for the refugees out of respect for the fact that, of all the former Soviet republics, Georgia was the most open and democratic. Tiny Abkhazia thus became an international problem. And with international problems came international meetings. That is why Osman Samir al-Husseini was in Georgia.

In truth, al-Husseini was completely uninterested in the plight of these miserable people from western Georgia. He was here using his cover as Syria's UN representative as an excuse to achieve far more important goals. His total time in-country would be no more than twenty-five hours. But the course of the world could well change as a result of his visit.

To the Refugee Conference

Tbilisi, September, 29

10:00 a.m.

Osman Samir al-Husseini arrived at the Chancellery Building in downtown Tbilisi at exactly 10:00 a.m. His UN driver, the English-less Temuri, had failed to show at the hotel. Irritated, al-Husseini had jumped into a cramped and dilapidated Czech-made Skoda that doubled ridiculously as one of the Sheraton Hotel's high-end taxis.

The driver took a scenic route into town. It was a pretty drive. Tbilisi in the daytime looked vastly different from the way it had the night before, when it had shown nothing but dingy griminess. On this bright morning, al-Husseini was surprised to find the city charming and beautiful. The turret-like domes of Georgian Orthodox churches were everywhere. The old city clung onto the cliffs overlooking the Kura River, and the old castle's fortified walls were visible from every angle of town.

"Tbilisi is one of the oldest capitals in Christendom," said the chatty taxi driver, oblivious to the fact that his client was from a Muslim country. "We were the last Christian stop of the silk route. From here, the caravans would depart into Islam on their way to Baku, Tashkent, Bukhara, and Samarkand. This was a land of traders and smugglers. It was never clear who was our friend and who was our enemy. I guess that happens in a land of smugglers."

That complex Georgian attitude toward foreigners could be seen in the gigantic steel statue that stood at the top of a ridge on the city's highest hill. The statue was of a winged woman denoting Mother Georgia. The monument held in one hand a welcoming bowl of wine and in the other a fearsome sword—not a bad symbol, given the fact that Georgia had, for so long, been the geographic crossroads of Christian and Muslim civilizations, caught between friend and foe.

Al-Husseini felt a sense of disgust. How was such silliness possible? A cup of wine in one hand, a sword in another? In Syria we know who our enemies are and how to treat them, he thought to himself.

"Then," continued the tour-guide wannabe, "the era of Soviet domination came and we found ourselves at the crossroads of nothing. Georgia became a small, insignificant part of the Kremlin's lands. Even under Stalin, a native Georgian, we withered. But now the smuggling has begun again. Oil contracts, opium, caviar, even humans looking for jobs in the West. Everything is again being smuggled through Georgia."

He seemed happy about this, thought al-Husseini, admiring the cabby's unusually erudite English. The driver babbled away.

"But we have become a strange country—a country of shadows. We live in both light and darkness. You know our first president was Eduard Shevardnadze, the last Soviet foreign minister? In the lights of a television camera, he was a hero of democracy; but after ten years, his name became synonymous with corruption. You see these beautiful buildings? They are beautiful on the outside, but inside they are gutted and horrible. You see what a beautiful day? Well, when the sun goes down, we do not have electricity or water in our houses. It all seems nice. But it is not."

Al-Husseini asked the driver other questions along the way: What was that building and this monument? The more the taxi driver talked, the more al-Husseini understood why Georgia was perfect for his mission. It was Christian. It was a recent democracy. It was a former Soviet satellite aspiring to become part of the West. All of these things meant that Georgia was now a Western ally; U.S. and European intelligence agencies would not look here first for danger. Yet, as the taxi driver made abundantly clear, it was a smuggler's paradise.

The taxi arrived at the Chancellery Building. It was Georgia's seat of power. Here the president and his senior ministers had their offices. It was a Soviet-style sandstone and granite monolith—eighteen floors high and surrounded by wrought-iron fencing and guards.

From the outside, the chancellery's sheer size communicated power. But, in reality, it was one of those Georgian opposites the taxi driver philosophized about. Inside was a very different story. Every floor was the same. Drab elevators gave way to drab hallways that extended hundreds of endless yards. A sickly, moth-eaten red carpet ran through the middle of each corridor. Doorway followed doorway, each leading to a cubicular office over-filled with three or four bureaucrats smoking cigarettes, drinking coffee, and doing nothing.

Al-Husseini, however, would see only the eighteenth floor. The elevator operator was under strict instructions to stop nowhere but the top. The penthouse floor was the only one designed to receive guests. It was ornate, with medieval Georgian furniture and art. Outside the president's office was a huge cabinet room that was to host today's conference on Abkhazia's refugees.

Al-Husseini stepped off the elevator and smiled at the obsequious young man who was there to meet him. He followed his young host down the hall and, as the Syrian diplomat passed a mirror, he looked at himself and approved. He only discussed human misery when dressed to diplomatic perfection. His conservative three-piece blue suit adorned a crisp white shirt and red-and-blue-striped tie. With al-Husseini, everything was small. He was thin and short. He sported a tiny, closely cropped mustache over his small mouth. He had short hair, parted from right to left and combed backward. As he entered the conference room, al-Husseini took his assigned seat behind the card that read "Syrian Arab Republic."

The large conference table was arranged in alphabetical order using Latin letters. He looked up and smiled at his neighbors around the table—the representatives of Pakistan and Portugal on his left and the ambassadors of Sweden and Thailand on right.

As the delegates sat down, he greeted each with a slight bowing movement and a practiced diplomatic smile. He immediately noticed that the handsome Pakistani representative with the salt-and-pepper beard sat ramrod straight, his hands folded on the stack of papers in front of him. Notwithstanding the man's elegant Western clothes, the Pakistani is clearly military, thought al-Husseini. The two delegates looked into each other's eyes in a split-second secret acknowledgment of their real mission in Georgia. Nobody else in the room noticed any hint of recognition between the two.

Al-Husseini's eyes turned from his colleagues to his meeting agenda and his mouth curled into a smile when he saw that nothing had changed from the agenda sent a week earlier to all participants. The meeting's schedule was tightly scripted.

After the presentation by the representative of the high commissioner for refugees, there would be a lunch break. Over lunch, the Georgian finance minister would speak about the financial toll the refugees' burden caused the Georgian economy. He would plead for increased international assistance. After lunch, each delegate attending the conference would have a chance to comment. The meeting would end at 5:00 p.m.

An hour later, a bus would pick up the delegates at the Sheraton Hotel for the hour-long drive to Kakheti, Georgia's wine-producing region. There, the minister of finance would host a traditional Georgian dinner, called a Supra, for the delegation.

Perfect. Osman Samir al-Husseini slid back in his chair and settled in for the next hours. His real mission would not begin until the evening.

Through the Mountains
The Pankisi Gorge, September 29
7:00 a.m.

Many miles to the north of Georgia's capital city, Professor Farooq Rahman did not know what had been worse: the exhaustion or the fear. He had been en route for days. He was overweight and not used to the difficult terrain. He was not accustomed to sleeping in the cold. He had never before been surrounded by unknown men armed to the teeth. This was not his preferred way of travel. But on he went. Professor Farooq Rahman did not belong here, but being here was God's work. He was certain of it.

Rounding yet another curve deep in the mighty Caucasus Mountains, Professor Rahman wondered if he would see the inside of his beloved Karachi laboratory again. One of the troika of scientists who had successfully exploded Pakistan's nuclear device in 1997, he was known as the proud father of Pakistan's nuclear bomb. Like many Pakistanis, Professor Rahman fervently believed that Islam needed to go on the offensive.

For years, as one of the country's leading experts in applied physics, he worked diligently at Karachi's Technical University. Recognizing his potential, Pakistan's Inter-Services Intelligence Agency (ISI) long ago started paying him the money needed to complete the research to convert Pakistan into a nuclear power. Whatever monies were left over went into a numbered bank account in Zurich, Switzerland.

Professor Rahman had always been comfortable with his handlers in Pakistan's intelligence services. Throughout the 1980s and early 1990s Pakistan's senior intelligence officers professed to be allies of the United States. But friendship with the CIA and the U.S. Defense Department only served a limited and temporary purpose: namely, to rid neighboring Afghanistan of Russian domination. Many in Pakistan's intelligence community lived with and aided the brave and devout freedom fighters in Afghanistan's war against Russian tanks.

The leadership of Pakistan's intelligence services was both proudly nationalistic and devoutly Muslim. Many intelligence officers became convinced that the dream of a real Islamic state in Afghanistan was possible. Dreams became reality when the Taliban—a troop of firebrand Muslims who were among the bravest of all who fought the Russians—took power.

In the Taliban, the Pakistani intelligence services had more than they could ask of any neighbor. They had the comfort of the Taliban's friendship. They had the protection of the Taliban's countryside for their operations. They had the serenity of knowing the Taliban's dependence on Pakistan. And, together with the Taliban, some key senior officers of the ISI shared the dream of creating a Muslim land ruled by Muslim law from the Indian Ocean to the Black Sea.

Professor Rahman became infected with that dream. He was sick and tired of India's Hindu hostility and the West's condescension. The United States had used his country as a base through which to smuggle weapons, money, and intelligence to Afghan guerillas battling the Russian invasion. Once the Red Army retreated and the Soviet Union no longer existed, the United States showed its true colors and disappeared from Pakistan. It left misery, lawlessness, and despotism in its tracks. As Pakistan became poorer, India prospered and exploded a nuclear device.

Professor Farooq Rahman was implored to find a quick solution—to make Pakistan a great power. He redoubled his research. Money flowed in. With his two colleagues, he slept four hours a night, ate in the laboratory, and spent every possible hour testing and retesting the machinery that would accurately slam together the fissionable material in such a way as to create a controlled nuclear explosion. Finally, after months of nonstop work, the three physicists succeeded—first with uranium and then, later, with much more difficult plutonium—in achieving detonation. Pakistan proudly announced to the world that it had become a nuclear power.

In the years after the device's creation, Professor Rahman joined the Ummah Tameer-e-Nau, or Reconstruction of the Muslim Ummah (UTN), an organization purportedly involved in relief and development work in Afghanistan. In reality, the UTN was a front organization of Pakistani scientists and intelligence officers designed to advise the Taliban and its al-Qaeda allies on the development of enrichment capabilities and nuclear capacity in Afghanistan.

Professor Rahman's scientific advances and his diplomatic missions to neighboring Afghanistan were exciting moments in his life. But the dreams that accompanied the great promise of nuclear prominence never materialized. India remained in Kashmir. Pakistan was still poor and bedeviled by corruption and disorder. The power of the intelligence services began to wane. And, worst of all, after 9/11 the Americans retaliated against the Taliban's protection of al-Qaeda, and in just a few pathetic weeks Afghanistan's Islamic purity ceased to exist.

In the spring of 2002, the new president of the University of Karachi told Professor Farooq Rahman that budget cuts would force the university to close his laboratory. Within months, Professor Farooq Rahman, the man who had given birth to the world's first Islamic-owned nuclear device, was retired and sent home.

That is why the professor was so excited when, just a few weeks ago, one of his old friends from the Inter-Services Intelligence Agency had arrived unannounced at his home. It had been at least four years since the professor had heard from him. They settled on the simple green sofa in the pretty house on Karachi's southern suburbs. Professor Rahman's wife served tea and almond cookies and silently disappeared back into the kitchen.

"What brings you back to me?" Farooq asked of the good-looking and well-dressed man with a salt-and-pepper beard whom he had always called "the Colonel."

"I will not lie to an old friend," said the Colonel, sitting very straight even though he was offered the deepest of couches in the house. "Things have not gone well for us in the past years. Our friends in Afghanistan have been disbanded. The dream is no more. We are under attack here in Pakistan. But we—and some friends of ours in an Arab nation—have an idea that can reverse this negative course."

The Colonel saw that he had the scientist's attention. "But I need you to again solve one of your nuclear mysteries. Would you be willing to help?"

"Colonel, I am honored that you still think me useful," said the professor. He felt the excitement growing inside. He was again being counted on. He could again make a difference. He leaned forward to listen.

"Professor, am I right to believe that one needs relatively little nuclear material to make a bomb?"

"Yes, Colonel, but it depends on what material you are using. One needs just a very few pounds of plutonium. If you remember our work at the laboratory in Karachi, the task was slow because of the dangers inherent in working with plutonium."

The Colonel raised his hand and stopped the scientist. "Professor, I am no longer the government. I am on a mission that is known only to a few. I do not have the time to linger. You will—you must—answer my questions very succinctly. Understood?"

The professor nodded his assent. He understood. Rahman now gathered his thoughts and spoke quickly and assuredly. "You need very few pounds, but a very sophisticated laboratory, to work with plutonium, because it is so toxic and dangerous. Your other material of choice is highly enriched uranium, known either as HEU or uranium-235. It is far less toxic. It requires less sophistication. Its radioactivity is less hazardous to handlers and it has little chance of becoming unstable. Yet the background neutron rate is so low that you can set off a high-yield explosion with very little sophisticated knowledge. It's the gold standard if you do not have access to advanced laboratories."

"On the other hand," concluded the professor, "you need more of it to create a serious explosion. Thirty pounds would suffice for a good-sized bomb."

"Thank you, Professor, that was clear. Now, if I was to tell you that we desire to explode a bomb made of uranium in another country—an enemy country—what would be our obstacles in transporting the material?"

Professor Rahman gave this some thought before he answered. "Colonel, trained physicists know how to transport the material. Will it be transported by competent nuclear experts?"

The Colonel smiled. He liked Farooq Rahman because, in addition to his academic training and laboratory skills, the professor was unusually practical. With this last question, Rahman had jumped to the core of the problem.

"No, Professor, the material will be transported by absolute amateurs. Some may not know even what they are transporting. And it will be very close to their bodies."

Farooq Rahman's mind was bursting with curiosity and admiration. How did the Colonel find such people? How would they agree to walk around with uranium? Was the target country the United States?

Rahman forced his mind back to the questions. "Plutonium is out of the question with amateurs. So, we move to uranium. The key problem to resolve is the issue of critical mass. A little bit—say a kilogram—of U-235 is somewhat radioactive, but it is stable. It is not lethal to transport for a short trip. But the more you add, the more unstable it becomes. At some point, as you keep adding uranium to the mass, the neutrons of its radioactivity cannot leach to the surface and dissipate in the air. These neutrons start looking for atoms to bombard, and each atom that is split gives off new neutrons that look for new atoms to hit. That is the chain reaction that is desired for explosion but must be avoided in transportation."

Professor Rahman was not finished. "Forgive me for sounding scientific, but I have no choice. The calibration of critical mass—how much is too much before an explosion—needs to be made by a scientist looking at the material and its purity, density, temperature, etc. If you don't have that expert, you cannot risk putting more than one half pound of uranium-235 together in one place. In other words, you will be compelled to transport thirty pounds of U-235 in about sixty separate half-pound pieces. Am I clear?"

Rahman was enjoying this. He had an unusual capacity to boil the most difficult matters to their most understandable core—he was, after all, supposed to be a teacher. But the Colonel had interrupted him to demand that the professor be succinct. Now the professor interrupted the lesson to ask if the student had understood. The Colonel smiled at the professor to acknowledge the academician's clarity.

"Very clear. Tell me, now, how damaging is it to walk around with a half pound of U-235?" said the Colonel.

"Without protection, it is possible that the carrier would eventually fall ill. But this problem can be resolved easily by shielding the half-pound of uranium in a thin lead or tungsten casing. This will add weight, but it protects the carrier and also reduces the chances that the material will be found on any radiation-detecting equipment. On the other hand, it can also be carried without shielding for a few hours.

The Colonel now leaned over and took the professor's right hand in both of his hands. He came very close to Rahman's face and his voice reduced to a whisper.

"Professor, I need you again. I need to send you on a difficult and dangerous mission. It is not the trip on which I would normally send a sixty-year-old man to whom our nation already owes much. But I know nobody else who can do this."

He looked deeply into the eyes of the scientist. "We are able to take delivery of thirty pounds of uranium-235 cut to the specifications you request. The uranium comes from materials stolen from Russian enrichment plants. It will be delivered to us in Chechnya. But we need an expert to verify that it is indeed what the sellers say. Thievery and fraud is easy in this business. Unless we have somebody like you, we may be sold discarded radioactive medical equipment and would never know the difference.

"But, Professor, once you have verified that it is uranium, you must then take it across the Chechen border to Georgia, where you will be met. This is extremely dangerous. It is not the mission for a professor; but a professor must do it. Would you?"

Silence enveloped the room. Professor Farooq Rahman seemed lost in thought. He slowly rubbed his face with his hand. He knew he could well end up dead. Yet, the retired university professor with the illustrious past was excited to once again be invited to participate in a plan that could change the course of the world. He had tried before to make a difference. Little had changed. Maybe this time?

"Colonel, working with you on the nuclear program in Karachi, I asked few questions and became accustomed to not having answers. But I don't want to be sent on a voyage that can end my life if the mission seems destined to fail. So, I would like to ask you one question."

"Please ask, Professor. You have earned the right," said the Colonel.

The more he thought about it, the more Farooq Rahman thought the idea silly. Citizens of Muslim lands were now the most carefully surveilled group on earth. Was the Colonel crazy? Did he think that he could organize a little squad of Arab, Afghan, or Pakistani smugglers and get thirty pounds of the most coveted material on earth into the United States or Europe without a leak? The idea was mad.

"Colonel, after the events of September 11, the toppling of Taliban Afghanistan, and the invasion of Iraq, we have become the most watched region in the world. Our area of the planet is full of listening machines, satellites, intelligence personnel, double agents, and traitors. Even some of al-Qaeda's cells have been penetrated. The United Nations International Atomic Energy Agency has just issued a report asking the Security Council to consider imposing multinational control over the production and transportation of nuclear material that could be used in weapons. With all of this international scrutiny, do you honestly believe that fifty or sixty men from Muslim countries can deliver thirty pounds of uranium secretly into an enemy country that I presume is the United States?"

The Colonel stared at his host. He sipped the sweet black tea slowly and answered quietly. "No, I do not believe that is possible."

Professor Rahman, flabbergasted, dropped his cup onto the table. Thankfully, it was empty. What did this old intelligence agent want from him? If the mission was doomed to fail, why does he want to send me to a near certain death? Rahman thought to himself.

The Colonel's calm voice stopped his anger. "Professor, listen carefully, I am not a fool. It is probably impossible to penetrate the United States from our region of the world—you are right. At present, we cannot count on the mission succeeding with our people, with those who believe like we believe. So, we must look elsewhere . . .

"Sometimes we Muslims have a hard time believing that there are others who can do things better than we can. We never look beyond our noses, dear Professor. And there exists one group of people who can smuggle anything into the

United States. In fact, they take large quantities of illegal items into the United States every day. Many times a day!"

"Who? Who?" shouted Rahman.

"The drug traffickers of Colombia. Day after day. Hour after hour. They smuggle their products into the United States. And now they will bring in something for us," answered the Colonel.

Professor Rahman's Voyage
September 18-29

===

Professor Farooq Rahman's odyssey had been incredible.

Eleven days ago, he had left Karachi early in the morning. He was put on a small jet to Quetta, a large Pakistani city nearly on Afghanistan's southern border. Quetta's population was Pashtun—the same ethnic group as those living in southern Afghanistan. Notwithstanding the coalition occupation of Afghanistan and the soldiers of the government of President Hamid Karzai in Kabul, Professor Farooq Rahman was driven by jeep—nicely stocked with iced drinking water and candies—straight over the border and into Kandahar, Afghanistan's second-largest city.

Once, the driver changed. Rahman presumed the change happened as he entered Afghanistan, but he could not be sure. There was no clear border on the mountain road on which he was traveling. Roadblocks peppered the way—manned with Pashtun tribesmen, making it impossible to tell if they were Pakistani or Afghans. At each stop, the jeep was waved forward. Nobody directed a word at the professor. Nobody asked a question.

He stayed overnight in Kandahar, a silent guest in an empty, beautiful house. Two men took him down a hall until they came to a door that opened into a huge suite. A king-size bed crowned the room. The walls were painted ochre and the furniture was upholstered in different hues of orange. On the coffee table lay plate upon plate of delicacies, salty and sweet. Rahman bathed and then put on the robe left for him. He ate voraciously. He waited for something to happen; when nothing did, he put out the light and went to sleep.

A knock awoke him at sunrise the next morning. In the distance, Rahman heard the voice of the Muezzin calling to prayer. He dressed in silence, wondering when somebody would explain where he would go next. At 6:30 a.m., the door opened and the same two men gestured that he should follow. He again climbed onto the jeep and was driven through dusty back streets.

They passed busy Afghani merchants. He marveled at all the roof-less commerce. An open tent was a welding shop. A farmer selling only string beans laid his vegetables on a dirty rug and haggled loudly with women wearing blue burkas fully covering their bodies and faces. Every few yards, grizzled men doubling as one-man filling stations sold plastic bags filled with a gasoline and oil mixture for two-stroke engines. Motorcycles stacked two stories high with anything and everything—food, hay, and commuters—zoomed in and out of traffic. The noise of commerce was overwhelming.

Professor Rahman was taken to a soccer field outside of town. Within minutes, he heard the chopping sound of helicopter blades hitting the air. A Russian-made medium-sized helicopter landed on the field, and on he went. There were no good-byes and no wishes of good luck. Noise filled the void, but the world immediately surrounding Professor Farooq Rahman was silent and sullen.

The volume from the chopper blades and the aircraft's groaning vibrations was painful. Two hours later he landed in Herat, a dusty city nestled into the Afghan side of the triangle border with Iran and Turkmenistan. The professor was again loaded onto another jeep—this one decidedly older and more abused—that lurched forward without a human sound being exchanged.

The jeep rolled straight north. Professor Rahman noted a sign in English that told him the Turkmen border was only seven kilometers away. Soon after that sign, the jeep stopped. The driver and guard were heavily armed. The driver spoke broken English: "At dark, you go to Turkmenistan. You travel at night and sleep in day for six days until reach Caspian Sea. Then cross to Chechnya by boat. You not ask question. You not talk. Turkmen are brother Muslim—but less said is better for all. Clear?"

And so it went. By car or jeep at night. From Bayram Ali to Kaakhka, around Ashkhabad to the waters of the Caspian Sea. He passed one dusty town after the next. After seventy years inside the Soviet Union, Turkmenistan was probably better off than neighboring Afghanistan. But each place the professor drove through looked eerily like the last. Shabby Soviet cinderblock construction lined main roads strewn with empty cans and stubbed cigarettes. Two-stroke engines—motorcycles, cars, and small lorries—buzzed about dilapidated roadways like flies on a carcass.

He was handed off from one group to the next. Sometimes the next drivers were waiting for him. Sometimes Rahman had to wait in deserted cafés with dingy wooden tables and chairs. But the trip proceeded forward.

Rahman marveled at the organization. The professor had now been traveling for days—by car, plane, helicopter, jeep. This was a vast and formless Muslim syndicate. It spanned borders and nations. It crossed languages and races. It survived the Soviet boot and refuted temptations to Westernize. It traversed deserts and mountains. The silent men transporting the professor did not know his mission, but they had been told to move him safely onward.

Each of these men belonged to organizations, mosques, schools, and groups that had money and were motivated by the dream of violence against a vastly more powerful enemy. Each believed in an anti-Islamic conspiracy by Christians and Jews. Each knew that violence against the outside enemy was now no longer a choice, but a necessity.

Indeed, violence with the West was a fact of life. It was unpleasant, but there were no options. It was the tax Muslims had to pay for regaining authority and respect. The sullen men along Rahman's way all shared the belief that the youth of Islam must carry arms and defend their religion with pride and dignity. For years, the West's implacable forces—on television, in magazines, politics, clothing, everywhere—had permeated their societies. Nobody seemed to object. This inaction had slowly bred despair. Now Islam's youth was rising in a Babel of languages with a force that would cleanse and restore.

To Westerners, it seemed that Islam was in the hands of those who advocated destruction and death. But to the Muslim believers living in the vast Fertile Crescent from the Indian Ocean to the Mediterranean, the death of Westerners—whether pinpoint or indiscriminate—restored a fearlessness and self-respect that had been missing for generations.

After six days in Turkmenistan, Professor Farooq Rahman finally saw the lapping, dusky waters of the Caspian Sea. The road followed the shoreline a few miles, and Rahman strained to see his surroundings. His vision hardly penetrated the darkness.

The car arrived in a small fishing village. There was a single main street with no more than a couple of dozen buildings. The town's restaurants, barbershop, and a single grocery store were long closed. A few men milled together in the street, smoking. Ahead of them, lights seemed suspended in midair, twinkling and swinging to and fro. Boats.

On the other side of the Caspian Sea lay the world's most dangerous place: the Islamic provinces of the Russian Federation. The southern Caucasus border of Russia was a region of remoteness and ethnic chaos. One ethnic and tribal loyalty lay upon another in a hot mix of nationalism and religious unrest. Kamykia, Dagestan, Chechnya, Ingushetia, North Ossetia, Kabardino-Balkaria were Islamic autonomous regions of Russia. And they were centers of poverty and resentment. Here, the new democratic Russia ended sharply, giving way to tough repression and control.

Rahman's boat was an aging thirty-five-foot wooden supply vessel used by

Azeri salesmen to resupply food, water, and goods to the hundreds of offshore oil wells that peppered the Caspian Sea. The professor tried to engage the crew in small dialogue, but the captain and his mate were clenched-mouthed toughies. Again, Professor Farooq Rahman found himself traveling in silence.

After nearly ten hours of nighttime rolling and rocking, the professor jumped off his boat in Dagestan. He was now in Russia. The old vessel entered the cove just as the first single ray of dawn fought away the night. It dropped its passenger and turned right around. So far, the trip had not been so bad—it had become a mixture of elation and boredom. But as he stood alone on a small wooden dock that spilled up the waters of the Caspian Sea, Rahman wondered if he knew what he was doing. A man of his age! Maybe he had gone too far.

Farooq Rahman looked around. As daylight began to penetrate the gloominess, he noticed that there was nothing in the little bay except the rickety pier he was standing on. One small path led up a steep hill. Above him, Rahman could discern a road—he occasionally heard the squishy splashy sound of car tires on damp pavement. He walked to the end of the pier, thinking that it might be less chilly at the other side, away from the lapping cold of the water.

Rahman sat for nearly an hour. He became increasingly agitated and nervous. Here was a Pakistani scientist, alone, on an abandoned pier in Russia. What a fool! He started imagining his imminent capture by a routine Russian military patrol.

Just when he had convinced himself that he had been double-crossed, he heard another car approach. This time it slowed. A car door opened. A balding man dressed in a well-worn grayish Western suit appeared as he leaned out over the cliff to see if someone was on the pier below. When he saw Rahman, he smiled and waved, beckoning him to come up the path.

When the professor had made the climb, the man shook Rahman's hand. "My name is Yusef. You have come a long way and the trip is nearly over. But this is the most dangerous part. Come with me."

The old, white, boxlike car roared off into the countryside. Rolling hills were lost in the morning fog. But in the distance, above the mist, rose the massive, snow-covered Caucasus Mountains. Across the mountains lay Georgia. He was nearly there.

"Professor, I am to accompany you the rest of the way. In five hours we will reach our first stop. There you must receive possession of the materials. But you must be in Telavi, in Georgia, tomorrow at 6 p.m. We have less than thirty-six hours."

Professor Farooq Rahman was surprised by the sound of a human voice. For nearly eleven days, he had been surrounded by silence. Nobody had talked. What a pleasure to exchange words with this man in an easygoing tone. Rahman asked about politics in the world, soccer, and weather. Anything, just to have a conversation.

They drove up and down hills, always staying on small back roads. The terrain became increasingly steep as they got closer and closer to the mountains. Time passed quickly. Yusef was easy to talk to as long as the conversation was neutral. Once, Rahman had tried asking Yusef where they were and he simply did not answer. Four hours into the up and down drive, Yusef announced, "We have crossed into Chechnya."

At some point before midday, in the middle of barren farmland, the car turned left and arrived at a sickly looking barn. Two thin cows and some bleating goats were eating their noontime hay just outside the structure. The professor entered the barn, following Yusef. As he adjusted his tired eyes to the dark, he could make out a number of large round bales of hay packed side by side.

Two men emerged from behind one of the bales. They carried two cases. One of them, tall with a closely cropped beard and wearing a tight leather jacket, was clearly the boss. The other man also carried a very modern-looking rifle.

"You are Professor Farooq Rahman, right?" asked the man in surprisingly good English.

The professor nodded. He was exhausted and scared—but he understood that the cases these men were carrying could contain the thirty pounds of uranium-235 he had come such a long way to acquire. I have traveled all this way to do a job. God give me strength to do it, thought Rahman.

"Do you wish me to look at the materials now?" asked the professor. As he reached for his bag, the second man raised the rifle. "I am going into my bag to get the equipment I need," Rahman assured the younger man quietly.

He opened the cases on the floor. They were heavy—made of some type of metal, they easily weighed forty pounds each. He opened both cases and looked inside carefully. They were identical.

When opened, he saw that each case contained a foamlike material that covered the inside. The foam had perfect indentations that fit four rows of small, dark metal boxes lined seven in a row. Each of these twenty-eight tiny boxes was made of tungsten—an excellent metal that shielded radioactivity. Every box opened with a tiny spring-loaded lock. Inside, give or take a few ounces, each box contained approximately a half pound of U-235.

Farooq Rahman chose one box randomly from each of the rows in the two suitcases. He worked slowly and carefully. After gingerly lifting each random sample from the foam, he slowly opened the chosen boxes and removed a small, silvery metal nugget about the size of a large marble. It was very heavy for its size.

It had been years since he had last seen highly enriched uranium, but he could tell just by looking at the metal's silvery coating that it was real.

A scientist's instinct was not enough, however. From his bag, he removed his American-made portable ionization spectrometer—a device that measures alpha emissions. Measuring four feet by four feet and resembling a common hair dryer, it was known affectionately among nuclear scientists as a "Cutie Pie." Years before miniaturization, the Manhattan Project scientists had christened it with this silly name because, even then, it was one of the few machines in nuclear research that was relatively small. A half century later, during the time of Rahman's laboratory work in Pakistan, Cutie Pies became smaller and more portable. Now they were shrunken to a gunlike form with a flat panel LCD screen and some plastic detectors. The moment the professor placed the detectors close to the silvery metals, the grids on the Cutie Pie's screen lit up, identifying the alpha emissions.

He repeated the exercise again and again. He knew that, in the past, smugglers had tried to pass off cesium and strontium—both radioactive derivatives—as HEU. Millions of dollars exchanged hands and the forgers disappeared before anybody realized that these radioactive materials were useless in creating a detonation. Cesium and strontium were gamma emitters; U-235 is an alpha emitter. The Cutie Pie now confirmed the presence of millions of jumping alpha particles. He smiled. There was no chance these suitcases contained forgeries.

"There is no doubt about it," said Professor Rahman, looking at the Cutie Pie's grids. "This uranium is enriched to levels over 90 percent."

The professor was done in less than an hour. He did not know who these men were or how they had gotten the enriched uranium. Professor Rahman was well aware that, in the recent years, the Russian government had hugely upgraded what scientists called the MPCA—Materials Protection Control and Accountability. All uranium and plutonium in the Russian Republic was now bar-coded with double markers. The Russians had even adopted the Los Alamos system of materials consolidation and control, meaning that each storage facility had cameras on access doors, double signature requirements for any movement of the materials, and clear records that precisely described any changes in the storage of Category One nuclear substances.

The Americans were also providing large amounts of money and know-how to former Soviet republics to increase the quality of care and control over nuclear materials. Minsk, in the Ukraine, still had one of the largest storage sites, and the Ukrainian government was successfully converting its facilities to MPCA standards. Much the same was happening in Belarus and other former Soviet lands where nuclear materials were stored. And in countries where MPCA standards were not adequate, there was now a large-scale international tightening of controls. American, Russian, and UN teams recently had confiscated Category One materials in Bulgaria and Serbia and transported the uranium to the newly stringent safety of Russian storage sites.

No, thought Rahman, these thirty precious pounds of HEU could not have been recently acquired. They were clearly taken years ago in the chaos that ensued after the fall of the Soviet Union.

Just before the Kremlin's collapse, Mikhail Gorbachev had ordered all nuclear materials, warheads, delivery vehicles, and scientists living in Muslim Soviet republics such as Kazakhstan, Uzbekistan, and Tajikistan to be moved to Russia proper. But, while the warheads and the missiles were accounted for, some of the uranium went missing along with the scientists responsible for the material. Obviously, a number of these scientists, fearing the oncoming chaos, saw an opportunity to make a lot of money by keeping behind a couple of kilos of the world's most precious and dangerous materials.

Rahman had no way to prove it. But he bet this stuff had been taken more than ten years ago and had since been kept in hiding in a former Soviet republic. The history, however, was relatively unimportant.

What was important was that, in a barn somewhere in Chechnya, Professor Farooq Rahman had just taken delivery of thirty pounds of one of the world's most dangerous objects.

PART V
THE UNITED STATES

The White House
Washington, September 28
9:05 a.m.

National Security Advisor Nelson Cummins hated being the target of a tirade. He had survived the pressures of major global crises. He had withstood the endless White House hours. He had held up well under the scrutiny of some of the world's smartest people. But he could not stand the fact that the everyday tensions at the White House turned some people into unbearable assholes.

Allyson Bonnet regularly hit the top of the White House asshole-ometer. Sure, the White House press secretary was great with the press—she knew how to keep her cool and banter at the daily briefings and had an innate instinct for what was news. It was also true that she had the president's trust. But more often than not, once the door to the press briefing room closed behind her, she morphed into an impossible bitch.

The complaints about her swirled fast and furious. Last month she had told Barry Sklar, the secretary of transportation—a twenty-year Washington veteran—that he needed to learn "Washington's ways." Just a few days ago, she had backed Ivan Jackson, the White House liaison to Capitol Hill, against a wall and lectured him on the fact that he had no right to talk to the press without first notifying her. When Ivan protested that he had a family dinner that included his brother, a reporter at the *Wall Street Journal,* she told him, "If you talk to a member of the press corps, I want to know about it—and I don't give a shit if they are from Mars or your family."

Today Nelson Cummins was the target, and he hated it. Here we go again—the lecture about the Bogotá trip. For nearly six weeks now, this was Allyson's favorite subject. Like a dog with a bone, she would not let go.

He was standing next to his black Lincoln Town Car, its door already opened to let him in. Nelson listened anxiously, hoping to catch a pause in Allyson's onslaught that would allow him to escape into the car's backseat. None came. Mike, the chauffeur, just stood there frozen, mortified to be listening to Allyson's tirade, but too embarrassed to walk away. The suitcases were already in the car, tagged for New York and ready to be loaded onto Air Force One.

"What were you doing, Nelson?" asked Allyson in her most grating voice. "Downing margaritas in Bogotá? How is it possible that he got away from you at this dinner party? Now, I'm about to leave you alone with him again. This time, be goddamn careful, Nelson. We're still getting reamed."

"Look, Allyson, chill out, please. You can plan trips; you can brief the president about most things. But when the man is with fifteen other heads of state, you cannot cover every permutation. There are things out of one's control. If two heads of state want to talk to another one without staff coverage, it can't be stopped."

The thought of more than 200 heads of state descending on New York City over the next few days at the opening ceremonies of the UN General Assembly made his head swim. If Allyson thought he did a bad job controlling Stockman in the company of a handful of presidents and prime ministers in a South American capital, she was about to be in for a nasty surprise with the controlled chaos of the annual opening of the General Assembly.

"Yes, but it's your job to know in advance if this new girl in Colombia had plans to hoodwink our boy. You should have seen it coming. How the hell did she get him into a room alone with Castro? And how the hell did you let them walk out together so that the whole goddamn world knows the meeting took place? The entire state of Florida is about to secede. Some of our best donors in the Cuban community are furious. They're worried that we are going to lift the embargo, and all their allies are making sure we feel the heat. We did not need this, Nelson."

There was more. "Since we returned from Colombia, I have had to stand there and answer questions. 'What was said between Castro and Stockman?' Though we keep telling them that nothing of consequence happened, they have kept asking about it. Now, after a couple of weeks of our protestations, the press may believe us. But, the questions are changing. Suddenly, they are less interested in *what* happened than in *how* it happened. And that is dangerous stuff."

"Why?" asked Nelson Cummins. "Doesn't that mean that the story is dying down? They heard nothing that gives any meaning to the meeting, so they're now asking process questions. I heard you being asked a couple of those—'Who invited President Stockman for the art tour in the Bogotá presidential palace, was it set up in advance, what did the room look like, how long did it take?'

"Allyson, what are you complaining about? This change of questions is a good thing—they are grasping at straws because there is nothing to report."

"My God, Nelson, you are a really a naïve nerd. Learn something and learn it now. When a story no longer has legs—I think you called it 'dying down'—the press stops asking questions altogether. The press doesn't 'do' gradualism.

They're either interested or they aren't. So, if they are still asking questions, but different types of questions, it means only one thing: They have something up their sleeves."

She had Nelson's attention now.

"I don't understand. What could they be after?" he asked. "We explained that the new president of Colombia took President Stockman on a tour of the Botero paintings in Colombia's presidential palace. They happened upon a small room where Castro was taking a phone call. President Pradilla introduced the two of them, but they said nothing to each other. Then, they walked out. What else is there to say?"

"I told you; the problem, Cummins, is no longer what was said but how Stockman ended up in the room with Castro in the first place. And let me tell you what the press is thinking: They are saying to themselves that he got there because he let Pradilla take him for a little tour that conveniently ended up with Castro. Specifically, they are wondering if the tough president of the United States of America got snookered by the hot Latin babe."

Cummins was agape. There was no disputing the fact that the new Colombian president had pulled a fast one on Stockman. Cummins and Stockman had talked intensely on Air Force One's ride home. The national security advisor and his boss concluded that Pradilla was trying to mitigate her weakness at being a female head of state in macho Latin America. So, in a vain play for early glory, she forced Stockman to meet Castro so that she could position herself as a leader unafraid to be tough on the United States. Given the upcoming General Assembly ceremonies and the need for Colombia's vote at the UN, they both agreed that the best thing was not to kick up a fuss now. Let some time go by and then find a way to publicly slap her down, they resolved.

But according to Allyson Bonnet, these conclusions now needed to be turned on their head. Until that moment, it had never occurred to the national security advisor that the gender issue could be manipulated against Stockman. Shit.

Now it seemed that the problem was not that an unmarried, woman president needed to project toughness. Instead, the issue was whether an unmarried, male president was too weak to deal with this woman's high-voltage femininity. Was it possible that Pradilla had thought it through and realized that this is where the story would end up? He dismissed the disconcerting thought. This woman was way too new to be that savvy.

"It's hard to believe that the press could be so suspicious and negative," said Cummins defensively to the White House press secretary.

"Don't try to hide your surprise, Nelson. I just saw the look on your face. You just put two and two together and realized that this chiquita took the president of the United States for a ride. She knew this would happen. But since you are both boys, you never saw it coming."

"How can we insure that this does not snowball?" asked Nelson. "Before the dinner, I tried to convince him to shake Castro's hand because I thought it was high time to move on from our forty-five-year-old Cuba quagmire. But it's one thing for us to initiate and proactively take a first step in a new direction. It's a whole different thing to get press stories that this widower president met his first foreign woman colleague and swooned. How do we kill this?"

"Only one way to do it," she answered curtly. "We have to go back to your original recommendation to the president. We have to make this his idea, his initiative."

"What do you mean?" he asked, now thoroughly confused.

"I'll arrange an exclusive interview for you with Peter Sempter from the *New York Times*. Trust me, he'll ask about this. We stick to the same basic story: She took him on a tour and they came upon Castro making a phone call. But now you need to say that President Stockman asked President Pradilla to introduce them. You will tell him that President Stockman had planned this all along. Tell him that the boss told you before the dinner that he would ask President Pradilla to effect an introduction of the two men if the appropriate occasion arose at the gala."

She scratched her chin as another thought occurred to her. "You might even tell the *New York Times* that you tried to talk him out of it but he was pretty determined. Tell him that you relented only because we were not changing policy, but rather making an effort to avoid irritating the other Latin American presidents. The Cuban community in Florida will scream bloody murder, but everybody else will be relieved that, at least, this isn't some wholesale change in U.S. policy."

Cummins shook his head in disbelief. He could not believe how this Castro thing had somersaulted. A month and a half ago, in Bogotá, the president told him—inelegantly—to fuck off after suggesting that he shake Castro's hand. Now he was supposed to tell the White House press corps that shaking Castro's hand was the president's idea and that Nelson actually tried to persuade him not to do it.

But, more than the irony of his own relationship with President Stockman, he was impressed with how the situation turned out for Marta Pradilla. Did she plan it exactly this way? Did she know that the press would wonder about her influence on the president? And even worse, how did she know that the only way for Stockman to avoid looking like he was love-smitten would be to convert the Castro handshake into his own idea?

"Allyson, do you think she read this thing all the way through? Do you think she understood that the only way to get out of this would be to pretend the idea was our own?"

"No doubt about it, Nelson—she had this thought out. Watch what happens when we communicate this version of events. The day after the *New York Times* runs your interview, the press in Bogotá will ask her for confirmation. I'll bet she lets us take the credit for the Castro handshake. Her press guy will come out and confirm our version of the events."

"Alright, we'll see. Now, which one of us runs this by the boss?"

"Normally, Nelson, I'd definitely love to watch you eat shit in front of the president of the United States. No better show in earth. But, because I'm convinced that this is really urgent, I'm going to do it. We can't risk the boss saying no just because he's pissed at how it evolved. I hate having to save your neck, but I'll talk to him."

"Now that I'm going to put out your fire, let me ask you a question." Allyson Bonnet leaned closer to Nelson. "You were with him at the party. You were closest to our man. Did he get a shine for this gal? I mean, how else do you explain that our diffident, difficult, hard-ass boss suddenly got himself on a one-on-one tour that ended up with Fidel Castro?"

Nelson stared at Allyson. It never occurred to him that Stockman might have fallen for her. To tell the truth, it never occurred to him that Stockman had any personal sentiments, period. The question was too difficult to contemplate.

"Stockman? Fancying someone? No way," said Cummins. He got into his car and closed the door.

To the Opening of the General Assembly
New York, September 28
10:55 a.m.

New York was a rush of activity, meetings, negotiations, speeches, and press appearances. The opening of the General Assembly is the world's premier international meeting. Every year since the UN's inception in 1946, most of the planet's leaders have traveled to New York to participate. Initially there were fewer than 51 countries. It was barely manageable then. With just under 200 nations today, it is out of control. Still, few leaders miss the meeting.

Meeting may be the wrong word; with *meeting,* you get the impression of people actually talking to each other. *Gathering* is more accurate. Each head of state gets to give one speech. That's the canned, rehearsed part that the world sees on television. But away from the cameras, real encounters do take place. The powerful get together in a flurry of face-to-face discussions and negotiations to talk about key world issues. The kings, presidents, prime ministers, sultans, sheiks, and princes who attend the Assembly's yearly opening don't go for the speeches; they go for the behind-the-scenes bilateral discussions.

John Stockman hated the ritual, but he went. The protocol and the niceties of the official Assembly irritated him to no end. Mr. Chairman here. Mr. Secretary General there. We have the pleasure now. We have the honor then. Yuck. He could not stand the diplomatic garbage.

But, for Stockman, worse than the canned protocol of the General Assembly were the one-on-one meetings. It was an endless array of breakfasts, coffees, teas, drinks, lunches with one bad English-speaker after another. Cummins briefed him before each meeting on the key issues that needed attention, but these guys never seemed to get to the point. The politeness made him ache. Each of these gatherings was scheduled to last for minutes, but to Stockman, they felt like hours.

Today, it would be worse than ever.

"Let me go over it again, Mr. President," said Nelson Cummins just as the plane touched down at New York's LaGuardia airport.

"Mr. Stanislav Radonovich, the president of Bulgaria, is going to be waiting for us in your limo. The issue is Bulgaria's role in the expanded NATO alliance. You have him for the twenty-minute car ride to the Waldorf Astoria, where we're staying the night."

Stockman groaned. Nelson Cummins ignored him.

"When we get to the hotel, you've got ten minutes to settle in. Then we have a coffee with Chancellor Schreker of Germany. Remember, he asked for this to repair some of the damage caused by his anti-American rhetoric during his election campaign. Then, Schreker walks down with you to the lunch with the heads of state of the Group of Eight. This one is important, Sir, they govern the world's richest countries, and this is your chance to talk about Syria."

If Cummins thought that would make Stockman happier, he was wrong.

"After lunch, President M'Brani of South Africa is stopping by your suite for a coffee. You and he have fifteen minutes alone. After that, Samuel Wolfman, the president of the World Bank, will join both of you to talk about the international response to the AIDS epidemic in Africa. At 3:00 p.m. we head over to the UN building. Your speech is at 4:00 p.m., so we meet with Chinese premier Teng for forty-five minutes before you go into the General Assembly."

Stockman literally winced. The last time he had met Teng, the Chinese premier had told jokes in Chinese for the first fifteen minutes of the meeting. Stockman recalled how bad Chinese jokes are when they have to go through an official Communist Party translator.

Nelson Cummins continued unfazed.

"The speech is twenty-five minutes long. After your speech, we'll take you out for a quick five minutes with the press. Remember, we want to express a lot of concern about Syria's harboring of terrorists. After the press conference, we walk to the office of the Indian ambassador to meet with Prime Minister Krishna for thirty minutes. We have to get back to the hotel by 5:15 because we have a coffee with Canadian prime minister Claude Sambert."

The plane was now parked. New York cops and Secret Service agents were everywhere on the tarmac, waiting for the president's limousine to pull up with Bulgarian president Radonovich already inside.

"Anybody from Latin America?" asked Stockman.

Cummins was leaning over to gather some papers into his briefcase, but his head rocketed upward at the question. Latin America? Why the question? This was the first time in history that Stockman ever uttered the name of the region without prior prompting. Cummins answered a careful "No, sir."

"Good. I was afraid that you had set up a meeting with that crazy woman from Colombia."

Cummins just smiled as they started walking down the aisle to the door. But, inside, he was wondering if the president was being totally honest with him. He thought of Allyson Bonnet's questions and wondered whether there was something he had missed between Pradilla and Stockman. He kicked the idea around for a few seconds and then banished it from his mind. Impossible.

The United Nations

New York, September 28

10:15 p.m.

President John Stockman was beat. Totally. The day had been murder. He had gone from one meeting to another, literally dragging himself into closed-door sessions with a parade of foreigners. The speech had gone impeccably. There was good attendance by many of the heads of state, and intense press coverage.

Most important, in each of his one-on-one meetings, he hinted that the United States was hardening its position toward Syria. Reactions were muted. Sure, all the heads of state had expressed perfunctory concern about another unilateral U.S. military action in the Middle East. But to one degree or another, there seemed to be agreement that Syria was a problem.

The growing international consensus on Syria made this a very good day, thought Stockman.

Stockman's positive mood spilled over into the evening. Even the usually horrid opening banquet hosted by UN Secretary General Barak Shampour was better than expected. Thank God he was seated next to Jordan Meyers, the Oscar-winning movie star, who served as the senior "special ambassador" of the United Nations. That made the conversation easy and kept him away from the usual diplomatic nonsense.

But the time had come to leave. Enough was enough.

He slowly made his way through the banquet, saying good night and telling the gathered leaders how much he looked forward to the meetings tomorrow. He glanced over at Cummins, who was waiting for him at the hall's exit doors. When he finally made it to the gaggle of Secret Service agents at the door, he slapped Cummins on the back and smiled.

"That went pretty well," said Stockman. "You should be proud of how diplomatic I was. I even said I was looking forward to tomorrow."

Cummins smiled as they walked to the waiting car. Stockman was incorrigible. Getting along with leaders from other countries was just not part of his character.

"You did well, sir," said Cummins perfunctorily. He stood beside the car as Stockman got in.

"Aren't you coming?" asked the president.

"I wish. I'm exhausted, but I have an 11:00 p.m. meeting with the national security advisors of the G-8 countries. We have to draft the communiqué for tomorrow. Good night, Mr. President."

It was a five-minute car ride back to the Waldorf Astoria from the United Nations Building. The president let the deep leather of the car envelop him. But just as Stockman was imagining the pristine, white down comforter of the hotel suite, lead Secret Service agent Tim Ordway leaned over to the backseat.

"Mr. President, we're going to have to go around the block once. Sorry about that. We're about four minutes early and they have a traffic jam in front of the hotel."

Stockman grumbled, but was not particularly put out. He didn't mind being alone. And he understood the way these things worked. Departures and arrivals of heads of states were prearranged and timed to the second. For the three days of the opening of the UN General Assembly, the front lobby door of the Waldorf Astoria converted into a Swiss-made precision watch of departing and arriving limousines. It was like an airport control tower talking through the take-offs and landings. Stockman had left the dinner a few minutes early, and now he had to wait for the traffic in front of the hotel to free up so that his limousine could park right at the hotel door.

They went around once, sirens ablaze. The motorcade turned right on Park Avenue and slowed down as it reached the elegant entrance of the old New York hotel. The black limousine in front was just leaving, now having dropped off its passenger. The yellow, blue, and red flag of the departing black Cadillac fluttered in the wind as the empty car sped away. Stockman squinted as he readied himself to get out. He had seen that flag before, but couldn't place it now.

Agent Ordway jumped out of the car, opened Stockman's door, and, together with two other agents, accompanied the president's purposeful stride into the lobby. Heading straight to the elevators, Stockman suddenly remembered where the flag was from—Colombia.

Stockman could not help himself. He looked left and right around the lobby for her and saw only diplomats and delegation members from various countries. The only place he did not look was straight ahead, and by the time they got to the elevator banks, Marta Pradilla was literally in front of him.

There she was, one Colombian security agent at her side, dressed in a peach-colored chiffon-like skirt that bloomed ever so slightly outwards as it came down. The dress fell discreetly below the knees, but there were still miles of legs left to

POINT OF ENTRY 113

admire. Toward the top, a V-neck linen blouse exposed only Pradilla's elegant neck. But it was the beauty of her face, the sculptured, fine outline of her aquiline nose and perfect chin that struck home. Her brown hair was pulled back in a ponytail and tossed around and over her left shoulder. This woman was even more beautiful than he remembered, thought Stockman.

"John, how are you?" said Marta Pradilla. "I thought your speech was very good and very sober." She ignored the outstretched hand and kissed him quickly on the left cheek.

Stockman caught himself smiling and tried to stop, but it was too late. He fought the mixture of irritation and attraction she caused him. Just as he was wondering what to say, Agent Ordway slowly pulled his charge toward the waiting elevator door. Stockman felt like a child, pulled away by an over-doting parent. He looked at her sheepishly and said goodnight.

"John, do you want a drink?"

Ordway had him practically in the elevator, but Stockman yanked his arm away and took a step back into the lobby. The other agents, clearly perplexed, jumped back out of the elevator.

"I'd love one," he answered, far too quickly. Then, to correct any lingering impression of over-eagerness, he added, "Whom are you introducing me to tonight? Castro again? Kim Jong II of North Korea? Muammar Qaddafi?"

Pradilla did not flinch at the provocation. "Just with me, John. No surprise guests."

"Mr. President, that is impossible," interjected lead agent Ordway. "The bar is way too exposed. We would need to clear it out. You don't want to do that to the other guests."

"The Secret Service agent is right," said President Pradilla. "Why don't you come to my suite—room 3021? I'm sure it's smaller than yours, but I have a minibar that is just as good."

Ordway tried to say something, but at this point Stockman had taken control of the situation. "That is fine, Marta. Lead the way."

The two presidents and four security agents entered the elevator, and it sped up to the thirtieth floor. Marta put her electronic key card into her suite's lock and opened the door. At this point, Ordway was in a state of complete agitation; this was totally out of the ordinary. He pulled the president back from the door and murmured to his ear that he could not allow the president to enter the suite because it had not undergone a previous security inspection. The president goes nowhere without the Secret Service having gone before.

President Marta Pradilla understood immediately. Rather than being offended or uncomfortable, she smiled easily at Ordway.

"Why don't your colleagues go inside with my security guard? Please feel free to look anywhere. I will wait with you and the president out here until your colleagues are satisfied."

The whole thing made Agent Tim Ordway shiver. What about the rooms next door? Or above? Or below? There could be security problems everywhere around them. But it was clear to the Secret Service agent that he had no choice other than to accept her reasonable offer. Ordway hesitated, but nodded to his agents.

A few minutes later, the two agents reappeared at the door. The room was clear. As the two presidents walked in, Marta Pradilla turned around and started closing the door behind her. Ordway immediately stepped in. Stockman looked at the head of his security detail with exasperation and held his hand up. Enough already.

"Tim, it's fine. We'll keep the door ajar, but I'm okay alone."

Pradilla's suite at the Waldorf exuded the typical heavy charm of old-fashioned hotels. Dense red curtains were drawn across the windows. The carpet was a plush color of soothing beige. The sofas and armchairs had a puffy, off-white, traditional turn-of-the-century French elegance.

Stockman turned to Pradilla. "I'm very sorry about my security people. They are just doing their job."

She threw her head back and laughed.

"Don't even mention it. Please sit down. What can I get you?"

Stockman sat stiffly on the couch and asked for a scotch on the rocks. As he watched her walk to the minibar, he tried to remember the last time he had been waited on by somebody not paid a salary to serve. It had been ages since a woman actually went to pour a glass for him. He had forgotten that drinks don't always come delivered on elegant silver platters held by white gloves. The whole situation felt completely new.

He shook himself out of his musing. Don't let yourself be drawn in by her, he thought to himself. She thinks she is too smart. She knows she is too beautiful. Don't forget the stunt she pulled in Bogotá, he thought to himself.

Marta Pradilla brought the two scotches and sat on the other end of the same sofa. She twisted toward him and slowly curled one leg under the other. It was an easy, casual gesture, designed to make Stockman feel comfortable. It was also designed to show that the president of the United States did not intimidate her. He was amazed at how she managed to be both in charge and informal at the same time.

"I'm glad you came, John. I'm glad we ran into each other," Marta Pradilla said simply.

"I appreciate your friendliness, though after our meeting in Bogotá I wasn't sure you wanted to be friends. Why did you do it?" He had considered not bringing up the Castro introduction, but it stuck in his craw. He had to get it out.

"John, if I offended you, please accept my apologies. That was not the intention. The United States has been a beacon of hope and light to the world. But a lot of people think that the beacon's shine is fading because of your government's stubbornness. Castro is an example of that. All your friends in the region advise you to stop the silly isolation of Cuba. They tell you that it only makes him more important. But the United States does not want to listen to friends."

She looked him straight in the eye and finished. "So, I wanted you to see Castro for what he was. Not a symbol of evil. Not the devil. He's just an aging dinosaur."

Stockman thought about her answer for a few seconds. He was not happy with it. The fact remained that a novice leader of a Latin America country had taken him for a ride. But her response was straight enough. He had a choice to make. Right now. He could let this fester or he could accept the explanation. John Stockman was not known for forgiving people who crossed him.

But this time he relented. "Why?" he wondered to himself. Sure, it was hard to say no to a woman this beautiful, but clearly she had some persuasive force that went beyond simple good looks.

"Fair enough. Let's start all over. But next time you want to pass me a message, just talk to me directly.

She smiled at him coyly. "Well, that's why I invited you to have a drink now."

He smiled back. People didn't see John Stockman smiling that often. "Well, I accepted because I don't get this type of invitation very often. I guess nobody has the guts to invite me over for a drink."

"It has nothing to do with guts. I learned long ago that you can't plan or prepackage everything. My parents were killed when I was a teenager. Tragedies strike without making an appointment, but so do opportunities."

She smiled, looking at him straight in the eye.

"And the same goes for life's small surprises. Like seeing you downstairs. You have to take advantage of things that aren't predictable."

She had the damnedest way of being brutally honest—and very intense. They had only been here for sixty seconds and she already mentioned her parents' deaths. Stockman felt forced to say something meaningful about his own life. He struggled.

"We—I mean, my family and I—had it different, Marta. When I was a kid in Nebraska, I grew up on a farm. I was homeschooled. My father was a Lutheran minister. Everything was predictable. There were certainties everywhere. God, country, service, study, and farm chores. That was my life. Only tornadoes were unpredictable."

"In many ways, I envy you," she answered. "You have the certainty of values that are unchangeable. It makes you a rock in the swirling waters of a fast-moving world. I, on the other hand, have strong political beliefs molded from the wrongs I've seen, and I also have my instincts. You are the steady hand, but I'm more adaptable and pragmatic. Which is better?"

"I don't know," Stockman said, trying to think it through. "The playbook I was given has done me good so far. But, sometimes it seems that the harder we run, the more we are stuck in the same place. What you told me in Bogotá is partially true. Against the onslaught, America needs to stand firm, but it must also stand for something. It's just hard to find the time to figure out how to talk about it."

Stockman could not believe he was engaged in this conversation. He had not talked this openly, clearly, about his own feelings in years. In the last years of her life, he had not even had an unguarded conversation with Miranda. The manic hours of political life had driven a wedge of silence between them. Now he was in a hotel room spilling his guts to this strange woman. Yet, he couldn't stop.

The conversation flew forward. He could not get enough of it. Correction— he could not get enough of her. Her looks held his eyes and her intelligence was like a magnet, drawing more and more out of him. They talked about youth, hopes, and disappointments.

"Is it hard to be a woman in politics?" asked Stockman.

"John, I've been criticized about my mouth for as long as I can remember. It's hard to tell whether the criticism would be any different if I were a man. But it's been like this since I was a beauty queen."

Stockman looked at her disbelievingly.

"Marta, come on, everybody knows that in the beauty pageant world, politics is like the plague. I'm sure they didn't allow you to give a political speech."

Marta chuckled, a deep guttural laugh.

"John, I fought with them all the time. They were always trying to keep me quiet—and I never blamed them. I knew that I was driving them crazy, but once I got the press coverage, it was too late. I was bitten by the politics bug and I couldn't shut up."

A Miss Universe who would not keep quiet. Stockman thought this was the funniest thing he heard in ages.

"What was the worst trouble you got into?"

"I'm not sure you are going to like the answer to that question, John."

"Marta, come on, tell me; how bad can it be?"

"John, on my wall in the office I have a framed letter from the Miss Universe organization. It's a letter of official chastisement; the first time I got into real trouble for something I said. It's on my wall not because I want mock the pageant or its organizers—that would be the last thing on my mind. It's hanging because the day I got the letter was the day I realized that words had consequences. That makes me a better person today."

Marta paused a moment. "I can remember it almost verbatim. The main paragraph thundered something like, 'It is our understanding that you repeatedly use occasions meant to celebrate your title to lecture audiences with strongly held political opinions.' Yes, that letter was a wake-up call."

"Wow, you must've really gotten under their skin. What was it you said?"

"It was a lot of things I said during the first half of my year as Miss Universe. But, one particular interview was the straw that broke the camel's back."

"So?"

"Well, it was during an interview with *Vanity Fair*. They were doing a spread on the travels of Miss Universe—I'm sure it was supposed to be a nasty and condescending piece. At some point in the interview, the reporter asked, 'You're from Colombia, what do you think of the drug problem?' and my answer to that question was a little controversial."

"Stop delaying, Marta. Tell me, what did you answer." Stockman chuckled.

"I said: Whose drug problem, ours or yours? They are different. You Americans smoke, swallow, shoot, lick, and ingest anything to get you high. In Colombia, we die trying to stop the supply of products that you require to do those things to yourself. The best of us are the ones who die most: Our journalists, judges, politicians, police, and academics are the ones who get killed on the front lines of your war on drugs."

"Yikes," said Stockman. "I can imagine how that got you some press coverage. And I can understand how that letter showed up in your mailbox."

"Look, John, the instant the words were uttered, I knew I had crossed the line. There was nothing untrue or imprecise about the words, but they cascaded out sounding so hostile and disagreeable. So, that is why the letter is on the wall—to remind me that words have consequences."

"How did they react to all of this in Colombia?"

"Back home, the press lapped it up. It was very strange. They converted me into a type of comic book superhero."

"Yeah, I can imagine the headlines—'The Colombian Miss Universe lashes out against injustice and rages for good,'" Stockman joked, making her laugh at the image.

"I know it sounds funny, but that *Vanity Fair* piece got me on television roundtables and radio shows. Magazines did interviews. Colombians of all ages couldn't get enough of Miss Universe. There was something irresistible about a beauty queen with brains."

"It wasn't only that—not at all. I don't particularly like what you said, but I'll tell you why it was so attractive, Marta. It's the simple, direct language that is refreshing. People in the news don't usually talk like that. Not here in the United States; not anywhere. Clearly you have a gift."

The conversation went on for hours. At some point, she took her shoes off. He matched it by taking off his suit jacket and loosening his tie. She broke into huge giggles, her green eyes blazing with humor.

"No, John, I'm not going to play chicken with you. That is as far as we go— my shoes and your jacket. Your Agent Ordway is out there."

Stockman broke into a massive smile. He remembered a passage from Mark Twain about the soft familiarity of a teasing friend. It had been years since he felt the intimacy and warmth of gentle needling. His daughter, Julia, used to pull his leg all the time, but now she was gone. Marta's smiling prank reminded him that it was something he deeply missed.

She stood up to get another refill of scotch. As he watched her walking back toward him, he finally understood what made this woman so attractive. It was not her stunning looks or her smarts. It was the fact that she refused to play by men's rules. More than any other business, politics was a man's craft. Most women in politics talked and behaved like men. But Marta Pradilla refused to give up her femininity and didn't give a damn what males thought. That actually made her a terrifying adversary.

She handed him the drink and stood in front of him and looked straight down his eyes.

"Somebody told me that you don't like foreigners. Is that true?"

"Most foreigners make me uncomfortable. Not you, though."

"John, have some patience. Listen to a story or two that is not an American story. You will find that the hopes and myths of other countries are very similar to America's."

He thought about it for a while. When he stopped wondering and glanced back at her, his heart jumped.

She had sat back down on the sofa, but not at the other end. She was now right next to him. Looking toward her, he could almost feel her breath. He could see the speckles of radiance in her green eyes and streaks of light in her brown hair. He could not remember the last time a woman was this close. Stockman started panicking. It was going too fast.

Marta put her hand on his arm. She held it there silently, never taking her eyes off him. Her body swiveled over and the other hand reached around his face to the small of his neck. He could feel her fingers on the back of his head, touching his scalp. A quiver went through his body.

She leaned over and put her cheek against his. John Stockman, the man who trusted nobody, closed his eyes and felt himself succumbing to a strange feeling of lightness. Their faces touched for just a few seconds. It was a gesture, a kiss.

But it was a good-night kiss.

"John, I don't know if we can ever do this again," she whispered to him as she slowly separated and got up. "But I need you to know that I want to." Her face was in the partial shadow of the sidelights of the suite. She looked more gorgeous than ever.

She was right; it could not go any further. Not now. He looked at his watch and saw that it was 3:30 a.m. Shit, it was late. But he smiled to himself because she had won the evening. She had shattered his predictable night.

As they walked to the door, she stopped at the suite's desk and wrote something down on the hotel notepad. Rather than hand it to him, she stuffed it into the side pocket of his suit jacket, which he carried neatly folded over one arm. It was a simple gesture of intimacy that would normally come between a man and a woman who had known each other for far longer.

"It's my e-mail address, John. Not the official one. Rather, it's my Yahoo address—just people close to me know about it. Let's be in touch."

As she opened the door, Stockman smiled at her. A lot had been said tonight, and he regretted none of it. He was profoundly grateful for their few hours together. She had made him laugh, talk, and look inside himself honestly. But as he left her doorway, John Stockman did not have the guts to confess that he had no clue how to use e-mail.

PART VI
THE CAUCASUS

The Sheraton Hotel
Tbilisi, September 29
5:45 p.m.

===

Osman Samir al-Husseini was more than a little concerned. Back at the hotel after the adjournment of the Abkhazian refugee conference, he slowly repacked his overnight suitcase. While the small, fifteen-pound Samsonite was all he had brought for his twenty-eight-hour stay in Tbilisi, his plan was to leave Georgia substantially heavier. The expected additional luggage was, however, not yet in his possession—and that worried him.

The day at the chancellery had passed slowly. The conference droned on and on. One speaker after another delivered the same message from a slightly different angle. Bottom line: More money was needed to clothe, feed, and shelter the growing number of refugees. Sometimes the UN was just too much, thought al-Husseini. With all the troubles in the world, why would anybody want to waste a couple of hundred thousand dollars to send twenty-five delegates to this far-away country to talk about some forlorn refugee group?

"There is no way to take care of everybody," thought the Syrian, allowing himself, for one rare second, to think as a policymaker who actually pondered international priorities. He quickly changed gears.

"Keep your eyes on the mission, you fool," Osman Samir al-Husseini chastised himself, raising a warning finger at his own face in the hotel mirror just above his open suitcase. "Stop complaining. These United Nations meetings and conferences are just the cover you need."

But it was late in the afternoon, and al-Husseini was seriously worried about his mission's success. He opened his conference agenda and looked under *P* for Pakistan and found the room number of the Colonel. It was so comfortable—all United Nations meeting agendas provided participants' direct contact information to facilitate backdoor discussions and deals. Al-Husseini picked up the phone and started dialing room 408, but hung up after pressing the second digit. He should know better. It was way too dangerous to call—the room's phone was probably bugged by Georgian intelligence services.

Al-Husseini took his suitcase down the elevator and crossed the immensely exaggerated lobby of the Tbilisi Sheraton to check out of his room. He handed his platinum American Express card to the smartly dressed concierge.

"Mr. Ambassador, all delegation costs have been covered by our government. It's been a privilege to have you here," said the young man, returning the American Express card with a quick flick of the hand.

The young concierge repeated the same exact phrase to at least three other delegations checking out. Not everybody was leaving on the Austrian Airlines flight in the middle of the night. Al-Husseini was on that plane, though, and the very thought of his departure again reminded him that he still did not have what he had come halfway around the world to get.

At 6:30 p.m. sharp a large tourist bus rounded the difficult curve of the hotel's driveway. Stuck on the right-hand side of its large windshield was a bad photocopy of the United Nations insignia. Sweating profusely, a pudgy Georgian man jumped off the bus and strode purposefully into the lobby. With nearly operatic effect, he spoke in a booming voice to anybody close enough to listen.

"Ladies and gentlemen of the United Nations, I am your escort tonight to the dinner at Telavi, in the heart of Georgia's beautiful wine district. We shall eat, drink, and be merry," the man hollered.

Al-Husseini merged into the short line to step onto the big bus behind the French and Canadian delegates. Suddenly, out of nowhere, the elegant Pakistani ambassador with the salt-and-pepper beard appeared at his side.

"Mr. Ambassador, it is a pleasure to see you," said the Colonel, amiably extending his hand. "I trust you thought the conference was interesting?"

"Interesting, yes. But the cost concerns me," al-Husseini lied. He didn't care about the cost of the damn refugees. He wanted to know where his packages were. But he did not ask. He knew the rules—they required restraint.

"Yes, there are so many other problems and worries in the world today. It's hard to prioritize," said the Pakistani, looking at the Syrian dead-on.

"Well, Mr. Ambassador, some of us are blessed with greater clarity than others."

"That is true, sir. And that is why I am pleased to be here," the Colonel said.

Then, with just a slight change in inflection, the Pakistani added twelve critical words.

"I should have something this evening that will clear away competing priorities." Then, "It's been a pleasure seeing you again, Mr. Ambassador."

Without a further word, the Colonel boarded the bus before al-Husseini and sat down next to the British ambassador, a move clearly designed to insure that the Syrian would not choose to sit next to him. As al-Husseini passed them down the narrow aisle to the back of the bus, he saw the two men greet each other with friendly smiles.

Al-Husseini sat alone in the second to last row. Relief rushed over him. This mission was going to be a success after all.

Into the Pankisi Gorge
Chechnya, September 28th
11:20 p.m.

The night before the Colonel reassured Osman Samir al-Husseini that his package was on its way, Professor Farooq Rahman and Yusef approached the Pankisi Gorge at dusk. It was amazing to the Pakistani that they had never once come across a Russian military or police block. Incredible, thought Rahman, how a disloyal population can work together to slowly dismantle the vestiges of authority. Armed only with a cellular phone, Yusef seemed to know exactly what roads to take and they were consistently empty.

While the Pankisi Gorge began in Chechnya, the majority of the gorge was located in Georgian territory. But the political geography of the Pankisi Gorge was just an ephemeral detail. Deep in the Caucasus, surrounded by snow-covered peaks that towered up to 15,000 feet overhead, the zigzagging gorge was cut into the rock as if a fiery serpent's tongue dug a steep gash in the mountains. The Pankisi Gorge's geography made it inaccessible to the authorities and their laws.

That is why the gorge was considered one of the world's most lawless places. For a while, after September 11, Western intelligence sources even speculated that Osama bin Laden was hiding in the impossible reaches of the Pankisi. Now, as in the old times of the silk route, the gorge had again become a smuggler's passage from the Muslim East to the Christian West and vice versa. It was the frontier of civilizations. And, like many borders in which radically different cultures lived side by side it was extremely dangerous.

The gorge was inhabited mostly by Kists, a Muslim mountain tribe of distant relation to the Chechens. Kist tribal law fiercely ruled the gorge region and its smuggling routes. Administering local control through absolute despotism and enforcing it with horrifying violence, the Kist chiefs levied fees on the passage of heroin heading from Asia's poppy fields to Europe. They taxed the smuggled cigarettes and alcohol moving from the West to the East. They monopolized the brisk movement of arms and weaponry. And, obviously, they controlled the export and import of humans into and out of the gorge.

Professor Farooq Rahman and Yusef started the winding climb up the mountain pass at about 9 p.m. As they approached an eerie tented village at 10,000 feet in the mountains, the professor almost had a heart attack when six armed men leaped off the embankment and stopped their car.

Testifying to the gorge's unique role in arms trafficking, the men pointed a mix of modern weaponry at the car—Russian Kalashnikovs, Italian Berettas, and American-made M-16 attack rifles. Their dress was equally eclectic. One could make out the blooming tribal pants, but their upper bodies were covered in modern, brightly colored ski parkas with "North Face" etched on the front of multi-toned winter jackets. Scarves covered the men's faces and twisted turbans capped their heads.

A young man approached. In his early twenties, he had an air of calm authority about him. He was dressed like the others, but as he approached the car he removed the scarf covering his face to reveal a handsome smile.

"We have been waiting for you. I do not know who you are, but you are obviously very important. My name is Armad, and my father is the head of the Nursultan tribe. He has sent me to take you across. Everyone here knows that I am the eldest son of the most important man in the gorge. You will be safe with me," said the young man, gesturing for Professor Rahman to come out of the car.

Rahman and Yusef collected their belongings. As they left the car, one of the armed men curved his thumb and forefinger together to make a rotating back-and-forth motion with his hand, indicating that he wanted the car keys. Yusef gave him the keys and the man drove away in the white Lada. The moon lit the inky night sky, as well as the mountains surrounding them.

It was freezing. Armad led them toward the tent village and into one of the larger structures. Around them, hundreds of tents—some were camping tents, some larger four-poled Bedouin-like edifices, and some just lean-tos—spread across the rocky site. The place stank of a mixture of human sewerage and animal carcass. The occasional bleating of a goat broke the silence.

"What is this place?" asked Farooq Rahman.

"These are Chechen refugees," explained Armad. "They are mostly pathetic villagers, with some Chechen rebels hiding among them. They are escaping the scorched-earth policy of the Russian Army that closed entire towns to the entry of food, water, and medicine. They come to these heights because it is the only place the Russians will not come. But it is a miserable sight. You should thank God you're here in the darkness."

Armad reached into a large pile of clothing and began to hand the professor and Yusef winter gear. They put on woolen pants and sweaters. Over that, they were instructed to put on the same North Face ski jackets used by the armed men who had stopped their car. The professor wondered if the American ski-clothing company gave these people a discount. Last, Armad handed each of them leather chaps to tie around their waists. One of the men in the tent helped them secure the chaps with a strap around each ankle.

"What is this for?" asked Professor Farooq Rahman.

Armad smiled. "There are few roads here. We are going by donkey. Come."

They walked out of the tent. Rahman nervously noted that one of Armad's assistants had picked up the two cases. He wondered if they had any inkling what was in the metal boxes. Forget it, he told himself; the Kists made their living transporting people and objects through the gorge. They learned not to ask or even care.

They walked for five minutes and reached what was obviously the edge of the refugee camp. Ahead were moonlit barrenness and more mountains. A turbaned man crouched on his haunches as he tended a campfire and drank tea.

Rahman was startled by a sudden noise from the darkness behind the campfire. He looked up to see an old man in dark woolen clothes leading five donkeys.

Armad led Rahman to the third animal. The donkey was unusual because it was pure white. It had white eyelashes, and its left ear rotated like a radar as the two men approached. "Meet Anis. The only white donkey in the gorge—she is my father's pride. He instructed me that only you must ride her. She will take you into Georgia."

As the professor rode, he could feel the precipice. On his right was the mountain. To his left, there was nothing but a sheer drop of thousands of feet. He imagined the caravansaries climbing the rutted path hundreds of years ago. When one camel stumbled, whole caravans—connected front to back—would plunge into the shrouded depths.

Now, six hours later, as the sunlight slowly crept across the mountains, an exhausted Professor Farooq Rahman fought the irresistible urge to sleep to the hypnotic rhythm of the donkey's movement. He was dead tired. He did not know if he could make it any farther. For the second time, he questioned his sanity. Was he doing the right thing? The professor reassured himself that he was still lucid by mentally beating back the onset of exhaustion-induced depression.

Armad broke the silence. "We are almost there—another half hour."

Indeed, within minutes, as the path rounded a wooded hill, the riders could begin to see the valley. Slowly, with each passing pace of the donkeys' slow movement, the valley far below opened majestically. In the ever-increasing dawn light, the professor could make out the panorama.

He suddenly felt very close to God. He was atop of the world. Sweeping around him were majestic snow-capped mountains that gave way to green meadows dotted with wildflowers. Shepherds' huts, with rounded roofs that clawed into the rocks, were the only sign of humanity.

It was no wonder that these mountains captured so much attention over the ages. Here, Prometheus, who stole the secrets of fire, was chained for eternity on Mount Kazbek as birds pecked his liver. On Mount Elbrus, the dove took flight toward Noah and the ark marooned on Ararat. In Colchis, where the mountains fell to the Black Sea, Jason and the Argonauts sailed in search of the Golden Fleece.

Many centuries later the Russian Anton Chekhov and the Frenchman Alexandre Dumas would wax poetic at the spiraling heights and impressive dangers of the mighty Caucasus.

The sudden halt of the animals interrupted his thinking. This was the first time Anis had stopped her movement in nearly six hours. Rahman saw Armad get off his donkey and walk toward him to steady his dismount. He began to wave away the younger man, but stopped because, as he attempted to get off the animal, his legs trembled and struggled to support his weight.

Farooq Rahman looked at the donkey. In the light, she looked even whiter—nearly albino—her ears again rotating to follow his presence around her. Professor Rahman felt a pang of shame at his life long derision of the legions of donkeys that clogged the streets of Pakistan's cities and villages with their over-size loads. Patting the warm muzzle, he smiled and made a silent promise to Anis to never again shout at a donkey.

They were at the edge of woods. Just below them, the trail crossed a mountain road and continued downward through yet more forests. On the road was a new red Toyota car. A man, dressed in a blue Izod Lacoste sweater with a curiously wrong-sized crocodile insignia on it, stepped out of the car. After traveling for nearly three weeks in rural Muslim lands, Professor Rahman's eyes were riveted on the car's occupant because this was the first man he had seen in days dressed entirely in Western clothes.

Armad descended the hill and kissed the man on both cheeks. "Meet Aslan Tungaridze. If you are forced to befriend a Christian, this man is an acceptable specimen." The man gave Armad a pat on the head and toyed playfully with his hair.

"Tell your father that he has my respects and that I thank him for his kindness and his trust," said the Georgian, his face serious and earnest. "Tell him also that he has made abundantly clear how important this mission is to him. Our friend will be delivered safely to Telavi," said the Georgian with the Lacoste sweater.

As the professor's cases were placed in the Georgian's car, Professor Farooq

Rahman turned to say good-bye to the men who served as his guides through the gorge. He was stunned that Yusef's hand was also outstretched. After so much travel in the company of silent men, Yusef had been the first to chat and talk with the Professor. In twenty-four hours, the scientist had developed an attachment to the man who picked him up on the shores of the Caspian Sea.

"How can a man called Yusef enter Christian Georgia?" joked Yusef in response to Rahman's inquiring look. "I have completed my mission. Now, you complete yours. Allah be with you."

Rahman sat in the car, and within minutes he was asleep. Exhaustion had taken him over. He tried to resist, but the deep comfort of the Toyota's front seat caught him by surprise—the cloth upholstered chair seemed to caress him in softness. It had been weeks since he had felt such luxury. The last thing he remembered was smiling at the Christian man Armad called a friend.

Four hours later—at about noon—the man gently shook his knee. The Pakistani scientist awoke to read a road sign announcing their arrival in Telavi, in the heart of Georgia's wine-producing district. They entered the charming old town, with its medieval buildings and rustic palaces. The car stopped in front of the Telavi Royal Palace Hotel.

To the Western businessman, it was just any rundown hotel in the ex-Soviet Union—it might have once been a palace, but seventy years of Communist rule removed any meaning from the word "royal" in its name. Yet, to a man who, in the last eleven days, had slept on mattresses thrown on hard floors and in the backseats of cars, the place looked perfectly splendid.

No check-in was required. Entering the hotel, the two men skirted around a hubbub of workers carrying tables and chairs back and forth in preparation for a large event at the hotel later in the day. Carrying both metal cases and the professor's small duffel bag, Aslan Tungaridze accompanied the scientist up the stairs.

Entering room 78, Rahman marveled at the bathroom and the white sheets. He ignored the cheap factory furniture made of pressed scrap wood. He did not see the scratches on the night table, nor could he feel the lumpy mattress. All that mattered was that he would be spending the next few hours in a real room.

"Professor, this is where I leave you," said the huge Georgian. "I have strict instructions for you. You must be ready by 6:00 p.m. You must wear the clothes I am bringing for you. These are the only clothes that you should have. I will take your duffel bag, as nothing must remain in your possession that could provide a hint of your trip. At some point this evening, you will be picked up. This is your hotel key, but I would prefer that you not leave this room until your pickup. When I go down, I will order you coffee and cake for the room."

The two men shook hands. Rahman could hardly wait. He could not stop thinking of the shower. He undressed quickly and nearly ran to the bathroom. It was his first shower in days—and it was hot! He let the warm water spray caress his body. He felt every individual sprinkle—his mind played games, segmenting the droplets that dribbled down to his feet from those that ricocheted off his body. He could not decide which he liked more.

Professor Farooq Rahman felt as though he was a sultan in palatial Turkish baths. He stayed in the moldy shower stall for over thirty minutes. Rahman dried himself with the old towels and, as he came out of the bathroom, he noticed that tea and yellowish pound cakes had been placed on the table.

There's no privacy in the ex-Soviet Union, he thought to himself, and then momentarily panicked as he spun around looking for his cases. Reassured they were exactly where he left them, Professor Farooq Rahman slipped into bed at one o'clock and fell instantaneously asleep.

The Royal Palace Hotel
Telavi, September 29
5:45 p.m.

Rahman woke up and immediately noticed that dusk was settling outside his hotel window. He showered again. Given his journey, it was his strongly held opinion that a senior Pakistani nuclear scientist had a right to two showers. He dressed in the clean pants and shirt his tall Georgian escort had left him. He turned on a wooden lamp, which threw a gloomy yellow glare into the dark room. There was still some light outside, but the room would have been dark without the lamp.

He lit a cigarette. Today his trip would end. The person picking him up here would get him back home to Pakistan. He never questioned the instructions or the promise to bring him home. Indeed, he never doubted the motive for his trip. Tonight he would deliver the potential for serious destruction into somebody's hands—he did not know who it would be. But he did know why. And the why was all that mattered.

His thoughts were interrupted by the sounds of a large number of people entering the hotel from the street below. He looked out the window and saw a large blue and white passenger bus with well-dressed people getting off. Looking very prominent, they were obviously not Georgians. The scene looked incongruous: All these elegant people were out of place in a hotel that, like the town itself, was pretty but suffered from disrepair and disdain.

Rahman looked at his watch and saw that it was 7:15 p.m. He wondered if the operation had been called off. For a moment he panicked: He had no passport. No means of identification. How would he get out of Georgia? What would he do with the uranium? The questions came fast and furious, but were stopped in their tracks by a knock on the door.

Rahman knew the moment had come. The end of his mission was waiting for him in the hotel hallway. He squeezed out the cigarette in an ashtray and got up to open the door. His eyes squinted to adjust to the hallway's darkness and he was shocked to see the elegant salt-and-pepper-bearded face of the Colonel. They kissed each other warmly on each cheek.

"Professor, I am proud of you. Pakistan is proud of you. If you are here, it means that you have achieved what nobody else has ever done," said the Colonel stepping into the room and closing the door behind him.

"Colonel, you never told me that you would be waiting for me here. How did you get here? I am so pleased that it is you who is here," said Professor Farooq Rahman to his old friend.

"My friend, I did not want to get your hopes up that it would be me personally. Please do not address me as Colonel," admonished the Colonel softly. "You see, I am today the Pakistani emissary—with rank of ambassador—to the United Nations conference on Abkhazian refugees. We will have much time together on the airplane, and I look forward to hearing about your trip. Please, just tell me about the materials that you have picked up."

"Colonel—sorry, Ambassador—I inspected the packages. It is indeed what you want it to be. Highly enriched uranium-235. And we have here approximately thirty pounds of the material, divided into half-pound pellets. Each is encased in boxes of tungsten. There are two suitcases, each with fifteen pounds of the HEU."

Putting his arm around the professor's shoulders, the Colonel smiled. "We are in your debt, Professor. You have done an amazing job. Now, I have brought you a passport and documents that will allow you to exit Georgia with me tonight."

Rahman felt a warm sense of pride wash over him as he watched the Colonel reach into his briefcase to get the documents. The Colonel snapped open the two locks and opened the light brown Samsonite. Instead of tickets and a passport, he pulled out a Beretta 515 revolver with a silencer. In one sweeping, slow motion, he arced the gun upward, placed it inches from the professor's left temple, and pulled the trigger. The gun spurted and the professor slumped. It happened so fast that Farooq Rahman never knew or understood what happened.

"Pity, but there was no choice. There was no way to get you out of Georgia. You died a hero—that is more than one says about most of the dead," muttered the Colonel to the slumped body.

The Pakistani intelligence agent reached inside his briefcase and took out a soft cloth that he normally used to clean his Giorgio Armani reading glasses. Nothing was better for removing fingerprints. He cleaned off the gun and placed it in the dead professor's hand. He curled the professor's fingers around the trigger.

The Colonel had been careful to kill the professor at a moment when the blood spatter would not point toward the two suitcases in the closet. Nothing supplanted experience, thought the Colonel. The blood and cranial fluid were all over the bed, but they were not in his way as he walked to the closet and reached in to take the two cases. He quickly toured the room to insure that nothing was left behind but the body.

He then picked up his briefcase and walked to the door. He thought of turning around for a last look, but decided against it. He walked out and quietly closed the door.

The Colonel slowly descended the two flights of steps with the two cases and his briefcase. It was a lot of weight, and he was breathing heavily by the time he entered the hotel foyer. He stopped to gather his breath and wondered why the dinner party was being held in the middle of a lobby area. All the UN delegates were present and in the process of taking their seats. A man at the front of the room was warmly greeting each delegate—the Colonel recognized the Georgian finance minister from his speech over lunch.

The Colonel stepped fully into the lobby. For a moment, the Pakistani became apprehensive when he realized that he had not considered where to store the two big suitcases during the dinner. But the Colonel's years in intelligence provided the cool calm needed to opt for the most logical of solutions: Give it to the bellman for safekeeping. The hotel would not lose the suitcase of one of the UN conference delegates. So he handed the overweight, mustachioed Georgian porter thirty pounds of stolen Soviet uranium and took his claim check. He walked to his seat.

The finance minister was already talking. "My friends, welcome to a Georgian *supra*. This is a special meal—it is a centuries-old tradition in Georgia. It is a special way of welcoming friends, relatives, and important visitors."

"Let me explain how this works," continued the young Georgian executive with a large smile. "I ask for your vote to elect me the evening's 'Tamada.' A Tamada is chosen for his richness of language and his stature. In this case, I would ask that you vote for me as your Tamada because I am the only Georgian among you. I would like your vote; please raise your hands."

The amused delegates unanimously voted for the finance minister as their Tamada.

"Thank you, it is an honor," continued the finance minister, smiling now that the delegates were clearly having fun at the *supra*. "Now I will tell you the bad news. I was elected democratically, but a Tamada rules over his dinner subjects with an iron hand. I will present you a theme as a toast, you must all listen, and at the end of each toast you must finish your entire glass of wonderful Georgian wine—Georgians do not sip wine! Guests are permitted two replies—called *alaverdi*—to each of my toasts, but it must be only on the theme of my toast. Is it clear?"

The guests applauded approvingly.

"So, my first toast is about friendship. Our friendship. The friendship established in this short trip to Georgia. Even if you will spend only twenty-four hours in Georgia, you will not be able to resist the friendship you now feel toward my country. The same thing happened to God, you see. After creating the world, he stopped for supper and rested on the high peaks of the Caucasus. He drank too much wine and spilled a little of everything from His plate onto the valley below. That is how Georgia became blessed with such riches. They were table scraps from heaven's platter.

"Friendship in Georgia is based on human contact. This friendship cannot exist through e-mail or on the Internet because there it lacks the warmth of a smile or the delicacy of an extended handshake. Friendships need to begin the old-fashioned way. Some may go no farther, but some may bloom, flower, and seed better horizons. I look forward to each of those horizons and thank you for your newfound friendship with my country and myself. So please raise your glass and drink to friendship."

And on the evening went. One flowery, velvety toast followed the next. To family. To children. To peace. To prosperity. To Georgia and to patriotism. To the importance of international institutions. To freedom. To respect for parents and elders. With each toast, wine cups were refilled. Georgia was not a vodka land. Ancient vines produced excellent red wines. As each glass of wine—poured in round water glasses as opposed to wine goblets—followed the next, the visiting delegates found their courage and began replying to the toastmaster.

Food arrived in little plates, mezze style. At first, it was just a few things on the table. Cabbage, pickled carrots, and fried eggplants stuffed with walnut paste, marigold powder, and pomegranate seeds were spread on the tables. *Khachapouri*—a Georgian-style pizza with a fried egg on top—followed thereafter. But, as the speeches went on and more and more wine was poured, the food accelerated. Chicken *Satsivi*—in walnut sauce—was placed in front of every other person in big bowls with huge serving spoons. Goat kid and *Gomi*, Georgia's version of polenta. *Kinkhali*—giant dumplings—filled with pork and boiled, were placed steaming on the table in long flat plates. The food spiraled out of control.

Hours later, the evening turned from pleasure to hardship. Too much wine, too much food, and too much structured talk melted away the novelty. That happened at all *supras*—foreign guests wondered how Georgians were able to bear the repetitious drone of this festivity.

Unlike most of their colleagues, neither the Pakistani nor the Syrian delegate drank or ate much that evening. They were not seated close to each other and did not interact. They listened and pretended to enjoy. Secretly, the two men shared the same disgust for the beastly overindulgence of the *supra* spectacle. They could not wait for it to finish.

The arrival of fruitcakes and half-moon-shaped sweet cheese dumplings signaled that the end was close. The finance minister, much the worse for the wear and slurring slightly, raised his hand one last time to demand silence.

"The last toast of the night is always the same. It is dedicated to our deceased kin—to those who came before. It is these forefathers and foremothers who make us who we are, who created our genes, our blood, and our taste. They made our parents, and our parents created us. Most important, they created our history and our culture. It is they that created the custom that allows us to sit with friends in this *supra*. To those who were, and today are no more, I give this last glass!"

The guests all stood and clapped wildly. The enthusiasm came from a mixture of emotions. Perhaps the most important one was relief that the evening was finally over. But there was also grudging admiration for this tradition. For to dine with Georgians and participate in the food, drink, and eloquent oratory was to watch an event that celebrated human life.

Slowly the party began to unwind and many of the delegates milled about. The Thai representative sought out the French ambassador to talk about the upcoming meeting on Cambodian refugees in Thailand. The U.S. ambassador and two African emissaries were deep in conversation about future U.S. contributions to the High Commission on Refugees. So nobody noticed when the Pakistani ambassador came up to his Syrian counterpart to shake his hand.

"Mr. al-Husseini, I understand that some delegates are going to be taken directly to the airport and that you are among those leaving tonight."

Osman Samir al-Husseini, Syria's delegate to the refugee conference, smiled politely. "Indeed, we are going directly to the airport. This country has the strangest departure times—my flight to Vienna leaves at 3:30 in the morning."

The Colonel looked straight into the eyes of his Syrian counterpart and handed him a small piece of paper. "I believe, Mr. Ambassador, that you dropped the claim check for the bags you left with the concierge. I wish you a nice flight. I trust we will see each other again." The Pakistani smiled and went to the bus.

Osman Samir al-Husseini stopped at the concierge and claimed two large suitcases. They were loaded onto a smaller, newer bus that arrived during dinner. This minibus was bringing nine of the delegates to the airport to catch the Austrian Airlines departure.

In less than an hour and a half, the Syrian ambassador was in his business-class seat on the Austrian Airlines Airbus A-320. The flight was nearly empty. He checked the two large suitcases all the way through to Rome. His plane arrived in

Vienna at 6:00 a.m. and he would have an hour for his connection. Once in Italy, his diplomatic status would prevent Customs from searching the bag. By midday, the cases would be at the Syrian embassy in Rome.

He smiled. So far, it had gone flawlessly. He would soon complete what many had tried to do but failed. Indeed, with takeoff no more than a few minutes away, he congratulated himself on the fact that thirty pounds of highly enriched uranium would soon be successfully smuggled out of the former Soviet Union.

PART VII
THE UNITED STATES

The Oval Office

Washington, October 4

5:58 p.m.

It was one of those classic political events that made Nelson Cummins's stomach turn. Small-minded, petty, narrowly focused. It was billed as an important decision-making meeting, but participants would be far too busy scratching each other's backs to discuss or make policy.

These events happen every day in the life of the president of the United States. All the time. Yesterday, Stockman had gone before the Corn Grower's Association for a "discussion" on price subsidies for maize. What a farce! It was nothing more than a forum to announce the administration's intention to raise crop supports for corn farmers. Stockman was introduced enthusiastically by the president of the Corn Growers Association, a couple of members of Congress from farmland states, and one of the senators from his native Nebraska. Then the president spoke. It was completely canned—there were no "discussions." Stockman was there to meow and the audience was in place to purr its approval.

Usually, Nelson did not get so hot and bothered with these horrid sessions of political masturbation. His job requirements did not have him attending every one of his boss's political events. He was the national security chief—it was somebody else's job to babysit the president's schedule. Anyway, he got to read about Stockman's events in nearly real time, courtesy of the electronically circulated wire reports sent by Allyson Bonnet's efficient press operation.

This invitation was different, though. If the president decided to attend this crap, it would weigh on Nelson. It would feel like being buried under pile after pile of water-soaked blankets. It would be morally wrong, politically backward, and, frankly, just plain stupid. There were times when one just couldn't separate the policies of the Stockman administration from longtime, strongly held personal beliefs. For Nelson, this was one of those times.

It was nearly twilight—a few short days after returning from the United Nations—and the president and Cummins each had a copy of the invitation in their hands. It said: "The Presidential Commission for Assistance to a Free Cuba wishes to invite President John Stockman and senior members of his administration to the final seating of the commission. At that time, it is our intention to present the results of our year-long deliberations on policies to accelerate the day when Cuba shall again be a free country." And so on.

"You can't go to this, boss. I'll go," said Nelson, wincing at the thought.

Stockman smirked. They both understood that this was a joke. Before his inauguration and prior to all White House personnel being subjected to Allyson Bonnet's stringent press straightjacket, Nelson Cummins had acceded to a long interview for the January issue of *Esquire* magazine. Billed as *the* interview with the new administration's up-and-coming foreign policy star, Nelson had called U.S. policy toward Cuba "the dumbest policy on earth."

No, Nelson Cummins was not exactly the representation Stockman needed at a gathering of rabid Cuban exiles.

"Why shouldn't I go?" asked Stockman. "I created the damn commission. It's good electoral politics. It will get me back on the front pages in all the Florida newspapers. What's not to like?"

"I know you created the commission, Mr. President," said Cummins, trying hard to contain his strong personal views on the subject. "But it was at a time when many people here thought that you would need a forum to project toughness in the latter half of your administration. Since then, we've been pretty tough on a lot of fronts. So, while it may be good politics, it's awful policy. And you don't need the additional muscles, sir."

"Okay, let's talk about it, Nelson," the president said. "Take me through their recommendations."

Cummins sensed an opening. He needed to present this well. Here goes. He started slowly.

"The commission's central political contention is that the U.S. embargo on Cuba needs to be made stronger, not weaker. The commissioners, almost unanimously, believe that Castro is debilitated and that tough measures would make him and the Communist Party apparatus in Cuba more vulnerable.

"They are recommending a number of specific steps to achieve this. First, they propose to restrict the ability of Cuban-Americans to travel back to the island by limiting returns to once every three years. Second, the commission wants to reduce the amount of money American citizens can spend in Cuba from $165 to $50 per day. Third, they want to greatly reduce monies being repatriated from Cuban-Americans in the United States to impoverished family members on the island. Right now that figure is at a billion dollars."

Cummins looked up at Stockman. Shit, he was taking notes.

"Two more central recommendations, sir. The commission feels we need to do more to assist pro-democracy organizations on the island. They are suggesting a 400 percent increase in funding—some of it to go through third countries that have full embassies in Cuba—for the more established pro-democracy groups. Last, since the Cubans have successfully jammed broadcasts from Radio Martí in Florida, they propose to dodge the interruptions by moving Radio Martí to an air force C-130 flying on a nearly permanent basis just off the island's international waters."

Stockman put down his pen and thought for a second. He knew what Cummins and some leaders like Pradilla would think about these suggestions. They would say that the policy had not worked for forty years, so why try more of the same?

But then again, they don't get the politics, thought Stockman. A million or so very wealthy Cubans lived in Florida, a swing state. It wasn't only their money and political support that was important to him. He actually believed that he had a responsibility to this important constituency. These were citizens, his citizens. And they felt strongly about Cuba and about an implacable U.S. opposition to Castro.

"Look, clearly the policy of isolating Cuba hasn't been successful in doing the one thing it was supposed to do: get rid of Castro," said the president. "But how the hell do you undo the policy? At a time when we're talking about democracy in the world, how the hell do you hand an olive branch to a communist dictator?"

Cummins started to answer, but Stockman wasn't anywhere near done.

"How can we proudly point to the elections in Iraq and say in the same breath that, gee, its okay for Castro not to have them. I'm not stupid, Nelson. I can see that forty years of Cuba policy did not work. But I'm just not convinced that undoing the policy will work either.

"We may all have to wait for this guy to die, that's all. Meanwhile, it's hard to quibble with these recommendations, Nelson," said Stockman. "Yes, they're tough, but people very close to me believe strongly that they are the right thing to do. I tend to agree. Let me hear your view."

"Sir, you know how I feel on this issue; maybe I should opt out and recuse myself," Nelson answered. It was the only honest thing to do, given Cummins's public outburst in the media.

"Gimme a break. Don't get holier than thou on me," said the president. "If you have something to say, say it."

Nelson fiddled with his papers for a few seconds. The blue felt-tip pen he had clipped onto the front of his yellow pad sprang loose, flipped up into the air, and landed point first onto the beige carpeting of the Oval Office. He leaned over the side of his chair to pick it up and noticed a blue spot spreading outward from the pen tip. Uh-oh. Not a good sign, thought Nelson.

"Look, I don't want to rehash my fundamental view on this. You know them. I think that forty years of failure deserves to be changed. Isolating the guy didn't work, and isolating him even more won't work either.

"I should also say, for the record, that there are a lot of people outside of South Florida who share my view of this issue. However, you decided not to put any of those people on the commission."

That was pretty tough, thought Stockman. Then again, he'd asked for it.

"But, let's stick to the substance of their recommendations," said Nelson. "Fundamentally, what bugs me about it is that we will divert attention to exactly the wrong issue. Rather than focusing the debate on Castro's cruel dictatorship versus a democratic alternative, we will allow it to be twisted back to an argument about the United States bullying a small island. He gets to play David to our Goliath. Why give him the chance?"

Cummins was warming up now.

"Whatever real political benefits we get out of it will be subsumed in an avalanche of bad publicity. The public relations damage will be tremendous at a time when we are looking for friends to support our positions on a lot more important issues. Like Syria. We make it real hard for allies to back us up.

"Speaking of Syria, can I remind you that we still have full diplomatic and economic relations with the Syrian government? Which one is the real enemy, Mr. President? Which one is the nastier government? Because if this is only about the level of a specific government's nastiness, then we should be lifting the embargo on Cuba and unilaterally imposing it on Syria.

"Last—and I promise this will be really the end—do you really think we can stop the movement of people and capital in this day and age? Come on! Already, U.S. tourists go to Cuba by the boatloads through places like Mexico City or Montreal. All we will be doing is forcing dollars to take similar detours through offshore banks in Bahamas or the Cayman Islands. This is just silly posturing."

"Tell me how you really feel, Cummins," snorted the president. Why in God's name does this guy get so up in arms about this issue? Stockman silently asked himself.

"Look, Nelson, many people—and, specifically, a lot of the commission's members—feel equally passionately and come to a diametrically opposite conclusion. Tell you what: Why don't I think about this for a few days? The event is not for another month and a half. I'll sleep on it."

Nelson Cummins was not happy. He looked down at the blue spot on the carpet. It seemed bigger than before; definitely a metaphor for his lack of success here. Clearly Stockman was trying to placate him. He could see it a mile away.

"Thank you, Mr. President. I appreciate your consideration of my views," he lied. Nelson Cummins walked out of the Oval Office dejected.

A Restaurant
Washington, October 4
7:00 p.m.

Nelson Cummins walked straight past his office and out of the White House. The meeting with Stockman on Cuba had him in a funk. Thank God he was going out this evening. It was not a day to go home to a Chinese take-out meal and some television. He said hello to his driver, Michael.

"Hi, Mike. We're going to this new place on the corner of Ninth and G streets. It's called Zaytinya. Do you know it?"

This may be a strange question for most chauffeurs. But not Mike. He had been a White House driver for the last seven years, but prior to his career in a car, Mike was a sous-chef for one of Washington's better French culinary masters. Then, after finally acceding to his wife's nagging to clean the upstairs windows from the outside, Mike fell from the second story of his suburban home. He badly damaged his lower vertebrae. Miraculously, he was able to walk again, but the doctors at Georgetown University Hospital told him that the pressure on his back would impede him from standing for long periods of time. Mike's time in the kitchen came to a sizzling end.

But he still loved cooking and knew all about new restaurants and culinary techniques. The White House staff called him their in-house *Zagat's*. There were lots of stories about Mike and his culinary interventions.

At the beginning of the administration, the president's secretary, Marjorie Orloff, had made the mistake of ordering carryout pizza from one of the chain operations. Mike got a message to her through Nelson Cummins that, in the future, he could gladly get pizza delivered on an exclusive basis from Pizzeria Paradiso, Washington's best homemade pizza shop. Unlike any others, the Paradiso pizzas would have buffalo mozzarella and deliciously thin crusts. Similarly, when the chairman of the President's Council of Economic Advisors wanted to impress the president of Japan's central bank with Washington's best sushi, he asked Mike where to find it. Mike was sure that the central bank president would love the eels at Mikado on MacArthur Boulevard.

So, it was no surprise to Nelson that Mike knew everything about Zaytinya.

"Absolutely. It is wonderful. The chef is in all the food magazines. It's like Spanish tapas, but from the other side of the Mediterranean. It serves Greek, Turkish, and Lebanese food—some of it is traditional and some revved-up to ultramodern. But it is incredibly popular and very noisy. Is this a business dinner, boss?"

"Yes, Mike, it is. I guess I'll have to shout." Nelson smiled, because it was just like his dinner partner to suggest a meeting at one of the loudest possible places. Unlike most spies, Willy Perlman disdained quiet places with low whispers in lieu of restaurants that roared. He figured that it would be harder for listening devices to decipher conversations where noise volumes veered dangerously close to rock concert range.

Nelson opened the door to the ultramodern restaurant and immediately noticed the whitewashed walls and huge cathedral ceilings. Just as he was muttering to himself that he had never been to a restaurant with such high ceilings, a delicate tap on the shoulder interrupted his upward gaze. His eyes came down to meet face to face with a handsome, thin man impeccably dressed in the most modern fashions.

Men this good-looking could only be gay, thought Nelson.

"My name is Raymundo, and I presume you are Mr. Cummins. There is a two-hour wait, but Mr. Perlman knows the owners, so we are able to expedite your waiting time," said Raymundo, signaling that he actually liked making people wait. He seemed both impressed and distraught that somebody had managed to skirt his tightly knit barriers.

Raymundo led Nelson through the bar, where the beautiful people thronged, and toward the far side of the restaurant. There sat Dr. Willy Perlman nursing a beer. Willy was one of Nelson's closest friends. It was Nelson who introduced Willy to the CIA ten or so years ago, and since then, Willy had taken the place by storm. He rose to become the deputy director for analysis. But, with the director of central intelligence now ailing with debilitating lung cancer, Willy was effectively in charge.

Dr. Willy Perlman was not your run-of-the-mill spook: He was a medical doctor, a senior epidemiologist who had made a name for himself in the bush of Africa and the slums of Calcutta. It was Willy who, over a decade ago, had identified a virulent, mutating strain of tuberculosis that was resistant to the usual cocktail of drugs. When combined with the immune system's devastating depletion caused by the spreading AIDS epidemic, TB and its new drug-resistant strain was quickly reclaiming its historical role as the world's principal killer.

The CIA station chief in New Delhi was deeply concerned with Dr. Perlman's findings and asked him to travel to Washington to brief the agency, the State Department, and Congress on this worldwide health threat. Nelson Cummins, then chief of staff of the Senate Select Committee on Intelligence, was high on the list of Washington insiders to get Willy's tuberculosis alert. That is how the two met.

Nelson was immediately impressed by Willy's insightfulness, his attention to detail, and his thorough research. Accustomed to briefings on military strength, intelligence assets, and electronic surveillance budgets, Nelson was fascinated by the painstaking discovery work of public health epidemiology. After the briefing, Nelson asked Willy out for drinks.

"It's not hard," Dr. Perlman had told Cummins a decade ago. "You have to understand culture, behavior, and motivation, and pay a lot of attention to detail. I'm like a public health spy."

Those words lit a mighty bulb in Nelson's head. A man like this belonged at the CIA, thought Nelson. It needed more people like this. For a year, he tried to convince Willy to talk to some friends at the agency. Willy resisted fiercely at first, but then relented. The rest was history.

Dr. Willy Perlman rose fast at the agency. He was a man of the world. Raised in numerous countries, Perlman spoke six languages fluently and had an unnatural ability to put himself in the place of people living in foreign countries and cultures. He could speak Portuguese like a surfer from Rio or Italian like a Roman politician. Yes, he understood foreigners—but that did not mean that he automatically agreed with their views and their policies.

No, Willy Perlman was not a cultural relativist. He was a devout Jew and had clear and definitive opinions of what was right or wrong, better or worse. For Willy Perlman, living in a Western secular democracy was more right and better than any other thing in the world.

Willy's father, Matthias, had been interned in the Dachau concentration camp until saved from death's door by American GIs. Matthias came to America penniless and broken, but rebuilt his life by joining the foreign service. The elder Perlman served his adopted country as a diplomat for thirty years.

In his free time, Willy's father advocated for Jewish causes. Matthias Perlman did everything with enormous passion right up to the day he died. In the late seventies, at the tender age of eighty, Matthias wrangled himself an invitation to the ornate Soviet embassy on 16th Street in Washington and, together with a delicious young blond partner almost sixty years younger, chained himself to the chandelier of the embassy ballroom to protest the Soviet government's veto of Jewish emigration.

That was Willy Perlman's family—people had opinions and took stands.

Perlman got up to greet his old friend. They embraced warmly. Nelson sat down, ordered a glass of Willamette Valley Pinot Noir, and smiled at his CIA companion.

"Mike thinks that the national security advisor and his CIA friend are crazy to have dinner in such a busy place," said Nelson to his CIA friend.

"Yeah, yeah, but remind that gourmet chauffeur of yours that he does restaurant reviews and I do intelligence operations. He gets to say the place is good and I get to say the place is safe to talk," said Willy Perlman. Willy thought that Nelson ought to rein in Mike's easy commentary about every aspect of policy, government, military operations, and intelligence gathering. Then again, thought Willy, Nelson probably enjoys it.

"Tell me, Nelson, where is the president on the Syria thing?" asked Willy, getting right to the point. Willy was like this. They had set this dinner to discuss Syria; so that was to be the subject from the very first minute. On the other hand, if the dinner had been defined as only social, he would have refused to talk about office matters. He liked his meals well organized and clearly delineated.

"He is all over it. We strongly believe that, based on your reports, Syria continues to avoid intervening against terrorist groups operating from its territory. It is increasingly isolated. Iran has made a deal with Europe on nuclear and biological weapons. Libya agreed to terminate all WMD research. Syria remains the recalcitrant outlier."

"We have broad policy tools available to us," continued Nelson. "At the very least, we believe that diplomatic, economic, and political isolation could force real change in Damascus. At the most, we would be willing to consider ordering marine and army infantry units to cross the border from Iraq into Syria. The march to Damascus would take a little more than two days from the Iraqi border."

"Careful on that last part, Nelson," recommended Willy. "We agree that the moment is right for pressure on Syria. It is weak and alone. For God's sake, when Bibi Netanyahu said it was an 'isolated backwater,' we all cringed—not because he was wrong, but because he was right.

"Syria is weak, and that is why the UN will back ratcheting up the diplomatic pressure," Willy continued. "But I really want you to think carefully about what you'll achieve from military intervention. If we enter another Arab country, we end up strengthening the Arab Islamists who think this is a holy war against Christianity and Judaism. What do we get out of putting the American flag on the hills around Damascus? Nothing but problems. Syria is weak. Be my guest and make it weaker. But don't make it *our* problem."

This was why Nelson loved Willy. He did not play games. You got clear analysis and good advice—all before the food was even ordered. Most people in Washington were not like this. They hedged. They talked about their own importance. They forced you to beg so they would own a chit for future favors. Willy was oblivious to this. That was what made him so good.

"Willy, you need to take a break because I'm hungry. Let's order before we get any further into it."

They called their waiter over and Willy did the ordering. Nelson could only make out a few of the names of the grazing meal of seven or eight plates Willy commanded—freshly made Spanakopita, Kibbe balls, carrot and apricot fritters, tiny stuffed pasta from Istanbul covered in yogurt and spices called Manti. "You ever eaten this Manti stuff?" Willy asked breathlessly. "It's the missing link between the Chinese wonton and the Italian ravioli."

The minute the waiter left the tableside, Willy jumped back into their subject. There was no transition. No pause. He started to analyze which countries were the probable naysayers at the UN and which countries could be cajoled into voting for the tougher U.S. position. He was just starting to take a guess at how the French would react when his cellular phone vibrated silently in his pocket.

Nelson always found it funny to watch somebody with a vibrating mobile phone. While vibrating telephones did not have a disruptive ringer, they sent their owners into sudden, silent contortions as they dug into their pockets to pry out the mobile unit. You could see it often enough in a restaurant: Upon feeling that first vibration, legs ratchet outward. Hands dive into pant pockets. Fingers troll for the phone among loose change and credit cards. Faces rivet in silent desperation. That was what Willy was doing now as he reached for his phone.

"Perlman," he answered tautly. Willy listened for less than thirty seconds. In that short time, Nelson noticed his eyes becoming darker and steelier.

"I understand," Willy barked into the phone, "I'm on my way.

"Nelson, we have to break this up. I have to go back to Langley. Something has come up—it could be serious or it could be nothing at all. But I can't do anything about it over the phone. I'm sorry about our dinner."

Willy Perlman got up to put on his jacket. He walked over to Raymundo to explain the situation. The manager was gracious. He understood that sometimes these things happened in Washington.

Willy straightened his tie and was in deep thought about leaving behind his dinner with Nelson. He greatly enjoyed their gatherings. So a thought occurred to him.

"Nelson, I regret this. You know how much I look forward to seeing you. You have a choice: Either enjoy the delicious things I ordered alone or let's ask for a portion of Kibbe and carrot fritters and eat it together in the car. Come with me to Langley—I figure you're cleared to hear anything, right? The meeting should not be too long. We can grab a drink after."

"Willy, eating with you in the car and driving on a dark road to the CIA is not my idea of fun. But it's better than staying here alone. Let's go."

They got into the car with Mike and told him where they were going. Willy was unusually silent as they passed the styrofoam box of twelve Kibbes and twelve fritters back and forth among the three of them. Nelson and Willy did not ask Mike if he wanted any and did not previously discuss whether to share the meal with him. They both knew that excluding Mike from a food-related activity had unthinkable consequences.

Nelson wondered if he made the right decision to come along. His friend's silence told him that the meeting would not be that short and that drinks were probably not going to happen. He even wondered if the sudden end to his dinner was entirely casual. Had Willy actually wanted him to come to a meeting at CIA headquarters without making a formal request of the national security advisor's presence? He would never know.

The car passed quickly through the multiple security stops outside the CIA headquarters in Langley. Once inside, however, Willy had to go through a rigorous process of checking his guest in. Although Nelson Cummins was the president's national security advisor, he was not a CIA employee. Anybody entering the building and accessing key floors was required to provide substantial background information that required cross-checking.

They got off on the fourth floor and walked left down empty hallways. It was now 8:30 p.m., and the building was empty. Cleaning crews were dusting down offices and emptying trashcans. Nelson wondered about the level of scrutiny that each of these Central American immigrants had to go through to clean the offices of the Central Intelligence Agency.

Willy stopped and went left into an office. The tag outside the door said "Office of Nuclear Proliferation."

Willy Perlman said hello to the two people in the office and introduced Nelson. "Guys, meet Nelson Cummins, national security advisor. He is a friend and he is not here in any official capacity. This is not a formal briefing. Nelson, this is Ellen O'Shehan and Ruben Goldfarber."

Nelson smiled. Two things amused him. First, both of these senior CIA employees, whom he presumed were in charge of tracking and following the movement of the world's nuclear materials, were completely stunned that Willy had brought the White House foreign policy czar to this meeting without a heads-up.

The two analysts' facial expressions showed they were impressed that Willy knew somebody so high up, but irritated that they were not forewarned of this VIP's arrival.

Nelson was also amused by the physical appearance of these two bureaucrats. They were everything a spy should not be. Ellen's light brown curly locks framed a cherubic Irish face with glistening, laughing eyes. She was, however, at least 400 pounds heavy. This woman was huge—neck, breasts, waist, hips, thighs. Everything about her was framed *XXL*. Next to her sat a gaunt, bald man with thin wire-rimmed glasses. He had this exhausted look that Nelson remembered from pictures in the Holocaust Museum of Jewish Yeshiva children in turn-of-the-century eastern Europe. Those kids spent their days and nights indoors studying Torah and Talmud. Playing outside was not a lifestyle option for these children. Ruben Goldfarber looked like he had last seen the sun twenty years ago.

The two of them made an incredible couple to look at. Nelson could not take his eyes off this oddball pairing. They all sat down at an oval conference table.

His amusement quickly turned into surprise as their voices became professional. They did not waste a minute as they locked into the reason for interrupting Willy's dinner.

Ellen started. "Sorry about dinner. Here is what we have. We have continued to try to trace the chatter about the uranium. Nothing concrete. Nothing believable. We are nowhere on it."

Willy held up his hand signaling that Ellen should pause and turned to Nelson. "Let me take fifteen seconds and get you up to speed on what Ellen is saying. Over the last four or five days, we have heard chatter about a successful smuggling of uranium into the West. This is not the first time we've heard this. We actually get it with some regularity. Groups brag. Somebody claims to have something they don't really have. Somebody wants to sound bolder than they really are. We listen. We follow. Usually it leads nowhere.

"We paid attention to this one because we heard about the same thing—a movement of highly enriched U-235—from two completely different places. The first source was electronic intercepts in Chechnya. The second was from Indian intelligence sources. But as you have just heard, it seems that we are nowhere on this. Please continue, Ellen."

"Right," continued Ellen, whose weight seemed to disappear under her in-charge and self-assured demeanor. "So, we mobilized informants and got our stations in and around Russia to prick up their eyes and ears on anything unusual. It's been four days since we first heard the chatter, and since then, we have had nothing further on any movement of uranium. We were about to file this one and go home when Ruben suddenly stumbled on something that you should hear."

Ruben took over. Notwithstanding his gray and drab appearance Ruben also surprised Nelson with his forcefulness. When Ruben Goldfarber stood up to talk, his laconic slouchiness suddenly turned erect. These two CIA analysts were amazing studies in contradictions, thought Nelson.

"As Ellen said, the electronic intercepts led us to tell our four stations around Chechnya—in Georgia, Azerbaijan, Armenia, and Moscow—to report all activities. So we got the usual. Surveillance reports. Public events. Police reports. Gets a little overwhelming, but I tried to plow through it. In the Georgian report, we got a copy of a newspaper article about a suicide death in a small city in Georgia's wine-growing region. I would have paid no attention at all, but for the police photograph of the dead man in the newspaper."

Ruben paused for effect. Willy had no time for drama. "No theatrics, Ruben. Move on," said Willy.

"Maybe I have been in this business too long. Who knows? But after working in this office day after day for twenty years, I've become a nuclear groupie. Some people look at *People* magazine and can name each movie star. Others read *Rolling Stone* and recognize every rock singer. I can identify and name every nuclear scientist of any consequence in the world."

Ruben continued. "So, this photo caught my attention. The man was disfigured and the picture was grainy. But part of the reason the picture was so bad was that the floor on which the body was lying was dark and the man's skin was dark. Sort of weird in Georgia, right? Georgians are white. The more I looked, the more I thought the dead guy in the picture looked familiar. Then it hit me. He looked like Farooq Rahman."

"Who the hell is Farooq Rahman?" asked Willy.

"Dr. Rahman is one of the three fathers of Pakistan's nuclear program. He is brilliant. He is a devoted scientist and a devout Islamist. He is believed to be responsible for starting to create a nuclear working team in Taliban Afghanistan. We suspect that he was responsible for giving nuclear secrets to the Iranians. He was retired in the post-Taliban cleanup of Pakistan's intelligence services."

"So you are telling me that the father of Pakistan's nuclear bomb is dead in some small city in Georgia at the same time we start hearing rumors of smuggled nuclear materials?" said Willy, his eyes now riveted on Ruben.

"I am saying that I think the picture could be Rahman and I am saying that the connection worried us enough to call you at dinnertime," said Ruben.

"Wait a minute, wait a minute," interrupted Willy Perlman. "I've known you guys way too long and way too well. You would not have broken up my Spanako-pita with Nelson here merely with speculation. I am sure that you guys told our people in Tbilisi to get us confirmation—dental records, fingerprints, DNA. Whatever."

"Yes, you know us well," answered Ellen. "And, yes is the answer to both of your assertions. Yes, we instructed our people to try to confirm Rahman. And, unfortunately, yes we called you on mere speculation. We will never be able to confirm it."

"Why the hell not?" demanded Willy.

"Georgia is now in the throes of an unusual autumnal heat wave," Ellen explained. "Their hydropower dried up over the summer and the usual electricity crises in Georgia have turned dramatic. The corpse was found in Telavi five days ago. The police posted the picture in all the country's newspapers asking for someone to identify the body. Nobody showed. But the morgue has no electricity for ten hours per day, and since they don't get a lot of killings in that country, the lab has no reserve generator. The dead guy started decomposing. So, after five days, they cremated the body and dumped the ashes in the river."

She looked at Ruben, who nodded gravely. "Everything is gone. We'll never know for sure who he was," she concluded.

Nelson and Willy sat in stunned silence. Potentially, they could be on the cusp of discovering a grave security threat to the United State and its allies. On the other hand, there was nothing to go on save for the similarity of a dead body in Georgia to a Pakistani man. On the surface, it seemed preposterous. How could a Pakistani scientist get into Georgia? What was he doing in this small town? Who killed him?

Nelson looked at Willy. "I don't mean to tell you guys how to run your business, but I can't see an elderly Pakistani waltzing secretly into a country thousands of miles from his own to trade in nuclear secrets. The dead body must be somebody who coincidentally looks like him."

"Possibly. Maybe even probably," said Willy. "But we can't leave it at that. In a single four-day time period, we received two separate alarms regarding illegal movements of uranium-235. One of the advisories is from Georgia's next-door neighbor in Chechnya. The other tip is from India, Pakistan's next-door neighbor. Now, we may have a dead Pakistani nuclear expert in Georgia. Until proven otherwise, I go with Ruben's intuition about who this guy is."

Willy now took over the meeting. "Ellen, get our Karachi people moving on what Rahman has been up to and where he is. Hopefully we'll find him playing with his grandchildren and this goes away. Ruben, can you follow up with Georgia? Have them press the local police for any missing detail. Bring in the FBI to see if there is any forensics we can come up with to match the body. Last, send out a message to all stations to press for information on illicit nuclear materials. Urgent.

"No, Nelson," Willy turned to his friend. "We have to follow this one. Too many coincidences in too short a period. Not good. Not good at all."

The Oval Office
Washington, October 5
11:25 a.m.

==

President John Stockman warmly shook hands with the legislators as he walked them to the door of the Oval Office. The four most important members of the United States Congress were the majority and minority leaders of the Senate, the Speaker of the House, and the House minority leader. The meeting had gone well.

He invited the four politicians to coffee to apprise them of the fact that his administration would be coming to them for a supplemental appropriations package of nearly $50 billion to cover the ongoing problems in Iraq. It had been a number of years since the United States had sent troops to Baghdad, and they were still not out. Well, that is a euphemism. U.S. forces were mired in what seemed like an endless war of attrition with faceless sharpshooters and nameless bombmakers.

And now, notwithstanding the problems in Iraq, Stockman was resolved to throw down the gauntlet to Syria.

This meeting was a first pass at revealing the president's intentions to Congress, and it went well. Stockman made clear that conflict was the last resort, but he convinced them of the need to look like they were serious. That was the reason for his administration's request for extra monies to "support U.S. goals in Iraq and elsewhere, if needed." That exact language was important because it would send a united message to the world that the United States was ready to engage "elsewhere, if needed." The four members of Congress agreed.

As he closed the door of his office, he looked quickly at his Omega Seamaster watch. Miranda had given it to him on his birthday the year she died. It told him that he had a free half hour. He smiled at the bittersweet contradiction. It was Miranda's watch that announced the fact that he had a free thirty minutes to contact another woman.

In the past few days, he had thought about whom he would ask to help him execute the connection. Above all, Stockman wanted nobody at the White House to know what he was doing. He felt a strange mixture of emotions. Personal embarrassment that he was even thinking about reaching out to her and trepidation that one of his controlling advisors would find out and convince him that this was not a smart thing to do. Shit, he wanted to do it! But, better that nobody find out.

He picked up the phone and dialed it. He smirked to himself as he imagined Marjorie's shock in the outside office when she saw the lit line. But he knew she would not say anything. He hardly remembered the last time he dialed a phone number on his own.

He punched in the 405 area code number and a sleepy teenager answered the line. It was nearly eight in the morning in California and his daughter was still in bed. Didn't she have class? Stockman suppressed the parental desire to ask her what she was doing asleep at this hour.

"Hi, Julia, it's Daddy," Stockman loudly. Father and daughter talked nearly every day, but almost always at night. He could imagine her surprise at hearing his voice first thing in the morning.

"Daddy, hi." Julia said something else, but a yawn made anything further unintelligible. "Sorry," she said, giggling, "I just woke up. What are you doing calling me at this hour? Don't you have a meeting to go to or something?"

Stockman laughed. His daughter was rarely impressed by power. Perhaps it was the result of growing up surrounded by authority.

"How is your paper coming along? You know, the one on, um, psychology and mass marketing."

"Okay. It's due next Thursday, but I was in the library writing until one o'clock this morning."

"And Michael—how's he doing?" asked the president, referring to Julia's present flirt. It was only a six-week thing, so Stockman wasn't paying a lot of attention to it—yet.

"Daddy," Julia exploded, "It's 8:00 a.m. here. I went to bed late and you are the president. You are calling in the middle of your morning. There is no way you want to chitchat about Michael at this hour. So, take off the fake friendly face and tell me why you are really calling."

President John Stockman grinned sheepishly into the phone. He figured he should get to the point.

"I'm calling to ask a favor. I waited until 8:00 to call. I think that is very polite of me, don't you?"

Her father was calling to ask her a favor? That was new. She sat up in bed.

"Sure. What's up? Let me change phones and get the cordless so I can walk around. I can wake up faster if I'm out of bed."

Stockman heard the click of the phones picking and hanging up nearly simultaneously. He also heard the scratchy sound of a Bic lighter. She was lighting up a cigarette. Jesus, his daughter was smoking! He started to say something and was interrupted by the menacing threat of his watch. He had only twenty-five minutes to go. The smoking lecture would have to wait.

"I need to learn how to use e-mail. Can you teach me?"

Julia paused for a second. "What? Don't you have anybody there to give you a crash course?"

Women were insatiably curious, Stockman thought. Yet, he expected the question from Julia. After all, she was his nineteen-year-old daughter, not a White House staffer. She was allowed to ask questions. He had already resolved to tell her the truth—well, not quite all of it.

"Yes, I can have somebody here explain it. But, I don't want a White House e-mail address. I want my own address so that I can write privately. To tell you the truth, I don't want anybody to know."

He knew she would love the intrigue. And he was right. What was not to love? The maximum authority was trying to skirt the authorities.

"Okay, I get it. Well, do you remember how to use the computer? I taught you a couple of years ago about the Internet. Do you remember?"

"Yes, you turn the computer on and then click on the blue *E* for Explorer, right?" Stockman had actually enjoyed learning to browse the Internet. Over the past year, he occasionally had fired up the machine in his office to get football results or look up famous speeches.

"Right. Well, we have a number of choices now. We can get you a hotmail account or Yahoo or MSN. We can even set up an Instant Messenger account." She was getting excited now.

"Julia," Stockman interrupted, his voice stem. "I want the easiest one."

"Please," he added, quickly realizing that he sounded angry. "You know me— I need it simple or I'll never use it."

"Fine," she said, disappointed that he was not willing to try more. "Is your computer up?"

"Yes," Stockman answered. He had pressed the on button before making the call.

"Okay, double-click Explorer. Once you are there, use the address line to type in 'Yahoo.com.' Tell me when you see it come up."

"Got it," her father answered.

"Good. Now, at the top right-hand side, you will see an icon that says *mail*. Click that." Julia talked her dad through the setup of an e-mail account. They answered all of Yahoo's registration questions. John Stockman used Julia's address.

"What do you want for a user ID name and a password?"

"Umm? Man From Nebraska? How is that?"

"Sure," she said. Make sure you write it all together, Dad. Now, you need a password that you will remember."

"Anything?"

"Absolutely anything, but you need to remember it."

"Okay, how about 'IloveJulia'."

"Perfect," she giggled. This was a blast.

"You're in, Dad. Now let me teach you how to write and send a message. I'm sitting down now at my computer and I'll send you something too. That way, you can open it."

They went through a practice run. It worked.

"Now, let's do the same for Instant Messenger," Julia said. "It's the best. IM is like e-mail but it happens instantaneously; so you get real-time chitchat. You don't have to wait for your message to get through. I do it all the time to arrange meetings, to talk about homework. It replaces the telephone."

"I can't, Julia, I'm out of time. This is enough."

"Dad, two more minutes. You called me. Now finish the lesson," she joked. Julia walked him through the basics of Instant Messaging. He heard the cybernetic doors opening and closing as they practiced a couple of back-and-forths. Stockman thought that she was right—it was fun and useful.

He was ready.

"Thanks, honey. I have to run. Remember what my password says. I mean it!"

She hung up with a smile that immediately turned into a laugh, wondering what her powerful father was up to now.

Stockman looked at his watch. He had ten minutes to go.

The Oval Office
Washington, October 5
11:48 a.m.

═══

John Stockman slowly uncrumpled the small piece of paper with the Waldorf Astoria letterhead. He had transferred it to his wallet the morning after she slipped the note into his suit pocket.

He wrote tentatively, pecking one finger at a time.

TO: BeautifulColombia@yahoo.com
FROM: ManFromNebraska
RE: Meeting

Dear Marta,

Congratulations. This is one of the first things I've ever done on impulse. I suppose you convinced me of the beauty of trusting one's instincts. Guess it's worth a little try.

I'm writing to tell you that I enjoyed our evening. It was a surprise. I was not sure you and I would get along.

I have a confession to make: This is the first e-mail I've ever written. So, I hope I have done everything right and this gets to you.

Yours truly,
J.

Stockman looked at the screen and reread his document. He moved the cursor and took a breath. He clicked Send.

TO: ManFromNebraska (Reply)
FROM: BeautifulColombia
RE: Meeting

Dear John,

Don't worry; I knew you had never sent an e-mail. The panic on your face when I told you what the note said was obvious. Who taught you?

And don't brag about your computer skills too widely. If somebody finds out, they will take the computer away from you. That is what happened to Bush—he was e-mailing too many friends.

I also enjoyed our evening. And it's true: I too felt as if we had known each other for a long time. Yes, it's surprising. We could not be more different.

Will we be able to again have a drink somewhere? What do you think? It seems awfully strange that two adults that might want to have dinner together will probably never have the chance.

One day, I should like to see your Nebraska. I'm one of those people who say that I know the United States well. But that's really not true. I know New York, LA, San Francisco, and Washington—the coasts. What's in the middle is a mystery. Which is the real America?

The real America? That is a good question, eh? Hispanics are now the largest minority and will grow and grow. (Another reason you should get closer to Latin America!) In a few decades, the real America may be speaking Spanish like I do. It would save me from writing this e-mail in your impossible language. How can any language be so devious? "Caught" and "Enough." What are the "gh" letters doing there? And, why do they behave so sneakily—one is pronounced one way and the other completely differently?

We have nothing to hide in Spanish—what you hear is what you get.

Remember that,

Marta

TO: BeautifulColombia
FROM: ManFromNebraska (Reply)
RE: Meeting

Dear Marta,

This is actually fun. Amazing, isn't it, how the world comes full circle. Here we are back to writing letters; like they used to do over the centuries. The telephone was supposed to replace letter-writing. And now technology brings us back to where we started. I presume e-mail will do marvels for young people who abandoned writing as old-fashioned.

Yes, I'll take you to Nebraska. With pleasure. I took a Mexican politician there once. Do you know what impressed him most? Not the cow operations. Not our grain storage technology. Nor our incredibly innovative rural credit. What impressed him was lunch at one of my dearest friends' place, Jim Barr. On his 960-acre cow-calf facility, Jim has a very large library. There the Mexican found books by Carlos Fuentes and Mario Vargas Llosa, poetry by Pablo Neruda. He looked at farmer Jim—maybe he thought nobody reads anything in Nebraska—and asked, shocked, "Do you really read this?"

Jim just answered: "It's a long winter out here, sir."

What's the real America? God knows, but surely it's partly Jim too. And, yes, Marta, now it's more and more Hispanics. That is great. More than great, it's wonderful! Immigration is the way to renew—to become younger, to reenergize. But, I'm not sure that we are doing Hispanics a service by allowing them to avoid mastering the naughtiness of the "gh." We're letting Latinos in the United States maintain a language totally apart. Is that a good thing?

My grandmother came from Moravia in Czechoslovakia—she spoke only Czech when she settled in Nebraska. These immigrants stuck together, created little Moravian communities and founded Moravian Lutheran churches. But they made their children learn English, because English was the way to move up. The same went for Poles, Italians, Germans, and Jews from wherever.

English was the common transportation to self-improvement.

And you, where would you take me in Colombia? Tell me about Cartagena. All I know is that everybody says it's beautiful.

Marta, I loved your stories about the political trouble you got into when you were Miss Universe. It's an amazing juxtaposition—a beauty queen who gets into trouble because of her strong opinions.

I've got to run. Write me.

J.

TO: ManFromNebraska (Reply)
FROM: BeautifulColombia
RE: Meeting

Dear John,

Be careful with those generalizations, John. The reason the Miss Universe organization and I were a misfit was not because I was a smart girl in a dumb system. Lots of the girls were pretty, smart, and had opinions. Unlike them, though, I just never went with the flow. I didn't believe that being Miss Universe was a reason to stop expressing what I think.

It was a hard experience, you know. In eight months, I went around the world. Indonesia, China, Japan, Hong Kong, London, Paris, Stockholm, New York, and almost every capital in South America. The pace was grueling. Murder, really.

The trips were a nightmare. I became one of those select few who know the dirty little secret of international travel. No matter what class of service I flew in or how many VIP lounges I went to, the glamour of flying wore off fast. Believe me; when you know the names of the flight crew working your airplane, it's time to start worrying. But if you find yourself reciting your frequent flyer numbers by heart and can state to the nearest ten thousandths the balance of your various mileage accounts, it's time to start considering a life change.

It was a job, John. Too many people one never really talked to. Too many places one never really got to know. Too many events that veered close to meaningless.

But I learned one terrible lesson as Miss Universe. I learned that violence is a human condition. It's not Colombian or American or Russian or Chinese. When a child suffers from violence, the whole world darkens a shade. It's something that should—must—concern all of us. That is a lesson that I will never forget.

One of the first stops on my inaugural trip as Miss Universe was the most unforgettable. It was at a classroom in rural Indonesia—on the island of Bali. Mark the words carefully: It wasn't a school; it was only a classroom—a hunk of concrete formed into a square. Months earlier, men had come and lifted the structure from the ground—one bulldozer, a portable cement mixer, and some wire bars. In less than thirty days, a gray, four-walled slab of concrete stood on the muddy Balinese soil a few hundred feet from the beach.

There were no windows. Just three round holes in every wall, each three feet in diameter, carved out of the cement. If you built windows, the hurtling rains and howling winds of the yearly monsoon would shatter them instantaneously. So the builders just left twelve small circular holes in the walls to let the air circulate and bring some light into the room.

I went to visit the classroom in the morning—and I'll never forget what it looked like when I walked in. The room was dusky and damp. Twenty children sat on tiny chairs slapped together from discarded driftwood. The schoolbooks were in their twentieth iteration, yellowed and held together with dirty Scotch tape. Muslim boys and girls—separated, in opposite sides of the room—were neatly dressed and combed.

The morning sunlight was just high enough to stream in through one of the holes in the wall. In the darkness of the classroom, the light funneled in and refracted its brightness onto one single little girl. It was an amazing sight—straight out of Michelangelo's paintings of God's divinity pouring down on the Christ. The little girl looked translucent in the singular flood of light that perfectly covered her body and desk while leaving the rest of the classroom in semidarkness. She smiled at me.

I gave my little speech to the children. What it means to be Miss Universe. I always stressed the importance of study for girls—because knowledge expands the mind and improves families.

After my presentation, I asked the teacher if I could talk to the little girl lit up by the sunlight. Along with my translator, I took the girl to the courtyard, strewn with plastic bags, discarded diapers, and metal cans. What a strange contrast; just inside was the orderliness of the small classroom with its rays of divine sunshine streaming through the holes. Outside, the visual and smelly stench of underdevelopment's garbage and insufficient hygiene permeated every possible barrier.

Through my translator, I tried to get the little girl to talk to me.

I asked her name. How does she like school? What subject does she like best? Does she do her homework?

Then I asked where her parents live.

"I live with my uncle," said the girl.

"Really?" I said to her. "I too lived with my uncle for many years. Are your parents working in the city?"

"No, they were killed in the fighting two years ago. The military men came to our village and just shot anybody they could find. My mother was cooking dinner." The girl said this matter-of-factly, as if reciting the multiplication tables.

I shook inside. I tried to push away the thoughts of my mother and father looking down the barrel of a terrorist's gun, but they came flooding in.

Here I was; in Bali. I was on the other side of the world from my home, speaking through a translator to a dark-skinned Islamic child with Asiatic features. The expanse of the Pacific Ocean lay between our countries. Yet there was no gap. Everything about this girl suddenly became familiar, close.

"What do you want to do when you grow up?" I asked her.

"I want to be a leader," said the girl, no hesitation in her voice.

I took the girl in my arms and squeezed her small body. Then, I took her by the shoulders and looked squarely into her eyes—eyes that I will never forget.

And I told her that I understood because I wanted to do the same thing.

Maybe I am here today because I had to keep my promise to the little girl in Bali.

This is now way too long. You are going to think that I am an emotional sap. So now it's your turn. John, tell me about Miranda. What was she like? What was your relationship like? What did you like to do together? There's an expression is Spanish: "You can judge a man by the woman he keeps." It's a little macho, but it still has a lot of truth. Tell me about her.

Bye,

Marta

CIA Headquarters
Langley, October 7
2:03 p.m.

Seventy-two hours had gone by. At CIA headquarters, Ellen O'Shehan and Ruben Goldfarber were now on their third day with practically no sleep. They had not gone home. They had not showered. Ellen was on her fifteenth Diet Coke and her seventh steak and cheese sandwich from the CIA cafeteria. Ruben Goldfarber seemed to exist on coffee alone.

They were exhausted. Mostly, they were physically tired. But they were also mentally beat from frustration. Two days had gone by, and nothing. Like Willy Perlman, they knew that the chance of coincidence was too great. But Perlman's urgent orders asking CIA station chiefs around the world to mobilize informants, contacts, and intelligence had not gotten them any further information.

Information flowed in, but none of it seemed relevant. Nonetheless, they followed every lead emanating from the approximate date of the discovery of the corpse in Telavi. They sorted through everything.

The CIA station in Baku informed them that the president of Azerbaijan had welcomed the prime minister of Malaysia. Ruben wired Baku to find out who was in the Malaysian delegation.

The U.S. embassy in Moscow reported on a convention of biochemists in Saint Petersburg. Ellen ignored the time change and woke up the ambassador's assistant in the middle of the night and ordered somebody to get them the list of participants.

Chechen rebels blew up a bus transporting Russian soldiers in downtown Grozny. Willy Perlman issued orders to CIA agents in Chechnya to query their rebel informants regarding plans to escalate their anti-Russian activities to nuclear levels.

The CIA Georgia station reported that the only activity in the country of any note was a regularly scheduled UN meeting on Abkhazian refugees. Goldfarber e-mailed back for the list of participants.

In Pakistan, India, Afghanistan, Uzbekistan, Armenia, agents of the United States government were pressing informants, paying for information, scouring newspapers for unusual events. Whatever was found was reported back to Langley, which, in turn, requested more information. Who met with whom? Who was on a delegation? Who attended a conference? Were there any unusual movements?

There was nothing. The only piece of news that seemed to be of any relevance was the absence of any information on Farooq Rahman. U.S. embassy inquiries with the University of Karachi, the Pakistani government, and officials in the intelligence agencies went nowhere. Nobody had seen or heard from Farooq Rahman in at least two or three years. Willy Perlman ordered an undercover operation to go directly to Rahman's home.

A secretary entered the room and dumped more paper on the conference table in Ellen and Ruben's office. Responses from embassies and CIA stations. More lists. More schedules. More reports on meetings, conferences, and summits in faraway places.

"Maybe we overreacted," said Ruben. "Maybe there is nothing here. Maybe the corpse is not Rahman," he concluded, looking up at the blown-up grainy likeness from the Georgian newspaper that was now pinned on the office's bulletin board.

"Maybe," answered Ellen, too tired to even talk about it. She reached for the top sheet of paper from the folder recently placed on the table. Sent from Tbilisi, it was titled "Memo to Headquarters re Additional Information on UN Refugee Meeting."

"Listen, Ellen, we may have to backtrack with Willy," said Ruben. "I am sure that this is a picture of Rahman lying there dead in some hotel room thousands of miles from his home. But if I can't prove it, if our people around the world cannot find a connection, we may have to tell Willy we were off base . . ."

"Ruben," Ellen said. He just kept talking.

"I'm racking my brains for something we missed. Is there something we did not ask for? I can't find it. I don't see it. So, we got to figure out when we call Willy and throw in the towel. What do you think?" Ruben rattled on.

"Ruben," Ellen repeated. Getting no pause from Ruben's defeatist stream of consciousness rants, Ellen shouted this time. "Ruben, shut up!"

"Let's wait for Karachi to come back with the operation to Rahman's house. If there is nothing conclusive, we may have to—"

"Ruben!" Ellen's unusual burst skidded him to a stop. He stared at her.

"Ruben, I may have something." Ellen felt her blood pulsing. Exhaustion suddenly seemed to drop off her body. "Ruben, Christ, we may have something!"

"Guess who the Pakistani representative to the UN meetings on Abkhazian refugees was? Ambassador Ali Massoud Barmani, otherwise known by us in the nuclear world as the 'Colonel.' This guy was in charge of creating the team that put together the Paki bomb. From the mid-'70s to the mid-'80s, he chose the scientists, funneled the money, and oversaw the tests. Jesus, Mary, and Joseph— Farooq Rahman's longtime handler was in Georgia at the same time as the corpse. Are we supposed to believe that an intelligence agent who dedicated his life to creating nuclear weapons was the best possible representative to an obscure refugee conference? Bullshit."

Ruben Goldfarber's white, pallid skin flushed with color. His eyes opened wide. He slowly took off his glasses. "Ellen, my God, we were right. God help us. What is going on?"

He reached for the phone to call Willy. Perlman was in his office and on a secure line. Ruben succinctly reviewed what Ellen found and thrust out his conclusion. "Willy, there can be no doubt. We don't know what they were doing. We don't know who killed Rahman. But if the Colonel was in Georgia at the same time as the body was found, we can definitely say that the body was Farooq Rahman."

All Ruben heard was a click. Willy Perlman hung up the phone without a word. Ellen and Ruben said nothing to each other. They were wide awake. Their analytical minds churned with possibilities.

It took less than forty-five seconds for Willy Perlman to burst open the door. He did not knock before entering.

"Give it to me again," Willy said. "Slowly."

They reviewed their requests to the CIA stations in different capitals. They walked him through the responses to their initial requests for further information. They told him about their frustration and then the sudden appearance of the e-mail from Tbilisi. They quietly and efficiently reviewed the Colonel's biography. There would be no Pakistani bomb without the Pakistani Intelligence Agency and its director of nuclear development. The Colonel and Farooq Rahman were intimates. They had worked together for decades. The fact that both were in Georgia was a strange and dangerous fact.

Willy Perlman asked many questions. He wanted detailed information about both the scientist and his handler. He asked Ellen and Ruben about their youth. Their schooling. Their links to extremist Islam. Their relationship to the Taliban regime in Afghanistan.

An hour later, Ruben and Ellen were still methodically debriefing Willy. They were used to this. They answered questions tightly. They included fact and hearsay—both were important in intelligence—but they clearly identified which was which.

As he listened, Willy Perlman absent-mindedly reached over for the critical memo from the CIA station in Tbilisi; it lay randomly among the many papers and memos strewn on the analysts' conference table. Willy was not reaching for anything specific; he just needed to play nervously with any piece of paper.

Willy realized that this was the list of names attending the UN conference on Abkhazian refugees. He noted to himself that good intelligence, like public health work, was still made up of hard, slogging research. This small list of participants had changed everything. It was from this list that they could confirm with near certitude that it was Farooq Rahman who died in Georgia.

As his analysts continued their briefing, Willy Perlman's eyes scanned the list. He was not reading with real purpose. It was just a researcher's old habit of looking at everything. But his eyes locked in on one name. All color drained from his face. He was no longer listening to Ellen or Ruben. His mind raced forward and backward. He took a deep breath to steady himself. He looked again at the list. And again.

Representative of the Syrian Arab Republic: Ambassador Osman Samir al-Husseini.

It was not clear how long Willy Perlman fixated upon the name on the list. But it was clear enough that something was wrong, because Ellen and Ruben had stopped talking about a minute ago and were staring at him. Ellen called him quietly by his name a few times, but Willy Perlman was in a trance.

He raised his head slowly. There was no reason why these two experts on nuclear proliferation would recognize the name of one of the most ruthless enforcers of the Syrian government. Ellen and Ruben were the world's best sources on nuclear proliferation. But Osman Samir al-Husseini's name—or for that matter, Syria's name—had never before been linked to nuclear issues.

Clearly, the Syrian government had found out about U.S. plans to isolate and, possibly, invade Syria. Clearly it was intent on arming itself with nuclear weapons. Clearly, the presence of three people in Georgia—the nuclear scientist, his handler, and the Syrian spy—meant that Syria was being given nuclear secrets or nuclear material or both.

He stared at Ruben and Ellen but did not engage with them. The pieces were falling into place in his head, but his mind's synapses were connecting so loudly that all outside noise was blocked out. He did not hear Ellen's ongoing incantation of his name. He simply allowed his mind to order the pieces of the puzzle.

What was less certain but could be safely presumed was that Syria had successfully managed to get what it was looking for. He would ask for Husseini's destination, but he presumed that the spy had changed planes a number of times to cover his tracks.

But the biggest question of all was the one to which he did not yet have answers. Presuming the Syrians had gotten some type of nuclear weaponry, what was it to be used for and where was it going?

His mind was much clearer now. He refocused on Ellen and Ruben.

"Guys, you have done a good job. There is another name on this list that is important. The Syrian name. He is Syria's senior spy in the United States. He's way too senior to attend a minor refugee conference without having a secondary purpose. You could not have recognized his name—it had nothing to do with nuclear matters until today. I want you to continue to find out everything you can about Rahman's death and the last three or four weeks of his life. We need to start putting the pieces of the puzzle together.

"But we have the three main pieces of the jigsaw in front of us. The combination of the three names in one place at one time adds up to very bad news. Unfortunately, what you have uncovered is serious shit. We are now in the midst of a national emergency," whispered Willy.

PART VIII
COLOMBIA

Bresso's Restaurant

Bogotá's "Zona Rosa," the Pink District, was rocking on Thursday nights. This ten-block area in the capital's northern reaches was an alphabet soup of restaurants, nightclubs, bars, and discos. One storefront crammed into the next, the Zona Rosa concentrated the best of Bogotá's nightlife.

The Zona Rosa always impressed first-time foreign visitors because it was symbolic of the incongruous nature of Colombian reality. While bad news dominated the headlines, Colombians refused to give up on life. So, for many of Bogotá's residents, the Zona Rosa was a connection to the better part of living. A good restaurant. A lively bar with a jazz quartet. Funky clothing boutiques. Art galleries.

Elegance and hip coexisted easily in the Pink District. Conservative businessmen sat at tables with women dressed in the latest sexy getup from Soho. Long-haired musicians smoked cigarettes in hazy-aired bars and talked for hours about art. Cafés were the favorite watering holes of intellectuals and academics sharing whiskeys and pondering social theory long into the night.

But it was not only the people that brought the place alive. It was also the architecture and design. Many of the restaurants and bars of the Zona Rosa looked taut and modern. Bright interiors splashed light on sleek, avant-garde open spaces, sporting thin tables dressed with oversized colored plates. Waiters, wearing heavily starched and perfectly white long aprons, ran around clucking over their favorite customers. The scene was more like New York or Milan than that of a Latin country in crisis.

Bresso's was a favorite for politicians in Bogotá. The food was simple Provençal French cuisine, but there was nothing cutely country-like about it. Bresso's was a place in which to see and be seen. Its long, curving tropical hardwood bar herded over a hundred people around drinks served by tenders resembling Calvin Klein models. Clients were lucky to get a table after only an hour-long wait.

Naturally, Senator Juan Francisco Abdoul did not have to wait to be seated.

Luis, the maître d', recognized him the instant he walked in and pointed the Senator to his favorite corner table where Ricardo Abdoul, the younger brother, was already seated. The senator was such an avid frequenter of Bresso's that the restaurant created a menu item in his honor: Steak Abdoulaise. It was a fifteen-ounce sirloin with Bordelaise sauce but, in keeping with the senator's fiery Caribbean palate, the kitchen added tiny red-hot chile peppers to the traditional French sauce.

It took Juan Francisco Abdoul five minutes to reach the table. On his way to the far corner where his brother waited, the senator stopped repeatedly. He slapped backs and laughed with fellow politicians, greeted wives and girlfriends with a vivacious kiss on the cheek, and, every once in a while, dragged somebody into the restaurant's aisle for a quick, serious conversation in bent-over whispers.

Ricardo marveled at his sibling. No matter how hard he tried, he was unable to pull off the political act as well as his brother. As mayor of Barranquilla, Ricardo was a local politician through and through. He despised the vapid national scene, full of party intrigue and posture. He hated Bogotá's sleek stiffness. Unlike his brother, Ricardo rarely wore a tie—in Barranquilla's sweltering humidity, you wore shirtsleeves or you died of heatstroke.

Two years ago, Juan Francisco had convinced Ricardo to run for the Liberal Party's nomination against Marta Pradilla. But for all of Juan Francisco's pretty talk about how nice it would be to have the Abdoul brothers dominating both the legislative and executive sides of Colombia's national politics, Ricardo understood the real reason that Juan Francisco did not run himself for president. It was simple: Juan Francisco was unelectable. Poll after poll reported that Colombians viewed him as the symbol of old politics, corruption, and the worn-out political machines. His brother, Ricardo, practically unknown outside his native Barranquilla, younger and better looking, was less defined. Ricardo was an empty vessel that could be filled by Juan Francisco's communications machine.

But the gambit failed. In the year-long Liberal Party primaries, a growing clamor for change inside the party meant that Ricardo Abdoul was always playing catch-up to Pradilla's exhortations to a "new" Liberal Party. She won the primaries handily and months later the whole Colombian electorate voted overwhelmingly for the change that Marta Pradilla symbolized. Everyone had enough of old-school politicians and, yes, their younger brothers too.

Ricardo returned to Barranquilla after the primary season—secretly happy to get back to his city, his money, and his family. With no real aspirations, he lived like a king, enjoying the political power of city hall and the financial treasures of his family's illegal trade. Ricardo ruled Barranquilla with zero tolerance for those who opposed him. Not one to negotiate, he just crushed those in his path. You can run a provincial city that way.

Ricardo was content with what he had; his purpose in life was to keep it rather than grow it.

But as he watched Juan Francisco coming his way, he worried that his brother was still unable to digest Pradilla's election. The backslapping and genial conversation in the restaurant was a front; in fact, her political victory was like an evil spell destroying him, chromosome by chromosome, from the inside. The younger Abdoul knew that his brother spent hours ranting at images of the president on television. He appeared on talk shows in Bogotá, spitting venom on her ideas, her political appointments, and her events.

What Juan Francisco clearly did not see was that this was exactly where Pradilla wanted him. In the past weeks, repeated leaks from the presidential palace had hinted at some coming bold move on extradition; recent press stories mentioned that the president was particularly focused on weeding out the corrupt influences from Colombia's politics. Everybody knew that this was code for stripping the immunity of targeted elected officials. And Juan Francisco Abdoul was a top target.

That was the reason for Ricardo's deep worry about his brother's furious television and radio appearances. The more Juan Francisco's anger became public, the more his protestations and accusations sounded suspect and contrived. The vitriol was becoming all consuming. Beyond his concern with his brother's psychological state, Ricardo feared that this was just the situation that could lead to serious mistakes and endanger the family's wealth. This was the trap Pradilla was setting.

That's why the younger Abdoul brother resolved to fly to Bogotá on the late afternoon Avianca flight. He spent the hour on the airplane rehearsing the conversation he needed to have with Juan Francisco. This very evening.

The brothers embraced warmly. No matter their differences, there was still an undeniable closeness between them. Juan Francisco ordered a bottle of Chilean cabernet sauvignon and began the conversation inquiring about Ricardo's family. But the polite chitchat did not last long.

"Did you see this slut at the speech on computer training?" sputtered the elder Abdoul. "She thinks she's still Miss Universe. It would be almost funny if it weren't for the fact that her ideas are so dangerous. This is what happens when we send kids to study in England or the United States!"

Ricardo wished the moment had not come so soon, but he had promised himself that tonight would be the night to confront Juan Francisco.

"Juan Francisco, we are all worried about you. You are overexposing yourself. You are everywhere—on television, in newspapers, magazines. She has become the sole focus of your existence. You can't let your hatred consume you. She will make mistakes; let's wait for those to happen."

"Ricardo, I can't believe you are telling me this. Do you not read the papers? Are you not talking to your friends in Congress? She has decided that extradition is the only way to get us. And you know what? She's right. If we don't stop her, little brother, you and I could well be on an airplane bound for a Miami jail for the rest of our lives."

"Of course I understand what she is doing on extradition," Ricardo continued. "But she is here and not going anywhere. It's a reality, so we have to be smart. Now is not the moment to fight her head-on; it's time for us to consolidate our strength, our money, and our friends. We will have to make some investments in new friends. Let's secure our position, Juan Francisco—both to defend ourselves against her and to attack when she is weak."

There was more to be said, but he never got around to it.

Juan Francisco Abdoul's large face first turned pasty green, then livid red. He was enraged. He leaned over the table and grabbed his brother's arm. It wasn't a gesture of brotherly friendliness; it was the squeeze of pure fury.

"Thank God you didn't get elected, you little coward. Your life was given to you by the hard work of our father, and then by me. You are just a backward, lazy, comfortable boy. Our money ruined you. You don't understand what is happening in this country. In my own goddamn country!

"This woman will finish us if we don't finish her first. Listen to what she says and believe it. She said that she will reinitiate the extradition of Colombian nationals. Believe her. The next step will be a public declaration of her intention to move against the immunity of a number of elected officials. Believe that too. We will soon have investigators up our assholes. Do you know what that means, silly boy? It means that people like us will be on the American Airlines flight in handcuffs."

"Juan Francisco, she can't get the Congress to strip you of your immunity without proving massive wrongdoing. Do you know how difficult that is going to be? It will be years before a prosecutor can get a case together. Meanwhile, what we have to do is expand our circle and grow our friendships."

"You still don't get it," said Juan Francisco, his face twisted into a grimace. "Do you remember how the U.S. government arrested Al Capone? Not on murder or embezzlement charges. They sentenced him to years in jail for mail fraud and tax evasion—the smallest, tiniest legal infractions. That is what she is going to do. She's not going to get bogged down in legal niceties. She will find one small thing—anything—and use it to take away my immunity. When that happens, I will be extradited from Colombia in less than an hour.

"No, little brother, this is not the time to consolidate," Juan Francisco said, his expression darkening. "This is the time to attack, attack, and attack more. And I have figured out how to do it."

With no further warning than that, he revealed his plans. Over the next forty-five minutes, his chest heaved heavily as he precisely explained the trap he was laying. His lips trembled as he rolled out his schedule, beginning tomorrow night, step by step. It did not matter what she would do or how she would respond. The beauty of his plan was that, once he started, she had no way to stop him without dooming herself in the process.

"The result is simple, Ricardito," he concluded. "She will be gone in a matter of weeks and, as president of the Senate, the constitutional succession means that I will take over the presidency."

The blood drained from Ricardo Abdoul's face. He had come to Bogotá believing his brother needed political advice. But he now discovered that what the older Abdoul required was medical attention. What he was proposing was sheer lunacy. Sure, the plan was so over the top that it could even be called brilliant. But thousands, even millions, could be killed in his obsession to get rid of her. Juan Francisco might think he, Ricardo, was a coward, a traitor, or just plain lazy. But he wasn't dumb. He wanted no part of such a plan.

Ricardo Abdoul looked at his brother and stood up.

"This one you are going to do by yourself," he said, with a long last stare at his brother. Then he slowly walked out of the restaurant.

The Cloisters

Manuel Saldivar sat at the small brown table trying desperately to concentrate. He had pushed the white plates in front of him off to one side. Nobody came to clear the table; the restaurant's maitre had given orders not to do anything that might disrupt the focus of the new president's closest advisor.

The Cloisters was the favorite restaurant of a certain, very particular Bogotá crowd—politicians, journalists, government officials, and policy analysts. A gorgeous colonial convent located right across the street from the presidential palace, the Cloisters made up in personality what it lacked in gastronomic finesse.

The food was purely local, Colombian fare. Grilled meats, served with rice and plantains were carried out of the kitchen to the table on wooden carving boards. For dessert, carts were wheeled up and down the aisles with assortments of rice puddings and flans, and all meals ended with wonderfully strong coffees. Clients loved the restaurant's simplicity.

But, the Cloisters' attractiveness was its setting—the circular porticos that centuries ago housed the nuns' living quarters surrounded the hustle and bustle of its tables. Everyone knew who everyone else was. In every corner of the establishment, handshakes and pecky kisses were distributed with largesse. Voices asked if certain articles had been read carefully, whether this or that politician's speech had been accurately scrutinized. It was a loud, energetic place.

Manuel arrived late and asked for a table by himself in a faraway corner. Eating alone in the convent was almost unheard of. Only those truly secure in their position could afford to be seen alone at one of the Cloisters' lunch tables.

Manuel Saldivar ate quickly and cleared away his plates to the far side of the table. He left only his tall glass of passion-fruit juice to his immediate right. Open in front of him to page 147 was a large blue book titled *Constitution of the Republic of Colombia*.

Earlier in the day, the palace's lawyers had tried to explain the steps required to remove a senator's or congressman's immunity. The two young lawyers had snickered at his obvious inability to follow their scholarly analyses of the constitution's mandates. It was true; Manuel had barely understood a word. One of them suggested that Manuel read the appropriate sections on his own and then come back to discuss it further. This sounded like good advice to Manuel, so he borrowed a copy of the constitution from their office and the lawyers pointed him to the appropriate sections.

Manuel Saldivar took the republic's laws across the street for lunch.

It was hard reading for the untrained eye. The legalistic language was twisted and circular. The words were written to sound pompous. Although each sentence of the written document was designed to resolve very specific situations, it often only engendered more questions. That was the problem with Napoleonic law—it tried to foresee every eventuality, but couldn't.

Manuel concentrated. His eyes closed and fluttered. How could any sane person write this way?

He forced himself to read on and focused on Section 187, Clause 9, titled "The Loss of Office Investiture." Wait a minute, Manuel said to himself. This sounded right.

It said: "Elected officials are immune from prosecution and sentencing while invested with the authority of national office. Criminal charges or prosecutorial motions can only be brought against a national officeholder if and when such person is stripped of his or her office and all immunities removed. The president may commence proceedings, but only the Congress, by majority vote, may remove an official's investiture of office. The reasons for removing immunities are a) illicit use of public monies; b) the illegal manipulation of votes in the Congress; and c) extreme absenteeism."

He read the tortured words slowly again. And again. There were nine members of Congress who, beyond any doubt, maintained their power through a political patronage system fed by illegal monies of a family mafia. These men were both symbolic and real-world brakes on the modernization of Colombia. They did not want Colombia to change—their politics could thrive only by keeping the country exactly the way it was.

Manuel went through each name—one by one he compared the criteria specified in Section 187, Clause 9, to what he knew about the politicians' illegal activities. To a certain extent, each one fit the description of wrongful use of public monies and vote manipulation, but these were hard charges to prove.

One name, however, jumped out because of his consistent abuse of the last of the constitution's criteria. Juan Francisco Abdoul. The arrogant son of a bitch was never there. The President of the Senate regularly waltzed around the world for so-called important meetings. Abdoul's missed votes throughout his career were innumerable.

He remembered his sister Susana's call of a few weeks ago. After talking to her, Manuel had pondered how to quietly confirm that it was indeed Abdoul's voice that Chibli had overheard in the Syrian embassy's basement. Manuel did not want Abdoul's informants in government to pick up on the fact that he was asking questions about their boss.

So, Manuel decided on one safe course of action. He telephoned the Ministry of Foreign Affairs to ask if Senator Juan Francisco Abdoul had registered his recent trip to Rome. It occurred to Manuel that Abdoul would want the privilege of diplomatic immunity wherever he traveled. But Colombian law required any official traveling with a Colombian diplomatic passport to register the trip with the Foreign Ministry prior to departure.

"Sure, Mr. Saldivar," said the young diplomat in charge of the ministry's passport section. "Senator Abdoul registered a three-day trip to Italy to attend the European–Latin American Inter-Parliamentary Conference on September 13."

Now, reading the legalistic words again, Manuel could barely contain his excitement. The new legislative session hardly started and Abdoul was again parading around the world. His absences during critical votes would be easy to prove.

Manuel started to reconsider his earlier protestations to Marta. Now, suddenly, he wondered if she hadn't been right all along. This was a fight they could win.

As she did every day, President Marta Pradilla punctually entered the small dining room in the palace's third-floor family quarters. Waiting for her were Manuel Saldivar, her chief of staff and communications director, and Hector Carbone, the taciturn director of the DAS, Colombia's state security agency.

Carbone, a black man from Colombia's northern Caribbean coast, was a tough ex-prosecutor who made his reputation by a successful crackdown on corruption. He had been one of Marta Pradilla's earliest supporters; he had never met the candidate, but he liked what he saw. As a result, in addition to his duties as the head of the DAS, he functioned informally as the president's domestic security advisor.

There were other dining rooms in the presidential palace. President Marta Pradilla hated them because they were too big and ornate. This one, in the family quarters, was comfortable—it sat no more than ten. A small room, it had just a few paintings to warm it up. The art consisted of dead-serious portraits of the heroes of the nation's struggle for national liberation from Spain: Bolívar, Santander, Miranda. She would have loved to replace those dark wartime portraits of generals and admirals with paintings by wonderful young Colombian artists who were enjoying growing international prominence. Manuel Saldivar counseled her to forget about it.

"Somebody in the press will find out that Colombia's first woman president is redecorating her dining room by taking down Colombia's national icons and replacing them with incoherent artwork by dubious modern painters. Marta, we have enough fights. We don't want this one. No redecoration," Manuel Saldivar had said when Pradilla asked his opinion.

The two men stood as the president entered the room. As she walked in, Pradilla smiled and just stabbed her index finger downward indicating that they should sit right back down. They attempted to stand every day, and every day she indicated that they should not.

"Good morning, guys. Gossip first," Pradilla dictated as she put her napkin on her lap.

There was a strange rhythm to these daily 7:00 a.m. briefings. There was rarely any chitchat—Pradilla began her business day early and was a believer in moving quickly through her appointments. Yet, before getting to Manuel's political briefing and to Hector Carbone's national security issues, their morning breakfasts contained a twilight zone which the president called gossip. It was chitchat dressed and delivered in a fast-clipped, formal briefing tone.

Hector Carbone rarely participated in this part of the conversation. He knew this was a chance for Pradilla and her alter ego to engage the day. Pradilla needed the five-minute interaction with Manuel like a car needed fuel before traveling down a highway. In front of Hector, the exchange was never intimate, but it was clearly private. Carbone knew that although his presence was tolerated, he was just a guest, not a participant.

Pradilla and Saldivar were just about finished with their morning-time fun.

"One last thing, Presidente," said Saldivar. "I was at dinner at the German embassy last night. After I said good-bye, I spent some time looking at the sculpture garden they inaugurated a few weeks ago. From behind a sculpture of the god Thor with his lightning rods, I saw the American ambassador get into his car. As the driver opened the door for Ambassador Salzer, I could see Alice Andrews in the backseat. Ms. Andrews runs the Drug Enforcement Agency's programs in Colombia. She carries a big gun in her purse and is a tough-talking woman. By the way, she's also good-looking.

"Now, since the ambassador's wife is back in Washington for the birth of their fourth grandchild, I am presuming that Ms. Andrews was not in the car at midnight for a drug briefing. Moral of the story, you have to make a point of being nice to the Drug Enforcement Agency. It will get you on the ambassador's good side."

"Got it," answered Pradilla with a smile. She made a mental note to ask Agent Andrews over to lunch and giggled to herself as she wondered how she would use such a useful piece of information.

"Hector, your turn, please proceed," said the president to her national security advisor.

Carbone took her through the security preparations for next week's planned visit to Bogotá by Panama's president. It would be a one-day affair, but they would afford Panama's elderly president every scrap of pomp and circumstance they could muster. As Panama was a Colombia's only northern neighbor and also a former part of Colombian territory, it was always important to be on good terms with that nation.

"Let me end with the United States today." This was unusual for Carbone. He either began with the gringos or did not mention them at all during his briefing.

"We continue to get clear signals that the United States will soon present a package on Syria to the UN Security Council. You will need to make a decision as to what our position will be at the Security Council. It's clear to me from my CIA friends that they are preparing for expanded operations in the Middle East."

Saldivar jumped into the conversation. He turned to Pradilla.

"At the inauguration, you asked Stockman for two things: help on trade and a change in Cuba policy. We have not even gotten the courtesy of a response. Abstaining on the Syria vote at the UN is a way to show our displeasure. We should send a message to the United States that we will not be pushed around without anything in return.

"Stockman can't be trusted to do anything for us," Manuel continued. "He is completely obsessed with himself and his war on terrorism. We are supposed to be neighbors. Instead, we are pawns to be used in international organizations and then forgotten. It does not work like that. The world is about dialogue. Our existence needs to be acknowledged."

Saldivar wasn't done. "You called it correctly on the Cuba issue," continued Manuel. "We used a little charm and mischief to force him to take ownership of the meeting with Castro. I confirmed their version of events to a *New York Times* reporter. It was fun to get them to say that meeting Castro was their idea, but it hasn't resulted in any opening in America's Cuba policy. I agree with Hector—we need to start thinking about the UN vote. We should definitely abstain. I would even consider voting against a U.S. proposal on Syria."

President Marta Pradilla held her hand up to stop both advisors. "We will deal with the UN vote at another time. I would remind both of you that this is a morning breakfast briefing, not a complaining session. Stop whining. What else, Hector?"

Both men nodded. They were not used to being cut off by Pradilla. Her irritation at his anti-Stockman tirade was a little strange, Manuel thought to himself. He would remind himself to ask her about it. Not today, though. She clearly had enough of him on this subject.

"Nothing else. That is all that is pressing on my side," said Carbone. He was about to close his files when he remembered one last thing he neglected to mention. The file opened up again.

"There is one last small thing. The French ambassador called yesterday and asked my advice on how to treat Senator Juan Francisco Abdoul's request for full protocolary and diplomatic niceties on his trip to France this evening. Seems like there is a European Chambers of Commerce meeting in Paris that Abdoul will speak at. Anyway, Abdoul requested a car from the French to use during his stay. The senator just can't resist being treated in a manner befitting his rank."

"The ambassador was calling because he knows how you feel about Senator Abdoul. He wants to make sure you are okay if they treat him with respect. It was quite delicate of him to check in with me. I took the high road on the issue and told him that we had no objections to France treating the president of the Senate like the senior government official he is."

"That is fine, Hector," Pradilla reassured him. "It kills me to see this criminal given all these diplomatic niceties, but you made the right decision. Seems strange, though, that he would go while the Senate is in session. Manuel, aren't they debating social security tomorrow and Friday?"

Saldivar did not hear her. He was still staring hard at Carbone. Shit. Did he hear this correctly? Abdoul was going back to Europe? It would be his second European jaunt in less than twenty days.

Two divergent thoughts went through Manuel's mind. The first was that this was one more proof-point to argue Abdoul's "extreme absenteeism." But, something else worried Manuel. It was just plain weird that Abdoul would again take off to Europe in the middle of legislative debates. Something was wrong.

"Manuel?" Pradilla repeated the question. What was wrong with Saldivar this morning? the president asked herself. "Manuel, aren't they debating the social security bill this week in the Senate?"

Saldivar got himself under control. He had to tell her about Abdoul, but not with Carbone. He decided there and then to go through his usual fifteen minutes of domestic political issues in less than sixty seconds.

"Yes, forgive me, the Senate is debating social security this week. It seems like our recommendation of raising pension payments will be okay. Also important this week is the announcement of your plan to open six hundred high-technology learning centers throughout the country. I had a thought about how to announce this: What if you did a press conference via the Internet. In other words, you would take and answer questions in Instant Messenger formats. I think that would be a nice, modern touch on a high-tech issue."

"I love that idea. Go with it," said Pradilla. "Anything else?"

"Nope, need to make it fast today."

"Fine, many thanks."

All three got up and packed their papers. Carbone said his good-byes. Manuel gladly allowed him to go out first. As soon as he was out of earshot, Manuel swiveled back around to the president.

"Do you have another couple of minutes? I need to tell you something. It is important."

She looked at her watch and remembered her 8:00 a.m. meeting. She would have to be late. He may have gotten on her nerves earlier, but she never said no to Manuel. She again jabbed her index finger in the direction of his chair and arched her eyebrows. Manuel understood that the gestures meant she had some time.

"I need to talk to you about Abdoul. First, let me tell you the good news. I may have found a constitutional mechanism to strip away his immunity that would be hard to argue against. I need to check it with the lawyers, but these two consecutive trips to Europe may be all we need."

Manuel briefed her in detail on the constitution's prohibition against "extreme absenteeism." Marta Pradilla smiled broadly.

"Now, let me tell you what worries me," Manuel continued. "We may also have a serious problem with Abdoul. I don't know what it is, but I smell trouble."

Saldivar told the president of all that happened three weeks earlier in Rome. He told her of his sister's call and Chibli's story of a Colombian senator in the basement of the Syrian embassy in Rome in the evening. He told her that the only Colombian senator in Rome on that exact day was Abdoul.

"I looked up all his press releases, and there is no mention of anything with Syria. He has a large Syrian Arab constituency in Barranquilla. Why would he not mention the visit with the Syrian ambassador? I asked our people in Barranquilla, and they have heard of nothing that Abdoul is planning to do politically with the Syrians.

"The whole thing is strange. If he was planning some big event with the Syrians, people in Barranquilla would know about it. In his neck of the woods, an affiliation with the Arab world is a good thing. Why is this so quiet?"

Pradilla looked at him closely. "So, you are now concerned about this second European trip, right? It worries you that he is going back in the middle of one of the most important political debates in the Senate? Now I understand why it is that you got so lost during Hector's briefing."

"Look, Presidente, this man wants to kill you. Figuratively and literally. I was concerned with my sister's story, but then the usual daily political crises consumed me and I proceeded to forget about it. But with Abdoul going back to Europe tonight, I am convinced something is wrong."

Pradilla knew that Manuel was not exaggerating. Juan Francisco Abdoul was a dangerous man. Politics bought him immunity from the police and from justice. Criminality brought him the money to buy the politics. It was a neat concentric circle of power. Abdoul had seen a great future for himself and his family with his ruse to run his far less astute brother straight into the presidency. Only, Marta Pradilla had gotten in the way.

"He is leaving tonight," said Pradilla. "Can we get Carbone and the DAS on it? Can we get him followed in France?"

Manuel shook his head. "Marta, the DAS is not the FBI. They can't turn around an international surveillance operation in less than twenty-four hours. Especially not on this guy. I don't know whom Abdoul may have bought inside the DAS. I trust Carbone, but we have not been around long enough to know who is on our side and who isn't."

President Pradilla stared at Manuel, lost in thought. Suddenly she turned around and grabbed the phone on the sideboard table. The Casa de Nariño operators answered without delay.

"Get me the French ambassador immediately," she ordered.

Manuel started asking her what she was doing when the phone rang back. Ambassador Jean Claude Pepin was on the line.

"*Cher* Jean Claude," cooed Marta into the phone. She knew him well. The ambassador had taken a particular interest in Marta two years ago and was the foreign diplomat closest to her. She was, after all, schooled in France, and perfectly bilingual. The ambassador had made her a press darling in France and, not coincidentally, impressed French reporters and editors with his closeness to the chic new president of Colombia.

She got straight to the point, in unaccented French.

"Jean Claude, I wanted to personally call to thank you for your delicacy in contacting Hector Carbone about Senator Abdoul's trip. Your concern for our view is gratifying and appreciated. I want to also reiterate what Hector told you today: Senator Abdoul is president of the Senate and he deserves and should get all the diplomatic privileges accorded to somebody of his stature.

"I do, however, have something to ask of you in regards to the senator's trip, Jean Claude," she continued. "I understand he will be in France for only one night. As he has asked the French government to provide a car and driver for his quick trip, would there be any chance for you to let us know if the senator deviates in any way from his predetermined schedule? You see, we have recently learned some things about the senator that concern us. I only ask this of you since he already requested your help and you will . . . how can I say? . . . have people around him anyway. But, Jean Claude, I will need to know of any change in Abdoul's itinerary in real time—I need to know about it as it happens. Can you help me?"

There was a half second of silence. But bar that slight hesitation, if Ambassador Pepin was taken aback, he did not show it. "Madame Presidente, you have our cooperation." He did not have to say that what she was asking was highly unusual. He was French. Subtle. All these things went unsaid.

"Should you need to get in touch with me during the senator's trip to Paris, Jean Claude, you can call me or Manuel Saldivar. I would be grateful if we were the only ones to have the pleasure of talking to you on this issue. Jean Claude, *je te remercie infiniement.*"

She hung up. She looked at Manuel with the smile that made her irresistible. "Abdoul will now be followed by the French Sûrété. They are even tougher than the FBI. It does not get better than that. If he does something, we will know about it."

Manuel Saldivar's Apartment
Bogotá, October 15
1:23 a.m.

Some forty-two hours later, the phone rang. Manuel Saldivar was fast asleep, but the phone kept ringing. He opened first one eye and then the other. His left arm was completely asleep and tingling so badly that he could hardly move it, so he twisted his body to allow his right arm to make a motion for the phone on his night table. The receiver came to his ear and, before he could say anything, he heard a dial tone. The phone kept ringing. Shit, it's the cell phone. Jumping out of bed to look for the mobile phone woke him up once and for all. Manuel found the phone in the pocket of his pants.

"Manuel, bon soir, c'est Jean Claude Pepin," said the French ambassador cheerfully. Manuel noted that his alarm clock confirmed the sad news that he had been awakened at 1:23 in the morning.

"I am sorry to wake you. But, I must ask you to pass along some information to Marta. Are you awake? Good. Yesterday morning, Senator Abdoul arrived in Paris, checked into the Hotel George V. A few hours later he went to the Chambers of Commerce, attended the conference, and gave his speech. He went to an afternoon cocktail party. He finished the day with an early dinner with a young Colombian woman who works at UNESCO. I have her name, should you want it. He then went to his hotel, accompanied by Mademoiselle. She left at about three in the morning."

Manuel asked himself whether the ambassador harbored a previously unknown deep personal dislike for him. It was now 1:30 in the bloody morning and this Frog was forcing him to listen to a recitation of Abdoul's political, gastronomic, and sexual activities in Paris. He was awake, though. So he listened on.

"So far, Manuel, nothing interesting. That is why I did not contact you all day. However, during the last few hours, things have changed. And the events are unusual enough to warrant calling you."

Manuel was now rethinking his disdainful opinion of this Frenchman.

"It is now 7:30 in the morning in Paris. Unexpectedly, the senator left his hotel—checking out—at 6:00 a.m. Before departing, he left instructions that the concierge do two things: First, to call Air France to reconfirm his 4:00 p.m. return flight to Bogotá. And second, to call the chauffeur provided by the French government to tell him that he would not be needed.

"Nonetheless," continued Pepin, "since we had asked that the senator be followed, our services were kind enough to continue their watchfulness, even without his official driver. Senator Abdoul took a taxi to Charles de Gaulle Airport and purchased a round-trip ticket on Alitalia flight 468, an 8:15 a.m. departure to Rome. According to the itinerary he purchased, he will spend less than one and a half hours in Rome before getting on Air France flight 933, departing back to Paris at 12:48 p.m. He has just checked in for the Rome flight. No luggage. Presently, Senator Abdoul is standing in line to go through security."

Manuel was speechless. Both because of the news and of how the ambassador reported it. Marta Pradilla had requested real-time information from the ambassador. She had said these guys were good, but this was amazing!

"Mr. Ambassador, I don't know what to say. Obviously, I am gratified by your government's ability to comply with the president's request. She will be very grateful."

"Manuel, you really must come to France," chuckled Ambassador Pepin. "We do more than cook well, you know. We are actually quite efficient. I will let you go. If you need more from us, call me. Anything at all. Manuel, we all want Marta to succeed." The ambassador hung up.

Manuel Saldivar did not know what to do next. Should he wake up Marta? Should he try to have Abdoul detained? But for what? Hello, Senator, you are under arrest for doing something suspicious? Abdoul did something suspicious every day of his life.

What the hell was Abdoul doing in Rome for an hour? Who was he meeting? This is what Manuel was thinking as he realized he needed to go to the bathroom.

But he held on until deciding upon a path of action. It was as if his need to relieve himself forced some tough, on-the-spot, choices. He hated where his mind was going. It went against every fiber in his body, every bit of sound judgment. But he knew also there was no other way. If he did not act now, he would never be able to find out why Abdoul was going to Rome.

He dropped his cell phone on the bed and crawled across the bed to his landline. He dialed the fourteen numbers needed to reach his sister's cellular phone. She would probably be in her car on the way to school.

The phone was answered on the other side of the Atlantic Ocean, and all Manuel heard was the blasting of car horns. Roman traffic. He had seen it on a trip to visit Susana. The deafening noise of the Roman rush hour was a mind-altering experience. Romans drove with permanent hand pressure on their horns. He could hear his sister's voice screaming in the phone.

"Susana, it's Manuel. Can you hear me?"

"Hi, little brother. Yes, Chibli and I are on our way to school. Hold on. Let me shut the windows so the noise does not blast us away. How are you? Girlfriends?" It was the usual Susana chitchat. She always wanted to know about girlfriends.

"Susana, you have to listen to me. It's nearly two o'clock in the morning here and we may be in some real trouble. I don't know who else to turn to."

"Wait, little brother, I am parking the car. You sound really worried. How can I help?"

Manuel tried to synthesize the story. After their call a few weeks ago, Manuel had done some investigating and found nothing. Now Abdoul was in Europe again. And was on his way to Italy for an hour-long visit. He needed to know why.

"So here is what I am asking: I need you to go to the airport and wait for that flight to arrive. But be careful to keep your distance, since he may recognize you as a Colombian. You know, politicians have a nose for constituents. In any case, can you follow him? See what he does? He is clearly meeting with somebody. The question is, who?"

He wasn't done. "One more thing, sister. Can you buy a ticket on Air France 933 to Paris? I need you to get on that plane with him. I need to make sure that we know what he does once he gets to Paris. And I have no way of doing that without you."

Susana laughed. "My little brother wants to turn me into James Bond. I never thought I would see this. Usually you are so overprotective, even though you're the youngest. Now you want to draft me into Her Presidency's Secret Service. Hold on a minute."

Manuel could hear muffled conversation. Susana was telling Chibli everything. He knew she would, and concluded that it was fine. If he had the audacity to involve his sister in something dangerous, he would do it on her terms. And Manuel understood that this meant telling Chibli everything.

"Manuel, we want to help you. But Chibli is asking me if you understand the obvious. It is most probable that Abdoul is coming to again meet the Syrian ambassador here. He needs you to know that this ambassador is a very powerful man in Syria. If Abdoul and Omar bin Talman are involved together, it is probably something very bad. I guess what we are trying to say is that if you want us to look after Mr. Abdoul, that is fine. But you need to understand that if the purpose of the visit is to see bin Talman, you are going to need better help than two school-teachers."

Manuel knew what Chibli was saying. It was polite talk for "you are in way over your head." He knew this was true, but he needed their help now. They had to get him through the next couple of hours.

"Susana, I know this is Latino-style, homemade rice and beans espionage. It's completely stupid to ask your big sister to play spy. But I am in the government of an underdeveloped country, and you are all I have for the moment. Do not call me on my cell phone. Use the Casa de Nariño operators. I'm going there now. I love you a lot." Manuel hung up.

Jesus, he really needed to pee now. Manuel ran to the bathroom, stood over the toilet for over sixty seconds, washed up, got dressed, and went downstairs. Like all senior government officials, Manuel had a group of bodyguards and a chauffeur. But neither was there at 3:00 a.m. Manuel shrugged. He went to the garage and stepped into his car. He had not driven himself since the campaign. He wondered if he would remember how. As he left the garage and turned onto the street, he noticed the police guard in front of his door. In his rearview mirror, he could see the guard in a total panic at the sight of Saldivar leaving the house unescorted. Manuel chuckled. Don't worry, Mr. Guard, thought Manuel. At that hour, guerrillas, criminals, and narco-traffickers are all sound asleep.

Manuel drove at breakneck speed—not because he had to, but because it was fun. Bogotá was a busy place most of the day and night. To be able to speed his way to the presidential palace, barely encountering another car, was a rare pleasure.

He swerved right into the palace parking lot and found the gates locked. He thought of honking, but then realized that he might wake up the building's sole permanent resident. So he got out of the car to look for a security guard. He found one at the main door of the building.

"Hi, sorry about the hour," Manuel said to the sleepy police officer. He tossed the man his car keys. "My car is sitting in front of the gates to the palace entrance. I need you to find somebody to bring the car in before a police patrol comes and thinks it's a car bomb. Then I need you to tell the operators that I am inside the building. I am expecting a call."

Manuel sat at his desk. He turned on only one light in his office that bled a yellowish tint over his desk. He knew this evening might change his life. He did not yet know how. But he could feel it. He hardly moved. Nearly an hour passed inside his office. It was now 4:15 a.m. Abdoul was landing in Rome.

Time inched by. Manuel tried to close his eyes and sleep, but he couldn't relax. He tried to do the crossword puzzle in yesterday's newspaper, but couldn't concentrate. He went on line to read the morning's news, but couldn't follow the stories.

The phone rang. He looked at his watch: 5:50 a.m. in Bogotá; 11:50 a.m. in Rome.

Manuel hesitated for a second and picked up the phone. "Manuel, this is Chibli. Abdoul came off his flight about one hour and ten minutes ago. He stepped into the terminal and was met by a man it took me a while to recognize. They walked together to an illegally parked Mercedes 450 SL with diplomatic plates. Somebody was in the back of the car. Abdoul got in and spoke to the person for less than five minutes, then got out. The driver opened the trunk of the car and took out two suitcases that looked quite heavy. He handed the suitcases to Abdoul, then got back into the car and drove away."

"What happened then?" asked Manuel.

"Then Abdoul calmly called a porter, and they walked the bags to the Air France counter. Abdoul checked in for the flight to Paris. Susana has a ticket on that flight. We had to buy a business ticket to make sure she gets off the plane ahead of him in Paris. Otherwise she could lose him."

"Chibli, did you get the license plate number of the car that Abdoul got into?"

"No, I did not need to. I recognized the car, and then it was clear who was waiting inside the terminal for Abdoul. The man is Hamid Tarwa, the driver of the Syrian ambassador in Rome—and that was the ambassador's car. I presume the ambassador was in the car.

"Manuel, Omar bin Talman is ruthless," Chibli pleaded. "He is the worst of my country now involved with the worst of yours. Do not go any further by yourself. You must get real help. From people who know what they are doing. Anyway, now Susana is on the plane, and she will let you know what Abdoul does in Paris. After that, you will be on your own. Get yourself help, Manuel. You need it."

Manuel was silent. Something very bad was happening, but he did not know what. Dealing with Colombians was one thing. Quite another was involving himself in Middle East affairs. Chibli was more than right. He needed help. He just did not yet know where to find it.

Casa de Nariño

Bogotá, October 15
6:02 a.m.

══

Manuel did not hesitate any longer. Time to wake up the president of Colombia. Ten seconds after Chibli's phone call, he picked up the receiver again and asked the operator to ring the president's bedroom. There were some seconds of palpable hesitation on the part of the Casa de Nariño operator.

"Please do it now," Manuel told the man quietly. A few seconds later he heard President Marta Pradilla answer the line with an easy voice.

"Marta, sorry to call this early. I apologize for waking you up."

"Manuel, give me a break. I've read all the newspapers and now I'm online reading the *New York Times.*"

"I need to see you. Now. Can I come up?"

"Up?" asked Marta, obviously confused. That meant he was already inside the building at nearly six in the morning. That fact alone told her how serious this was. She knew how hard it was for Manuel Saldivar to make the daily 7:00 a.m. briefing breakfast.

"Absolutely. I will order coffee. You will have to accept me in a robe, though."

Manuel went down the hallway and called the elevator. It was funny, he thought to himself. The two of them had gone through so much together in the last months. The campaign. The inauguration. The first two months of the presidency. Every day brought them closer together. But this would be the first time he would see her in nightclothes. He was sort of curious.

She had obviously alerted security and the kitchen about his arrival, because the burly security officer on duty in the hall just waved as he walked by. Although security knew his position and understood how close he was to president, he wondered if they would allow him through at this hour without her approval. He knocked on the door of her bedroom suite.

Marta answered the door. It wasn't quite the disheveled robe she warned him about. She was dressed in silken, dark-blue pajamas. They looked more like men's pj's. The shirt was collarless, buttoned up to the neck in a Chinese, Mao Tsetung–like fashion. Her light brown hair was twisted up in a bun and fixed in place with a chopstick. How did this woman always manage to look this attractive? Manuel asked himself.

She did her index-finger-pointing thing toward the chair, indicating that he sit on the loveseat in the small foyer outside of the bedroom itself. He did not hesitate—it was shortly after 6:00 a.m. and Manuel was already exhausted. He started right into the story.

He told her everything, leaving out no details.

"Marta, there is one more thing," Manuel concluded. "Chibli and Susana have said it to me twice in the past hours: We are in over our heads. It is one thing to deal with Abdoul. He is a criminal, but he is our kind of criminal—a Colombian, a known entity. But now we know that he is tied to a Middle East state that has known terrorist links and is on the verge of being singled out by the United States as its next military target. This is beyond our frame of reference."

President Marta Pradilla soaked in the information quietly. Then she slowly started to speak.

"I want to break this down into its component parts, Manuel. First, let's speculate as to what is in those suitcases. Let me go first. A Colombian politician that is a mafia family leader does not have much to offer the Syrians except for money. So the question is, what has he purchased? The only answer I have is that he has gotten some sort of sophisticated material to use against the Colombian state to get at me. It could be eavesdropping and spying equipment. Or it could be bomb-making materials to blow up something important in Bogotá. Clearly, it is something to use against our administration. Do you agree with this?"

Manuel answered quickly. "Yes, I agree. Short of money, there is nothing that a Syrian government would want from a Colombian. And clearly Abdoul's motivation is to do everything in his power to hurt you."

"Okay, good," said President Pradilla. "Now, the question is, what we can do about it? He lands in Bogotá this evening on Air France, right? Can we arrest him at the airport?"

"For what?" answered Manuel? "Possession of two suitcases? The man has done nothing out of the ordinary. We happen to know that he met with a dangerous man from Syria, but Abdoul is of Syrian descent. If we let on that the meeting in Rome is the reason we suspect him, most people will tell us that meeting with the Syrians is no big deal. There are also clear political consequences to stopping him at the airport. What if we stop him and find nothing? We will look like idiots and the press will roast us. It could be a tough blow within weeks of beginning your administration."

Manuel was not finished. "Anyway, it may not be legally possible to stop him.

There is no way to get an arrest warrant against him without some serious proof of wrongdoing."

"Yeah, I imagine you are right. Okay, here is what we do. It's time to get the DAS involved. You are right that they are not the FBI or the Mossad, but they are good enough. And Carbone is completely trustworthy. He was a fabulous prosecutor in Santa Marta. He impresses me. He doesn't seem to mind people asking questions—even a woman. That is a good sign. Manuel, we have to take the risk."

Manuel looked doubtful, but he knew that they needed some professional help. There was no choice but to trust the DAS.

"We will see Carbone at the 7:00 a.m. meeting; that is in less than twenty minutes," she repeated. "We'll tell him we have two requests. First, he needs to know that we have been given serious intelligence that the Abdoul family is planning something out-of-the ordinary, possibly against the government. He needs to help us confirm what that might be. The second one is a lot more delicate: He has to put Senator Abdoul under some type of surveillance from the moment he lands this evening. It's less about following Abdoul than about following those suitcases. We need to know what is in those suitcases."

"There is one thing I would not do yet," continued Manuel. "Don't tell Carbone about the Syrian link and what we know from my sister. I don't want to start a file on her at the DAS. And I don't want him to feel compelled to start asking the Italians and the Americans for information."

She thought about it and disagreed. "No, Manuel, this is a team. If we do not work together there is a strong chance that we could fail. And this is way too important to take that risk. We have to trust Carbone. He is talented, he's a professional, and he's on our side."

She looked at her watch. It was twenty minutes to seven. Manuel read her mind; she wanted to be on time.

He left quickly, took the elevator one floor down to his office to collect his papers, gulped down a small coffee, and walked right back for the return trip to the third-floor residential area. He stepped off the elevator and walked slowly to the dining room in the family quarters. He was in no rush, since he knew she would be late. As he opened the door, he was surprised to see the president already at the table with Carbone. Waiters were serving breakfast. How the hell did she get ready this quickly?

"Late night, Manuel?" said President Marta Pradilla in the most casual of tones as she pointed her index finger to his usual chair.

The president asked the waiters to serve everything at once and leave coffee on the table. She did not want to be interrupted. Once the staff distributed the breakfast, Marta Pradilla and Manuel briefed Hector Carbone on all that they knew.

Casa de Nariño
Bogotá, October 15
8:06 a.m.

═══

"Manuel, its Susana. This is sort of fun. But there is way too much stress. I keep thinking I'm going to lose him. You know, when I got off the airplane, I could not see him with all the people in the terminal. And I—"

Manuel interrupted. "Susana. Please, tell me what has happened."

She smiled. He might be a big-shot government official, but she knew her chatter always drove him nuts.

"Yes, no problem. I'm in Terminal 2F at Charles de Gaulle Airport. I'm at the gate of the Air France flight to Bogotá and Abdoul is at the coffee bar just down the hall. He got off the Rome flight, went to the first-class transit desk and checked in for this flight. He introduced himself as the president of the Colombian Senate and asked for somebody from Air France Special Services to meet him at the gate. A nice lady came just a few minutes ago. I was close enough to hear it all. Abdoul told her that he was carrying critically important government papers in two suitcases and it was imperative to ensure that they transferred safely from the Rome flight to this flight. She asked him for his baggage tags. Five minutes later, she came back and confirmed the bags were on the airplane."

"Susana, has he done anything unusual. Has he made any phone calls? Did he talk to anybody?" asked Manuel.

"Except for the Special Services desk . . . Hold on, they are announcing the flight, I can't even hear myself talk."

There was a void on the phone line that slowly filled with the sounds of the Paris airport. First in French. Now in heavily accented English.

"*Madames et Monsieurs,* this is the first boarding announcement for Air France flight 456, nonstop service to Caracas, Venezuela, and on to Bogotá, Colombia. We will begin by boarding our first-class passengers and any passengers requiring special assistance. Air France wishes you a good flight."

Susana's voice took over again.

"Anyway, what I was saying was that he spoke to no one and made no calls. He looks relaxed. I can see him paying for his coffee. I'll wait until he boards,

Manuel, and then I'm getting out of here to buy myself a ticket back to Rome. There is nothing else I can do at this point, right?"

Manuel agreed. "Just wait until you see them close the door of the airplane. Then go back, okay? You've been the most wonderful sister. I'm sorry I did this to you, but you are completely amazing. I am going to research what medal I can give you. There must be something like the Medal of the Patriotic Citizen or the Order of the Good Sister. I'll figure it out," laughed Manuel.

"Pay for this damned business-class ticket is what you need to do! I'm a teacher, remember," teased Susana.

He hung up, promising to pay in both money and brotherly hugs. Manuel wasted no time and walked to the president's office. The president's secretary told him that Marta was busy with the mayor of Medellín, Colombia's second-largest city. He thought of waiting but instead wrote her a note. "He's on the airplane with his things. Landing tonight."

He asked Mabel, the president's secretary, to bring the paper in right away.

The rest of his day melted away. He went from one event to the next. He only saw President Pradilla once that day, at the announcement of a special presidential commission to study energy supply issues for the Andean areas of the country. For nearly six months of the year, there was just not enough water in the highland region's hydroelectric reservoirs. As a result, the government was often forced to ration electricity. Marta Pradilla said this would be among the first things she would tackle. And she was true to her word.

She looked his way right after her speech. It was perfectly normal for them to huddle at the beginning or end of an event. Everybody knew that the press would hit her on the way out of the meeting. They chatted for a minute about what the highlights were for the press. Just before she walked out the door, she leaned over to him.

"Carbone is on top of it. You have to start trusting this guy," she told him.

So he hoped. The DAS was a strange institution. The Colombian DAS— Departamento Administrativo de Seguridad or, in English, Administrative Security Department—was a mixture of the CIA, FBI, and Secret Service all rolled up into one. They served at the pleasure of the president. Three thousand strong, the DAS was lean and tight. It tended to be free of the bureaucratic and corrupting political pressures that too often afflicted the far larger military and police.

The DAS was in charge of presidential protection and special investigations. The DAS did not look into robberies, murders, and common crimes. Its purview was crimes against the state—things like terrorism, narco-trafficking, guerrillas, major corruption, and some particularly heinous homicides. Tough duties. As a result, it was also Colombia's link to Interpol.

The DAS was fanatical about protecting the president of the Republic. DAS agents were not the only intelligence-gathering network in the Colombian state. The police and the armed forces also had intelligence directorates. But, while those other organizations did lots of other things too, the DAS was solely dedicated to intelligence and information-gathering about security threats to Colombia and its president. During the harrowing days of Pablo Escobar, the vicious drug kingpin of the Medellín cartel, then-president Gaviria and his director of the DAS became the first- and second-most threatened Colombians in history. Escobar had more than one hundred contracts out on their lives.

Notwithstanding all this power, reach, and access to Colombia's presidents, the DAS remained in the shadows. Its directors rarely made press comments. They were not seen in public. They hardly ever issued a report. No, the director of the DAS worked privately. In past administrations, the director tended to arrive at the presidential palace late at night to brief the president verbally over a drink. Decisions were made in the dark privacy of Casa de Nariño's third-floor suites and remained unknown to most people, even the closest of presidential advisors.

The whole thing bothered Manuel. It offended his sophisticated sense of openness and transparency. He believed strongly that a real democracy could not abide the informal, late-night decision making that the DAS wanted of the president. He understood that every country needed an efficient intelligence service to protect it from enemies inside and out. But the DAS was too shadowy, too murky. It lacked public accountability.

He had to admit, though, that Hector Carbone was an unusual appointment. Usually, DAS directors were picked from a roster of retired police generals and commanders. Marta, however, specifically wanted a civilian. As prosecutor, Carbone had a successful record convicting corrupt politicians and unsavory bureaucrats. Marta admired the man because he took on the status quo. Carbone was from Santa Marta on Colombia's northern coast. He was also black. While most Colombians were of some sort of mixed heritage, there was no mixing in Carbone's genetics. He was 100 percent black—"like carbon," they said in Santa Marta. And he was one of the first black men appointed to a prominent national position in Colombia's history.

Manuel admired Carbone, the man. But within just a very few weeks in office, he came to realize that Marta's relationship with Carbone was one of the few places off-limits to him. He knew that Carbone, like his predecessors, started to come late at night to the palace. He knew that sometimes Carbone was in Marta's limousine on the way back from an event. Those were the times he was not given a ride. He tried not to take it personally. These were affairs of state.

So, for the rest of the day, he tried to force himself not to think of Abdoul or

Carbone or the suitcases. A long drink at five o'clock with an incredibly sexy, blond, thirty-five-year-old reporter from the BBC made the job easier. This woman had everything going for her: just the right twinkle in her eye; a sexy, stylish sense of clothing; a great body; and tons of smarts. She was in Colombia to do an extended TV segment on Pradilla. The British TV network had promised a thirty-minute special on Colombia's new president—an amazingly generous amount of time for television.

Manuel ended up taking Maggie James on a tour of the palace. He peppered his mastery of Colombia's history with details about Marta's work, rest, and eating habits. He probably said far too much. But he could not shut up. This reporter had all of that sly wit that came with higher-end Brits. But, with her lithe and breasty body, she also had looks that were oh so rarely part of the English, shall we say, makeup.

He was in the process of saying good-bye to Maggie when he got a call on the internal phone. He looked at his watch. It was close to 6:00 p.m. He answered fast and heard Marta's voice.

"Please come in," she ordered and immediately hung up.

He pushed Maggie out of the door and put her in the capable hands of his driver, Alfonso. Manuel promised to do everything possible to extend tomorrow's thirty-minute interview with Marta a little longer. The moment Alfonso turned the corner with Maggie in tow, Manuel turned on his heels, ran past the elevator, and bounded into the ornate office of the president.

It was a classy place. In a palace that was a seesaw of magnificent taste and offensive drab, the presidential office was a feast for the eyes. Paneled in dark caoba wood and furnished with colonial antiques, it was formal but not heavy. Original works by classic and modern Colombian masters hung on the walls and sculptures stood on side tables. The art was majestic in quality.

He noticed two things immediately. First, Marta was not alone. Second, she was not happy.

He turned and saw Hector Carbone sitting on one of the antique chairs against the walls. Manuel never actually thought this chair was designed for sitting in. It was one of those delicate colonial antiques that slid tightly against a wall; a piece designed for observation, not interaction.

Manuel walked over to shake the director's hand. Carbone did not stand. It was not a sign of disrespect. It was worry.

"Director, please tell Manuel what you have told me," ordered President Pradilla.

"Air France 456 landed in Bogotá at 5:23 p.m. We had men stationed in the terminal and outside the airplane in case Senator Abdoul left without going through immigration formalities. Manuel, Abdoul was not on that plane," said Carbone.

Manuel felt sick. How was it possible that Susana had made such a mistake? She promised him that she would watch the plane's doors close. He replayed his conversation with his sister again in his mind. Suddenly, his brainwaves skidded to a stop. He remembered the airport's loudspeakers overpowering his phone conversation with Susana. The Air France gate agent had announced the flight to Bogotá with a stopover in Caracas, Venezuela.

"He got off in Caracas!" Manuel spit out. He thought himself a genius for figuring this out.

Carbone was well ahead of him. "Yes, we believe that is correct. We are confirming this. We will also confirm if the suitcases went with him."

He was not done. "If, as we all suspect, the answers to both those questions is yes, we have a problem. Venezuela is in a state of total disarray. Abdoul can buy himself into and out of the country, leaving us with no ability to monitor and control his entrance into Colombia. There are thousands of miles of coastline, plains, and high Andes borders with Venezuela. Abdoul can fly in on a small airplane; he can take a jeep or jump on a boat."

"Director, what exactly are you saying?" asked the president.

"I am saying that you should consider Juan Francisco Abdoul as already having effectively entered Colombia with his two suitcases. Crossing the border from Venezuela is simply not an obstacle for a man as rich and resourceful as he is. We do not know where he is or how to find him. At this point, we have absolutely no way of controlling his actions," said the director of the DAS.

PART IX
THE UNITED STATES

Dear Marta,

My God, your description of the day in Bali was deeply moving! Clearly the girl had an indelible effect on you. One day, if you are comfortable talking about it, I would like to know how you survived the brutality of your parents' deaths. I know what happened; but I can't even imagine how it changed you.

I have to confess that, since I've met you, you have been uniquely single-minded in asking me questions and putting me in situations that require a lot of thought. You're new at this, but you will find that thinking is difficult in our job. We are overscheduled and move with a fire hose from one flame to another. So, it's hard to gather my wits when you start throwing questions up that take time to think about.

Miranda. Where do I start? She was my teenage love. We went to high school together—I was a year older. I invited her to my senior prom. I applied to Stanford (where Julia is now) and Yale and Johns Hopkins. I got into all those places, but decided to go to college at the University of Nebraska because I dared not move far away from Miranda.

I almost have no memory of life without Miranda. She was part of me. With me. She believed in me—without questions. She listened a lot; but her answers were short. She helped me immensely, but you could not call what she gave me "advice." Often, she would listen to my complaining for a half hour and then would say, "Why don't you ask so and so?" And that would be just the right person to talk to.

I guess she would have been a very different presidential wife than Hillary Clinton.

Miranda was a wonderful mother to Julia. She tried to pass on so many of those values that we believe are good, healthy, and sane. Yes, those small-town values of Moravian, Lutheran Nebraska. They may not prepare you for the big world, but they hold you together from the inside.

She's been gone nearly three years now. I miss her deeply. But I have also come to the conclusion that there was a lot left unsaid and unaddressed. We were together because we were supposed to be together, and sometimes I fear that it was not because we asked ourselves every day whether it was right to be together. It is true that in the end, with Julia older, we did not engage much.

Damn you, Marta. This stuff is hard! Hard to admit to yourself and hard to speak of with another woman; particularly one so different from my wife.

I would not have expected to talk to anybody about this and certainly not to you. I hardly know where you come from. I haven't seen your home. I can't imagine having parents killed by terrorists. Nothing about you is remotely similar to my background.

Yet, there is something so very appealing about that fact that you recognize no boundaries or limits.

Enough of this.

I think of you fondly,

J.

TO: ManFromNebraska (Reply)
FROM: BeautifulColombia
RE: A Return Invitation

Dear John,

It seems strange that you cultivate this image of tough impenetrability. You are not that way at all!

The way you describe your Miranda is beautiful. You say "life has no memories without her." As a woman, I can't think of anything more flattering or moving than this.

You sound almost embarrassed to admit to yourself that life also changes and that your relationship with her changed too. Miranda and you probably would have always been together—it was the way things were determined to be. But now that destiny has taken her away, it is not wrong to ask yourself what was missing or what else you want.

We all change, John.

A few days ago you asked where I would take you in Colombia. Yes, it's Cartagena. The city's beautiful, even magical. But it's also gritty, noisy, and dirty. All those things and more.

Behind the walls of the colonial city lies the whitewashed town. Cartagena is my grandmother's city. But it's not what I imagine your grandmother's well-organized Moravian community in Nebraska to be like.

Cartagena is a jumble of humanity, activity, and life. Controlled chaos.

Cafés, rum bars, restaurants, street salesmen, elegant shops mix together with filth and poverty all through the night. It's a hard place to quantify. One thing is a constant—music is everywhere in Cartagena, all the time.

Speaking of music, we Colombians are hooked on music, and we have great musicians. I will send you some CDs of Carlos Vives and Juanes. And one of our top Colombian stars, Shakira, is making it big-time in the United States. She just put out her second English album.

So, be warned: If you come with me to Cartagena, you will have to dance late into the night. Dancing is a national obsession in Colombia.

I appreciate the invitation to Nebraska. I would love to see a U.S. presidential campaign up close. Perhaps you'll let me be a volunteer in Nebraska on the next one?

On second thought, that might not play so well at home, no? I can see the local newspaper writing their story: "President John Stockman today returned to Nebraska in the company of his new volunteer, the former Miss Universe who is today president of Colombia." Hmmm? I'm not sure that sounds very helpful.

Speaking of helpful, I need to appeal to you again on Cuba. I read in the *New York Times* online edition that you are about to receive a 500-page report from a blue-ribbon panel on Cuba. And, while the report hasn't yet been published, we all know that it advocates retightening whatever small opening there has been for travel, and for sending medicine and food, to Cuba.

Why are you doing this? What can this possibly get you? Why wasn't I or President Flamengo of Brazil or President Granada of Mexico on your blue-ribbon panel? This is our business too; after all, we live in the same damn neighborhood. Why do you appeal to this narrow constituency in Florida rather than the broader community of our Americas? The communist regime in Cuba is still there after four decades and you want to pretend that more of the same will get it out? What does it take to understand that something new is required?

If you approve your commission's recommendations, you will give Castro another ten years of life. You will make miserable those of us struggling to be your friends, while our voters will see you as just a bully. We have all told you that your Cuba policy is a forty-five-year failure. I am just the last one in a long line. But friends' views seem not to matter. Yet, you will want our support later, behind you for your causes in Iraq and Syria and Bosnia and so on; and you will be surprised when you don't get it.

Why is it so difficult to break new ground in politics, John?

Marta

TO: BeautifulColombia
FROM: ManFromNebraska (Reply)
RE: Your Note

Dear Marta,

Today I will do two things of transcendental, fundamental, and consequential importance. First, I plan to strip away the United States citizenship of my national security advisor, Nelson Cummins, and then I'm going to revoke your visa. God, you two drive me nuts on the Cuba issue!

I'll tell you what I told him: I'm thinking about it. But both of you need to accept that nothing in life is as clear-cut as you wish it to be.

Most countries are not able to rid themselves of their historical baggage just by wishing it away. Look at your own country. Without Colombia, there would be no drug problem. Yet, I—everyone—understand that it's not something you or any other leader can change overnight.

That's why I disagreed so strongly with what you said in your inauguration speech. I well understand that you weren't proposing anything specific—but even musing about drug legalization is dangerous.

We all have our political traps, Marta.

Best,

John

TO: ManFromNebraska (Reply)
FROM: BeautifulColombia
RE: A Return Invitation

Dear John,

If we are going to have a real friendship, there is no avoiding this argument. So let's have it. And I'm sure we will keep coming back to it—because drugs are, unfortunately, the most important thing in the relationship between our two countries.

During the last twenty years, the United States has spent nearly $450 billion in federal, state, and local funds devoted to different antidrug activities. Yet today you have close to 18 million twelve-year-old or older consumers of illicit drugs. You throw money into the drug war and don't get very far.

The U.S. set out to improve eradication to discourage peasants from cultivating illicit crops. You tried to strengthen interdiction in processing and transit countries to decrease the availability and potency of drugs in the United States. You attempted to enhance seizures at U.S. borders to elevate the domestic price of narcotics.

What have you gotten? The result is that most illegal drugs are more easily available, with greater purity and at lower prices, than in the early 1980s.

In your courts, you instituted a zero-tolerance policy with mandatory sentencing. Judges have been forced to give ten-year sentences to students found with grass. The result is unprecedented levels of incarceration: more than 50 percent of federal prisoners and 30 percent of state inmates are in jail for drug offenses.

I am not sure about legalization, John. I said it to be provocative.

But it seems to me that blaming Mexico for your high consumption of marijuana, bashing Myanmar for the rise in heroin addiction, or identifying Bolivia as a scapegoat for U.S. cocaine abuse just will not solve America's drug problem or the worldwide narcotics trade. The problem will need a complete refocusing.

I don't have the answers. But just like the Cuba issue, the international narcotics problem is begging for something new.

Yours,
Marta

President John Stockman went to his room early. It was rare to even contemplate going to bed at a decent hour—meetings, speeches, dinners, fundraisers regularly packed his evenings and got in the way of retiring early. But, to tell the God's honest truth, John Stockman did not mind occupying his evenings. Since Miranda died, bedrooms had symbolized loneliness and introspection—two very human sensations with which he was intensely uncomfortable.

Yet, today, he wanted to be alone. He went upstairs and asked Ronnie, the steward on duty, to get him a cognac. Notwithstanding Ronnie's cheerful "yessir," Stockman had no problem picking out his steward's sideways glance at Barney Holloway, the Secret Service agent posted at the door of the presidential bedroom. John Stockman had been president for more than two years and an early evening with a cognac was entirely out of character.

Stockman lay down on his queen-size bed dressed in what Adidas called "sportswear"—a gray sweatshirt and gray sweatpants. His inelegant getup was incongruous with the Ralph Lauren paisley sheets that had been pulled back and the pillows that were propped and puffed. He aimlessly zapped at the television.

The Thursday lineup—*ER, CSI, Dateline*—zoomed by aimlessly. Zap, zap. John Stockman was not watching.

He was nervous and jumpy. His orderly mind wandered uncontrollably and ideas bounced around. Overall, he was irritated. Mostly at himself. And, mostly, because he detested disorder. Since he had met Marta Pradilla in Bogotá, disorder was the order of the day.

His mind kept replaying short snippets of his quick meeting with her in Bogotá and then their long evening together in New York. Now the e-mails. Few people talked to him anymore with that level of clarity. He could hear her voice inside him. Her slight accent reverberated and beat rhythmically in his mind.

Two things really impressed him. First, she was right that the United States again needed to demonstrate hope for the world, not just fear of the world. Second, there was no doubt that politics had created some dead-end issues and that new solutions were needed.

Marta Pradilla's two points were linked. Great American presidents rolled the dice. Franklin Delano Roosevelt had unveiled his revolutionary New Deal; Lyndon Johnson had promoted a Great Society; Ronald Reagan had stared down the Soviet Union. These men were not universally loved, but nobody doubted their courage and conviction. Yes, thought John Stockman, unless you broke new ground, history would see you as a caretaker. There was nothing wrong with caretakers—Eisenhower, Carter, Bush I were transitional figures. Good men. But not great.

Somehow, this woman managed to make him look in the political mirror in ways he had resisted for years. He knew that his own psychological dependency on order, predictability, and stability was both a strength and weakness. His focus on security would convert him into the national security president—Americans were kept safe under his watch. He was successfully pursuing terrorists in faraway lands. But it would not—it could not—be enough to make him a great president.

Of course, she was right that change was needed. Yet, despite the obvious, every issue was entwined in a web of political straitjackets, economic handcuffs, and emotional taboos. On Cuba, Florida politics and its large congressional delegation froze any change in policy. Similarly, a small number of very rich and powerful corporate interests impeded a real discussion on trade. Needless to say, admitting defeat on drugs was political suicide.

Yes, it would take a lot of shaking to create real change on any of these issues. And, shaking required political guts. That is why John Stockman was so irritated tonight. He felt challenged by a beautiful woman, and he was not sure he had the stomach to do something really different.

Zap. Zap. *Queer Eye. CNN with Aaron Brown. Law and Order* reruns. John Stockman was not watching.

Stockman was pacing at this point. His heart was thumping away. His face was tightly stretched in a strange grimace. His brain jumped around to politics, legacy, courage, Castro, and drugs.

Every minute made John Stockman more irritable. He hated doubts. He despised questions. He abhorred the unpredictable. Damn, he could not control his jumpy mind.

Zap. Zap. A baseball game on ESPN; a John Wayne western on AMC; the local news. John Stockman was not watching.

Suddenly, at 11:20 p.m., just as the local weatherman finished predicting an unusually wet morning commute, it came to him. John Stockman realized that he had missed the real reason for his disquiet. He stopped cold in his tracks, midway between the television and the bay windows overlooking the Rose Garden. He suddenly understood his deep agitation. But knowing did not calm him down. It worried him more.

John Stockman realized then and there that he had fallen for this intelligent beauty from Latin America. Maybe it wasn't love yet, but it was close enough to it to scare him.

"Oh shit," whispered the president to himself.

Willy Perlman sat with Ellen O'Shehan and Ruben Goldfarber around the conference table in his outer office. This was their fourth day in the building since identifying the connection between the Syrians and the Pakistani nuclear team. Straight. Clothes were brought in. Showers were made available in the gym below. But nobody asked to go home—not even for a few hours. They all knew how serious this was.

Willy was not a monastic fellow. Actually, for a spy, he was pretty gregarious. Never married, Willy enjoyed going out—he liked good movies, restaurants with friends, and a nice bottle of wine. But, like everything with Willy Perlman, it had to be methodical. He liked his life well organized and perfectly balanced. And at present, his life was severely out of kilter.

"We're fucking nowhere," shouted Willy.

"Forgive me, Willy, but you are not being fair," Ellen O'Shehan said with a cold stare back at him. "I know there is a long way left to go and we don't have a lot of time. But telling us that 'we're nowhere' is neither helpful nor accurate. We are faced with a completely new threat and we know a lot more today than we knew a few days ago."

He had known Ellen O'Shehan for years. Nobody knew more about the spread of nuclear armaments than this overweight woman. She dedicated her life to following radioactive materials, interpreting reports on processing plants, tracking the comings and goings of nuclear experts in more than 200 countries. She did this while maintaining a wonderful, cheerful calm. And Willy never heard her raise her voice or answer back. Today she did both.

Willy Perlman completely ignored the tension and struggled to maintain his calm. He considered himself lucky to have her around—yes, he could forgive the fact that she was crabby. He backed down quickly.

"Okay, guys, let's go through it calmly again. Tell me where we are. Tell it to me like you would tell the president, because that call will come any minute."

Ruben Goldfarber went first. He always let Ellen start, but today he wanted to avoid any further tension. So, in his mournful, languid tones, Ruben summarized what they knew.

"We know Farooq Rahman had been retired for three years when Colonel Ali Massoud Barmani went to visit him approximately two months ago. We know this because his wife has confirmed to Pakistani intelligence that the visit took place. She heard nothing of interest. She served almond cookies.

"We also know that Rahman's beaten and morose demeanor lifted considerably after the Colonel's visit. Let's be clear, Farooq Rahman was a devout anti-Westerner, a fanatical Muslim. If this guy became happy, it's because the Colonel gave him a mission he liked. Farooq Rahman disappeared from his house about two weeks later. He had a small travel bag with him.

"Third, we squeezed—and paid nearly a million dollars to—our assets in Chechnya and got our first serious confirmation of what the objective of Farooq's mission might have been. They heard through the grapevine of a purchase of highly enriched weapons-grade uranium that took place a few weeks ago. They knew nothing of the purchaser, but curiously noted that the sale was conducted in English—not Russian. That is another sign that points to Rahman—all Paki elites speak English."

Ruben leaned over and took a long swig of his bottled water. Ellen could not resist; she grabbed Ruben's silence to teach Willy some background.

"It seems like our years of warnings have been right on," said Ellen. "We have long known that weapons-grade uranium went missing from a number of Soviet plants, nuclear power stations, and processing locations right before the collapse of the Soviet Union. While we suspected that some small quantities of this stuff have gone on the market before, this is the first real, concrete clue of a sale made of former Soviet uranium.

"Our Chechnya contact told us that this stuff came from the former Soviet nuclear enrichment plant sixty-five miles south of Almaty in Kazakhstan," continued Ellen. "Two months prior to the collapse of the Soviet Union, Mikhail Gorbachev ordered that location—and three others like it in the Kazakh Soviet Republic—closed. He instructed Russian scientists to come home to Russia and ordered all nuclear material transported. But many of these scientists were ethnic Russians who had lived in Kazakhstan all their lives. Their wives, kids, extended families were all in Kazakhstan. They were Russians, but they had nothing in Russia to go back to."

"They appealed to stay, but Gorbachev ordered them repatriated. Most obeyed. Two scientists—Vladimir Prostov and Gyorgy Aspartin—disappeared days before the evacuation order took effect. With them went about 100 kilograms of 90 percent–enriched uranium-235. In the immediate chaos of the evacuation of families and materials, nobody noticed. Drs. Prostov and Aspartin and the nuclear material have never been seen again. Until now. This is the stuff that we believe was sold to Rahman."

"Have we learned how much uranium is involved?" asked Willy. He had asked this question twice before in the last twenty-four hours. It was as if he needed to hear the bad news over and over again.

"Who knows, Willy, what the truth may be?" answered Ruben. "Our sources are saying between fifteen and thirty kilos. That is thirty to forty-five pounds. Detonated in the proper form—and it's not difficult to do—this is way more than enough to make a very serious bomb."

"Right. Keep going, Ruben," ordered Perlman.

"We are almost at the end of what we know nearly positively. We have not been able to confirm that Rahman was in Chechnya. But again, the sale was made in English. So, we think that there is a high probability that it was to him. Next he shows up in Georgia—dead. He probably crossed the border at the Pankisi Gorge. That is an amazing feat of organization. Money alone is not enough for a stranger to cross that border."

Ruben now accelerated to the conclusion.

"So, we have Rahman in Georgia—in a hotel in Telavi, a provincial town—at the exact time that a UN refugee conference is having its farewell dinner in the same hotel in this small town. The planning was extraordinary."

"The Pakistani representative to the UN conference was the Colonel, Rahman's longtime trusted handler. The FBI team we sent to Georgia confirms that the killing was professional, notwithstanding a desire to disguise it as a suicide. Although we don't have the body, the police report details one bullet to the temple, at close range, with a silencer. Ellen and I believe the Colonel did it. He has the training."

"But why would he kill his longtime friend and associate? Why would he kill a man he has worked with for twenty years?" Willy had asked this question previously too. It was crystal clear now that Willy was rehearsing his own, inevitable conversation with the White House.

"Because there was no way to get Farooq out of Georgia," answered Ellen. "It would be too risky to fly him out. Sure, he could retrace his steps back through the Pankisi Gorge, but the Colonel knew that a successful, undiscovered one-way trip was nearly miraculous. Chances are that he would get caught going backward. There was no way around it. He had to kill him."

"Finish up," spat out Willy. Ellen and Ruben both wondered if Willy understood that it was he who kept interrupting with questions they already answered hours ago.

"Now, the Colonel has the uranium," Ruben says, closing out the story. "But not for long. The bellboy clearly remembers putting the suitcases on the airport bus. The Georgians reported that the Colonel left the next morning on a flight to London. But the Syrian delegate to the conference, Ambassador Osman Samir al-Husseini, was on the airport bus and left on the Austrian Airlines flight to Vienna that very same night. No doubt in our minds, Willy, the Syrians have the uranium."

"Where?" asked Willy.

This question had been asked not once or twice, but hundreds of times in the past few days. Unlike other questions Willy asked over and over again, this one did not have a clear answer. It was the million-dollar question. The answer would dictate the policy decisions that had to be made in the next hours.

Ellen answered.

"Osman Samir al-Husseini is the al-Assad family's principal spy in the United States. He is the number two at the Syrian mission to the United Nations. We have to presume that he is a good spy. So we have to believe that he probably heard we are planning to get tough on his country at the United Nations. He found out that we have some sort of military planning going on that involves engaging our troops on his borders.

"Our conclusion, therefore, is that the uranium is in Syria and that they have the detonation mechanisms. If U.S. troops cross the border from Iraq, they will use nuclear weapons on our soldiers. Even if we prepare for this and we fan out our entry into Syria, they will inevitably kill a lot of Americans. They may kill a lot of Syrians too. But they will become heroes in the Arab world. They will be the first to launch a successful nuclear attack on the United States Army."

"Is there any other scenario?" asked Willy.

"Yes," said Ruben. "The other scenario is that they will try to bring the uranium into the United States to launch a state-sponsored nuclear terrorist attack on U.S. soil. But, frankly, that one is hard to fathom. How do they get the stuff in? Who smuggles it? Al-Qaeda has been successful in the past because it is a web of small, tightly knit cells. They are hard to follow, because we don't know who is al-Qaeda and who isn't."

"But a terrorist attack sponsored by Syria is another thing entirely," interrupted Ellen. "It is not easy to pull off after September 11. We have such vastly improved assets in the Middle East now. If money is moved, we know it. If assets get shifted around, we hear about it. The NSA has the conversations of most important people in the region covered."

"So, you would not recommend to the president to raise the alert level to orange?" asked Willy, referring to the silly color codes devised by the Homeland Security Department to inform the public of an elevated possibility of a terrorist attack.

"Willy, two days ago we ordered massively heightened surveillance and coverage of Syria and its friends," said Ellen. "We rerouted satellites that are now in permanent geostationary orbits over Syria. We augmented surveillance of Syrian diplomats and personnel everywhere in the world, but especially in Europe. We notified governments in key banking nations that we want to know about any Syrian-related money movements."

Just then Willy's cellular phone started vibrating. Ellen and Ruben could tell, because Willy's legs stretched out and his hand started spastically patting his pants pocket. Willy flipped open the cell phone and listened. The conversation lasted less than ten seconds.

"Yes, Nelson. I'll be there in half an hour," Willy answered, then closed the phone.

They did not have to say anything to each other. This was the expected call from the White House. The president would want a briefing and then would ask for clear policy advice. Willy stood up and looked at the analysts one last time. He asked for any parting counsel.

"We'll know if the Syrians are planning to move anything this way," concluded Ellen. "There will be time yet to raise the alert level. Our best guess today is that we must face the fact that the Syrians now have a theater nuclear weapon to defend Syrian territory and repel a U.S. invasion. The president needs to factor this into any decision to cross Syrian territory from Iraq. We believe that they will not hesitate to use it."

Willy nodded his agreement. Without a word, he turned around and walked out.

===

It took only two minutes from the moment Willy's car arrived at the White House grounds to the time he was knocking on Nelson Cummin's door.

Willy had done the trip many times. He reckoned that between security checks, registration, elevators, and a little wait in the outer office of the national security advisor, the average entry time to see Nelson—from entering the White House grounds to shaking his hand—was fifteen to twenty minutes. This time his car was waved through and a secretary waited for him at the side door of the building. An elevator was blocked and waiting for their arrival. Willy was taken to a back entrance to Nelson's office and told to knock.

This only made Willy more nervous, for all this speed was not a reflection of his level of intimacy with this president's White House. It demonstrated the clear agitation inside the building.

Nelson got up to greet him, but there was no smile. "Willy, we've got five minutes before we see the big man. Review what you know."

Willy took him through the entire story. He concisely detailed their level of knowledge of each stage of the story. He wanted Nelson to understand the difference between what they knew, what they surmised, and what was an educated guess.

Nelson listened carefully. His eyes never left Willy's face. He was fully, totally concentrated. Even when Willy finished, Nelson did not let Willy's eyes go.

Okay," Nelson said. "Keep your part under five minutes. We'll let him lead the discussion after."

Willy was accustomed to power. Years in Washington made him immune to the pompous titles and puffed-up men and women who populated this town. He had met both Clinton and Bush before. But those encounters were at CIA headquarters in a larger, multiperson briefing. This was his first time in the Oval Office, and he was surprised to hear his heart pounding.

The president got up from behind his desk as they walked into the room. He

greeted Perlman with an outstretched hand and pointed to one of the two famous sofas in the Oval Office's sitting area.

"Thank you for coming, Dr. Perlman. Nelson has told me that you two are
friends and that he has the utmost respect for you. Since you are the person who
uncovered the nuclear material, you get to be on the hot seat. Give it to me," the
president concluded.

"Thanks for having me, President Stockman. It's a pleasure to meet you in
person. Let me be brief and concise. I'm glad to fill in details if you want them."

Perlman waited for a nod. He knew that powerful people liked to be in control of every aspect of a meeting—including the perception of controlling those
who were briefing them. The president gave him what he needed with a slight
movement of his face.

"We believe, Mr. President, that around forty pounds of highly enriched
uranium from the former Soviet Union—that is more than enough to make a
good bomb—has made its way into the hands of the Syrian government or renegade elements of that government. It was smuggled by a Pakistani nuclear scientist who has clear connections to Islamic zealots. This Pakistani put it into the
hands of a well-known Syrian government spy. We don't know where this material is now."

Willy ignored the cloud developing on Stockman's face. He went on.

"Mr. President, in thirty seconds, you have just heard what we know. Now, let
me tell you what we speculate. We believe the Syrians have acquired this uranium
in order to create a bomb. They have done so in order to use it to repel a U.S. attack on Syria from the Western Iraqi border. The Syrians are well aware of this
administration's view that the government in Damascus continues to play a
hugely negative role in the Middle East by harboring and sponsoring terrorism. If
we attack Syria militarily, we believe they will use the bomb against American
soldiers.

"Their thinking is this, Mr. President: Regardless of whether we reach Damascus or not, they will be heroes for killing many thousands of American soldiers.
If we respond in kind—with nuclear weapons—we will indiscriminately kill
many civilians. We will be forever reviled in the Arab world for launching nuclear
weapons against ordinary people. If we don't respond in kind, then al-Assad and
his cronies will say that they had the unique courage to acquire and use nuclear
weapons against a weak-kneed America.

"Syria's leaders will become heroes and martyrs and will be protected by
their huge popularity in the Arab world," Willy concluded.

President John Stockman slowly took in what he just heard. His plans for pressuring Syria were becoming more difficult and complicated by the minute. He knew that on today's call list were a couple of scheduled phone conversations with world leaders to lobby for support of a tough UN resolution against Syria. He couldn't remember which leaders, though.

Nelson Cummins quietly interrupted.

"Mr. President, while I believe Willy is correct in his analysis of where and how the Syrians plan to use the nuclear material, I think we should consider raising the alert level in the United States to Code Orange. We have lost track of forty pounds of the world's most dangerous material. If we are wrong about where it is going, we need to be prepared. Further, it is important, in case something does happen, that you are seen to have done everything possible."

Stockman shook his head.

"I can't do that, Nelson. If I raise the alert level, I have to tell police and emergency personnel why I am doing it. Do you know the panic we will sow if we tell people that we believe that Syrians could have forty pounds of U-235 in their back pockets and might be smuggling it this way? It's suicide."

The president was talking faster now. "I won't have my government raising alert levels and ascribing it to some ill-defined chatter. If we believe that the Syrians are planning an attack on our soil, I won't hesitate to raise the level, and we will have to tell everybody why we are doing it. But that is not what I am hearing from you. Is that correct?"

"Yes, Mr. President. We believe that, if they have the weaponry, they will use it in the Middle East against American soldiers."

"That makes this a Pentagon matter," said Stockman, turning to his national security advisor. "Nelson, I would like a meeting with the Joint Chiefs. I will not be dictated to by a terrorist state, whether it has nuclear bombs or not. I want to know what our military options are, and my guess is that we need to accelerate our plans against Syria."

President John Stockman looked at Willy Perlman. "I assume I don't need to tell you to spare no resources in following every possible lead to find the uranium. It is now this nation's highest priority."

The president stood. "Dr. Perlman, thank you for the good job. I appreciate your clear advice."

Two hundred and twelve miles to the north of the White House, the thin man with the small moustache picked up the phone and dialed the international cellular number he knew by heart. Although he was on a scrambled line, his intention was to keep the call as short as possible.

It was late at night in Rome, but Ambassador Omar bin Talman's voice responded after the second ring.

"Mr. Ambassador, as always it is a pleasure to hear your voice," said Osman Samir al-Husseini.

"Hello, my friend. I was hoping this would be you. Do you have news for me?"

"I do, my old friend."

"Then don't keep me in the dark. Tell me."

"The plan has worked perfectly. All packages have safely arrived in Latin America with our friend."

"That is excellent. And do we think that the Americans are aware of all this?"

"Surveillance of the homes of the two intelligence analysts in charge of proliferation tells me that these agents have not come home in days. That would indicate that the Americans have discovered the existence of our precious materials."

Ambassador Omar bin Talman sighed into the phone. "That is unfortunate, but not lethal to our plans. But the question is, do they suspect where the cargo is going?"

"A meeting of the senior military staff has been scheduled at the White House tomorrow. To me, this means that they believe our materials have gone to our country."

Bin Talman never ceased to be impressed by his friend's capacity to glean information. How did he do it? Never mind; he preferred not to know.

"So, does that mean that they suspect we will use it to defend the homeland in case of attack?" asked bin Talman.

"That is exactly what it means."

"Excellent, my friend. The deception is complete," Ambassador Omar bin Talman smiled broadly.

"Our hopes now rest with our friend from Latin America."

"He is a determined man. Still, we should pray tonight for his success."

Osman Samir al-Husseini quietly put down the phone without a further word.

PART X
COLOMBIA

TO: BeautifulColombia
FROM: ManFromNebraska (Reply)
RE: Your Note

Dear Marta,

Alright, we've had our drug interchange. As you said, it was unavoidable. I understand what you are saying—let's promise to think together about new directions.

The fact is that I've been thinking of you often in the past days. And it's not only because you scold me about Cuba or the drug issue. Rather, I seem to carry your voice around these days. I catch myself asking what you would think or do about certain things. It's silly, frankly.

Yet, it also feels right. It's hard to remember how long it's been since somebody told me exactly what was on their mind. It seems as though you never hold anything back. You are not afraid of nearness. And somehow that makes me want to close any distance between us. So here I am writing you things so close that I don't ever remember telling anybody before.

Our little exchange has become something important in my life. God knows where it's going. I can't imagine that we'll be allowed to take it anywhere at all.

Last night, I smiled to myself thinking that I might order my press secretary, Allyson Bonnet, to announce that "the president today called President Marta Pradilla in Colombia to ask her to accompany him on a visit back to his home state of Nebraska." She would then add, "The visit's purpose is entirely social, and no official agenda is planned. The president has come to admire President Pradilla and requested the pleasure of her company back to his native state."

But the smile quickly turned to laughter as I thought of the frenzy that would follow. The press would dig into both our lives. Talk shows would mobilize, call-in radio stations would ask the public for their opinions. Historians would comment on parallels and we would be compared to Mark Anthony and Cleopatra.

Forget it. Instead, I shut off the light and went to bed.

Hope you are fine.

J.

TO: ManFromNebraska
FROM: BeautifulColombia (Reply)
RE: Your Note

Dear John,

Your note had me in tears of laughter. I needed it. We are going through a real crisis here that I will want to tell you about, but it's too complicated for me to fill in the details now. Put bluntly, I think we have uncovered a plot by my political enemies to attack me physically. I will write you more about it in the coming days.

Please don't think that I was laughing at what you are thinking or how you are feeling. It was your description of the reaction to Ms. Bonnet's press conference that made me double over in stitches. Here it would be just as funny. They would accuse me of ceding the sovereignty of Colombia; I would be indicted in Congress for treason. But, who knows? Colombians are practical people. Many of them would say that perhaps I could knock some sense into you!

I don't have answers for you. I don't know if these notes to each other can be catapulted into something more. I find myself wishing at times that they could, and asking myself the best way to do it—though I confess that the feeling surprises me. Having a relationship with you right now is not exactly—how can I put it delicately—what the doctor ordered for my political career.

But, I want you to know this, John: If Ms. Bonnet ever held that press conference, here is what my communications director would say to the press corps in Bogotá: "President Marta Pradilla today accepted the generous invitation of the president of the United States to visit him in Nebraska. Mr. Stockman is a man who has earned the president's respect and her sympathies. She is delighted to learn more about President Stockman's home state and expects that he will visit her family home in Cartagena in the near future."

It is a nice thought, John. I like the sound of that press conference.

Kisses,
Marta.

Casa de Nariño
Bogotá, October 15
7:05 p.m.

===

President Marta Pradilla held her head in her hand. She knew that Stockman would have answered her last note by now. But it would be hours before she got a chance to log on, look for it, and answer. She badly wanted to write him. But the nightmare that filled up her office now was all consuming. It would have to wait.

Since finding out that Juan Francisco Abdoul had escaped their reach by getting off the plane in Caracas, Hector Carbone, Manuel Saldivar, and Marta Pradilla were unable to think of anything important enough to break the ornate silence of the president's office. Not a word was uttered. She got up to pace and the sound of her clicking heels spilled over the room, drowning their thoughts. A ruthless enemy was planning to hurt them and the country—they had few doubts about this. One question was top-of-mind: How would they stop him?

Manuel spoke first.

"Marta, I've prepared a memo on the constitutional questions that you asked me—and it's ready for your approval. The upshot is this: There are a number of ways we can strip Abdoul of his congressional immunity, but most of them are difficult and complicated. It would take lots of time. But I found one thing— it's a big, wonderful thing—that put me in a great mood."

"What is it?"

"Extreme absenteeism."

"What are you talking about?" asked Marta Pradilla.

"I know it sounds silly, but hear me out. We are never going to be able to conclusively prove any case against Abdoul that centers on his illegal drug and smuggling activities. The man created companies within companies owned and directed by people loyal to him. He will obfuscate, weave, and lead us down dead-end alleys. It could take years, and we might never get the votes in Congress because we'll never have conclusive proof."

"So, what is this thing? Extreme something or other."

"Absenteeism. The law provides for the stripping of immunity of any member of Congress who has been absent from his job—remember, a congressman's job is to vote, Marta! In the last legislature, Abdoul missed 53 percent of his votes. In the few months of this congressional cycle, he missed nearly 70 percent of his votes."

Marta Pradilla was silent. She crossed her legs slowly and was about to react. But Manuel continued.

"It isn't perfect. It doesn't allow us to make the case that we want to make—that this man is a criminal, that he represents the political machines, that he symbolizes the past. But it will accomplish our goal. And we can do it fast. There is no arguing with his voting record. You can bully a majority of Congress for this vote, Marta. He has no defense."

"Yes, Manuel, you're right. It's not perfect—but it will do the one thing we need most. We'll be able to extradite him to the United States," said Marta, her hands gesticulating excitedly. She was warming to the idea.

"Okay, Manuel, you can talk to the prosecutor tomorrow. I want to initiate proceedings to strip the immunity of Senator Juan Francisco Abdoul of Barranquilla for dereliction of duty due to his extreme absenteeism," Marta paused for a second. She liked how that sounded. A lot.

Manuel interrupted her train of thought. "Can we do that while he is out of the country? Don't we need to wait until he comes back?"

"Are you kidding, he's absent again! Right now. This is exactly the time to do it. You need to prepare a press release and get me an interview on a news program that will give me no less than five minutes. We're doing it tomorrow!"

Hector Carbone had not said a word during the exchange between his boss and Manuel Saldivar. The more they talked, the more he worried. This was the problem with politicians. When it came to security issues, they had trouble understanding the dimensions of a potential threat. Clearly, the president and Manuel did not comprehend the dangers his country was facing.

He decided to interrupt.

"Marta," Carbone said in a soft voice.

She looked his way.

"Forgive me for being disrespectful. But this conversation between Manuel and yourself misses the point completely."

He did not allow her to answer. He knew she would be angry.

"We are facing a serious national security threat. There is a prominent Colombian citizen somewhere near our borders trying to smuggle some type of serious weaponry back into our country. It is clear that his intention is to use it to harm the president and country's democratic institutions.

"I fear that political solutions like extradition may be too late to implement," Carbone continued. "Senator Abdoul is today a major security risk. Sure, if we catch him, we'll have lots of time to talk about the political options. Right now, though, the only thing that counts is catching him. Can we concentrate on that?"

Marta and Manuel looked at each other, searching for something to say. They just were not sure what it should be. They felt chastised because Carbone was right.

"Okay, Hector, thanks for bringing us back to reality." Marta Pradilla said to the DAS chief, her eyes blazing with intensity. "I want Manuel to move ahead with his meeting with the prosecutor tomorrow, but you are right to remind us to keep our eye on what is important. Do you have a suggestion?"

"Just one," Carbone said. "I hate to ask the gringos for any favors. But they have the capacity to redirect satellites that can track communications and transportation. We have done it before on drug interdiction missions. Why don't we ask them for help? It may be a long shot, but if we want to find Abdoul, the Americans are our best bet."

That was as far as he got. Marta Pradilla already had the phone in her hand and was barking out orders to find Ambassador Morris Salzer.

Carbone thought for a few moments. Even though it was his idea, he disapproved of any precipitous movement. "Presidente, it may be better to go directly to the CIA or to Southern Command for this. We may get it faster."

It was too late. Marta Pradilla was already well on her way. She had the United States ambassador on the line.

"Morris, it's Marta. I need to discuss something of some urgency with you. Forgive me for the late hour, but I need to impose on you now. Can you come by? Great. Thanks."

Pradilla ordered hamburgers and fries for everyone in the office. The evening would be a late one. Better to eat when one had a chance and they had a dead hour ahead of them right now.

The food came. It was the silliest of sights. Cheeseburgers and fries were delivered from the palace kitchens on hundred-year-old German plates kept warm with pompous-looking sterling silver plate covers, as if each plate was crowned with the cupola of a Russian Orthodox church. Two waiters passed around the plates and offered tropical fruit juices with white-gloved hands. The serving ceremony resembled that of Michelin's best three-star French restaurant. The food was a Colombian version of McDonald's.

The intercom buzzed, announcing the ambassador's arrival. The president ordered him brought up immediately to the living room of the third-floor residential quarters. That would make him feel important.

Morris Salzer's posting to Colombia was the grand finale of a star-studded diplomatic career. The ambassador was a highly intelligent and well-known man.

So far, he was not happy with his relations with the new government and, specifically, with the new president. In a meeting with senior embassy staff, he had described Marta Pradilla's behavior with President Stockman on her first day in office as "completely infantile." He expected her to be trouble for the United States.

The three Colombians stepped off the elevator and into the living room, where Ambassador Salzer was already sipping a cognac. A steward walked in to take their drink orders, but Marta waved him away. Salzer was going to drink alone that evening. She wanted him to feel a little out of place.

"Mr. Ambassador, thank you for coming and forgive me for interrupting your evening. I think you know my chief of staff, Mr. Saldivar, and the director of the DAS, Mr. Carbone. Mr. Ambassador, we have an urgent request of the United States."

She wasted no time getting to the point.

"As you know, Senator Juan Francisco Abdoul has declared himself a sworn enemy of my government. You also know that his family's narcotics trade regularly feeds the drug needs of the United States. As such, I am presuming he is a sworn enemy of your country as well.

"Senator Abdoul is believed to be in Venezuela, having returned from a highly suspicious trip to Europe," continued Marta. "A few hours ago, he got off an Air France flight to Caracas; he may be carrying materials designed to do serious damage to this government. We think it is some sort of sophisticated weaponry. We don't know what. However, the fact is that we lost him. We require some technical help in monitoring the borders—namely, we need satellite intelligence on airplanes, boats, and any unusual movement from Venezuela into Colombia.

"We consider this request to be a priority. We would be grateful if you would give this the highest degree of attention. Mr. Ambassador, your help is only useful if it happens fast. I will await your answer tonight."

The ambassador started to protest.

"Marta, I appreciate the urgency. But you have not given me much to go on. To transmit this type of request, I need to have some more details. More importantly, I don't think I can do this within the few-hour framework you have given me."

President Pradilla started to get up. The meeting was nearly over. The ambassador and the president clearly disliked each other. From a protocol point of view, it was a miserable encounter. It was about to get worse.

"Morris, I want you to be under no illusions as to the importance I am placing on this request. It will be a clear harbinger of the tone and tenor of my future relations with the United States embassy in Bogotá. Please try to do this for us. I would like Director Carbone to be the point of contact on any follow-up tonight."

They all stood up. Marta Pradilla was the last to shake the ambassador's hand. As she took his hand in hers, she locked his eyes in a cold stare. Manuel recognized it instantaneously. It was the stare that happened before Marta Pradilla played a trump card.

"Again, thanks for coming on such short notice. Please give Ms. Alice Andrews at the DEA my very best regards. I will be calling her to ask her to lunch. Girl to girl." President Pradilla never took her eyes away from the ambassador's.

Morris Salzer looked at her in a rage. How had she known of his affair with Alice? For God's sake, this woman would do anything to get what she wanted! He said nothing. The U.S. ambassador walked out the door without a further word.

Hector Carbone's eyes bolted upward to Marta Pradilla for some explanation. Then he remembered Manuel's gossip about the ambassador's car at the German embassy. He turned to Manuel and saw the huge smile on his face. Carbone started to laugh. His handsome face warmed up the room left chilly by the ambassador.

"I can't believe you just blackmailed the United States ambassador," Manuel said to Pradilla.

"Well, we'll see what it gets us. Okay, I want to make some phone calls. I played this to the maximum. It will either backfire or it will work. We'll see. I will be up until midnight. If it is later, you can wake me up. I want to know the answer."

Back to the Palace
Bogotá, October 16
12:00 a.m.

Hector Carbone had called Manuel on his cell phone at 11:30 p.m. Manuel had left Casa de Nariño a few hours earlier thinking very seriously about calling Maggie James, the BBC beauty, and passing by her hotel. He was sure that the British television public would benefit by some additional "texture" on the functioning of the Colombian government and its new president.

Manuel knew that his weak spot was his easy infatuation with beautiful, intelligent women. Should he call? He closed his eyes and had visions of her leaning close after dinner, her breath warm against his cheek. What does an important man like you do so late in the office? she would ask. Just push papers, he would answer. She would come closer. Tell me what you reaaahhhly do, she would say in the irresistible British English that so fully formed even the most normal of words. Oh, Manuel would say, we just blackmailed the American ambassador into rerouting spy satellites so that we could track the president of our Senate.

Nope. He could not see Maggie tonight. Way too dangerous.

So, he went to his gym club to sit in the steam room. He was on his way home, still enveloped in the eucalyptus-induced haze of the Turkish bath, when Carbone called.

"How did it go?" asked Manuel.

"Badly. Very badly. We need to meet back where we left her," said Carbone. Manuel wondered why spies never talked clearly. Were all the half tones, inferences, and codes really necessary? They sounded like a cheap movie.

"Okay, I will call and arrange. See you in fifteen minutes." Manuel hung up and called the switchboard. He asked the operator to advise the president that they would be there shortly. He told his driver to turn around and go back to the office.

Carbone was waiting for him at the elevator. They rode up together. The elderly elevator operator, Don Ignacio, was off duty at this hour, so a young policeman had to run the elevator. Within seconds, it became evident that he had never done it before. As he pulled the handle toward him, the elevator lurched downwards rather than up.

Manuel looked at Carbone. The DAS director said nothing, but his fists were clenched in impatient rage. Manuel became seriously worried about what he knew. Hector Carbone had always come off like a man in control. But the person now sharing the lurching elevator with him was consumed with worry.

They walked into the familiar sitting room. Marta Pradilla was waiting for them, dressed in blue jeans and a T-shirt. She wore light blue Keds shoes. The president greeted them with a can of Coke in her hand.

Carbone did not even wait for instructions to start talking.

"I don't have good news. I have very bad news."

"The fucking Americans," Manuel interrupted. He couldn't help himself. "Unless there is something in it for them, they will not lift a finger for us or this country."

Marta Pradilla lifted her palm toward Manuel, imitating a policeman at a traffic intersection. She wanted silence.

"I think you want to let me finish," Carbone continued, throwing Manuel a cautionary glance. "I was called by the CIA station chief here. I have met him a number of times. He is a good guy. He told me the ambassador passed on our requests to the highest levels. He said that Ambassador Salzer was very eager to help. He had called the State Department, the CIA, and the National Security Agency directly. In case you don't know, the NSA is the American agency in charge of electronic espionage."

Carbone leaned over to drink some of the water a waiter had placed on the table in front of him. He was very nervous.

"My CIA contact told me that everybody was very understanding. He reiterated to me that the U.S. government was committed to assisting Colombia and this new government. But, he said, now was not the time.

"He told me that the information he was going to give me was highly classified, but that it was important that we understand that America's inability to help us now was not due to a lack of motivation. He said that the American intelligence apparatus was—to use his words—on "high alert." All the counterespionage, satellite, human intelligence, cybernetic warfare, and eavesdropping capacity of the United States of America presently are being focused toward the Middle East. The director of Central Intelligence has ordered that no resources be redirected for any other purpose.

"You see," continued Hector Carbone, "my CIA contact told me confidentially that the United States suspects that the Syrian government has gotten possession of significant quantities of 90 percent–enriched uranium. However, it does not know where that uranium is and what the Syrians plan to do with this material."

The time was shortly after midnight and the three people in the room were exhausted. But Carbone's words hit the room like a high-voltage electrical jolt. Slouched backs turned ramrod straight. Pulses quickened. The ensuing silence in the room was the quiet that often happened when the mind had to bend to grasp the unbelievable. The DAS director's words did not require translation or interpretation. They were all thinking the same thing. Juan Francisco Abdoul was smuggling nuclear material into Colombia even as they spoke. Was it possible that one of Colombia's largest narco-traffickers was seeking to destabilize the country by detonating a nuclear explosion in Colombia?

"Did you tell the CIA guy anything about what you know of the origins of Abdoul's suitcases?" asked the president. She formulated her question slowly and deliberately.

"No, I did not. I imagine the three of us are convinced of the same thing, but we have no proof that Abdoul is carrying uranium. We know the Syrian ambassador in Rome gave him two suitcases. Until I know for sure what is in them, I prefer not to speculate."

Manuel looked at the president. Before talking, he waited until their eyes locked and he had her complete attention.

"Marta, I agree with Hector. This is our problem. We need to deal with it. First, we need to confirm if Abdoul has the uranium. Second, we need to find the suitcases. This madman is planning to use nuclear weapons in Colombia in order to hit at you. He figures that it does not matter if he kills you or not. By killing thousands in Bogotá, Medellín, Cali, or Barranquilla, he will neutralize the presidency for the rest of your mandate. We can't tell the Americans, because they will believe that Colombia has spun out of control—on your watch."

Carbone agreed. "This man clearly sees you as the single greatest threat to his family, his riches, and his own life. He will stop at nothing. Even if he does not use the uranium, he may use it to blackmail you into keeping away from him for the next four years. The idea that a Colombian criminal organization has its hands on materials to make a nuclear bomb fills me with dread. But it is also proof of how worried they are about you. We need to find him and the suitcases."

"How do we do this?" asked Marta.

"Marta, you will have to trust me on this," said Carbone very slowly. "If you agree to let me find out what I can, you must also agree never to talk to me about what was done to acquire the information. There are some things that even a president cannot know. The same goes for you, Manuel."

So here we are, thought Marta Pradilla. How soon the moment had come! She knew when she ran for the job that there would be times in which the exercise of power would force her into difficult decisions. Decisions that hurt. Indecent decisions. She knew when she swore an oath to the constitution that leading a country of Colombia's size, with its problems and its complications, would eventually bring her to unforgiving pacts with the devil. She took the job because she knew that with leadership came opportunity. But she also understood that it would also bring personal pain.

That started right now. She was in the second month of her presidency and a man she knew only moderately well was asking her to approve something so horrible that he refused to talk with her about it. Damn it.

"Yes, I trust you," nodded Marta Pradilla to Carbone, after a long pause.

The director of the DAS got up and walked quietly toward the elevator. He did not say goodnight.

Plaza de las Flores
Barranquilla, October 16
8:23 a.m.

The spiking sun was already burning in the northern Colombian city of Barranquilla. You could become sun-obsessed in Barranquilla. The sun was everywhere.
Always. But Barranquilla pretended not to notice.

The traffic was infernal. Policemen shouted at cars blocking intersections.
Horns wailed. Old decrepit automobiles stood in winding car lines that went on
for kilometers. Most of the cars were old; their air-conditioning systems could
not handle the combined onslaught of sun, heat, and traffic. But they had stereos
that made their owners proud. Competing merengues, salsas, bachatas, and Val-
lenatos blared from each window.

Nobody seemed to care much. The citizens of Barranquilla had learned long
ago to smile over the noise, the heat, and the traffic. How else could you live in a
city of such troubles? Children were taught from a young age that there was a lot
to love about the city as long as you pretended not to notice the bad stuff.

A few blocks away from the traffic of Avenida Miranda, schoolboys in uniform played a game of pickup soccer in a shady park called Plaza de las Flores. It
was a beautiful oval-shaped plaza with one-way streets going up on one side and
down the other. The park was permanently in the shade, protected by hundred-
year-old palm and mango trees. Thousands of yellow Alamanda flowers spilled
over the short walls of the park, giving it a sense of a tropical Garden of Eden.

At the northern end of the plaza, the nuns of Saint Mary Our Savior welcomed the kids to another day of school. Saint Mary's was an elite institution, attended by the sons and daughters of the city's richest and best—a mix of children
from the families of industrialists, exporters, landowners, and politicians.

Sister Francisca had the duty of helping to unload the arriving students from
the cars and vans that disgorged their passengers in front of the school. She
looked at her watch and noted that it was time. She blew her whistle to call over
the boys, just fifty feet away in the park. It always took them forever to finish the
game and once again capitulate to the sad truth that adults ruled the world. As expected, the first whistle was summarily ignored, and Sister Francisca ended up

having to blow six or seven times before convincing herself that the soccer game in the park was over and the boys were packing up to come her way.

Assured that they were walking over, the nun again turned her attention back to helping the arriving children and their oversized backpacks out of the backseats of cars. Mothers and fathers drove some of the children. Most were ferried to school by the family chauffeur.

Sister Francisca hardly noticed when she heard an adult voice yell "Daniel!" But she certainly heard the children screaming. She picked her head up just in time to see a white van with sliding side doors careening in front of her line of sight. Inside, she saw two masked men struggling to throw a small, handsome six-year-old boy with dirty blond hair onto the floor of the vehicle. The boy screamed. As the van drove by, a third man, also masked, was sliding the door shut. As the door closed and locked, it permanently cut off the wailing scream of the child.

Oh my God, thought Sister Francisca, they just kidnapped little Daniel Abdoul, the son of the mayor. In Colombia, kidnapping was a national sickness. Thousands of parents and children were taken from their homes and used as bargaining chips in exchange for money or political favors. You had to be nuts, however, to kidnap the son of the mayor of Barranquilla. She crossed herself repeatedly as she sprinted to the school building to phone the police.

The Mayor's Residence
Barranquilla October 16
9:40 a.m.

Across town, just over an hour later, at the end of a tree-lined street, Hector Carbone sat in an air-conditioned car with his eyes closed. He had not slept a minute
the entire night. Forty-five minutes ago he had gotten a one-word SMS message
on his cellular phone. "Done," it had said. He had waited, impassive, over the last
three quarters of an hour, as the level of activity in and around the house at the
other end of the street spread from a steady churn to near hysteria. Cars came and
went. Vehicles belonging to the Barranquilla police, sirens ablaze, set up a protective perimeter around the palatial home of the mayor.

It was nearly time. As a man walked toward Carbone's car, the driver muttered "Director" to get Carbone's eyes to open. The director of the DAS rolled
down the car's rear window. The man in the street stopped just long enough to
give Carbone a small rectangular box that looked like the small packages that fit a
watch or a bracelet. Carbone looked up and saw the man's disgusted look. Carbone understood. This was not a nice assignment.

"Where's it from?" Carbone asked.

"A five-year-old girl who has been in the morgue for over a week. Nobody
claimed her," was the dry answer.

Carbone nodded and turned to the man behind the steering wheel.

"Drive," he ordered. In seconds, the director's driver had the car in gear
heading toward the mansion. As he drove, his right hand attached flashing lights
to the dashboard and placed on the far right-hand side of the windshield a sign
that identified the security agency.

Police let the car through immediately. It surprised nobody that the DAS was
here. The son of a prominent politician had just been kidnapped and the DAS
would want to know if there was a link to guerrillas or any other threat to the
state. But all the activity ground to a halt and the cops just stared when they saw
who stepped out of the rear of the vehicle. This was not the DAS administrator in
Barranquilla. It was the director himself—from Bogotá. How had he gotten here
so quickly?

Hector Carbone was let through the multiple levels of security in the house. If Carbone was uncomfortable as a black man in a white world, he never showed it. The director of the DAS walked into the mansion, exhausted from a sleepless night, but perfectly dressed and totally in control.

He thought back to his youth, to the fact that his father had shined shoes in the streets of Santa Marta, and to how long and hard he himself had struggled to become a lawyer and then the chief prosecutor. He was not proud of what he was here to do, but he was convinced that the road to profound change in Colombia was lined with nasty events. What was about to transpire was one of them.

Ricardo Abdoul, mayor of Barranquilla and brother of the president of the Senate, appeared within minutes of Carbone's arrival. He was far better looking than his older brother—a tall, athletic man with a full mustache.

Ricardo Abdoul lived in the shadow of his more famous brother everywhere—but not in Barranquilla. Here, in this city, he was the better-known Abdoul. He lived with a psychological need to prove every day that he ran things, took decisions, and was in charge. That often meant the physical enforcement of his rules. In Barranquilla, Ricardo Abdoul demanded subservience.

Hector Carbone knew of Ricardo Abdoul's need to assert supremacy and had decided long before entering the house that only one thing could work: to take total control of the meeting. Ricardo Abdoul could be given no choices. Carbone would have to instantaneously create the impression that life or death danced on a knife's edge—Carbone's knife.

"Mr. Director," the younger Abdoul said to Carbone, "I am gratified by your personal attention. I presume you have heard about little Daniel?"

Carbone took a deep breath. He had won his reputation as a prosecutor by enticing hardened men to talk—he traded up. Carbone had made them believe he was tougher than they were. Carbone always attacked—piling one charge on top of the other, squeezing witnesses, and threatening to go after family and friends. But he always had a carrot, too. He believed that the moment a suspect turned was not when frantic and desperate, but rather, when offered hope to end the desperation. That is when men were most vulnerable.

Now, he needed the mayor of Barranquilla to trade up and turn on his brother. He needed it fast. Carbone had to do in five minutes what had taken weeks to achieve with the criminals he had prosecuted.

"Mr. Mayor, please sit." Hector Carbone was barely whispering. "Please listen carefully to what I am about to say. You are about to be faced with the choice of a lifetime, and I will give you almost no time to weigh your options. Today you will betray somebody you love. You will have no way to avoid it."

The mayor got up and tried to say something. Carbone cut him off before he could finish the first word. "Sit. Now." Carbone's voice turned from a whisper to a shout.

The mayor sat back down.

"Mr. Mayor, we know that your brother Juan Francisco Abdoul is smuggling uranium into Colombia. This is uranium that he got from the Syrians. We know that he is in Venezuela. We need to know—and we need to know now—how he is entering the country."

Ricardo Abdoul smiled. So this is what this visit was about, he said to himself. He wondered how they had found out.

"That is crazy," Abdoul answered. "Why would Juan Francisco do such a crazy thing?"

"Mr. Abdoul, do not treat me like an idiot." Carbone reached down, raised his briefcase onto his knees, and took out a butcher's hack. It was one of those instruments that looked like a miniature ax. Butchers used them to cut pieces of meat with thick bones.

"If you do not tell me where your brother is, your son will die. I have already used this hack to chop off his left pinky finger. I will order the other fingers hacked off one by one, beginning in ten minutes. If I have to walk out of the house without the information I seek, I will personally kill your child. I will do it painfully. Tell me now and your son is saved."

Carbone instantaneously recognized that he had hit home. He had seen the same look with many of the men he wanted to scare. Abdoul's mouth became dry and his tongue tried to swivel around to create some saliva. Eyes could remain hard. Bodies could communicate disdain. But when a man was scared, his mouth became dry.

It was not enough, though. Carbone had to beat him down more. So, he slid across the coffee table the small, rectangular package handed to him a few minutes earlier in the car. Abdoul reached over to pick it up. There was a clear tremor in his hand.

Ricardo Abdoul opened it and winced. There was no mistaking the finger of a child. It was slender and small. The base was covered with blood. He closed the box and looked at Carbone.

"I will kill you," Abdoul said.

"No, you will not. You know that if you try to do that now, your son will die. And you will be under arrest. No—you will talk to me and you will deal with me."

Carbone allowed a minute of silence to pass. Abdoul was mulling his options. He knew Abdoul was already considering whether he could make a pact with the devil—his son for his brother. Now it was time to make the offer complete.

"Mr. Abdoul, we need the information on what your brother is doing and where he is. He's escalated this to levels that we can't tolerate. When we find him—with your help or not—he will probably be killed. The family will be yours to run. It will be nice to have your son grow up with you as the boss."

Abdoul stared at him. What was this man saying? He could have his son back and assume the family's leadership? This was interesting. He knew Juan Francisco had gone too far this time. He understood that his brother's hatred for Marta Pradilla was completely overboard. Over the edge. He made a split-second decision.

"My brother has become consumed by hate. He devised a horrible plan. He used his Syrian connections to get a serious quantity of uranium-235. And he is bringing it into Colombia."

Carbone interrupted him. "We know this. I know he is a criminal. But I never thought of him as a mass murderer. If he uses the uranium to make a bomb to kill Marta Pradilla, he will kill thousands of Colombians. Even bringing the uranium into Colombia endangers himself, his family."

The younger Abdoul looked at him with questioning eyes. Then he started chuckling. Ricardo Abdoul now understood that Carbone had no clue what Juan Francisco's plans were.

"You have it completely wrong. You don't understand anything about Juan Francisco. He despises Marta Pradilla. But he is a patriot. He would never hurt his fellow citizens."

Now it was Carbone's turn to be completely confused.

"Juan Francisco is bringing the uranium in from Venezuela. I don't know where he or the uranium is. That is the truth. All I can help you with is to tell you what is happening and when it will happen. You see, the uranium is not staying here. Sixty *mulas* are lined up and ready to go on Thursday, two days from today. They will leave from Cali, Barranquilla, Bogotá, Medellín, and Cartagena, and are flying into Miami, Dallas, Atlanta, New York, Newark, and Los Angeles. All on one day. That way even if some get caught, the rest cannot be stopped. They will each have bits of the nuclear material in their guts. It gets delivered to Syrian agents in the United States. Then, it is up to them to blow up millions of gringos."

My God, thought Carbone. This was starting to come together. How had he not seen this before? He had been completely off base. This was not about a sale of Syrian uranium for Colombian money. That was not at all what was happening. The Syrians did not need the money. They needed the smuggling skills of Colombian drug dealers.

That is how they could bring the product into the United States. There they would create a nuclear device and explode it. It would create complete havoc around the world. It would reduce the United States to the role of a flailing paper tiger.

For Juan Francisco Abdoul, this was a win-win deal. Even if most of the nuclear material was captured or even if the Syrians were unable to create a bomb, Juan Francisco Abdoul would still get what he wanted. What mattered most to Abdoul was getting the nuclear materials into the United States. From Colombia. Their country would be accused of being the transit point for a massive terrorist attack on the United States. Colombia would become a reviled pariah. And, with that, Marta Pradilla's presidency would come to an end. It was complete lunacy, yet utterly effective.

Carbone took out a walkie-talkie and gave an order to come in. Instantaneously, five agents leapt out of waiting cars, showed their badges to the police outside, and strode into the house. They came into the room with Carbone and Abdoul.

"Mayor Abdoul, these men are placing you under arrest. For now, it is a temporary arrest. We will tell the police and the press that you are in protective custody because your life is in danger. You will be taken to a safe house in Bogotá. If what you told me is true, then my part of the bargain will be upheld—with regard to your son, your brother, and your position as family leader. If what you have told us turns out to be a lie, both your son and you will meet again in the afterlife."

"I have to tell Stockman," shouted Pradilla.

They had known each other for many years and had been the closest of confidants for the last two years. They had never raised a voice to each other. Manuel Saldivar and Marta Pradilla were soul mates. They continuously checked out each other's compasses to make sure there was no drifting. They became accustomed to seeing eye to eye on almost everything.

This was not the case now. For the first time ever, there was clear, palpable tension between the president and her chief of staff. Over a secure speakerphone, Hector Carbone had just told them of his discoveries, and all hell had broken loose between the two friends.

"Look, Marta, you can't trust the Americans with this. It will be the end of your presidency. They will come at Colombia with everything they have. They will not be delicate. Potentially, we could even risk an invasion of our country to find Abdoul or the uranium. I know you want to do the right thing, but you swore an oath to protect Colombia. Not to protect Americans."

"It is one and the same, Manuel," answered President Pradilla, her voice strained with emotion. "It is my responsibility as a citizen of the world and the head of state of a friendly country to advise the United States that their security is in danger from Colombia. It is our fault that we produce people like Abdoul— not theirs. They just make him rich by providing him with a market. This is no longer just about narcotics. Millions of lives are at stake."

"Marta, please think about it. Anybody who gets near the United States gets burned. Look at Goni Sanchez de Lozada in Bolivia. Peasants revolted against him because he was close to the United States. They asked him to eradicate coca leaves and gave nothing in return. He is out. Look at Aznar in Spain. He was Bush's closest friend and backed Iraq. Aznar is out. You will get nothing in return. They will run over you and you will be forced to resign here because you gave up sovereignty."

"Explain yourself," she asked coldly.

"Once you tell them, they will do one of the following: They may invade parts of our country to find Abdoul. They may take out our airports to stop the smugglers. They could order a blockade, like the one they instituted around Cuba during the missle crisis.

"And if they don't take military action, you will still have given up sovereignty because you did not stop the crime in Colombia. You give the United States the power to arrest the sixty Colombian *mulas*—who may or may not know what they are carrying. The gringos won't keep it quiet. Our citizens will be paraded in front of the press as more proof of their success in the war on terrorism. At best, we will look like fools and accomplices. At worst, we will be blamed. Most Colombians will say that this is a problem you should have taken care of, and that, instead, you abdicated your powers to the United States."

Pradilla turned to the phone box and addressed Hector. "Can you guarantee that we can catch these people as they leave Colombia?"

"No, Presidente. If we want to keep this quiet, there is no way to promise you that we can stop them from leaving Colombia. We can probably catch a number of them. But unless we shut down Colombian airspace, I cannot make promises to you. Abdoul may have people on planes to Panama and Ecuador, and flying from there to the United States. To stop them here, we will have to make public what is happening."

Manuel jumped in again. "Marta, that is exactly my point. The Americans will not keep this quiet. Stockman hates you for the Castro play on Inauguration Day. So, the American propaganda machine will skewer you. Let's do our best to stop them here and try to control the aftermath."

Marta turned to Carbone. She could hardly think straight. Her mind went back and forth. "Hector, make arrangements to implement a shutdown of our airports in Colombia and all Colombian airspace as of midnight Wednesday. If we decide not to do that, give me another plan for how we actually inspect outgoing passengers on Thursday."

Manuel exhaled a huge sigh of relief as Marta Pradilla walked out the door.

The Family Quarters
Bogotá, October 16
12:37 p.m.

The president turned left into the corridor and headed toward the elevators. She knew that she had four congressmen waiting for her to discuss oil contracts in northern Colombia. She did not care.

Once in her private quarters, Marta Pradilla gave orders that she not be disturbed, then picked up the phone. "Get me the White House. I want to talk to the president."

It took over ten minutes. When the operator called back, she was connected with Stockman's secretary.

"Madame President, I'm Marjorie Orloff, we have passed President Stockman a note. He said he would adjourn his meeting for a few minutes to take your call. I'm sure he'll be right with us. Yes, here he is, please hold."

She heard John Stockman pick up the telephone. "Marta," he said with a joking snicker, "this is a change. Maybe you won't enjoy my company as much over the phone."

"John, how are you?" Marta Pradilla was all business. "Look, I need to discuss something, but I won't do it over the phone. I don't want any tracks left regarding what we talk about. I need you to use our usual communications, John. You know what I mean. But, I need you to IM me."

"What's that," Stockman said.

"Instant Messenger. I know you are in a meeting, so I'll wait for you to get on. John, this is very important."

"Sure, I know what IM is," said Stockman, now remembering his practice sessions with Julia. "But Marta, please tell me what this is about. If I can help with something, you know I'll try. Give me a sense of the problem."

"No, John. Not on the phone. I will wait. Bye, John."

President John Stockman stood there with the phone against his ear. It occurred to him that years had gone by since someone else had disconnected a telephone line on him.

In Bogotá, Marta Pradilla had one more call to make. She picked up her phone and instructed the Casa de Nariño operator to connect her to President Fidel Castro in Havana.

PART XI
WASHINGTON

The White House

===

Stockman paced once around his desk. He looked at his watch. In the small meet-ing room next to the Oval Office, Jasper Thompson, the secretary of Housing and Urban Development, was still waiting for the president to complete his phone call and return to their lunch meeting. Stockman's tuna and hard-boiled egg sandwich remained half eaten.

John Stockman picked up the intercom and called Marjorie.

"Something has come up. I can't finish the meeting with Jasper. Tell him I apologize and will reschedule for tomorrow."

She started to protest, but he had already hung up. Not a man to cancel meet-ings midstream, Maggie worried that this was highly unusual for the methodical president of the United States. Was something wrong with him?, she wondered. He never behaved like this.

Stockman turned on his computer with some apprehension. The machine was still a difficult experience for John Stockman. He had ongoing troubles with the mouse, struggling with the differences between single-clicking and double-clicking, right-clicking and left-clicking.

He double-clicked the IM icon and then looked for the plus sign, which sig-nified "add a buddy." He wrote the words "beautifulcolombia" in the empty space. Immediately, he heard the sound of a door creak open. She was there.

He clicked on her name and waited for the box to appear. Then, he typed. "Hello, Marta." Nothing happened. He waited, and still nothing. Shit—he forgot to press enter. He punched the key.

Suddenly, the machine came alive. He heard a mechanical bell and saw her answer simultaneously.

"John, it's me"

"Good, I remembered how to do this," he wrote.

"Thank God. I need to talk to you urgently."

"So why couldn't you talk on the phone?"

"No. Can't do it over the phone. I need to see you."

Stockman stopped cold. He was confused. This woman drove him nuts. He felt awash in a strange pleasure that she needed to see him, but her direct proposition made him supremely uncomfortable. He was not ready to have an open relationship with a woman, much less another president.

"That would be nice. I want to see you too," he answered coyly.

"John, it's not a proposition. I need to talk to you urgently. It's an emergency."

He felt a pang of disappointment that this was not about them. It was business. Still, he was intrigued. With anybody else, his natural politician's defenses would have kicked in.

"How do we do that?" he answered.

"I want you to meet me tonight. Halfway."

"Tonight? Halfway?"

"Yes, in Cuba. It is the only place in the Western Hemisphere where the press doesn't run rampant. We will not be seen. It will not be reported. Any other place is too open. I have already asked Castro."

Stockman was shocked. Furious was the right word.

"Marta, I am not coming to see you tonight in Havana. That is ridiculous."

The computer hesitated. He could feel her pausing. He knew that she was disappointed. But the one-word answer that came next was totally unexpected and shook him to his core.

"Syria."

"What!"

"John, I know your government is looking for something very dangerous. I can help. But I can't do it in the open. I need guaranteed secrecy. Havana is the one place that can be managed. Castro controls everything. He gave me assurances."

Stockman did not know what to do. How was it possible that this woman knew about the uranium? How could he go to Havana? His mind swirled uncontrollably. The computer's bells rang again.

"John, trust me. You are in danger, and I can help you."

"I need to think about it."

"Don't. You will not regret it. I will see you there at midnight tonight. I am leaving for the airport in an hour."

He needed time. He was in the middle of repeating his need to think when he heard a loud thump. Her electronic door had closed. She was off-line. Gone. Stockman was alone.

The Oval Office
Washington, October 16
2:10 p.m.

About an hour later, Nelson Cummins opened the door to the Oval Office. He saw the president sitting at his desk staring blindly into space. It was unusual to see this guy in quiet mode. Cummins braced himself.

"Sorry, Mr. President, I heard you were looking for me. I was downstairs getting a coffee."

The president got up and walked around his large walnut desk. He sat down on one of the ornate red chairs in the seating area and pointed Nelson to the sofa. Cummins was immediately wary. This seating arrangement was the exact opposite of the one Stockman usually chose. The president habitually took the right-hand couch to himself and had staff sit on the chairs. Something was wrong.

"I just had an interesting conversation with Marta Pradilla," said Stockman.

"Is it smart to have an informal conversation with this woman? She did not exactly treat us right in Bogotá," Cummins asked.

Stockman was impressed that the Secret Service had kept his nighttime meeting with Pradilla at the United Nations a secret. He was not about to detail the fact that he had seen her in New York and had been exchanging e-mail letters with her pretty much continuously for the past few weeks. So he answered precisely, but not exactly truthfully.

"I don't know."

"What did she want?" asked Cummins. He clearly was not happy. White House press secretary Allyson Bonnet had been the first to bring to his attention the fact that the president might have a shine for his Colombian colleague. But now it was amply evident to him that his boss was infatuated.

"She wants to meet me in Havana tonight." Stockman was perfectly aware of how unusual this sounded. Correction. He was perfectly aware of how totally strange this was. But even he was surprised by Cummins's response.

"What?" shouted Cummins as he rocketed off the sofa. "You want to go on a love fling to Havana?" Cummins regretted the instant the words left his mouth. But he could not help it. He had always criticized the president for being a brilliant but unfeeling politician. Now that the president had revealed a sentimental weak spot, he hated him for it. Go figure.

Stockman stared at Cummins. No staff person ever talked to him like this. Under normal circumstances, it was a firing offense. But these were far from normal circumstances. He let Cummins's anger slide by.

"Sit down, Nelson. I'm not done. She wants to meet because she has information about the Syrian uranium. Information we do not have."

Nelson Cummins had trouble gathering his thoughts. This was a once-in-a-lifetime meeting. Just when he thought he had heard something incredible, something more incredible popped up next. He realized his jaw was agape. A minute ago, his boss had announced that he was thinking about going to Cuba to meet the cute president of Colombia. And now he was saying that she had information that not even the CIA had.

Nelson tried to close his mouth, but couldn't. He kept fumbling for words that did not come out. How did she know about the Syrians? What information did she have about the uranium? Why did she not go through channels?

Since Nelson was having trouble answering, the president just kept going.

"She said that we are in danger. That meeting me is urgent. She chose Cuba because the press there is controlled. There is no chance for us to be seen. She has spoken to Castro about it. He promised her that he could keep the meeting completely silent."

Nelson was up again. "She spoke to Castro about it? Castro promised secrecy? How dare she speak to Castro without talking to you first! She is out of control. You can't go."

"Nelson, sit down. I won't ask again. Why can't I go?" Stockman knew the answer, but wanted to hear it out loud.

"Are you out of your mind, Mr. President? I don't need to tell you why. Imagine what would happen if it came out. In short, here's how the story will play: On the day your intelligence officials told you about Syria's possession of lethal amounts of highly enriched uranium, you did a couple of things. First, you decided not to warn Americans of the danger. Second, you took a jaunt to an enemy nation to have a midnight summit with the single most beautiful woman president on the planet. Mr. President, I know that these are not your intentions. But that is how it will read. You will never be forgiven."

It was true. If he went and was found out, it would be political suicide. He would be impeached. There was no possible explanation that would work. Moreover, Fidel Castro would own a chit on the American presidency. He could always threaten to tell the story. There might not be free press in Cuba, but there were a lot of government agents with cameras. Stockman was depressed.

"Call her and tell her that you are sending me to Bogotá. Tell her I'm leaving now," suggested Nelson.

"That won't work. She will only talk to me. I know her."

Jeezus. Either this man was completely in love and was projecting qualities onto a woman he hardly knew, or there was more here that the president was not telling him. How in God's name was he able to say that he knew her? He saw her once in his life for a very short time.

Or had they been in touch clandestinely?

Silence enveloped the room. Cummins watched with real worry. In all the years they had worked together, this was the first time he had seen his boss really struggle over a decision. He made tough choices all the time. Stockman always projected a pretense of listening to all sides, but the president's mind was usually already leaning heavily in one direction or another. This was new. The president of the United States honestly did not know what to do.

Minutes went by in silence. Cummins decided to shut up. He knew this man well. Stockman's conservative, risk-averse nature would take over and make the right decision. John Stockman would never put his entire career on the line for a single roll of the dice. Best to let him come to that conclusion on his own.

After what seemed like an eternity, the president of the United States stood up. "I took an oath of office to protect this country—whatever the lengths and whatever the risks. President Pradilla has something urgent to tell me about a major danger to our country. It must not be easy for her to help the United States. It used to be an attractive thing to be on our side, but now most foreign leaders who stand by this country become hexed. She is unusual, I'll admit to that. But she has balls. I trust her."

Stockman looked Nelson in the eye. The questions that previously clouded the president's face had vaporized. The cocksure, undoubting Stockman was back—only, with a dramatically wrong decision. Nelson could not believe what was happening.

"I am going to Cuba. Now. Make it happen, Nelson."

PART XII
CUBA

The Colombian Presidential Plane
Over the Caribbean, October 16
8:30 p.m.

At 39,000 feet, the Colombian 757 was flying smoothly above the Caribbean Sea. Inside the airplane, however, the air was rough.

Four hours ago, Manuel Saldivar thought he had won the argument with Marta Pradilla. She had asked Hector Carbone to make a plan to close down Colombian airspace on Wednesday night. Manuel was sure they convinced her that capturing the majority of smugglers as they left Colombia was doable. With that, they would avert any danger to the United States, while preserving Colombian sovereignty and dignity.

Now he was with the Colombian president on a government plane heading to Cuba to meet with the American president who might or might not be coming. For the first time in his life, he felt that Marta Pradilla could not be trusted to make the right decision. Without having had any discussion with him or any other advisor, without having previously negotiated any arrangement with the Americans, this Colombian president was about to tell the gringo head of state that their country was the source of a serious threat to U.S. security.

It would not matter to Stockman that Colombia was only a transit point for the uranium and that the smugglers were renegade, criminal elements of Colombian society. The U.S. president would not care that the Colombian government was willing to help. All that would matter to the Americans was that a serious, imminent threat was gathering from Colombia. There would be no delicacy or understanding. There would be no desire to cooperate. Their response would be brutal and overwhelming.

They were both exhausted. For the last two hours, the flight had seen a pattern of frigid verbal combat interspersed with stony silence. At first Manuel doubted she understood the danger in which she was placing her country and her own political future. He patiently reexplained the risks to her, listing them one by one and pointing out that they were not mutually exclusive.

First, Manuel went through the possible military responses. Within hours of telling Stockman, the United States Southern Command in Panama could mobilize, and could invade Colombia within a day. U.S. Delta Force special operations units could parachute into every Colombian airport. U.S. Air Force fighters could shoot down any plane leaving Colombian airspace. U.S. Navy warships could blockade Colombia's ports and board every boat leaving the nation's harbors.

Now he listed the political measures. If the Americans captured any of the poor Colombian souls smuggling the uranium, they could show them off like cheap advertising of America's determination in the war on terrorism. The U.S. administration could blame Colombia for endangering its security and could cut off economic and military assistance. Worse yet, the Americans could punish Colombia by blocking its legitimate exports of flowers, coffee, oil, and seafood. Within hours, they could decimate Colombia's economy.

How could she not understand that the dangers inherent in telling the Americans about the uranium completely outweighed any possible benefits? How could she not understand that Colombia had the wherewithal to arrest the perpetrators and stop the attack on America on its own? Damn it, she had been elected president to protect Colombia, not to be a good world citizen.

Therein lay the problem. As time clicked by and the plane passed over the snowy Andes Mountains, above the darkened Caribbean waters, and across the Windward Islands, Manuel Saldivar came to the scary realization that she understood all of it. All the dangers. To her country and her political career. She got it all.

Yet here they were, hurtling through the night to disaster. They were one hour from landing. Fifteen minutes had gone by in silence. Manuel seethed and finally exploded.

"Who are you? I thought I knew you. Millions of Colombians put their trust in you, and you are turning your back on them. At first, I thought you hadn't considered this through all the way. But I realize now that you know the dangers. You understand what will probably happen, and you are doing it anyway. Who gave you the right to do this?"

"Manuel, we are going in circles. I was elected. It's my decision. There are risks everywhere. But the greatest risk of all is that the first nuclear bomb since Hiroshima and Nagasaki could come from my country and could kill millions of innocent people in the United States. There is no risk greater than that."

"But chances are we can stop it ourselves!" answered Manuel plaintively.

"And what if we don't stop it? Can you live with not having told the Americans as they run around trying to bury millions? I can't and I won't."

"Hector Carbone says that the DAS can probably get most of them. We should try, and if we feel that we were not successful, we can tell the Americans at that point. Marta, do the right thing and turn this airplane around."

"No, Manuel," said Marta quietly. "I won't do it. I understand that you feel strongly about this. I know you think I am mistaken. You will have a choice when we land. You can stay on the plane or you can come with me, even though you think I am wrong."

She wasn't finished.

"This is where politics differs from journalism, Manuel. In journalism, you keep your distance, convincing yourself that you bear the righteousness of the neutral observer. In politics, you make your argument, but you are still expected to be loyal to your president and your party, even if you think I'm way off base. Yes, Manuel, I still count on you to walk off this plane at my side."

He stared hard at her. He could not believe what she said. A few hours ago, they were the best of friends; now they sat together on an airplane looking into an abyss that could end their friendship. This was what people meant when they shook their heads in disgust and muttered "politics are dirty." Marta Pradilla was ready to give up on everything they had built together just because she stubbornly believed she was right.

He ached. Manuel Saldivar was not in love with Marta Pradilla, but he had come to love her—as a friend, a soul mate, and as a fearless new leader who represented so much hope for his country. Tears of rage and hurt welled in his eyes as he realized that she was perfectly capable of dispensing with him. She wanted him there, with her. But she did not want that more than accomplishing what she set out to do in Cuba.

A mechanical hiss droned out of the plane's loudspeakers. The captain's voice soon followed. "Thirty minutes to landing, Presidente. Seat belts, please."

Manuel Saldivar looked at Marta and nodded. He understood that he had a half hour to cross the abyss or forever stay behind.

Air Force One
Off the Florida Peninsula, October 16
9:00 p.m.

Nelson Cummins closed his eyes. An hour ago, Air Force One had crossed over the beaches of Cape Fear, North Carolina, and roared out over the Atlantic Ocean. By now they must be halfway between Gainesville and Miami.

Tired was not the word. Since takeoff an hour ago, his mind had scrambled from one direction to the other. He reviewed all the arguments and rationales that could successfully negotiate President John Stockman away from this madness. He wrote them down as talking points, prioritized them, and practiced his delivery. In a few minutes, he would get up and walk to the 747's presidential suite. He would try one last time.

All hell had broken loose at the White House in the hour that ensued after the president's order to move. Nelson had made four phone calls, and within minutes people began to appear in his office.

Nelson waited for the foursome to gather. Marjorie, the president's longtime trusted assistant; Tim Ordway, the head of the president's Secret Service detail; Colonel Nicholas Markoff, the military liaison to the White House; and Allyson Bonnet, the White House press secretary—all walked in within a few seconds of each other. He did not bother offering chairs. They would be jumping right back out of their seats in a few seconds.

"You won't believe what I have to tell you," Nelson had started. He had tried to maintain an outward air of neutrality and impartiality. But he knew that what he was about to request was the political equivalent of the pope suggesting that the Curia take a field trip with him to a Roman bordello. It was more than unprecedented—it was completely impossible. Yet, Nelson shook himself out of his misery, here he was.

"The president wants to leave on a top secret mission within one hour," Nelson announced. "The mission is to meet tonight with President Marta Pradilla of Colombia who has urgent, confidential information regarding the security of the

United States. At the request of President Pradilla the meeting point is Havana, Cuba, because, as a police state, it is the safest place in the hemisphere from the press and any other intruder. We will be on the ground for as short a time as possible."

He had made the right decision not to offer them a seat. The room broke into a complete frenzy. They all talked at once. Correction: They shouted in unison. Nelson hardly understood any of it over the din of confused voices, but he could safely vouch that the noise was negative.

"Stop!" Nelson shouted. No use.

"Shut up, goddamnit!" he tried again.

This time the four quieted down. Nelson looked from one to the other.

"Each one of you can talk. One at a time. You have one minute to say why this is a bad idea. But I have probably already said all of it and more to the boss. After your minute is up, I need you to tell me how we do what the president wants. Start with you, Nick."

Colonel Markoff, tall and athletic, was out of uniform this evening. But you could tell a mile away the guy was military. He stood ramrod straight when he spoke.

"Nelson, it's crazy. Sure, we always have a flight crew ready, but there is no flight plan. We are flying into a country with which we have no diplomatic relations. How do we even know they will let us into their airspace? And even if they do authorize entrance, once we are in Cuban air, we fly unsecured. I don't need a minute. That alone should be enough to tell you we shouldn't do it."

"He is, unfortunately, aware of this. So, what if we have to do it?" snapped Nelson.

Markoff thought for a minute. He did not want to favor the question with a reply, but he was a military officer and, thus, was loyal to the chain of command. A question from the commander-in-chief's national security advisor needed a response.

"We can take off in an hour. I recommend we load the plane with a special operations commando group that can stay on the plane but will be ready to engage in case anything happens on the ground. We will be in touch with Cuban controllers an hour before reaching Havana. The good thing here is that the plane will be in U.S. airspace until we leave Key West, which is about ninety miles from touchdown—that is less than twenty minutes from landing. The Cubans will only give us permission to enter if they are aware we are coming. If they don't, we turn around.

"One last thing," added Markoff. "I would ask Homestead Air Force Base in

Florida for a squadron of F-16s to be on combat air patrol just outside Cuban air-space during the whole time we are there. We will also mobilize Guantanamo to high alert."

Nelson was always impressed by the can-do attitude of the military. They might disagree violently, but they were ready to go, regardless.

"Nick, go ahead and make the arrangements. Do we use helos to get to Andrews?"

"Absolutely. I'll get on it." Nick Markoff walked out of the room.

"Marjorie, you are next," Nelson dictated.

She was aghast. In twenty years with John Stockman, she had learned that he almost never made off-the-cuff decisions. He liked predictability and control. He stuck to his schedule religiously. But the same twenty years had also taught her that once he made a decision, there was no talking him out of it.

"I can only imagine that you have done anything and everything to convince him that this is madness. So, I won't even try to dissuade you. The first public event tomorrow is at 3:00 p.m. He speaks at the National Governors Association. Until then, the secretary of Housing and Urban Development, whom he so gently dumped today, is at 8:00 a.m. and then the Joint Chiefs at 9:00 with the secretary of Defense. He had calls from 11:00 to 12:00. All of that can be moved. He has lunch at 12:00 with Senator Carles, but he's a friend and we can postpone that too. The speech to the governors is at the National Building Museum. Get him there by 2:55 p.m. and maybe we can still be friends, Nelson."

Nelson smiled. She had a crusty, intolerant air. But she was loyal to the end.

He looked at the Secret Service man. "Tim?"

"Nelson, I'm not worried about random security problems. Cuba is a communist, authoritarian state. There are no crazy people with guns in that country. But they have a very crazy president. If we get on the ground and they want to hold our man hostage, there will be nothing I can do about it. I would need hundreds of agents to protect the president from fifty armed soldiers pointing AK-47s at us. We have been sworn enemies for over forty years. I would not discount the possibility that they would attempt to keep us there."

Nelson had not actually thought about Cuban troops keeping the president of the United States in Cuba against his will. The thought made him shudder.

"Here's what I would ask," Tim Ordway continued. "I want ten agents with us. And I want a three-minute hall pass before Stockman gets off the plane. I will get off first and look around. If I don't like something, we get back on, close the doors, and ride away. Understood?"

Nelson nodded his agreement. Marjorie and Tim lingered on for a moment and silence overwhelmed the room. After a short while, it became clear that Nelson wanted Allyson alone. They turned around and walked out. Nobody said good-bye. Everybody's head was racing too fast to stop for polite adieus. They closed the door.

Nelson looked at Allyson for a long minute. Allyson's instincts had been right all along on Pradilla.

"Allyson, I don't know how, but those two have been in touch with each other. He talks about her as if he knew her. He says things like 'I trust her' and 'I know her.' At first, I thought he was out of his mind. But then it became clear to me that they have connected in ways we don't know about."

"Do I need to know what the information she needs to impart is about?" asked Allyson.

"Not yet, Allyson. But Pradilla told him the magic word to get him there: Syria. She says the information is vital to the security of the United States."

"I told you that this woman was amazing. First, she played you guys like puppets in Bogotá. Then, she finds a way to have a clandestine relationship with the president that we didn't know about. Now, she has secret news that can only be told to him. In Cuba. She is incredible."

Nelson knew this was not the end.

"I believe her, Nelson. Woman's instinct. I've been right so far. She wants to change his mind about things. That is what the meeting with Castro in Bogotá was about. She does not play by the rules, but she won't lie. I believe her."

Nelson was floored. Allyson, the world's biggest cynic, was now painting Pradilla as just a sincere little girl from down south who wanted to do the right thing. How the hell could she know that?

"Look at it from her point of view," said Allyson. "If she really has something, she is taking a risk to tell it to the boss. For God's sake, we are incredibly unpopular down there. And the Cuba meeting is absolutely brilliant. We'll never get caught in Cuba. Sure, Castro will have something on us, but he won't waste a golden chit by embarrassing us in the press. He will use it to negotiate quietly. He has stayed in power for four decades—he knows how to use people smartly."

"What happens if we do get caught by the press here?" asked Nelson.

Allyson smiled. "That, my friend, is a different story. If that happens, we're totally and completely fucked."

Those were the words that kept going around in his head as the Boeing 747 sped southward over the Atlantic Ocean. We are totally and completely fucked. We are totally and completely fucked. We are totally and completely fucked.

He was rudely disconnected from his trance of negativity by the soft ring of the phone in his armrest. It must be Stockman. For a short second, he was elated by the hope that the president had come to his senses. He was calling to announce they were going back!

It wasn't the president. Colonel Jeffrey Swan was in command of Air Force One and was now on the phone with him.

"Nelson, I thought you might want to come up here. We're three quarters of the way down the Florida peninsula. We'll be calling Havana in a few minutes. Let's see if they have any clue we're coming," said Swan.

Nelson told the captain that he was on his way and climbed the front stairwell to the 747's upstairs cockpit. He walked in and Colonel Swan handed him headphones and pointed him to the jump seat in the doorway.

He adjusted the headpiece and pushed the voice-activated microphone to his mouth. "Try it, Colonel. Hopefully, they won't have a clue and we can go home."

Jeff Swan turned the dials on his UHF radio.

"Havana Approach, this is a United States government flight . . . with you at flight level three-niner-zero," intoned Colonel Swan. Tim Ordway and Colonel Swan had previously agreed not to initially identify themselves as Air Force One. While the airplane usually used confidential U.S. military frequencies to transmit, he was now talking to controllers at a commercial airport. It was an open mike. A few seconds passed.

"United States government flight, this is Havana Approach. Please switch to secure frequency 118.23."

Colonel Swan glanced back at Nelson. Was this good or bad news? This first concise communication was inscrutable. Jeff Swan switched frequencies and tried again.

"Havana Approach, this is U.S. government flight with you at flight level three-niner-zero," Swan repeated his previous words exactly.

"United States Government flight, this is Havana Approach on secure frequency. Please specify your identification."

Colonel Jeff Swan turned around to look at Nelson. His clear green eyes silently asked one question only: Do we tell?

Nelson took a deep breath and nodded yes.

"Havana Approach, United States government flight is a Boeing 747, call sign is Air Force One."

This time there was no hesitation in the response.

"Air Force One, this is Havana Approach. You are cleared to José Martí International Airport via the Varadero intercept. Plan to land runway 27. Kindly advise when beginning descent at Key West. Remain on this frequency only, please."

Swan was now in total professional mode and repeated back the instructions. "Cleared to Havana via the Varadero intercept. Will call back at Key West on this frequency only. Air Force One."

He turned around to Nelson.

"Well, they did not have the marching bands out and it didn't have the welcoming feel of a ticker tape parade. But you heard it—there is no doubt that they knew we were coming."

Allyson Bonnet was right. Marta Pradilla was amazing. The fact that a Cuban air controller was providing landing coordinates to Air Force One was nothing less than remarkable. It was not the result of delicate government negotiations. Nor was it the end of a long road of quiet persuasion by a Nobel peace prize winner. In less than an afternoon, Pradilla had managed to clear the landing of the airplane of the president of the United States on enemy soil. How had she done this?

Right then and there, Nelson decided he would not try to talk the president out of the trip. He knew it was useless. Stockman had come this far. He would never turn the plane around. Cummins realized that his furiously written talking points were really only about keeping himself happy. He wrote them because he wanted Stockman to know where he stood. Stockman knew. It did not need repeating.

Cummins thanked the colonel for allowing him to listen in. He turned left out of the cockpit and slowly came down the spiral staircase. He headed toward the presidential suite to tell Stockman that the last impediment had been removed. The Cubans were expecting them.

As he walked to Stockman's closed door, he could not stop Allyson's words from repeating dully into his brain: We are totally and completely fucked.

José Martí International Airport

Havana, October 16

10:43 p.m.

===

Colonel Jeff Swan landed the enormous airplane uneventfully on runway 27. Really uneventfully. As the 747 hit the tarmac, nobody inside the airplane said a word. Nobody breathed. Landing the U.S. president in Cuba was not an everyday occurrence, and all on board knew it.

The airplane followed the tower's instructions to taxi past the civilian terminal toward the far end of the field. This side of the airport obviously belonged to the Cuban armed forces. Military helicopters and old Russian-made Mig-21s were lined up in an orderly fashion. The U.S. airplane was directed to park next to a Boeing 757 with a large Colombian flag painted on its tail.

As the engines wound down, Tim Ordway got up and walked toward Nelson.

"I've got three agents with the president. They are not letting him off until I say so. Remember our agreement."

Nelson nodded and Tim walked to the door just as the air force crew was giving the thumbs-up sign to the airport staff to open the doors. Tim Ordway walked off and went down the ladder.

As Nelson looked out the window, he could see a small, elegant man in a coat and tie shaking hands with the senior Secret Service agent. He instantly recognized the Cuban foreign minister, Esteban Montealegre. So did Tim Ordway.

"Mr. Minister, I'm Agent Tim Ordway of the United States Secret Service. I'm in charge of the president's security. I have asked to come off the airplane first. Frankly, my job is to assess threats to my boss. Is there anything you want to tell me?"

"Agent Ordway, welcome to Cuba," said Montealegre. His English was practically accent-less. "Yes, come with me and let me tell you what we have. The airport is closed. The first flight that lands here is at 7:30 a.m. tomorrow morning. We presume the airport will be reopened and that you will be gone by then, so we have not issued any advisory about the airport's closure."

So far, so good, thought Tim.

"We have surrounded the airport and its access roads with over one thousand men of the Cuban army," continued the foreign minister. "They are outside the perimeter fence and their instructions are to have their backs to the airfield—they are looking for threats from the outside. We know this might make you nervous, Mr. Ordway. But on the other hand, we cannot risk any accidents during your stay.

"We don't allow accidents to happen in Cuba," the minister added.

Tim Ordway looked to the perimeter and saw men in army fatigues fanned out on the other side of the fence. They were facing the other way. He shuddered. "Where is the president going?" Ordway asked.

"To the VIP lounge of this terminal." Montealegre pointed. The terminal was less than fifty feet away. "There are three rooms there for your use."

Tim thought for a few seconds. The terminal was ultraclose. That was comforting. If he had to get the president back onto the airplane quickly, he could do it. On the other hand, he had no idea if there were other troops inside the airport that the foreign minister had not told him about.

"Mr. Minister, we have a special operations force of twenty-five men on board. I would like your permission to have them come out and surround the airplane. They will be armed. I know this may be unusual, but this whole mission is unusual. I hope you will understand. Their purpose is only defensive and to assist me in case we must leave in an emergency."

The minister nodded. He expected this.

"I will enter the building with the president and will take three other agents with me," Ordway continued. "Last, sir, I need to tell you that there is a squadron of F-16s that will be on patrol off your international waters during the time we are here. Should anything happen that would require us to leave, they will be asked to assist."

Montealegre smiled. The Americans were incurable. They just could not resist showing off. It was as if their subtlety chromosomes had been genetically spliced away generations ago. What this Secret Service agent had just said was something a ten-year-old could have imagined. Of course they had airplanes ready to come get the president. On the other hand, did they seriously think that the Cuban government would be so stupid as to cause injury to Stockman? My God, they are like children, Montealegre muttered to himself.

"Thank you for telling me this, Agent Ordway. Nothing will happen to the president while he is here. President Castro is providing a confidential place for your discussions with President Pradilla. He—we—are glad to do it."

Tim nodded his agreement and raised his hand to talk into the small microphone in his jacket sleeve. "Let's do it," he ordered.

Within minutes, President John Stockman stepped off the plane and into

Havana's balmy Caribbean breeze. Nelson Cummins followed him. One agent led the way; two others brought up the rear. The president walked down the stairs to where Esteban Montealegre was waiting.

"Mr. President, I'm Esteban Montealegre, the foreign minister. Your visit here will remain confidential. But one day I hope to welcome you here publicly."

Stockman looked at the man. He appreciated the foreign minister's direct approach. He was similarly honest.

"Mr. Minister, we're grateful that you agreed to allow this meeting. It was President Pradilla's idea. It clearly makes me uncomfortable to be here. Given the right conditions, I too hope that, one day, we can become friendly neighbors."

Montealegre nodded. He was not going to get more than that from Stockman—this conservative politician was not going to be the one to open up to Cuba. Both men knew it. He asked the president to follow.

They entered the terminal building through a badly lit doorway. Over the top of the entrance, the words *Bienvenidos a Cuba. Viva la Revolucion* were sculpted into the concrete. The Americans all got an eerie feeling.

Once inside the building, a man in a white Caribbean guayabera shirt opened the door to a lounge. It was a well-appointed room, interspersed with sofas and coffee tables. Big tourism books of Cuba's natural beauties lay haphazardly arranged on each table. In the middle of the room, a dining table was set with plates of cold meats. Three large metallic buckets rested on the table containing soft drinks, white wine, and beer on ice.

Stockman noticed none of it. The instant he entered, his eyes darted furiously to each corner of the room. He wanted to see her.

There she was. The juxtaposition of the two presidents was a study in opposites. The American leader was dressed stodgily in a woolen blue pinstripe suit, a white shirt, and a red and blue tie. He was surrounded by security and accompanied by an advisor. Stockman communicated the essence of power and security, yet he was nervous and unsure of himself.

She, on the other hand, was alone; poised and smiling. Dressed in medium heels, blue jeans, and a white button-up shirt with a single blue lapis lazuli necklace around her elegant neck, she held a drink in her right hand. It was the usual—a scotch on the rocks. Her hair was not the way he had seen it earlier. She had it combed back and set in place with a band that revealed her radiant face. She was even more gorgeous than he remembered.

As she turned around to greet him, he felt a rush of heat. He wanted to take her in a huge embrace. He had never felt this way. Not even at the beginning with Miranda. Yet this woman had a magnetic effect on him. It was as if he could not resist the magic.

But he did resist. Stockman walked toward Marta slowly. He looked into her eyes with intensity. He needed to know now, right now, that this was legitimate. This could not be one of her little games. She walked toward him with a smile and let his eyes pry open her mind and intentions. She never left his eyes as she crossed the room. When she reached him, she stood right before him for a few seconds and let their gazes meet.

"Hello, John, thanks for coming. I know it was difficult."

He nodded and stretched out his arm to shake her hand. She did not take it, but instead leaned over and gave him a friendly peck on the cheek. The kiss left him with an intense warmth on his face. She laughed.

"Don't get formal on me, Mr. President. I'm from Latin America and we don't just shake hands. It's either an *abrazo* or a kiss. But it's definitely not just a handshake."

Stockman introduced his national security advisor and the security agents. She remembered Nelson Cummins from her inauguration. An uncomfortable silence fell over the room. Here they were. Having drinks at a secret midnight meeting in Havana, Cuba. There was no agenda. No protocol. Hell, nobody knew where to start.

"John, can I speak to you alone in the other room?" said Pradilla softly.

Two agents leapt in front of the president to block him from moving as Ordway went to the door of the adjoining room to take a first look. Stockman brushed them aside.

"Tim, don't overdo it," snapped Stockman.

He followed Pradilla as she opened the door. It was another sitting room. This one was much smaller, with only two wicker chairs and a small coffee table in between. On the walls hung a couple of bad paintings of landscapes with farmers plowing distant fields.

Behind closed doors, they sat down. She smiled and put her hand over his for just a few moments. They looked at each other.

"John, we don't have a lot of time. I want to start by saying that there is something between us. We are both adults and we both feel this. You are a widower and I am an habitual single. There would be nothing more natural than a relationship, except for the fact that you are the president of the United States and I the president of Colombia. The bets are against us. Who knows if one day we can be more open? I can tell you that in the last few hours, I've learned that the people I trust most do not want it to happen."

Stockman smiled. How in God's name could she be this direct? Was it the age difference? He knew that Julia was a lot more honest about her feelings than he had ever been. Was it cultural? He didn't think Latin Americans, with their strong

Catholicism, were that open. It was both horrifying and refreshing all at once. He would try to return the intimacy.

"Marta, I have been stuck much of my adulthood without questioning the way things should be. I lived my life that way. You have made me think about the world differently. Christ, I'm here in Havana. I don't think I would have done this for anybody else. I hardly know you, but I do know that you have touched my life as few people have before."

"But there isn't a way for us to try to make this work, is there?" she asked sadly. It was a statement more than a question.

Her presence filled the small room that was their world for these few minutes. He wanted to grab her. He wanted to pull her toward him, to kiss her. He wanted her lips touching his. She was so beautiful. The desire for her was almost painful. He looked deeply into her eyes.

"Probably not," he whispered.

Her eyes sadly agreed. "Yes, that is right. I have already lost my best friend by coming only this far. He is on the plane. He refused to come off with me. I can only imagine what else I would lose if it went further."

"Why did he do that?"

"Because he does not trust you. It's not so much about you as it is the United States in general. He believes you and your colleagues are uninterested in the world. He believes you will walk over everyone—and burn all bridges, with no loyalties—to get what you want. He told me that this is what you will do to me and to Colombia when I tell you what I know."

What can she know? Stockman asked himself. What can she tell me that is so terrible? What did Syria have to do with this?

He let her go on without interrupting her.

"I will tell you everything, John. I pulled it all together this afternoon. I will leave nothing out. I am doing this because it is the right thing to do and because I trust you will do the right thing. You should know at the beginning that you have all our cooperation. But I am asking you now, John, to prove me right. Prove to me that being America's friend is not a suicide mission."

She took a breath. She did not want or expect a response to that request. She knew that whatever he said here and now was meaningless. Actions were all that mattered now. The next days would show whether her gamble had been worth taking.

"The United States is in great danger. The Syrians have acquired a serious amount of uranium-235. I imagine you know that much. What you probably don't know is that the uranium will be smuggled into America from Colombia."

He instinctively drew back, his mind instantly swirling. Good lord, the CIA was completely wrong. The Syrians were not looking for a weapon to repel an American invasion of their soil. They were planning to bring the uranium into the United States and detonate a bomb in a major U.S. city. And he had just decided not to raise the alert level!

Stockman needed distance. He had to get out.

She picked up on it instantaneously. There it was. Stockman's—America's—distrust of foreigners. The sense that they could do it better. The instinctive belief that they needed nobody. She had to bat it down. Now.

Marta reached over and touched Stockman on his forearm. She did not remove her hand while speaking.

"John, listen to me. Don't start raising the walls. You cannot do this without me. There is nobody in your government, nobody in your intelligence services, nobody in your military who can help you more than I can right now. Even though I am not an American, you will have to trust me. Listen to the same goddamn instincts that brought you here."

His shoulders relaxed. Yes, he had come this far. He needed to listen to the rest.

She pieced together the whole story. She told him of Juan Francisco Abdoul's connections with the Syrians, how they had tailed him and how they discovered the suitcase transfer from the Syrians. She recounted how they came to know of the missing uranium from the DAS's contacts with the CIA and how they only realized hours ago that Abdoul's suitcases probably contained the nuclear material. She told him about the younger Abdoul's confirmation of a plot against the United States by trafficking the uranium into the country with drug smugglers on Thursday. Finally, she confessed that they had lost track of both Abdoul and the uranium somewhere in Venezuela.

She was exhausted. It had taken her thirty minutes to recount the story step by step. The more she got into it, the clearer the lines of pain became drawn across John's face. His country was in mortal danger.

He now felt conflicting reactions to Marta. He was furious that a country in his own backyard could participate in such singular evil. How could it be possible that Colombia could produce such opposites as Marta Pradilla and Juan Francisco Abdoul?

But more than anything else, one thing was clear to him: He had made the right choice in coming to Cuba. For once, he had opted for blind trust and it paid off. This single moment, alone in an airport VIP room with her, would probably turn out to be the most important one of his life.

There was little more to talk about. He had to leave. He had to get out now. The next forty-eight hours were now his to dictate. She knew this. She also knew that any offer to help would be rejected. The Americans simply could not—would not—trust the Colombians to interdict the uranium on their own. She took one look at Stockman and understood that he would never agree to put his country's fate in the hands of others.

She tried to smile. The beauty was still there, but she was now alone. They both understood that what had just been recounted would probably separate them forever. Her perfect eyes were shadows, covered by the opaque sadness of an imminent loss. There was nothing more to say.

He did have one question.

"Marta, what do you want?"

"Let me tell you first what I don't want," she said. Her eyes now flashed anger. "I do not want your military near our country. I do not want you to name us as a conspirator in terrorism, because we're not. We are fighting our own ghosts, and Abdoul is one of them. I do not want our name dragged through the mud because of what Abdoul has done. I do not want you to gloat in our misery.

"I want the impossible," she glowered at him. "I want Colombia kept out of it. I want Colombia and Colombians to be more, not less, respected, because of what I have done here."

The last words rebounded in the room. She was indeed amazing. Through it all, facing political demise, she still demanded respect for her country.

John Stockman got up and took a last look at this beautiful woman. She had entered his life as a whirlwind. And that is how she would exit.

He nodded gravely. Without another word, he turned around and walked out. Left behind in the small room, the last sound Marta heard was his voice ordering the security entourage to depart.

"Tim, let's move. We need to get home fast," said Stockman to the group.

PART XIII
COLOMBIA

Back into Colombia
Uraba, October 17
6:40 a.m.

The sun was rising on Wednesday morning in the Uraba-Darien region of northern Colombia. When most well-educated, sophisticated people imagine the far corners of the planet, they often think of the Sahara in Africa or the Gobi Desert in Mongolia. Those are Mickey Mouse destinations compared to Uraba. This is the true end of the world.

It is not so much that Uraba was poor and isolated. It is, but lots of places in lots of countries are like that. It is that Uraba lives in a separate reality. It is geographically and psychologically sliced off from the rest of the planet. Indeed, the Pan-American Highway, built years ago to connect Texas in the North to Chile in the South, has only one gap in its thousands of miles of concrete. The road makes it through Mexico's Sonoran Desert, across the volcanic highlands of Central America, through the majestic Andes, and down to Santiago, Chile. Only one place along the way refuses to allow itself to be conquered by the highway's engineers: Uraba.

A huge swath of territory just south of Colombia's border with Panama, Uraba is nearly impossible to reach. And impossible to understand. It is an impassable lowland jungle region of constant rainfall. The daily, oppressive rains wash away more than just the concrete of the roads. They loosen the rivets of the mind and soul.

Uraba's isolation makes it a Promised Land for bad men. There is no way for the laws of a democratic state to reach Uraba. So, it is often forgotten and left alone by the bureaucrats in Bogotá. There are bigger fish to fry than trying to fix Uraba.

Long ago, the place became infected with guerrillas and right-wing militia groups. Drug traffickers used it as a hiding ground for their laboratories and transition stops. Competing mafias ruled bits of its land and administered a horrible, personalized justice over Uraba's sparse population. One group massacred the other. Killings happened every day. All the time. Nobody even tried to understand why. They just happened.

Once you were in Uraba's grip, it was nearly impossible to get out. A few years ago, a long-standing leftist guerrilla group called the Popular Army of Liberation, or EPL, decided it was fed up with the killings and violence. It issued a statement solemnly stating its intention to put down its arms and join civil society. It was to convert itself into a political party. "Enough," the EPL declared. Within months, rival groups from the Left and Right assassinated every single leader of the EPL. No, you could not just leave Uraba.

Uraba's "qualities" made it the perfect place for Senator Juan Francisco Abdoul's final assault on Marta Pradilla. Abdoul had reentered Colombia by boat with his precious cargo. Getting back in had been easy.

Two days ago, he had landed in Caracas's Maiquetia Airport on the Air France flight from Paris. He had calmly walked to baggage claim and found his two suitcases swinging around the luggage belt in the company of hundreds of other bags disgorged from the French jumbo. He smiled thinking about the irony of his two lethal cases in the innocent companionship of luggages full of underwear, blue jeans, and gifts from arriving family members.

Showing his diplomatic passport, he went through customs without a hitch and turned right back into the main terminal. There, he headed to the dingy counter of Aeropostal, a local Venezuelan airline, and joined the line of smiling tourists dressed in shorts waiting to check in for the flight to the nearby Caribbean island of Aruba. Less than an hour's flying time away, Aruba was a favorite destination for Venezuelan families needing a little time off. He joked happily about his favorite beach on the island with the cute lady who gave him his boarding pass. "Have a nice vacation," she had said.

Aruba is nominally Dutch. It belongs to the Netherlands, but is governed by local authorities that make millions off tourism and the generous subsidies of the Dutch welfare state. Oh yes—one other thing. Aruba also makes a pretty penny as a smuggler's paradise. Every day, dozens of ships leave its shores for Colombia, laden with illicit loads of contraband cigarettes, DVDs, videos, and case upon case of whiskey.

Curiously, most of the whiskey was Old Parr scotch. Fifteen years ago, when Juan Francisco Abdoul first bought ten small cargo boats from a bankrupt Greek merchant, his investment had dominated the smuggler's trade between Aruba and Colombia's northern coastline. Back then, he experimented with all types of liquor. But nothing moved like Old Parr. Not Chivas Regal nor Johnnie Walker. God only knows why Old Parr was so popular. He always found it hilarious that this most basic of scotches was the mainstay of Aruba's smuggling trade.

Awaiting Abdoul just outside Aruba's arrivals terminal was Captain Antonio Sierra, a longtime trusted employee of the Abdoul family business. They drove the pretty, five-minute distance to the port and, within a very short time, one of Abdoul's very first boats, the *Patmos,* weighed anchor and left. Captain Sierra ordered his boss a scotch—obviously Old Parr—and sat him comfortably next to the skipper's chair on the bridge. He steered to a compass heading of 210 degrees—south by south-west—straight to the Guajira Peninsula. Sierra knew every cove, every riverway, every inch of the Colombian coastline in the peninsula of the Guajira. There was no better captain. Eleven years of illegal smuggling and he had never been caught.

Ten hours after boarding the *Patmos,* Abdoul stepped off the boat onto Colombian territory. Captain Sierra's walkie-talkie alerted his local men on the ground to a chosen landing spot. Part of Sierra's magic was that he never told anybody where he was going to disembark the merchandise until the last minute. On that day, in particular, Sierra's routine did not change. After all, this time he had his boss on board.

From the Guajira, it was simple. His local smuggling crews drove Abdoul to a fully fueled Piper Aztec, waiting for him on a nearby landing strip. There were thousands of those small strips in the Guajira. After all, those hundreds of cases of Old Parr arriving every day had to get quickly distributed throughout the country. Three hours after takeoff, Senator Juan Francisco Abdoul's Piper six-seater landed in Uraba.

Abdoul got off the plane and was pleased to see nine other Piper Aztecs parked under a huge green camouflage canopy that hid them from aerial photography. It was the entire Abdoul family fleet. The senator shook hands with Alfred Villas, the Abdoul family's chief financial officer. Well, that title might be a tad official, but it showed how highly Abdoul thought of him. Villas had built the business. He organized the smuggling, kept track of the drugs, laundered the money, and paid the bills. Without Villas, a brilliant logistical organizer, the Abdouls would be nowhere.

"Alfred, I see we are ready," said Abdoul. It was a question as much as it was a statement.

The two men walked up the grassy incline toward a farmhouse a few hundred feet away. There they would review the final plans.

"Senator, we are completely ready. Though there is one problem," said Villas with some hesitation. "Your brother was arrested yesterday. The news said the DAS arrested your brother as a protective measure to ensure his safety, but it was very unusual. Your nephew, Daniel, was kidnapped from school, and within an hour the DAS took your brother. The two events are connected; they have to be. I believe the DAS kidnapped Daniel to get to his father."

Abdoul thought for a long minute. This was not good.

"How do you read it, Alfred?"

"Our sources in the police tell us that there is no warrant out for you, but I am sure that your brother's arrest is connected to this mission. They suspect something, but they do not know what it is. And Pradilla does not have the balls to come after you publicly. Anyway, they cannot get you, so they got Ricardo."

"Does it change anything?" asked Abdoul.

"Only if you decide it should, Senator. Even if your brother tells them of our plans, he does not know the logistics. You do not even know them. They are mine alone. Nothing he tells them can stop the plan. However, I would perfectly understand should you decide not to go ahead, given the circumstances."

Villas was so professional, thought Abdoul. But what if Ricardo had told them enough to go to the Americans?

Villas read Abdoul's mind.

"Even if Ricardo should confess the outlines of our project, there is no way for them to cover and track down sixty disparate persons in different places. Pradilla can't find the uranium. And she cannot go to the Americans."

"Why not?" snapped Juan Francisco Abdoul. He stopped at the door of the farmhouse. Abdoul knew the answer to the question. But he wanted to hear it again, because this was the most beautiful part of the whole thing.

"Because it would be her end. The Americans would react violently. They would most probably send forces into Colombia to try to stop the shipments. She could not survive that politically—imagine, our first woman president, and she causes an invasion of our country sixty days after her inauguration. Even if they didn't invade, they would shoot down any planes traveling across our borders. And even if they didn't do that, they would publicly and violently arrest thousands of innocent Colombians arriving in the United States. They might even find the uranium.

"But the result would be the same," Alfred continued. Villas reached out and touched his boss's arm. Smilingly, he reassured the senator. "Every politician in this country would be screaming that the United States treats Colombians like pigs because of Marta Pradilla's weak presidency. She wouldn't survive a nanosecond of the pressure."

Abdoul nodded. Forget Ricardo for now. Pradilla would have to resign and the succession would inevitably go to the president of the Senate. Ricardo would be freed when Juan Francisco took the oath of office of the presidency upon Marta Pradilla's resignation. You see, that was the beauty of the plan. It made no difference to him if the Syrians actually got their uranium. It made no difference if the nuclear bomb exploded or if it didn't. Either way, Colombia would become a public pariah. Public Enemy Number One in the United States. That would be

Pradilla's undoing. Villas was right and had said it perfectly. She would not survive a nanosecond.

"I agree," Abdoul said finally. "Let's proceed with one final review." They walked into the empty house. A maid immediately took a waiting pot and poured hot coffee into two small cups set on the kitchen table. They sat on stools in the rudimentary kitchen. Abdoul had no clue whose house this was. It was just one of Villas's many statistics.

Villas assented. "We send about forty mules out to the United States every week. Tonight we will have to send out ninety. Not only are there more people involved, but half of those are going to another country before getting on international flights to the United States. That is unusual for us—as you know, I have always preferred nonstops for people with stomachfuls of drugs.

"For the last three weeks, I slowed our trafficking of *mules* to a trickle. So, our usual carriers are impatient. They need the money. They are anxious to move. This morning we called and told them that they would leave tonight. Every one of them but three agreed to go. It's wonderful what holding back for a few weeks does to their desire to work.

"The ten planes outside are ready to move on your orders," continued Alfred. "They are going to all the cities where we have people. We usually let the *mulas* pack the merchandise in plastic by themselves and swallow it on their own. We will do some things differently today. First, we will prepack the uranium in the latex before we leave here. I don't want any questions about what it is. Second, our distributors will pick up the uranium pieces and deliver them to the *mulas* and actually watch them swallow it. We don't want anybody changing their minds.

"The rest is airplane ticketing, and all of that is ready," Alfred was concluding now. "Some will go the usual direct routes. Others will go to Panama, Venezuela, Ecuador, Mexico, or Costa Rica to change planes. The U.S. destinations are completely varied. We do not want any single airport lucking out. By Thursday evening, the uranium will be in Dallas, Houston, Miami, Fort Lauderdale, New York, Newark, Chicago, and Los Angeles. It will be picked up at predetermined hotels by our usual U.S. people and put in UPS packages destined to an auto parts shop owned by a man called Rashid Sarqawi in Newark. As you know, that last part was at the request of our clients in Syria."

Abdoul looked at his man. There was no doubt he was absolutely brilliant. The plan was not complicated, but it required a logistical sophistication that only Villas could achieve. Alfred Villas looked back at this boss.

"By Friday afternoon, the Syrians should have what they need to make a bomb. What they do with it will no longer be any of our business," proclaimed the CFO.

Casa de Nariño

Bogotá, October 17
9:46 a.m.

Marta Pradilla sat in front of Hector Carbone. Her eyes were a mix of sadness and steel. She had just washed down her fourth cup of coffee. Juan Francisco Abdoul was still missing. There was no clue as to where he was.

"Hector, fate will dictate what the Americans do. But, while destiny works its ways, I won't just wait. We're not going to find Abdoul, I'm convinced of that. What are we doing to stop the *mulas*?"

"Presidente, I haven't given up on finding Abdoul. But you are right, we have to change direction and concentrate on stopping the smuggling operation. We'll do whatever we can to stop the uranium from leaving the country."

"How?"

"I've ordered all DAS and police personnel to work. Full alert. No vacation, no sick days. We know that this will alert Abdoul—he's got people in his payrolls. But it doesn't matter."

Carbone laid out the plan. "I requested double coverage at all airports and for all flights. Passengers will enter airports and will see nothing different. I don't want to scare them off. They will get their boarding passes and proceed through all the same DAS controls they are used to seeing—passports, papers, questions—nothing different."

Marta was listening intently.

"Once they are through passport controls and after the normal security checkpoints that X-ray hand luggage, passengers will be inside the airports' hallways that lead to their flights' gates. Here we will have totally new DAS and police checkpoints. Passengers will not be able to go backward and get out of the airport. There will be no choice but to go through the secondary inspection."

"That sounds right, Hector. Can we get them all?"

Carbone cast his eyes downward. He knew this question was coming. He had no choice but to tell her the truth.

"No, we can't. We may not even get most of them. Most of our units are loyal and trustworthy. But there are bound to be some agents who are corruptible.

Some of the smugglers will get through that way. Others will get through because we just don't have the manpower to rigorously interview every one of the thousands of passengers leaving Colombia. Anyway, *Presidente,* without X-raying every single passenger's insides, there is no way to know for sure who is a carrying the uranium."

"What if we closed down the airspace? Isn't that a way to guarantee nobody gets out?"

"Yes, it is. But then they will try another day, and we won't know when that will be. That puts us in an even worse position. At least we know for sure that tomorrow is the day all the smuggled uranium will leave Colombia.

"I know this is not encouraging. But you have my word that we will do our best," said the DAS chief, his dark lips trembling slightly.

Marta Pradilla covered her face with both hands. She was exhausted. She felt her energy seeping away, draining into nothing.

"My God, it never even began," Marta thought. It was obvious that her short-lived presidency was nearing a premature end.

PART XIV
THE UNITED STATES

To the Cabinet Room
Washington, October 17
10:00 a.m.

Back in Washington, John Stockman chaired an early-morning emergency meeting of the National Security Council.

The ride back on Air Force One had been eerie. Nelson Cummins watched John Stockman climb aboard the airplane and quickly noted that the president looked like he had seen a ghost. The shadow on his boss's face terrified the national security advisor. What had he learned?

After takeoff, Stockman called Nelson into his quarters and told him the entire story. He recounted Pradilla's information word for word, methodically revealing the reason for his horror. The United States now knew that it was going to be attacked. Pieces of scattered uranium were on their way into the country, to be brought together to create a powerful nuclear bomb.

The horrible puzzle was finally falling into place. The CIA had been off by a mile. Stockman and Cummins were now cognizant of most of the macabre truth. They knew who was doing it. They knew why it was being done. They knew when it would happen. But they still did not know what was, arguably, the most important piece of information: They did not know how to stop it before it happened, because they still did not know where to find the uranium.

The two men talked for an hour and realized they were going around in circles. It was 2:00 a.m., and they would probably not have any sleep for the next two days.

"Nelson, we need to try to sleep. The forty-eight hours coming our way will be hell on earth. And after that, we may find ourselves trying to clean up our country's worst disaster ever. Do one thing, and then get some shut-eye until we arrive. Call an emergency National Security Council meeting for our arrival— CIA, FBI, Defense, and whoever else needs to be there. Not too big, though. This still cannot leak."

With that, Stockman stood up and, without a word, walked to the 747's adjoining presidential bedroom and closed the door on Nelson. Cummins was left alone with the terrible news. As he walked down the corridor to the communications office of the presidential airplane, he thought of Pradilla.

The president of Colombia had now become the main player in a great Shakespearean tragedy. Pradilla had come through big-time. Nelson's distrust of her motivations had been proven completely wrong. Having gone to Cuba to meet with her might yet save the lives of millions.

Yet, in the precise instant she became the best and most trusted friend of the United States, she also converted herself into its enemy and target. Nelson could see no way to avoid military action against Colombia. No amount of police work could guarantee that the uranium would be caught before entering the United States. It was a cold, hard fact: The only way to be sure to stop the uranium was to ensure it never left Colombia. This meant that U.S. armed forces had to stop everything emanating from Colombia. All movement. All traffic. All goods.

And she would be destroyed in the process.

Nelson walked into the ultra-high-tech communications room of the jumbo jet. Two air force signal officers were on duty. From there, they could reach anybody in the world.

Nelson shook off the depressing thoughts as he cobbled together a terse electronic message convening the key members of the U.S. government's national security apparatus to the Oval Office.

Against the president's wishes, he made one phone call to the one other person whose future would be doomed by Pradilla's news. Willy. His dear, good friend would not survive. Willy had gone out on a limb with the president of the United States. He had told the president flat-out that his best guess was that the uranium was in Syria and would only be used to head off a U.S. invasion. He was wrong.

Nelson made the call. He told Willy everything. The doctor-turned-spook would be the only person outside the White House to know of the president's relationship with Pradilla, their overnight trip to Cuba, and what she had told them. He even hinted of his suspicions of Stockman's feelings toward Marta Pradilla. Willy would have an advantage tomorrow at the White House. It was the least Nelson could do for his old friend. But nothing would save him.

The National Security Council
Washington, October 17
10:15 a.m.

"Here is what I know," said President John Stockman to his National Security team as they settled down in the executive chairs of the White House Cabinet Room. Present at the meeting was Averell Georges, the secretary of Defense, General Johnson Jackson, the chairman of the Joint Chiefs, David Epstein, the secretary of State, and Frederick Carver, the director of the FBI. Willy was there for the CIA, still standing in for his ailing boss. Alongside the president were Nelson Cummins and Allyson Bonnet.

"The United States is in grave danger," continued Stockman. He had everybody's attention. "As most of you know, over the last few days we have been following very troubling leads that the government of Syria may have illicitly purchased enough highly enriched uranium to make a nuclear bomb. The best guess we had from the CIA was that the uranium was in Syria and that it would be used to repel a U.S. invasion from Iraq. Based on that information, the Joint Chiefs were ordered yesterday to recommend plans on how the United States Army should factor this new Syrian weaponry into their plans.

"Unfortunately, the CIA's conclusions were wrong and we are now facing a far more ominous situation. Thanks to the friendship that the president of Colombia, Marta Pradilla, has shown for the United States, we learned that the uranium is in Colombia and will be smuggled tomorrow into the United States by major drug traffickers who have a well-known success record of getting illegal items into this country."

Willy winced hard. He knew he was going to be badly bruised. Nelson had warned him. But he hardly expected it to be this blunt and so early on in the meeting. Didn't matter. Willy understood his career was over.

President John Stockman briefed the group. He did not reveal anything about the face-to-face meeting with Pradilla in Cuba. Nor did he share any of his feelings about Pradilla. Nelson was not surprised. He caught Allyson Bonnet's eye. She knew what he was thinking. It was inevitable. Pradilla was being thrown to the wolves.

When Stockman finished, a stunned silence reigned over the room. Slowly, the secretary of Defense raised his hand and asked to speak. Before taking over the Pentagon, Averell Georges was considered one of the leading spokespersons for the neoconservative movement. From his perch at the conservative American Traditions Foundation, Georges had written tome after tome about the need to reassert America's military power. There was precious little doubt about Secretary Georges's coming opinion.

"Mr. President, what you have told us here today is one of the most ominous messages I have heard in my forty-year career in Washington. There can be no question of immediate action or resolve. I propose we ask General Jackson to come back in a few hours with a plan for the complete blockade of Colombia. As of this evening, we must warn Colombia to ground every airplane, block every boat, and stop every car from leaving its borders. We must be clear in telling the Colombian government that we will shoot to kill on any infraction of this warning. Colombia needs to be cut off and completely isolated from the rest of the world until the uranium is found. Our navy and air force must guarantee this blockade. And the army needs to be prepared to go in and look for the stuff if the Colombians can't find it themselves."

John Stockman inhaled deeply. He had not slept all night thinking of this very moment. He knew what he felt for Marta Pradilla. Alone, on the airplane back from Cuba, he admitted it finally and fully to himself. And yet, all night long, he had played out all the options. All roads but one were dead ends. There was only one way forward, and Averell Georges had just outlined it. There was no beating back the moment.

"General, can this be done?" asked Stockman.

"Sir, I have just heard all of this for the first time. I can't give you a firm answer as to how we would achieve the mission the secretary of Defense just outlined. Give me two hours to present a plan. But, in general, Mr. President, I believe it can be done. It must be done."

Stockman nodded. "You're excused, General. We will be waiting for you in two hours. Thank you."

Stockman looked to his secretary of State. "David, is there anything else we need to do?" David Epstein was a last hope. He was brilliant, creative, and incisive. And he always disagreed with Averell Georges. They were more than rivals for the president's ear. The two cabinet officials despised each other.

"Mr. President, military action will set back our efforts to stem drugs and violence in Colombia. It will also severely injure our relations with President Pradilla. You began this meeting, sir, with a statement of appreciation for President Pradilla's friendship toward the United States. You need to be fully aware that Secretary Georges's plan of a blockade of Colombia is in essence an act of war. President Pradilla will probably not survive that."

Stockman felt his heart picking up speed. Had he missed something? Could Epstein think of another way out? He looked at Epstein hopefully.

"Having said that, Mr. President, I'm forced to agree with Secretary Georges that we have no other options," continued the secretary of State. "There is no choice but absolute action in the wake of such a threat. We can't trust this to the Colombian police—Colombia's security services are much improved from the past, but I can't swear that key officials are beyond corruption.

"No, sir, I would add to the plan of the secretary of Defense by suggesting we make calls to all of Colombia's neighbors asking for their cooperation in closing down Colombia. This would mean that Panama, Venezuela, Brazil, Peru, and Ecuador would shut their borders and place their armed forces on alert. This will be difficult for them to do to a neighboring nation, but, given the gravity of what we face, I am sure that they will understand the urgency of our request."

Shit, thought Stockman, Marta won't even get the decency of some local support. The United States was going to lock up her country militarily, diplomatically, and economically. Good God, thought Stockman, this is what we wanted to do to Syria. Here I am about to do it to a friendly nation and to a woman who had the key to saving the United States. It hurt badly.

Stockman suddenly noticed that he was blinking back tears. He had no clue if it was exhaustion, rage, or a terrible sense of guilt about sacrificing the woman who had risked so much to tell him the truth. Next on his agenda was a discussion of coordinating domestic security through the FBI, but that had to wait a few minutes. He needed to get out for a moment.

"Let's take five minutes," Stockman said. He got up and disappeared behind closed doors. In his absence, the room erupted with noise. Little groups quickly formed and action plans were discussed. There were shouts about what had to be done first. Who had to be called? What about the alert level? Did they need to get the health authorities involved?

Willy looked at Nelson and Allyson and asked if he could talk to them alone. They left the room together and went into Nelson's office just down the hall.

"Nelson, thanks for the heads-up last night. I know I am dead meat," said Willy.

Yikes, thought Nelson. He wished Allyson had not heard that Nelson had forewarned his friend. He looked at her. If she disapproved, she did not show it.

Willy continued. "I did not sleep last night. Not a wink. Not because my career is over. That is a fact I have to live with, and I will. I didn't sleep because I was thinking about what this woman did last night. It's outstanding. And I refuse to believe that helping the United States must necessarily end in tragedy. We can't do what we're about to do to someone who is so clearly a friend.

"And this president needs friends—this friend. The United States needs friends. We lose them by the bucketfuls." Willy was nearly shouting now.

Allyson looked at him sidewise. Where was he going with this? Everyone agreed with Epstein that it was tragic to sacrifice relations with a friendly country like Colombia. But all agreed there was no choice. Willy, however, was talking in highly personalized tones. Had Nelson told him about Stockman's feelings for Pradilla?

"What are you saying, Willy?" asked Nelson.

"Remember, I was a doctor before becoming a spook. If I leave the CIA, I will go back to being a doctor. And the first thing I learned in epidemiology is that it is the job of the government is to protect the public health of its citizens. So, I had this idea."

In three minutes flat, Willy outlined his plan. It was completely simple and completely crazy. But, it also had a Willy-like methodological rationality about it. It answered all the right questions tightly. He looked at Allyson and she was smiling. Yes, Willy might well be on to something. Nelson jumped on the phone and told Stockman that he had to see him before the meeting.

"Don't come, Nelson, I'll drop by on my way back to the Cabinet Room," said Stockman.

This wasn't perfect. Nelson did not want the president to first hear of this plan from Willy. Dr. Perlman was no longer the most credible source of ideas and information in the president's eyes. Nelson was about to suggest that Willy wait for them outside when Allyson interrupted him. She knew what was going through his head.

"Nelson, eventually Willy will have to defend it. He should explain it to the boss now."

Stockman walked into the room. He was visibly shaken. Lines were drawn deep in his face. His light-blue eyes, usually powerful and demanding, were empty of all feeling and emotion. President John Stockman looked like a beaten man.

He saw Willy and stared for an instant. A nod was all Willy got.

Allyson took over. Women were somehow better at clearing the air.

"Mr. President, we recognize that you feel let down by the CIA's information and recommendations. We all do. However, you need to listen to this before you go back into the Cabinet Room and make your final decision."

Willy went through his idea one more time. As he talked, Allyson Bonnet could literally see a physical change come over the president. The more he listened, the more upright he became. His eyes began to clear and focus. His lips firmed up. When Willy was finished, the president looked at him for what seemed an endless amount of time.

"Where did you get this idea? How did you invent it?"

"Invent, Mr. President? I got it from the history books as I wrote my doctor's thesis on communicable diseases. At the turn of the century, it's what this country used to do to thousands of people every day, seven days a week. You should visit the quarantine rooms of the immigration center on Ellis Island. We separated families and threw sick people into horrible rooms. It was barbaric, but we thought it was the right thing to do. So, if we made the mistake in 1900, why not make the same mistake again?"

John Stockman looked at him and asked the question straight out.

"I want to be clear. You are willing to take responsibility for this mistake if we knowingly decide to make it, correct?"

"Correct," Willy said. "I will have to take some responsibility—either for the mistake I made yesterday or the one I will make tomorrow. Doesn't make any difference."

Stockman looked at his two closest advisors. They were the closest anything could come to the word *friends* in his life. He knew they were both aghast at his relationship with Marta. Yet, today, right now in this room, their looks could not be confused. With a smile and a movement of their heads, they were siding with him on a plan that might just save everybody.

"We have to sell it in there," said Stockman, pointing to the Cabinet Room. "It will be a fight. Clearly we need to turn Epstein around. Forget Georges."

Stockman cocked his head back and assented. It was as if he was convincing himself the more he thought about it. He decided right there and then to come clean with Allyson and Nelson about his feelings. He could not recall the last time he spoke to anybody about emotions. Willy was there; but hey—timing was never perfect.

"There are two reasons I like this idea," said the president. "First, because it finds us the uranium. Military action would probably avert an attack but might not get us the nuclear materials. In a way, Willy here has come up with a more conservative solution."

The three listened and waited for the second.

"The second reason is because it gives her what she wanted. She asked that Colombia be spared the rhetoric and accusations. And I want to help her. She deserves it."

Stockman expected the group to be blown away by his open confession. He did not realize that what seemed like a hard-to-admit declaration of emotion to him, sounded only like a mildly stated expression of friendship to the others. Only Allyson Bonnet, the most cynical of all of them, understood how deep a statement of sentiment this was.

She reached out her hand and touched his shoulder. "They are very good reasons, Mr. President. Both of them."

Back to the Cabinet Room
Washington, October 17
11:30 a.m.

The four of them walked back into the Cabinet Room and the president called the meeting to order. Averell Georges, the secretary of Defense, immediately took over.

"I have an update from the Joint Chiefs, sir," said Georges.

"Averell, I'd like you to hold on for a minute. Something has come up which I believe merits some discussion. It is Dr. Perlman's idea, and, frankly, I find it very attractive."

"Mr. President, we don't have time to chew on other ideas. We have less than a day to put a plan to bed and execute."

"Averell, there is always time to chew on other ideas. Particularly, ones that I like. Dr. Perlman, would you kindly present the outline?"

Well, at least he was floating upward from the bottom of the barrel, thought Willy. He forcefully presented his idea for the third time in the last half hour. Willy concluded exactly where the president would want him to finalize the argument.

"There are two reasons for doing this. First, it is a more conservative solution. It basically finds us the uranium. Military action would successfully avert the attack, but we might not find the nuclear materials. The second reason is because it avoids a practical declaration of war against a friendly country and its president who has risked a lot to help us. In the last twenty years, thousands— perhaps tens of thousands—of Colombian soldiers, judges, journalists, human rights activists, police have died in the front line of a war created by our drug addicts. Colombia deserves more respect . . . President Pradilla deserves it."

The first thing Willy noticed was that it did not happen like in the movies. He didn't leave everyone agape. There wasn't a pregnant pause filled with patriotic music and tear-filled eyes as people came round to his point of view. No, it did not happen that way in real life.

"Mr. President, we are sitting in the Cabinet Room talking about a national emergency. Would you kindly restrict the deliberations to cabinet members?" demanded Averell Georges. "While I am saddened by the ailment of the director of Central Intelligence, I can't help wondering why we have to listen to a second-level analyst."

"Wait a minute," cut in David Epstein, the secretary of State. "I will listen to anybody who has a good idea about avoiding military action. And I think I just heard a damn good one. I want to hear it again from the top. With all due respect, Averell, there are other ways to achieve one's objectives than through the use of military power. Until now, I could not think of one. But this is very attractive."

Yes, this was more like it, thought Stockman. The two men were at each others' throats again. The world was in equilibrium.

"Willy, I too would like to hear it again. Try to outline an hour-by-hour run of show for us," directed Stockman.

So, Willy went through it for the fourth time. This time he concluded differently.

"So, Mr. President, the run of show might go somewhat like this. At 10:00 p.m. you call the Immigration and Naturalization Service and U.S. Customs and tell them we may have a problem and that we are moving in equipment in the ten or so key places. We move at 11:30 p.m. Our job will take a number of hours, and we won't be done until dawn. At 10:00 a.m. tomorrow, Allyson makes a public announcement. Not earlier than that, because we actually don't want to give them a heads-up. In a nutshell, sir, that would be the plan."

"Mr. President, you are not going to agree to this," said Averell Georges. "We are facing the most serious threat to our civilian population since September 11 and you want to let the CIA play pretend games? Mr. President, this is lunacy."

John Stockman was now back. In full force. The president of the United States had walked into this meeting with his mind made up. As usual, he allowed an airing of views. But he would not allow anybody to question his authority.

"Averell, don't question my views or motives. And, careful with the word 'lunacy.' I have made up my mind and will sign a top secret executive order authorizing this operation. You, Averell, will be witness to that. If any of this gets out, I will know where to look for leaks. Remember what the *New York Times* says about me. I'm obsessed with leaks."

Everyone heard the clear threat. If there was one thing that Stockman abhorred, it was leaks. Stockman already ordered the attorney general to spend millions on seven investigations into leaks about the administration's internal debates on everything from abortion to the Middle East. Sometimes the Justice Department investigations found their man. Most often they didn't. No matter. After shouldering severe financial burdens in legal fees, the persons investigated were left in financial and political tatters. You definitely did not want to be a target of Stockman's leak investigations.

"Mr. Secretary of Defense, it is my stated order that the Joints Chiefs present you with a plan for military execution. I want to see it when it gets into your hands. However, you are not authorized to go any further than the plan."

Stockman turned slowly and raised his finger at Willy. It was like a parent scolding a child. No words were necessary. The finger said: Don't fuck it up a second time. He bore into Willy Perlman's eyes.

"Dr. Perlman, implement your proposal," the president said finally.

U.S. Customs
Miami, October 18
3:46 a.m.

From about midnight until five in the morning, Augustus Johnson usually enjoyed peace and quiet in the customs hall of Miami International Airport. He was the senior Customs officer on the graveyard shift five nights a week. With his kids in college and his wife working late as a legal secretary in a big-shot downtown law firm, he never much minded working nights. Nobody was home anyway.

He and the two other Customs officers on night duty had to attend to the occasional ultradelayed flight from Latin America or Europe, but mostly there was nothing to do but drink Diet Coke, chat about the evening's games with his two colleagues, and sleep. That was not, however, the case tonight.

It was nearly 4:00 a.m., and Senior Customs Officer Johnson had not gotten a second of shut-eye. Four hours ago, Bill Stevenson, his boss and the director of Customs at the airport, had called to tell him that there was a major health emergency happening in Latin America that would require the immediate installation of some large technology at the airport.

"Run that by me again," Officer Johnson asked his boss.

"Augustus, I know as much as you know. I just got a call from Washington and they told me something about the CIA being all in a panic about an outbreak of something in Latin America. They told me it was highly contagious and that we had to start screening all arriving flights as of tomorrow. They're making the same call to ten other airports."

Ten minutes after the phone call, six medical men presented themselves in the Customs office. They introduced themselves as Doctors this and that. Augustus couldn't remember the names. They had laptop computers, six large, flat panels that looked like white chalkboards, and a similar number of large cameralike machines. Portable X-ray equipment, these guys told him.

They spent the next hours setting up the equipment in the far side of the wide Customs hall of the airport. Augustus Johnson tried getting an explanation, but they wouldn't engage. The doctors were singularly tight-lipped. These guys went about their work in total silence.

About an hour ago, the activity in the Customs hall became frenetic. Four other men arrived and were introduced to him by the medical teams setting up the X-rays. These newcomers were not doctors, however. They were a construction crew.

At this point, Senior Customs Officer Augustus Johnson was clearly irritated. He did not like interruptions to his nighttime routine.

"Doctor, you have to tell me what's going on here," said Johnson to the older medical officer. He had no clue who was in charge, but he gravitated to the guy with the most gray in his hair.

"Officer Johnson, all arriving passengers this morning will have to pass through here. These men have come to build makeshift cubicles with drawback curtains. We'll place an X-ray machine in every cubicle. We are going to have to privately screen every single passenger coming into Miami."

"What?" gagged Johnson. "Do you have any clue about the bedlam that will create? Seventy-six thousand passengers go through this airport every day. On a good day, half of them come through this hall. That is about 35,000 people coming through here in a day. We'll have planes choked on the taxiways and people backed up to the gates!"

"Yes, I'm afraid that is right," agreed the gray-haired doctor. But he did not look like he cared too much. With a nod to Johnson and not another word, he turned right around and walked back to the construction activity.

Shit, thank God he got off duty at 8:00 a.m. thought Johnson. He did not want to be around when this place imploded. Good lord, it would be an unholy mess. And, needless to say, he wanted to be as far away as possible with some horrible sickness spewing through the airport's hallways.

The first flights from Argentina, Chile, and Brazil were scheduled to arrive at the airport at 6:00 a.m. That was less than an hour away. This was the initial spurt of the airport's daily activity. Flights from South America's farthest southern cone flew through the night and landed in Miami after an eight- or nine-hour overnight flight. He walked over to the medical guys busy pricking at their machines.

"You guys know that we have eleven flights from Brazil, Argentina, and Chile due here within the hour?"

"Yes, we do, Officer. We are almost ready for them."

Indeed they were. Johnson was amazed at what a few men could do in a couple of hours. Six little cubicles were set up, each one containing an X-ray machine, one of the large flat panels, and a laptop. The cubicles were tiny, but there was enough room for one passenger and an X-ray technician to do his job. The construction guys were now busy setting up a rope line that would funnel every passenger toward the cubicles as they came down the escalator after passing through Immigration.

"Here is what will happen, Officer Johnson. First, all Immigration, Customs, and airline personnel working in the restricted areas will be issued medically certified surgical masks."

Johnson heard a large duffel bag being unzipped by one of the guys in a lab coat. Inside were thousands of surgical masks wrapped in plastic. The medical technician reached in and handed Officer Johnson his mask.

At this point, Augustus Johnson was seriously concerned. Over the last ten or so years, he and his colleagues had become accustomed to wearing latex gloves on the job. Their expert hands rummaged through thousands of suspicious suitcases every day. Gloves were one thing. Surgical masks were another.

The senior doctor ignored Johnson's concerned look.

"Second, once passengers go through Immigration, they will then come down the escalator to the Customs hall, where they will be routed to our X-ray machines. It will take us about a minute and a half to two minutes per passenger. Once they are considered free of any medical problems, they can pick up their luggage and check through Customs. Once you have them, Officer, they are to be treated like any other passengers arriving on any other day.

"Third, there will be federal agents coming through that door any minute. I fully expect there to be a lot of screaming and protests. Unfortunately, passengers will have no choice but to be X-rayed or be deported. The agents' purpose will be to provide any assistance to passengers that are older or unwell. These people will all speak Spanish and Portuguese and will explain the situation to the passengers waiting in line."

Johnson was now impressed. There was obviously something serious and unexpected going on, and, in precious little time, the government had thought the situation out as best they could. It actually made him proud to know that the U.S. authorities were able to mobilize this fast to protect the country against life-threatening illnesses. But what the hell was so serious?

He walked back to his desk and saw his message light blinking. He picked up the receiver and punched the code.

"Johnson, bad news," said Customs director Bill Stevenson's voice. "I need you to stay on. I'm calling everybody in and nobody's going home. Tell your shift. The airport will be a mess today."

Shit, thought Johnson, for the second time that night. Now he was stuck here with some scary disease. But the crackling of his two-way radio cut off any further thought.

"American Airlines 963 is in from São Paulo," announced the disembodied voice.

The medics were now in full distribution mode. Airline employees coming into the Customs hall for the first time that morning looked stunned as they were asked to put on the masks. Johnson and his colleagues put theirs on. One of the guys wearing a white lab coat came down the stairs and announced that all the Immigration guys on the floor above had their masks on too.

Shit, Johnson thought again, for the third time. Imagine what the passengers would think when they got to the large hall upstairs and gazed upon fifteen or so passport control officers all wearing white masks. They would be petrified.

Fifteen minutes later, the first passengers off of the American flight from Brazil came down the escalator. Most of them froze as they realized they were not going to be allowed access to their luggage until they went through some medical examination.

As promised, technicians in white coats started hollering instructions and explanations in English, Spanish, and Portuguese. "Ladies and Gentlemen, we have been warned of a serious illness in Latin America. The United States has ordered a medical quarantine on all flights arriving from the region. You must pass through an X-ray inspection before entering the United States. Thank you for your cooperation."

Johnson knew instantaneously that his predictions of bedlam for the rest of the day would be on the mark. Within minutes, all hell broke loose. Parents asked if the machines were safe for kids. Elderly passengers in wheelchairs were unable to get up for the procedure. Young Brazilians, already furious at the United States for fingerprinting them upon entry into the country, were now incensed at yet another slap in the face by the American authorities. People had to go to the bathroom. Families were waiting outside.

Yet, slowly, person by person, the medical personnel did their tests and discharged the passengers. It was disorderly, loud, and unpleasant; but it was working. One by one, passengers were getting X-rayed. Furious, they then went to pick up their luggage and approached Customs. Johnson gave a hand signal and the other agents nodded.

"Go easy" was the translation of the quick movement of Johnson's hand.

Miami International Airport
Miami, October 18
9:51 a.m.

═══

It was shortly before ten o'clock in the morning, and Augustus Johnson was over-whelmed with exhaustion. He sat down, surgical mask dangling around his neck, with his fourth cup of coffee of the morning and surveyed the scene.

The Customs hall was nearly empty. Since the first rush of arriving flights, the airport had processed over 3,000 arriving passengers, most of them from South America's most remote southern corners. The lull in the hallway was, how-ever, only a momentary illusion. There was always a hiatus between the early morning flights from the southern cone and the mid-morning arrivals from the closer countries of South and Central America and the Caribbean. Those flights started arriving around 11:00 a.m.

The medical inspections of the first flights had been chaotic, but they had gotten through it. If the doctors and medics manning the X-ray machines were tired, they hardly showed it. Taking advantage of the lull, they were busy tinker-ing and recalibrating their machines. What they don't know can't hurt them, thought Augustus Johnson. He, on the other hand, understood well that process-ing these first arrivals was a simpleton's job compared to what was coming.

Beginning with a TACA flight from San Salvador at 10:49, the airport's arrivals would spring into action. 10:51 was BWIA from Barbados. 10:53 was Air Jamaica from Montego Bay. 10:54 was American from Panama City. 10:55 was another American from Tegucigalpa, Honduras. 10:56 was COPA from San Jose, Costa Rica. 11:00 was American from Caracas. And on it would go. From Bogotá, Barranquilla, Maracaibo, Quito, Guayaquil, Mexico City, Managua, Guatemala, Lima, Cartagena, La Paz, and so on.

Thank God it was the fall off-season in the Caribbean, because those twenty or so additional flights from all the little islands would be less full than during the rest of the year.

Augustus Johnson dreaded what was coming, but what made him even more nervous was that nobody at the airport really understood what was going on. Sure, it was clear that Washington was worried about some contagious disease.

But what was it? As they shifted positions, his Customs colleagues monitored their televisions and radios. Nothing.

Johnson could understand that this had not yet converted to a major news story. Journalists were famously late risers. And all the action was contained to a spot in the airport that was not visible to the public. The lack of swarming reporters outside Customs did not bother him; they would be around soon enough as word of the story ebbed out. What bugged him was that there was no official word from anybody on the airwaves. It was as if the emergency were restricted to the ten Customs halls of the major U.S. airports.

He was just completing the thought when Rita Omera, one of his oldest colleagues in the Customs service, called over to him.

"Auggie, come here and look at this," she said.

Three agents were huddled around Rita and her television in the main office of the Customs service. The television was locked onto CNN.

"Ladies and Gentlemen," said Michaela Urquell, smartly coifed, as usual. "We are going straight to the White House Briefing Room for an urgent announcement from White House press secretary Allyson Bonnet. John Davidson, at the White House, do you know what this is about?"

"All we know is that the White House has called an urgent briefing regarding a health-related matter," CNN's White House reporter intoned. "We are waiting for Allyson Bonnet, the White House Press Secretary to . . . well, here she is, Michaela, let's listen in."

The camera switched to a shot of a tall, sandy blond woman walking purposefully to the podium. Allyson Bonnet was a recognizable face. The White House press corps admired her daily briefings on terrorism and the situation in Iraq. She defended her president energetically but never misled reporters. The cynical Washington press grumpily admitted that she was a strong, skilled, and tough woman.

"Good morning," said Allyson Bonnet. "I have an announcement to make regarding an important health issue. I'll tell you everything we know, which is not a lot. I won't take any questions now, because the situation is evolving. But I will be back to you with updates throughout the day.

"We were informed yesterday by the CIA of a potential health threat to this country. In the course of their regular drug interdiction and antiterrorism duties in Latin America, the CIA has come to the conclusion that there may be an acute outbreak of multidrug-resistant tuberculosis spreading throughout Latin America. This particular form of tuberculosis is highly contagious and very dangerous.

"Tuberculosis is a disease that has killed millions throughout the world over the centuries. While tuberculosis is nearly unheard of here in the United States, it is still the world's biggest killer disease. Over the last few years, scientists at the World Health Organization have warned that tuberculosis in Africa and Asia has mutated into strains that resist usual drug treatments. Until today, we did not believe that these strains existed in the Western Hemisphere."

Allyson Bonnet reached for her water glass and took a swig.

"While the CIA is not the normal source for health-related warnings, the President is taking this information very seriously. As you can imagine, the CIA is discreetly, but deeply, involved in intelligence operations throughout Latin America. Its information tells us that this particular tuberculosis strain was identified in the Andes region and in Central America.

"Dr. William Perlman is the deputy director for analysis at the CIA. Prior to his career in intelligence, Dr. Perlman was one of the foremost epidemiologists specializing in contagious diseases and, specifically, in tuberculosis. His research identified the multidrug-resistant strains. The president considers himself fortunate to have the advice of Dr. Perlman.

"I want to repeat that we consider the information on tuberculosis serious, but preliminary. The CIA will be providing its information to the Centers for Disease Control in Atlanta, the National Institutes of Health, and the Department of Health and Human Services. Together, these agencies will analyze the extent of the threat and formulate a common response.

"Meanwhile, the president has authorized the federalization of every airport that serves as an entry point for airplanes from Latin America and the Caribbean. Since early this morning, all passengers arriving from Latin America are being administered a simple chest X-ray which will identify the existence of tuberculosis. Notwithstanding the belief that the TB may be limited to certain regions of Latin America, I wish to repeat that passengers arriving from all of Latin America and the Caribbean, regardless of their nationality, are being given the tuberculosis test.

"That is what we know so far. The president asks all Americans to remain calm. We believe that everything that needs to be done to protect our citizens is being done at the moment. I will have an update for you sometime this afternoon."

As Allyson walked out, the room erupted into an uproar. Reporters were shouting questions hysterically at the woman leaving the briefing room. What are the symptoms? When did you know about this? Have international health authorities been warned? Have we received cooperation from Latin American countries?

Allyson Bonnet left the room without acknowledging any of the questions.

As she walked through the door, Nelson Cummins was just on the other side. Allyson waited until she heard the door to the briefing room close behind her before letting down her guard. Once she was safe in the White House hallway, her shoulders sagged and her hands trembled. She almost fell into Nelson's arms.

"Twenty years of doing this for congressmen, senators, cabinet officials, and now for a president, and I have never knowingly lied," said Allyson. "This better fucking work or I will be back in Madison, Wisconsin, selling used cars."

Nelson had her in a gentle hug. He was smiling, but he too was nervous to the point of losing it.

"We need to stall for six more hours. Yes, it will get worse before it gets better, but we only need six hours. So far, it has worked. Willy called to tell me that there were no leaks from any of our airports on the early-morning arrivals. We waited just long enough to allow most of the flights from Latin America to get off the ground."

Nelson allowed himself a smile. "Allyson, these sons of bitches are in the air and can't get turned around. They are heading straight for the trap."

Allyson just shook her head in resignation. "This better fucking work," she repeated.

They both walked down the hall and turned left to head to her office. President John Stockman was waiting. He wasn't smiling, but he looked appreciative.

"Allyson, I know how hard this was. We're doing the right thing; I just want you to know it," said Stockman, patting her gently on the shoulders.

"I don't know how much of it was believable, sir. The only thing I said with any conviction was the part about inspecting all nationalities arriving from the region, regardless of origin. I hope I did that well enough."

Stockman smiled his assent.

"Forgive me, Mr. President, have you heard from . . ." Allyson trailed off before finishing. She shouldn't be asking this question.

John Stockman chuckled. No matter the crisis, she was insanely curious. Typical press hound.

"No, Allyson, I have not heard from President Pradilla."

Nelson had gone to Cuba and seen the two presidents together. He was now an official grudging admirer of Pradilla. He was in favor of what they were doing today—protecting the nation and an ally at the same time. But none of this made him comfortable with the notion that the president of the United States had feelings for this woman. The fact that Stockman's closest group was now talking about it openly made it worse, not better. So much for the psychologists' babble about open feelings. He changed the subject.

"Within minutes, the calls will start. God knows how we managed to get this far—there are ten airports that have been slowed to a crawl with X-ray inspections. Anyway, I suspect that the first calls will be from Secretary Simonsen at Health and Human Services and Dr. Frangiotti, the director of the National Institutes of Health. But the worst one will be from Dr. Gayle Amar at the Centers for Disease Control in Atlanta."

Allyson looked agitated. Nelson said to himself that, for her, being nervous must be a once-in-a-lifetime experience.

"These public health guys are going to come crashing down our gates," Allyson said. "There will be three prongs of attack. First, they will ask how in the hell can the president declare a medical emergency without consulting them. Second, they are going to demand scientific proof of the TB. Third, to cover their asses, they will all ask for a meeting to show they are upset."

"Correct," said Stockman. "The first two questions are the real hard ones to answer. But our little secret to avoiding them is in the third question."

The three nodded. They had been over this fifty times in the last twelve hours. Now, in the eye of the hurricane, all three felt a need to quickly review the plan.

Stockman continued. "I'm going to the office right now. Rather than wait for their calls, I'm calling them. I will ask them to come to the Oval Office for an emergency meeting to be briefed by Dr. Perlman from the CIA and to formulate further policy measures. Gayle is obviously my last call. I will tell all of them that we need to hold the meeting as soon as possible, but that I will not do it without Gayle. The CDC is too important in this decision. So, to accommodate the time it takes for her to get here from Atlanta, we're convening at the White House at 3:00 p.m."

Nelson closed his eyes. It was half prayer and half exhaustion.

"That gives us another five hours. Willy says that should be basically enough time," said Nelson.

"What if he's wrong?" Allyson asked.

Nobody said anything. On this one, Willy could not be wrong.

The next five hours were hell on earth for the White House. Every local television station in the ten cities with major international airports now had crews camped out in front of exit doors from Customs. Interviews with passengers coming off the planes were harrowing. Three- to four-hour waits to get to the X-ray machines. Children were hysterical. No water. No food. No seating. Outraged passengers shouted at the cameras that the medical inspections infringed on their rights. Occasionally, there was a more rational person who said that the sacrifice was reasonable, given the dangers of a major medical emergency.

The cable channels went wall-to-wall. Medical experts were recruited to explain the seriousness of TB. Historians droned on about how TB-diseased immigrants of the 1900s were separated from their families on Ellis Island and quarantined for months. There was coverage about the nationwide run on surgical masks. Reporters staked out in front of hospitals reported on a tidal wave of emergency room visits from people with coughs worried that they had contracted the disease.

Roundtables set up on Fox, CNN, and MSNBC analyzed the poor air quality on airplanes, concluding that the in-flight air circulation mechanisms could provide a rampant breeding ground for the bug. Television producers dug out experts from the World Health Organization to comment on the drugs needed to combat tuberculosis. Most worrying were the growing leaks from "U.S. Government sources" that the leading medical and public health organizations were furious at the president and the White House for embarking on drastic measures with only the CIA's input. Nobody but the CIA had gotten wind of any health problems in Latin America.

At 12:30, Allyson Bonnet sent out a news release saying that the president had convened an emergency medical summit with the Centers for Disease Control, the National Institutes of Health, and the Department of Health and Human Services for 3:00 p.m. By 1:00 p.m. interns in the White House press operation reported a substantial increase of reporters and cameras on the White House grounds.

Allyson hid her head in her cupped hands and remembered how Nelson had closed his eyes in what looked like a prayer a few hours ago. She did the same. Allyson Bonnet was petrified. But she also had to confess to herself that she was excited. For once, this administration was not reacting with an insular, fuck-you attitude to the world. Pradilla deserved this, she thought.

The minutes ticked by. Allyson walked down the hall to Nelson's office and looked in. She saw the national security advisor staring at the wall in front of him. There was no pretense of action. Nobody was hiding their worries.

"Have you heard from Willy?" Allyson asked.

Nelson shook his head.

"He asked that nobody call him. I've respected that request. What the hell, he'll be here in forty-five minutes."

At 2:35 p.m., Nelson's secretary walked in to say that Dr. Perlman had just come through the White House gates. Willy's car went straight through security and around the driveway to the mansion's main entrance. This time, it was not a secretary waiting at the staff entrance. Rather, two uniformed Secret Service agents were covering the main entrance to escort him upstairs. Willy smiled ruefully as he got out of the car.

In his usual, methodical way, he had timed the entrance to the most powerful building in the world. Calculating the distance to the elevators as he walked inside and the time required to get upstairs, he figured that from the gates to Nelson's office would be just about a minute. It does not get better than that, thought Willy, though he knew this would be his last entrance ever.

The White House

Washington, October 18
2:50 p.m.

===

Willy stepped off the White House elevators behind the uniformed agents and walked down the hallway toward Nelson's office. He was sorry things ended this way, but he had no regrets about his decision. It was the right thing to do. Period.

Washington was a town where few ever paid a price for mistakes. Failed policies, operational errors, wrong decision-making rarely exacted a price in the vast bureaucracy. People who authored failure never left, or ended up coming back dressed in new clothes. When was the last time somebody resigned because he or she was wrong? When was the last time somebody had the balls to admit that something had happened on his or her watch and the right thing to do was to go? Nobody paid a price at the FBI or the CIA for 9/11. Nobody at the Energy Department resigned over the mismanagement of nuclear waste dumps. Iraq was still a mess. The army was still trying to explain away the torture at Abu Ghraib. And, of course, New Orleans!

The list went on and on.

To Willy, this had nothing to do with Republicans or Democrats. It was an issue of morality. He remembered his father's tears on the Jewish holy day of Yom Kippur as the rabbi repeated the Bible's lessons over and over again: "For the Sins you have committed against the Lord, atone and God shall pardon. For the sins against your fellow man, God shall not pardon. For those, you must ask forgiveness from those you have wronged." In the Jewish religion, you confessed your sins and mistakes. You took responsibility. It brought you closer to God.

Willy was shaken from his thoughts when he reached Nelson's open door. The hallway entrance to the office of the national security advisor was never open. Willy stepped in and was surprised to see the president standing in the room along with Nelson and Allyson Bonnet.

"Dr. Perlman," the president acknowledged. "This has been an anxious day here."

Christ, thought Nelson, that was the understatement of the century. We're hysterical. There is a false national medical emergency underway, drug smugglers are trying to enter the country with highly enriched uranium, and the administration could be open to huge political attack. That added up to more than mere anxiety.

Willy Perlman pulled at the day-old stubble on his cheeks and slowly looked at each of them. These were good people, Willy thought. Don't let them suffer further. His face broke into a big smile.

"The Colombian authorities stopped eleven people from boarding airplanes this morning. We understand from our Colombian friends that each of these people has been tested and is carrying highly suspicious materials."

"As for us, by 2:00 p.m." Willy continued, "we had inspected nearly 11,000 people at the country's ten airports with incoming passengers from Latin America. We have taken forty-two persons into custody. Quietly. All were carrying an ingested metallic object in their guts. Only one of those, a woman, has, so far—how do I say this elegantly?—passed the object through her body. We have confirmed it to be uranium-235. I have no doubt the others will be the same. This means we have interdicted about twenty-six pounds of the uranium."

Nelson quickly looked up. That wasn't enough.

"That's not all of it, Willy. You said that there could be up to thirty-five pounds of the stuff."

"Yes, Nelson, I still believe that. There are still up to eighteen planes due to land between now and 5:30 p.m. This was an incredibly sophisticated smuggling operation. Without the medical dragnet, we would never have caught most of them. But with fifty-three people now in custody here and in Colombia, we are convinced that the rest are coming the same way. There are probably only ten to fifteen people left, and they are in the process of landing in one of the airports. We'll get them."

A huge flood of relief swept through the room. Stockman closed his eyes and spoke quietly under his breath. Allyson smiled at her president. At some point today, Nelson, the president, and Allyson herself had each closed their eyes in prayer. All this introspection was unusual at the White House. But the president's quiet words now were no longer appeals of hope. They were prayers of gratitude.

It was a strange scene, though. Notwithstanding the gut-wrenching sense of relief that a major national disaster was on the verge of being successfully averted, nobody celebrated. This was a bittersweet moment of success. Everybody in the room knew that this moment of joy would be dampened by the next moments of personal tragedy. In less than five minutes, Dr. Willy Perlman would be offered as a scapegoat to the bureaucracy's vultures. So there were no smiles.

Willy Perlman looked at his watch and saw that it was 2:55 p.m. "I am ready if you are, Mr. President.

Stockman nodded. In the Cabinet Room, waiting for the president and Dr. Willy Perlman, were three very angry public health officials. Yes, the vultures were swooping down.

"After you, Dr. Perlman," said the president. As he went through the door first, Willy Perlman could feel the president's arm come around his shoulders and squeeze gently in an unusual gesture of appreciation.

One hour later, the White House issued an advisory telling the press to expect an important statement from the White House press secretary in about fifteen minutes. That would give all broadcast, cable, and local affiliates time enough to prepare themselves to cut into ongoing programming.

At exactly 4:15 p.m., Allyson Bonnet strode to the podium at the front of a packed White House briefing room. It was not standing room only. It was barely breathing room. Reporters, cameras, photographers jammed every single square inch of the room. After all, the SARS fright and the avian flu warnings had given the press an acute sense of how well public health scares played on the news. Now, this multidrug-resistant tuberculosis epidemic was potentially a far more serious public health threat than all the others. Nobody was going to miss the story.

"Good afternoon," Allyson began. "I again have a statement to read, and I'll take questions afterward."

"After consultation with his senior public health experts, President John Stockman is happy to report to the nation that he is canceling the public health emergency announced earlier today. The president no longer believes multidrug-resistant tuberculosis to be an immediate threat to Americans."

Allyson ignored the collective groans from the press as they were seeing their big story fizzle out before their very eyes. She went on.

"The president acted this morning on what seems to have been incomplete intelligence furnished by the CIA. Initial tests conveying the existence of a virulent multidrug-resistant TB strain in the Andean region and Central America have now been deemed to be, at best, imperfect. We now believe this to have been a false alarm.

"Together with his national security advisor and the director of the Centers for Disease Control, the director of the National Institutes of Health and the secretary for Health and Human Services, the president today asked for, received, and accepted the immediate resignation of Dr. Willy Perlman as acting director of Central Intelligence and as director of analysis. The president respects and salutes Dr. Perlman's long-standing service to the nation as an intelligence officer and as a specialist in the epidemiology of this very dangerous disease. Yet, while Dr. Perlman was acting upon his belief of what was in the nation's best interests, the fact remains that the announcement of a health emergency was based on what now seems to be less-than-precise intelligence.

"The president recognizes that many people were gravely concerned by this morning's announcement. He also understands that many thousands of people around the nation's airports were severely inconvenienced. For this, he offers his apologies. Orders have been issued to cease all airport inspections by six o'clock this evening.

"He would also like to make public his regret that all our neighbors in Latin America and the Caribbean were unfairly singled out for being the cause of an alarm that now seems to have been false. The president intends to personally call many of his colleagues around the hemisphere to express his personal regrets at having unnecessarily targeted many Latin Americans at our nation's airports today.

"Finally, the president would like to make clear that, while this particular alarm has turned out to be erroneous, he will not take a backseat to anybody when it comes to protecting our nation and our citizens. This president was elected to act strongly and decisively on behalf of Americans. He will continue to do that.

"Thank you," Allyson finished.

She looked around the room. This woman could read the press room instantaneously. What she saw made her happy. A riveting public health story with legs to last days, if not weeks, had suddenly turned into a barely compelling angle about a CIA mistake and how Washington's competing bureaucracies were exacting revenge. It was mostly for the print media. There was nothing here for television, and Allyson took pleasure in seeing the cable channel producers ordering their crews to start packing.

As Allyson went back and forth with reporters for another twenty minutes, Willy Perlman went out through the White House visitors' entrance. He got into his car. His Blackberry chirped and he looked at his messages. There was one from his office consisting of only five words: "58 present and accounted for." There were only a few more to go. He had the smugglers beat.

Willy let himself sink into the backseat of the black car as it swung out of the White House grounds. He had made a mistake. The uranium had not gone to Syria. It nearly entered this country. He had a price to pay, and he was comfortable paying it.

For sins and mistakes against your fellow man, you must request forgiveness directly, ordered the Book.

It was done, thought Willy.

PART XV
COLOMBIA

Casa de Nariño

═══

At her desk at the Casa de Nariño, Marta Pradilla was glued to CNN. She caught every sentence of Allyson Bonnet's press conference. With every passing word, Marta Pradilla's face broke out into an ever-increasing smile. There would be no invasion. No blockade of Colombian airspace and waters. Most important, Colombia would not be the object of attacks and recriminations.

She knew she had done the right thing. Who knows if she would have felt the same way with American troops parachuting into Bogotá's El Dorado Airport? Probably not, she surmised. But the question no longer mattered.

All her life, Marta Pradilla had trusted her instincts. She had gambled on them again by confiding in John Stockman, and it had paid off. In those fleeting e-mails, she had seen a man struggling against the chains of convention. She knew that if a way existed to help her and Colombia, he would do it. Now, live on CNN, she was being proved right.

She was so good at analyzing and peering into everyone else's inner soul. It conveniently left her no time to look at her own. She hated self-analysis. But, faced with the knowledge of what this man had done for her today, she had to ask herself what she felt for him. Sure, she was attracted to him. Yes, he was intriguing. But how deep did it go?

The phone saved her from further agony. She let it ring a few times. There were only two calls she wanted to take. Marta brushed away a strand of hair as it fell across her face. She reached out to take the call.

"Presidente, it is Hector Carbone."

Yes, this was one of the two calls she badly wanted.

"Hector, have you watched CNN?"

"Yes, I have. I was very gratified to see this." It was vintage Carbone. Completely understated.

"Presidente, I have something to tell you," continued Carbone. "The DAS has discovered a landing strip on a farm in the region of Uraba. With the help of American satellites, we saw that the serial numbers of two airplanes on the ground belong to a holding company run by Alfredo Villas. Mr. Villas is the principal business manager of the Abdoul family. The satellites then confirmed two persons are at the farm—namely, Senator Abdoul, together with Mr. Villas."

"I see," said the president. She was taking her time to think this one through. "Hector, you have instructions that the DAS should arrest both men. However, I would be grateful if you returned them to Bogotá slowly."

"Slowly?" asked Carbone.

"Yes, slowly," Marta said again, a smile slowly forming on her lips. "Uraba is very far, isn't it? By car to Bogotá will take a couple of days. And I have to arrange a few things."

"By car? It will take—" Suddenly Carbone stopped in mid-sentence. He understood. He chuckled over the phone. "Yes, Marta, it will take a few days by car."

She thanked him and hung up. As she replaced the receiver, she heard the door to her office open and shut softly. She dared not look up. She so hoped it was him. He was the only person who would enter without knocking.

Without even looking, she said hello. He answered quietly. There was no hello back.

"What a day you have had, Marta. I heard Hector has Abdoul."

She had been hoping for a phone call from him. Now, Manuel Saldivar was in her office, and it filled her with joy. She walked slowly around the desk and went to embrace him. They held each other for a long time. For the first time in all these days of extraordinary tension, she let herself go in his arms and felt tears well up in her eyes.

They walked together to the sofas in the presidential office. They talked for a long time, like they used to do during the long nights of the campaign. They talked about their extraordinary country, so full of problems and so replete with hope. They remembered how they managed to cajole and attract that hope to her government.

"New blood," Marta Pradilla had ordered upon her election. And the search had begun for a new breed of public servant. It was hard, because those most often suited for public service don't often seek it. The "Kindergarten," as those cynics called her young government ministers, now represented the optimism of Colombia's future.

"Manuel"—the president was bringing the conversation back to reality—"did you talk to the prosecutor?"

"I thought I did not work here any more."

"I don't have a resignation letter from you," Marta said with a huge smile. "Anyway, I know you better than that. You won't let a good idea float away without taking action. So, did you talk to the prosecutor?"

"Yes."

"Come on, Manuel! What did he say?"

"That our understanding of the constitutional requirements to remove a member of Congress's immunity is completely correct. He can submit the request to remove Abdoul's immunity for 'extreme absenteeism' this afternoon. I have the press release ready to go, and an interview is set up for you at 3:00 p.m."

"Okay, Manuel, pull the trigger," Marta ordered. "Only one thing is left for this to work. I would like to meet with Ambassador Salzer and his lady friend from the DEA, Ms. Andrews. I need an urgent extradition request from the U.S. government for Senator Abdoul."

Manuel laughed. "Morris will help. He is probably regretting the fact that his initial impressions of you were somewhat off the mark."

Manuel was amazed at how quickly he fell back into her optimism and energy. She was beautiful, but that wasn't it. She was unlike anybody he had ever known. She believed that something better was possible and infected everyone with the same belief.

Finally the conversation slowed to a lull. There had to be a time to ask, and this was as good as any, thought Marta.

"Manuel, it has only been hours, and I missed you. Will you come back?"

"I talked to my sister and her boyfriend, Chibli. We had an hour-long phone call."

"What did she tell you?"

"Susana said that, after what happened at the Syrian embassy, she tried to leave Chibli. She was wracked by guilt about his torture. She was convinced that what happened to him was her fault—that it was due to her insistence that he publish his tough anti-Syrian articles. She told Chibli that she could not live with the guilt of having put him in the crosshairs of the Syrian government's intelligence services."

"What did he say?"

"He told her flat-out that she could not leave. He told her that every human chooses his own destiny; every person selects by him- or herself which boundaries to exceed. Some cross the boundaries of the law, stepping into sin and crime. Others cross the boundaries of conventional wisdom. Most of these are fools, but you can never be sure. Because every once in a while you come upon somebody who sets a unique path. Somebody who sees around corners and can envision the way the world should be.

"And Chibli told her that she could not quit before finding out whether he was just another fool or somebody with vision. He said that she could not leave before the show was over."

"Wow. That is beautiful. I can imagine Susana was impressed. Has she stayed?"

Manuel smiled. "Of course she has."

He looked at her for a long time.

"So, for me to stay for the final scenes, I need to know something about that unique path you took. I need to ask you two simple questions," he said.

She nodded.

"Are you in love with him?" asked Manuel.

She smiled a strange, mixed smile that was one-half regret and one-half joy. Six words, but they formed a hard query. She answered the truth.

"I honestly don't know. But it's possible."

He pursed his lips. It was not disappointment. He was steeling himself to ask the next question.

"Marta, I need to know this. Did you go to Cuba to meet with Stockman and tell him everything because you were in love with him?"

This time her smile was wide open. This question was easy.

"No, Manuel, I didn't," said President Marta Pradilla. "It was just the right thing to do."

PART XVI
THE UNITED STATES

The Syrian Mission to the United Nations
New York, October 31
11:00 a.m.

════════════════════════════════════

Osman Samir al-Husseini could not stop the trembling in his hands as he hit the ground floor button in the UN building's old elevator.

Nearly two weeks had passed since the plan had failed. It had collapsed without warning. He had gone to bed sure of success. The next day, he awoke to find the news plastered with minute-by-minute coverage of the tuberculosis scare. It took a few seconds' worth of television for al-Husseini to understand there and then that his plan had been foiled.

What worried the Syrian diplomat even more was the silence that ensued. The government of the United States, so quick to publicly blame and assess damages, said nothing. Al-Husseini scoured the major media and mobilized his informants. Yet, no mention was made of the terrorist plot. It was as if it had never happened.

Day in and day out over the last thirteen days, al-Husseini and Omar bin Talman had talked regularly. The initial wave of panic that the discovery of the terrorist plot would unleash military action against Syria slowly gave way to a different view. The two men now agreed that the U.S. government was going to do nothing. Stopping the uranium was an intelligence success that would never be revealed. And, if not revealed, it could never be used against their homeland.

Slowly, the two men drifted into a comfortable lull.

Until yesterday. At 11:00 a.m. New York time, two things happened—nearly simultaneously—that shocked the two Syrians to their core. Omar bin Talman was the first to see the reports and immediately called New York.

"Turn on the bloody television," he ordered when Osman Samir al-Husseini answered the phone.

First, CNN's Bogotá correspondent reported a long story about the extradition of a prominent Colombian politician. He was to be tried in the United States on charges ranging from drug trafficking to organized crime after a vote in Columbia's congress to strip his immunity. Television footage showed former senator Juan Francisco Abdoul in handcuffs and ankle chains boarding a Miami-bound American Airlines flight.

The CNN report ended with a short interview with the U.S. ambassador in Bogotá. The quote aired by the cable news service had Ambassador Morris Salzer gushing over the newfound cooperation between Colombia and the United States. Asked about the new Colombian president, Salzer described Marta Pradilla as "a woman of extreme courage and determination."

The second news item came quickly thereafter and shocked them even more.

"In an exclusive, CNN has just been told that President John Stockman will travel tomorrow morning to New York to personally represent the United States at tomorrow's long-scheduled Security Council discussion about Syria. Clearly, the United States government intends to use the UN discussions to ante up the pressure on Syria. We'll bring you more on this story as soon as we have it."

"Oh my God," groaned Osman Samir al-Husseini, breaking the silence that had enveloped the international phone line.

REUTERS WIRE SERVICE

U.S. PRESIDENT DROPS BOMBSHELL
AT UN SECURITY COUNCIL

New York, November 1. Two weeks after the tuberculosis health emergency fiasco, U.S. president John Stockman minutes ago regained the political initiative by stunning the United Nations Security Council debate on Syria with a surprise announcement that the United States intends to unilaterally end the decades-long embargo on Cuba.

"I have come to the realization that we cannot expect the world to see the clear realities in the Middle East while the United States remains the prisoner of its own mirages," said Stockman. "To lead today's battles, we have to leave behind yesterday's wars. We cannot be hostage to old, ineffective policies that were molded for a world far different than the one we live in."

"It is impossible for me to argue before this body for a political and economic embargo against Syria without talking about the political and economic embargo against Cuba. In an age of terrorism and fear, the fact that we dislike a government cannot be enough to seek the censure of the international community."

The U.S. president essentially proposed a rethinking of the use of international sanctions as a policy weapon. Today, the United States argued that active support for international terrorism must replace ideology as the litmus test for international sanctions.

The United States president presented an implacable hard line against Syria.

"The Syrian government today harbors leaders of Hamas, an organization that plans and executes the killings of civilians on city buses. It allows terrorists to use its territory to organize the destabilization of Iraq.

The Syrian government is actively attempting to acquire weapons of mass destruction—not to defend its own territory, but to use against the territory of others," said Stockman.

"On the other hand, the government in Cuba continues to be oppressive and authoritarian. It imposes a system of government that virtually guarantees the poverty of its citizens. But, let's face it, there are lots of objectionable governments around the world with whom we have regular diplomatic and economic relations. In an age of terrorism and extremism, we need to be clearer about what actions must require the censure of the international community."

"International sanctions must have teeth. They must be grounded in modern day realities and backed by the political force of worldwide condemnation," he continued. "This they cannot have while the United States employs sanctions against a neighboring country whose principal fault is having an unpleasant leader. There may have been a time when sanctions against Cuba were grounded in meaning. Today they are a distraction from far more menacing dangers."

Lowering his voice and pausing to look at the delegates, Stockman became most grave when he stated, "I know that a country as powerful as the United States will always be the target of some scorn. We recognize that leadership brings a measure of resentment. But while I don't always agree, I have come to understand why many in the world call us capricious and fickle. Policies like the Cuban embargo tear away at the legitimacy of our arguments, and slowly sap the strength from those who want to help us."

The U.S. president added, "I have never exchanged a word with Fidel Castro. I am quite convinced that he is a dinosaur. I have become equally convinced, however, that our policy toward Cuba belongs to a similarly Mesozoic era. It ends today."

Recalling the failed UN debate on Iraq of a few years ago, President Stockman ended his speech with an urgent appeal for a heads of state discussion of Syria by Security Council members.

"The United States today has taken action to give new meaning to the power of international sanctions. I ask this council to convene an immediate, urgent meeting of its members to discuss the world's response to terrorist states such as Syria. This is not a meeting for second-in-commands, ministers, or lieutenants. This meeting requires the participation of principals; I expect nothing less than the presence of heads of state," Stockman concluded.

- End of Story -

The White House
Washington, October 31
8:00 p.m.

Late that evening, President John Stockman sat in the Oval Office nursing a scotch. Allyson Bonnet had just finished reviewing press reaction to his UN speech. Conservatives hated it. That was to be expected. Liberals loved it. That too was predictable.

He did not really care one way or another. A controversial policy move like the one he had just taken on Cuba was bound to get the chattering classes debating the pros and cons of the policy itself. What caught his attention was the insiders' analyses of Stockman's leadership.

"Transformational," "newfound initiative," "clear drive," "willingness to explore new ground" were the descriptors in the online previews of the next day's newspaper editorials. As one particularly blunt editorial from the *Chicago Sun-Times* put it, "This was a bold speech from a man who, until today, was seen merely as a defender of the status quo."

"Am I really 'merely a defender of the status quo,' Allyson?" asked Stockman as she was straightening out her papers to leave.

Allyson was true to her reputation. Straight.

"Mr. President, people did not elect you because you were original. They voted for you because you were a safe choice."

"But Allyson, I've come to understand that I don't want history to say 'safe choice' when describing me. Who remembers the safe choices?"

They both thought about it in silence.

Stockman broke the silence in a hushed voice, as if he were talking to himself.

"In a way, she has a harder time. She was elected because she was different and original. Now, the cross she has to bear is proving it every day. That is a tough show to run. I only have to change a little bit and I get headlines like 'transformational.' Hell, this was easy."

Allyson did not know what to say. It was all true. Expectations of a leader like

Pradilla were much higher. Stockman's bar was low, but today his country had gotten more than it had bargained for. Who knew if this was just the beginning of something very different?

For once, Allyson felt she could not say any of this. So she got up, smiled at him, and said good night. President Stockman just nodded his good wishes in response.

Stockman took the last gulp of scotch in the glass and sucked a small ice cube into his mouth. He got up to leave the Oval Office and head upstairs to the private quarters. A Secret Service agent opened the door to the corridor. How the hell do they know I am about to leave? he wondered irritably to himself.

He changed his mind right there and then. He looked at the agent and with a wave of his hand commanded him to reshut the door.

Stockman sat behind the desk and looked at the flat-screen panel. He could not resist looking to see if she was there. He clicked on the Internet Explorer and logged into Yahoo Instant Messenger. She was there.

He wondered how to start? What should he say? He was jolted out of his doubts by the bong of the computer. BeautifulColombia jumped onto the screen.

"Nice speech."

"Thanks, you watched it?"

"Every minute. Pretty bold stuff!"

"A friend recently taught me that one should not shrink from doing bold things. Are you saying it's unusual for me?"

"Maybe a little. How's it feel?"

"I was not nervous at all when I gave it."

"No, my question is, how do you feel now?"

"Excited, elated. It's both controversial and right. It's aggressively generous. We asked nothing in return. Well, it's a different positioning for me."

"John."

"Yes?"

"I'm very, very grateful for what you did. It's not me that you protected, it's my country. You don't know how it feels to be seen as a pariah, though we struggle every day against all the stereotypes. Colombia deserves a break. You gave it to us."

"No, Marta, what you did took real courage. We were just clever."

The computers hummed on in near silence. For a short while, nothing happened.

"John."

"Yes?"

"What's this about a Security Council meeting of principals? Heads of state only? Did you really mean that?"

"Of course. Why do you ask?"

"Because it's the most awkward invitation to dinner I have ever gotten!"

President John Stockman swung round in his chair and roared with laughter.

bonusPAGES

© León Darío Peláez; Revista Semana

PETER SCHECHTER is an international political and communications consultant. He is a founder of one of Washington D.C.'s premier strategic communications consulting firms. He has been the senior consultant for numerous presidential campaigns around the world, advised the United Nations Foundation, the World Bank, and the World Health Organization on key strategic communications and assisted countries, including Colombia, Ecuador, Spain, Peru, and Portugal, in business and tourism promotion programs. Mr. Schechter has lived in Europe and Latin America and is fully fluent in six languages. He lives in Washington, D.C. *Point of Entry* is his first novel.

**AN INTERVIEW WITH PETER SCHECHTER,
POLITICAL CONSULTANT AND AUTHOR OF *POINT OF ENTRY***

You've helped presidents get elected around the world and have been privileged enough to have been in behind-the-scenes world power-broker meetings (both in America and abroad) to make your life a nice subplot on The West Wing. Do your kids think you're a spy?

My kids think that I'm a weird combination of silly and cool. Depends on the time of day you're asking. But, they do get irritated by the interruptive nature of my job. Clients call at weird times asking for advice. What do you tell a six- and eight-year-old when a client calls in the middle of bedtime reading to discuss responding to Venezuelan President Chavez's threats against his company. My kids don't get what can be better than that gripping moment when Harry Potter puts on his invisible cloak.

But, it would be difficult to imagine doing anything else. I've been privileged to see things, hear things, and do things that I could only have dreamed about. The experience runs from the sublime to the ridiculous. It's been a real ride; from writing a eulogy for an assassinated South American presidential candidate to organizing a balloon launch in a provincial Nigerian town to inaugurate a political campaign

Point of Entry deals primarily with the horrific reality of a terrorist plot to detonate a nuclear device on U.S. soil. With our current climate of skepticism over just how thorough a job our government can do in protecting its citizens, why go there, now?

The most basic social compact in democracy is a government's pledge to protect the safety of its citizens. To be effective, there must be credibility—citizens must believe that the government is doing its best, with the best people, to insure that protection. Here in the United States, that trust has been chinked in the past months.

We live in a scary world—natural disasters, contagious diseases that spread on the back of modern transportation, and terrorism. But, nothing is more worrisome than the spread of nuclear arms to terrorists. Nothing.

Point of Entry looks at a very unusual scenario for smuggling nuclear materials into the United States. But, it's not implausible. After all, the Colombian drug mafia has a stellar track record of knowing how to get illicit materials into our country. Every day. All the time.

Are the agencies that protect us from the illegal spread of nuclear materials looking south as well as east? Who knows? I think they should. But I'd be humbled if this story spurred our nonproliferation specialists to look at a new angle.

The novel contains the unbelievable: Fidel Castro aiding the United States during a time of urgent need. Do you think this could really happen? Would he really step up to the plate, if the United States was in desperate need of help?

Sure, why not? And, if it would happen, we'd never know about it because up to now both countries' politicians have vested interests in our mutual hostility. But, what we see on television is the staged, highly choreographed, perfectly planned posturing of government. What happens behind the scenes in the shadows is vastly more interesting.

Strange things happen in the shadows. We just reestablished relations with Libya. Few knew those negotiations were happening. During the Cold War, an improbable, aging United States oilman named Armand Hammer was the principal conduit to the Soviet Politburo. Or, how about the fact that while they were bitterly accusing each other in public, Ariel Sharon's son was, for years, his father's personal secret emissary to Yasser Arafat. I know of a number of instances in which Cuba has indirectly helped the United States and the United States has thanked Cuba for its help. The reverse is also just as true.

But, always in the shadows.

Intelligence gathering plays an exciting role in the novel. In fact, your novel strongly suggests that the CIA can very easily misinterpret information, thereby placing us all at risk of a new terrorist attack. Do you have any hope for the future of the famed agency?

I have lots of respect for the agency. Imagine, it's the only place in government where most of the mistakes are aired publicly, while none of its successes can be talked about. There is no external recognition for a job well-done. But, as a person who has lived in a lot of places and speaks six languages, I'm concerned about what clearly has been an over-reliance on technology to gather intelligence. If you don't speak the language, you can't know the culture; if you don't know the culture, you don't understand politics and society; and if you don't understand politics and society, you are not getting the intelligence you need.

That is why there is such a debate now about the need for enhanced human intelligence. *Point of Entry*'s three CIA analysts are a huge part of the book. They are principled, dedicated, patriotic, and knowledgeable. The book traces their struggle to make sense of signals they instinctively know must mean trouble. They are close to the truth. In the end, though, they get it wrong. But, maybe the book's heroic CIA analysts would have gotten it right were they to have had the benefit of human intelligence from the ground.

Women in power play a particularly visible role in Point of Entry. *The female president of Colombia is arguably the most self-assured, principled world leader to be brought to life in a thriller. What do you think about women in politics? And if you were to choose a female candidate for the American presidency, who would you say has the best shot to not only run, but win?*

Let me state my bias up-front: I love women—particularly attractive, strong, and intelligent women. My wife is one. The potential mix of style and substance makes women a lot more interesting to write about. It's been fun, as a guy, to create a Colombian woman president. I've met unusual numbers of powerful women in Colombia who are not ashamed to combine their femininity with their smarts. The same is often less true of American politics. Somehow our system sucks the femininity and style out of the political equation for women. We have admirable women in United States politics; it's just a pity that they often seem to feel a need to downplay their gender. The next time we have a glass of wine in our hands, let's toast to an election in 2008 between Hillary Clinton and Condoleezza Rice. We United States voters should only be so lucky!

You very plausibly suggest that a romantic relationship between a widowed American president and a foreign leader is possible. Is the world ready for such a thing? Would the tabloids survive?

The tabloids would have the serious media for lunch! But let me ask a question: what makes you think it hasn't already happened? Maybe not in the United States, but elsewhere? Marta Pradilla and John Stockman fall for each other. But they are adults and pros. They know what will happen if they let themselves go. So, I think the question isn't about falling in love; it's about acting on that love. And, for that, you have to wait for the sequel.

A COLOMBIAN PERSPECTIVE ON POINT OF ENTRY

Ms. President
In Peter Schechter's book, Colombia is a vibrant country
governed by a woman.
By Sandra Janer, *Semana Magazine*
February, 2006

When Colombia falls into the hands of an American author
or movie producer, it is often depicted as a place where chickens
scurry down dusty roads or are tied to the roof of a rundown
Chevy. Almost always, the touch of local color comes in the form
of a crumbling colonial church in a tropical-looking Bogotá,
where an overweight mafia gangster with a Hawaiian shirt, a
thick mustache, and a Mexican accent is never too far.

However, a novel has now been published in the United
States that defies these stereotypes. It's called *Point of Entry*, and
it was written by Peter Schechter, a well-recognized international
political consultant based in Washington, D.C., who has worked
on Colombian presidential campaigns for the past twenty years.
"He even sets one scene in Bogotá's lively Zona Rosa, a fashion-
able center of bars, restaurants and music, which had me
improbably thinking Bogotá might be a cool place to visit," says
the literary critic Patrick Anderson in his *Washington Post* review.
The author himself admits that in the pages of his novel he
describes Bogotá as a place more like Soho in New York than like
the capital of a country in crisis. But the most interesting aspect
of the novel is that the vibrant country described by Schechter is
governed by a woman. Her name is Marta Pradilla, she's single,
43 years old, an ex-Miss Universe, a Rhodes scholar, a senator for
six years, and more importantly, she's the first woman to become
president of Colombia.

The novel begins on August 6, the day of her presidential
inauguration, set some time in the near future.

"Negotiations with guerrillas broke down late last year, and
voters sided with Pradilla's hard line. Fluent in four languages,
the new president was raised from the age of sixteen in France

by her uncle, Francisco Gomez y Gomez, after terrorists belonging to one of the principial guerrilla organizations stormed her
family's ranch in the early eighties. Her father, then the country's foreign minister, and mother were killed in the attack," we
learn in the book. Schechter assures that Colombian President
Álvaro Uribe has inspired his character's directness, as have the
many women in politics he had a chance to meet in Colombia,
such as Noemí Sanín, Ingrid Betancourt, and María Emma Mejía,
all important political figures in the Colombian political arena.

"This year, female presidents are the hot topic. There's Ángela
Merkel in Germany, Ellen Johnson-Sirleaf in Liberia, and Michelle
Bachelet in Chile. Ségolène Royal is a strong candidate in the
upcoming French elections, and Hillary Clinton and Condoleezza
Rice may very well be so as well for the 2008 elections. Colombia
has a significant number of women in politics, more than any
other country in Latin America," explains Schechter. Another
one of his motivations in writing *Point of Entry* was the United
States's growing concern with nuclear proliferation in the Middle
East. This is why the other central figure of the novel is John
Stockman, the president of the United States, who has to deal
with a terrorist plot from Syria. The connection with Colombia
becomes evident when we learn that the terrorists plan to use the
Colombian drug traffickers' routes to smuggle uranium into the
United States.

But perhaps more original than the political and terrorist
activities involving the CIA, the FBI, and the DAS (the Colombian
FBI) is the romantic relationship that arises between the
Colombian president and her American counterpart. The liberal
Pradilla sweet talks conservative President Stockman into considering the legalization of drugs, the negotiation of a new TLC
agreement, and ultimately talks him into ending the embargo on
Cuba. Although facts like these can seem like sheer fantasy, the
author assures us that "five years ago no one would have imagined that two airplanes would bring down the Twin Towers."

In *Point of Entry*, Schechter realized his dream of writing a
story that began to take form in his mind since the very moment
he stepped on Colombian soil. He wanted to write a spy novel

á la Tom Clancy, author of *The Hunt for Red October, Patriot Games,* and *Clear and Present Danger.* In *Clear and Present Danger,* whose film adaptation features Harrison Ford, the bad guys—members of Colombia's mafia cartels—cannot escape the stereotype of the mustache. With over 102 entries into Colombia, as attest his last two passports, Schechter takes pride in being one of the gringos who knows most about Colombian politics; a knowledge he began to forge when, as an international relations expert from John's Hopkins University, he was a foreign political consultant to Congress on Latin America. Later, he came to Colombia with the New York political consulting firm Sawyer & Miller to devise a campaign that the government of Virgilio Barco wanted to put in place to improve the image of Colombia in the United States. Later, he was a consultant to the governments of César Gaviria, Ernesto Samper, and Álvaro Uribe.

Schechter lends his experiences with these presidents to his protagonist Marta Pradilla. This is why he didn't hesitate to include in the pages of his novel the memory he has of his first visit to Colombia. When he arrived at Casa de Nariño (the Colombian presidential palace), he was surprised by what he calls a "strident music." It was the five o'clock changing of the guard, which apparently used to torment president Virgilio Barco who had thought of eliminating the ceremony all together. To avoid the horrendous noise, the president closed his office window and said to him: "Amigo, this is life in the tropics."

—*Semana* magazine